Hearts and Minds

KU-050-836

ALSO BY ROSY THORNTON
FROM CLIPPER LARGE PRINT

More Than Love Letters

Hearts and Minds

Rosy Thornton

W F HOWES LTD

CARDIFF
CAERDYDD

This large print edition published in 2008 by
W F Howes Ltd
Unit 4, Rearsby Business Park, Gaddesby Lane,
Rearsby, Leicester LE7 4YH

1 3 5 7 9 10 8 6 4 2

First published in the United Kingdom in 2007
by Headline Review

A CIP catalogue record for this book is available
from the British Library

ISBN 978 1 40741 394 5

Typeset by Palimpsest Book Production Limited,
Grangemouth, Stirlingshire
Printed and bound in Great Britain
by MPG Books Ltd, Bodmin, Cornwall

In affectionate memory of Sue Benson,
who was always on the side of the angels.

ACKNOWLEDGEMENTS

There are many people I would like to thank for their help and support with the writing of this book. Mum and Dad read and encouraged. Louise Fryer gave me the benefit of her unerring eye for detail. Eleanor Spaventa corrected my execrable Italian. Phillipa Ashley, by sharing my madness, kept me sane many times. My friends at C19 were a prop as well as an occasional distraction. Clare Foss, my editor, maintained faith in me despite all the evidence, which means a lot. Claire Baldwin was cheerful and efficient, as always, like everybody else at Headline. Robert Dudley was the one who turned a joke about C.P. Snow into the idea for a book; he is also the best agent anyone could have. And of course Mike, Fadela, Natalie, Treacle and Snuffy, who between them bore the brunt, have my love and gratitude most of all.

CHAPTER 1

*O*n *the basis of these data it can tentatively be contended that . . .*

But could it? And if the contention was unfounded, labelling it 'tentative' would hardly make it less so.

Sighing, Dr Martha Pearce glanced away from the stubborn half-paragraph before her on the screen and down at her wristwatch. Three fifty-two, she noted in mild frustration. But far worse were the small inset letters and digits which reminded her: SEPT 23.

The accommodation required to refocus her eyes from computer screen to watch face took more effort than it would once have done – more effort than it should. That was one further unwanted thing she would have to contrive to jiggle into her complicated diary over the next week or two: a visit to Dollond & Aitchison. Martha removed her reading glasses and laid them down on top of the scatter of papers on her desk. With finger and thumb she massaged the soft indentation at either side of the bridge of her nose. The skin here – unlike that underneath her chin, for example – was still tender and elastic, and felt fragile to the touch; when she closed her eyes, a small vein fluttered just beneath the surface.

The students would be here in a few minutes, at four o'clock, and she was still wrestling with the pivotal central section of her article, which she had promised would be with Professor Styles by tomorrow. It was really a personal kindness that he had saved a slot for her in next quarter's *Review*; she could not possibly let him down. As for facing the students, Martha was not sure she had the stomach for the fight, not just at the moment.

It had been the Bursar's idea to bring forward the annual room rent review for the following academic year from mid-November to the pre-term meeting of the Finance Committee on 26 September. No doubt Kate had been trying to save Martha from confrontation: the very confrontation which was about to ensue in eight – no, six – minutes' time. But as college Bursar Kate Beasley was not so close to the lives of the undergraduates as was Martha as Senior Tutor. Kate was not to know, as Martha did, that Karen and Deepa, president and vice-president respectively of the St Radegund's College Student Union, did not live in college accommodation but shared digs in a private house. They were therefore not thrown out of their rooms in the Long Vacation to make way for revenue-generating conference delegates; the privilege of occupation and the responsibility of rental liability were theirs

in vacation as much as in term. This meant that
they were on hand to check their college pigeonholes on a daily basis – there to discover yesterday
the Finance Committee agenda with its accompanying papers, including the Bursar's relentlessly
upward-curving graphs. Now Karen and Deepa
would note the change of timetable and smell
subterfuge, and Martha would be tainted with its
odour. Student representation on college committees, with full voting rights, was something Martha
herself had fought for, two decades ago. Naturally
it remained for her a given, now that she sat on
the other side of the table. But she had to concede
that sometimes it did make her job more difficult.

Martha saved the tangle of her half-written
article and clicked to quit the file. In two minutes
the students would be at the door, and in five days
he would be arriving at St Rad's. She had just
eight days to update the term's lectures, as well
as to finish writing the sixteen new ones she had
to give because of Jane Billington's sabbatical
leave. Eight days before the new intake of freshers
would arrive, requiring the annual round of introductions and greetings, and bringing with them a
whole new set of tutorial headaches as yet
unguessed. And everything would be different this
year, in a way which Martha could not quite
succeed in picturing. One of the introductions –
which she must remember to fit into the draft
induction programme lying next to her article on
the hard disk – would be *him*.

The knock at the door, though expected, made Martha start. She rose from the swivel chair at her desk as she called to her visitors to come in and then invited them to sit down. Instead of resettling herself in her swivel chair, back to desk, Martha pulled over a footstool and sat down, waving Karen and Deepa towards the two ill-matched armchairs. Never arrange the seating so that you are higher than the students: she had once read this in a counselling manual, and had taken its symbolism to heart. The footstool, oddly sloping and heavily carved (left in the room no doubt by some previous occupant, who had used it to rest her swollen feet, or perhaps as a prie-dieu), was topped with red velvet, and was not prohibitively uncomfortable if you crossed your legs in front of you. Deepa hovered uncertainly between one armchair and the floor before choosing the former; Karen plumped uncompromisingly into the other armchair.

There was no need to ask, as was Martha's usual habit, how she could help her young guests. Kate Beasley's paper on room rent increases lay on the arm of Karen's chair, annotated (unreadably, from Martha's lowly position) in bullish red. It was the Student Union president who opened the bidding.

'We are very concerned about these proposed rent increases, Dr Pearce.'

Dr Pearce. Martha had always been Martha to almost everyone in the college, staff and students alike (with the notable exception of the Head

4

Porter). Her colleagues only ever addressed her as Senior Tutor in committee meetings if they were about to shoot her down in flames. Similarly, if Karen chose to address her by title and surname it could only be in order to create distance. In these negotiations, clearly, the college authorities were to be Them – which was particularly needling to Martha, who liked to think of herself very much as Us.

'This is the third year running that college rents have gone up by more than inflation,' Karen was continuing in her best shop steward voice. 'As you know, the value of the student loan has risen only minimally. How are the students supposed to be able to afford the increase?'

All the sound financial logic of the college's position sprang to Martha's lips without the need for reflection.

'I am afraid that student rents have historically been held at a level which is increasingly unrealistic, given the economic environment in which we are now living. Fee income from the government has fallen rapidly, and we cannot hope to make up the whole gap with increased conference income. The simple fact is that we can no longer afford to continue what has in effect been a generalised subsidy of students' living costs. We must move gradually towards room rents which reflect the hidden "sunk" costs, that is to say, the capital which the college has invested in the land . . .'

God, I sound like Kate, thought Martha, suddenly

hearing herself through the students' ears. But how to say what she really felt, without giving offence? That she had come to believe that it was an unjustifiable use of the college's charitable endowment – held for the furtherance of education, learning and research – to subsidise the rents of the comfortable majority of undergraduates who came from affluent middle-class homes? She gazed impotently at Karen, whose vowels were pure *EastEnders* but whose parents were in publishing and who was herself the product of a prestigious north London girls' grammar school; at Deepa, who was from a stratum of Bengal society entitling her to take tea and jalebis with the Nobel Prize-winning Master of another college and to address his wife as Auntie. They didn't even live in college; the parents of both could clearly afford to pay a market rent for their daughters' accommodation twelve months a year. A quick resentment flared, but was as quickly suppressed. Of course, they were speaking on behalf of others, Martha reminded herself, and not for themselves.

Abandoning the detached reasonableness of the bursarial arguments, Martha leaned forward on her stool with palms open on her crossed denim-clad knees and strove to engage the students, to get them on side.

'But at the same time we must cushion the increase for those in greatest need. Don't worry, nobody's going to go hungry or get into serious

6

debt. The college will not allow any student to suffer real hardship as a result of the rent rises. Yes, we are moving away from general subsidy, but I am determined to ensure that at least part of the extra income generated is used to increase targeted subsidy to poorer students.'

Deepa was gazing at her from earnest brown eyes, but Karen was studying the opposite wall, clearly already planning her next assault. Martha knew that she was losing them but plunged on regardless, for lack of any better plan.

'We already have the college hardship fund. I want to create alongside it a specific fund for rental bursaries . . .'

CHAPTER 2

James Rycarte hoped very much that it was not a portent when he missed the college the first time. The signboard announcing St Radegund's College to the passing motorist in reassuringly unfeminine black capitals was all but obscured by foliage, which seemed to have been allowed to burgeon unpruned since his last visit in February. But then, of course, he had arrived by taxi from the station. Having hailed the cabbie with the words 'St Radegund's porter's lodge', he had been free to sit back and worry about the ordeal ahead: trial by fire, water and the massed ranks of the St Rad's Governing Body. This time was different: he was bringing his own car up from London, along with the personal effects which he had not felt safe in entrusting to the removals men sent by the college. Spotting the half-hidden sign only at the last moment, Rycarte had checked his mirror and wisely decided against the sudden application of his brakes, continuing instead as far as the next convenient side road before executing a U-turn and coming back. From this direction the college entrance was more obvious;

he slowed safely and turned into the small car park.

His next dilemma was a tricky one. The car park was marked out to left and right with spaces for half a dozen cars, leaving enough room in the centre for taxis – or the merely lost – to swing round and turn. Two spaces were vacant, but which to select? That to the left, close to the steps leading up to the porter's lodge, was designated 'Mistress' by a discreet wooden notice; that to the right was signed 'Visitor'. Rycarte knew what he ought to do, what they would all expect of him, but could not quite bring himself to do it. He pulled the wheel round to full lock and nudged the nose of the Alfa up close to the word 'Visitor'.

A twist of the ignition key silenced both the engine and Bach's Mass in B Minor, but when he opened the driver's door a barrage of noise assailed him. It was coming from above. The row of elegantly pollarded limes which screened the perimeter of the car park was alive with screeching. For one dizzying moment Rycarte had the impression that the trees themselves were chattering and cackling over his arrival, before his eyes homed in and he saw that they were full of starlings.

Shooting the central locking from the hip, he pocketed his keys and mounted the steps to the lodge two at a time, feeling the bore of dozens of imagined eyes, human as well as avian. The Head Porter was understated in his welcome, for which Rycarte was grateful, although it would have been heartening if his 'Good to see you again, sir' had carried just a little more conviction. The formalities took an inordinate amount of time. Swipe cards, key codes and keys themselves more numerous than it seemed possible could be necessary were located, activated, logged, and handed out with unhurried method by the bowler-hatted Head Porter, while Rycarte tried his hardest to listen to what they were all for and not to shift too visibly from foot to foot. Were Cambridge porters, he wondered, the last men in England to wear bowler hats? He could not recall having seen one since watching *Mr Benn* on television when Paul was a toddler.

During the interminable procedure, a number of students drifted by on their way in or out of college, individually or in twos or threes, some casting upon him their incurious gaze, others ignoring him completely. A junior porter entered the lodge with a large pile of mail for distribution to the Fellows' pigeonholes arrayed behind the counter. The newcomer, who was introduced as Terry, acknowledged Rycarte with a grunt and a nod before beginning the sorting and dispatch of his envelopes. Somehow, none of this was quite how Rycarte had imagined it. In his nightmares he had pictured himself like the unnamed young heroine in *Rebecca*, facing a welcoming line-up of the entire college staff in their Sunday best, with the Head Porter in the role of Mrs Danvers. The more mundane reality was, of course, a relief. He wanted nothing more than to slip in quietly. And yet he found himself prey to a curious sense of anticlimax. Apart from anything else, did none of these people watch television?

Finally, the reception process complete, the Head Porter turned to more domestic matters.

'The Mistress's Lodging should be ready for you. The Bursar had the maintenance department give the central heating a blow through yesterday, just to take off any damp, even though college heating is not normally switched on until the second week in October. And housekeeping have put fresh linen on all the beds.'

Rycarte made appropriate noises of approval and obligation.

'And, er, it might be better to move your car round to the lodging, sir.'

The Head Porter's tone made it clear that Rycarte's choice of parking space had not gone unnoticed.

'There's a garage there,' he added, indicating a small silver key on one of the formidable bunches. 'The driveway to the lodging is the third on the left, sir, if you go back to the main road. You can't miss it.'

Back in the car park a moment later, Rycarte clicked open the central locking. He was surprised to find the Alfa's door already slightly tacky to the touch from the lime trees' secretions. It would play hell with the paintwork; he would have to wash the car tomorrow. Or perhaps there would

11

be staff whose functions included this task. Somehow he doubted it. The juxtaposition of limes and car park made him suspect that trees, in general, were held in higher regard than motor vehicles in these parts. Fastening his seat belt and running the windscreen wipers for a minute or two to remove a tenacious deposit of starling excrement, he engaged reverse and backed out.

'Mistress's Lodging', reflected Rycarte a short time later, was perhaps not such a misnomer, given the interior decor of the place. The phrase 'tart's boudoir', indeed, rose unbidden in his mind. It was not simply that the fittings and colour schemes reflected a feminine touch. Nothing here would have been to his ex-wife's taste – hers had run more to the primary and minimalist – and Rycarte had never had a mistress you could really call the name. The public reception rooms downstairs were not so bad: in the dining room there was in fact a very fine oak refectory table and a set of twelve dining chairs with understated sepia upholstery. But the curtains were richly sprigged with rosebuds, and elsewhere in the house the rosebuds had been allowed to ramble and blossom wholly unchecked. Worst of all was what Rycarte enjoyed the irony of thinking of to himself as the master bedroom. Here were frills and flounces so garlanded that the room could have served as the set for a school production of *A Midsummer Night's Dream*. This is where his predecessor, Dame Emily, had presumably slept for the fourteen years

12

of her reign at St Radegund's. The idea was an incongruous one. What he had seen of the august lady (at his previous visit and in snatches on television) had left an impression of corduroy trousers and bicycle clips – or perhaps, on the most formal occasions, a crumpled linen suit. To uncover this predilection for flowers and furbelows felt like the glimpse of a secret vice, like an uninvited peek into her underwear drawer.

Careful investigation revealed that this was the only bedroom with en suite facilities. Of the remaining five, the least pink and floral was a narrow mezzanine off a small landing at the final turn of the stairs. It contained only a single bed and an old-fashioned leather-topped desk, and appeared to have escaped the ravages of Dame Emily's decorative tastes. As the Head Porter had promised, this bed, like all the others, was made up in readiness for his arrival, and Rycarte sat down upon it tentatively. Quite why he might want six bedrooms all equipped with ready-to-use beds was clearly not a question it had entered anybody's head to ask. No doubt in Dame Emily's day the place had been constantly filled with house guests: homeless research students, impoverished visiting scholars, and archaeological volunteers recruited for her next Assyrian dig. Rycarte suppressed an unexpected wave of homesickness for his untidy and overbrimming London flat. Even one of the anonymous hotel rooms in which he had spent much of his early professional life would have been preferable just then. At least in a hotel bedroom there was always a television, but none had been apparent anywhere in the lodging. Still, tomorrow the removal van would arrive, with one or two pieces of his smaller furniture, his clothes, his books and music, and his television. Squaring his shoulders, Rycarte returned to Dame Emily's bedroom and Dame Emily's ruched and valanced bed, kicked off his shoes, and lay down.

At around the same time that evening Martha Pearce was finally thinking of going home. The article for the *Review* was finished – though not greatly to her satisfaction – and dispatched to Professor Styles with a contrite note about its tardiness, and she had spent the afternoon mapping out her sixteen new lectures on Microeconomic Theory for Part I of the Tripos. It was years since she had lectured in Part I, and recently she had even ceased to supervise the St Rad's first years, confining her teaching to her own specialist topics in Part II. Getting up this material was going to be a lot of work, she had realised, when she began to look over the syllabus, her old notes and the gaps between the two. She really should have said no, when the secretary of the faculty's Teaching Committee had asked her to cover Jane Billington's lectures this term. She had more than enough on her plate without it – her college responsibilities, even without the arrival of a new Head of House, were more than adequate grounds for her to have declined the invitation. But Jane was a friend, and people had to be able to take up their entitlement to sabbatical; Martha was nothing if not a collegial being.

Anyway, how could she possibly refuse any request which the faculty might choose to make of her, this year of all years? When her college appointment was due to come to an end – having indeed already been extended by this one further academic year beyond the expected period of tenure in order to see in the transition to James Rycarte's headship? The annual round of faculty lectureship appointments was due in February and, by all accounts, posts would be few and hotly contested: probably just three openings – and one of those specifically for an economic historian, a description which Martha could not possibly spin her CV to fit. The other two posts were likely to be open as to subject area. But would she be able to sell herself as a desirable product in the current market? To compete against the latest generation of bright young scholars, with their shiny new PhDs on electronic money and the other sexy subjects of the day? In the ten years since her research had been relegated to second place behind her duties as Senior Tutor of St Radegund's, Martha's subject had altered beyond recognition. Her own brand of liberal Keynesian theory, and her particular specialism of women in the labour market, were decidedly out of fashion. Everything now was neoclassical econometric

15

method: far too many equations and not nearly enough words for Martha's liking.

Having made depressingly little progress on her lecture notes, Martha decided to check her e-mails one last time and then call it a day. It was already well past seven thirty, and she had promised to cook supper for Douglas and Lucia tonight – that they would sit down together, the three of them, the way they used to do, like a proper family. She had picked up some mushrooms for a risotto at lunchtime, but already now she would be coming in on the run, as too often before. Martha ran her eye down the inbox, clicking to delete unopened the dozens of University circulars and external spam messages which had accumulated since her last visit. Still nothing from Karen about the rent situation, she noted with unease. The Finance Committee meeting on Monday had ended in bitterness, with Karen and Deepa stalking out angrily after the rent increases were voted through, the situation helped not at all by the Bursar's self-justificatory crowing. Really, Kate Beasley knew her stuff financially, but she could be so bloody *managerial* sometimes, so blind to the reality of what the shared life of a college was all about. To Martha, of course, fell the task of attempting to heal the breach, and she had invited the students to come and see her to talk things through. But to no response: it seemed that Karen was not answering her e-mails. Oh well, she would just have to resort to the old-fashioned method of a note in her pigeonhole. Shutting down the computer, she reached for a pen and a sheet of college notepaper.

As she crossed First Court towards the mail room which housed the undergraduate pigeon-holes, Martha's mind was already on her risotto. As well as the fresh mushrooms in her bag she was fairly sure that there were some dried porcini left from their last trip to Italy. They were never quite as good without a nice long pre-soak, but that could not be helped now. And there was certainly still plenty of the good Arborio rice in the cupboard. What a pity the flat-leaf parsley in the pot by the back door had died for lack of regular watering; she should have picked up a bunch when she bought the mushrooms.

All Martha's guilt – professional, familial and horticultural – was banished in an instant when she entered the student mail room. The noticeboards which covered the wall opposite the entrance were usually awash, once term approached, with posters of all shapes, colours and sizes, advertising forth-coming plays, gigs, debates and speaker meetings, but tonight the wall had a strikingly monolithic air. It was papered from top to bottom and side to side with multiple copies of one single, red A3 poster. It bore the logo of the St Radegund's College Student Union, and out from the surrounding text leapt two belligerent words: RENT STRIKE.

Martha stepped closer, extracted her spectacles from her bag and read the rest. The message was

17

unequivocal: college rent rises in real terms for the third consecutive year and now nearing market levels; students unable to afford the rises without hardship; the time having come to take a stand. The tone was all Karen. Never mind the obvious (to Martha) objection that the increase the students had been outvoted in opposing in Monday's Finance Committee was not due to take effect until next October – in protest at which they were planning to withhold rents agreed peacefully last November. Why had Karen refused even to meet Martha again, to give her a chance to outline further her plans for a rental bursary scheme? Why was she seeking confrontation? Why this year – why now?

But of course she knew the answer to that. The Student Union had made no secret of their opposition, last year, to the election of a male Head of House. Room rents merely gave them an excuse to stir things up, to make life difficult for James Rycarte even before his formal investiture. Certain now that her note would go straight in the waste bin as soon as it was opened, she deposited it in Karen's pigeonhole regardless and went back outside. Before turning towards the Fellows' bicycle shed to make her way home, she paused and looked through the archway in the direction of the path to the Mistress's Lodging. He had been due to arrive this afternoon; he was probably there now. She could check with the porters whether he had signed out his keys. She wondered

18

whether anyone had thought to instruct house-keeping at least to put a pint of milk in his fridge, or lay out a few guest sachets of coffee from the conference office, and maybe some soaps in the bathroom. Perhaps she should go over herself now, just to bid him welcome, check he was all right, see if there was anything he needed?

No, she told herself firmly: she had her own priorities. Even as things were, she would not be home much before eight fifteen. Lucia would probably have grown impatient and devoured most of the loaf from the crock. Douglas would have opened the wine without her and be on to his third glass. Home was where she needed to be; James Rycarte would just have to fend for himself.

CHAPTER 3

It was to the irascible whine of an electric hedge-trimmer, and the digits 07:13 blinking on his travel alarm clock, that James Rycarte awoke on his first morning as head of St Radegund's College, Cambridge. 'Head of House': that inclusive and gender neutral but impeccably ancient term used in Cambridge to denote the miscellany of Masters, Mistresses, Presidents, Principals, Wardens and Provosts who stand at the helm of its constituent colleges; a term which in his own case masked a political minefield. Picking a delicate path through that would come soon enough, but most immediate was the question of the hedge-trimmer.

Pulling back one of Dame Emily's rose-bedecked curtains, Rycarte looked out of the stone-mullioned casement. He had never really been quite sure how a casement differed from any other window, bay or bow – if indeed it did. Architecture was not going to be one of his strong suits over High Table; perhaps he should buy a book. But if there were still such a thing as a casement, this was surely it. Out of just such a window must the Lady of Shalott, sick of shadows, have dared the curse and gazed down on tower'd Camelot. The lodging was not an old building: certainly not by Cambridge standards, not even by those of St Radegund's. The central college buildings were contemporary with its early Victorian foundation; the lodging post-dated it by five decades. But the architect had indulged a taste for the Gothic, and in addition to the extravagant windows the house boasted a six-column portico and a complete set of battlements.

Directly below him he could make out the fore-shortened figures of two gardeners working in opposite directions round the edges of the lodging's lawn with long-handled shears, in addition to the one attacking the laurel hedge with the querulous electric trimmer. Three groundsmen tidying his garden, and all before seven thirty a.m., seemed to Rycarte to smack of unnecessary cosseting, even for a newly arrived Head of House – particularly in light of the parlous state of the college finances, of which so much had been made at his pre-interview briefing with the Bursar and the Senior Tutor. He wondered idly what the total strength of the college ground staff might be, to spare three of their number in one place at such an early hour. A direct linear extrapolation might be inappropriate, of course, for perhaps gardeners tended to hunt in packs. But certainly, everything he had seen of the college's green spaces was immaculate – in contrast to the air of distinctly down-at-heel gentility he had noticed about the

21

decoration and furnishings of the SCR on his previous visit.

Before he could begin to apply his mind to the question of the payroll, however, or any other aspect of his new responsibilities, it was badly in need of an invigorating injection of caffeine. A search of the carvernous kitchen, equipped throughout in professional-grade stainless steel for purposes of college catering, did not yield even a small jar of instant coffee. There being apparently no shower in his new home either, Rycarte sluiced himself down in Dame Emily's Victorian clawfoot bath, put on a suit and tie befitting his status, and headed off through the grounds in the direction of the main part of the college. Surely coffee must be available in the mornings somewhere in a Cambridge college, and possibly toast or even bacon.

Probably his best approach would have been to inquire about breakfast at the central nerve centre of the porter's lodge, but amongst the many things Rycarte could not face before his first coffee of the day he found was now numbered the St Rad's Head Porter. He could remember his way to Hall. In common, no doubt, with the other candidates for the post of Mistress, each on the evening of her own interview, he had been required to dine at High Table with the entire assembled Fellowship, to offer for general scrutiny his manners and his small talk. He shuddered faintly at the recollection. But Hall was now echoingly empty, the long benches still stacked upside down upon the tables following last night's floor mopping. The SCR – scene of the interview itself – was also deserted. Opposite its double doors Rycarte noticed a smaller entrance, over which were painted in black copperplate the inviting words 'Fellows' Breakfast Parlour'.

Fighting down an impulse to apply his ear to the keyhole before entering, Rycarte pushed open the door and went in. Inside was darkness, and the aroma which greeted him was not that of the blessed roasted bean but of wax polish and an underlying hint of damp. Groping around, he located the light switches – not before his shin had collided painfully with the corner of a mahogany sideboard – and flicked the room into sight. Deserted, it lacked even a self-service coffee dispenser. By now Rycarte would have welcomed the worst kind of insipid leachings in a polystyrene cup, but there was not so much as a water-cooler. Just two circles of assorted and somewhat threadbare armchairs, gathered convivially around a pair of coffee tables which, however, were failing to live up to their name.

On the nearer of these there was at least a fan of neatly folded newspapers: today's, he discovered with satisfaction. The papers were as essential to Rycarte in the morning as caffeine, and although he preferred the two in tandem, for now one without the other was a lot better than nothing. His eye had just been caught by an article in the *Independent* about the reintroduction of the European beaver on the river Rhône – he must send a copy to Paul in Lyon; probably he knew about it already, was even involved, but it would at least show an interest – when the door opened again and in walked one of the dons. She was a tall, uncompromisingly self-contained woman, and he recognised her at once as the prime mover behind the bombardment of aggressive questioning about the gender issue at his interview. *What difficulties would he foresee as a man required to represent, either internally or to the outside world, the interests of a women's college?* He remembered thinking that she would feature large among them. Dr Carter? Dr Kirk?

'Mr Rycarte, welcome to St Radegund's. Clarke, Ros Clarke.'

The welcome he was to receive was not to be a warm one, if her tone was anything to judge by, but he smiled as he took her outstretched hand.

'Ah yes, Dr Clarke, I remember. I look forward to working with you.'

Dr Clarke released his hand from her cool grasp and bent to fish the *Times Literary Supplement* from amongst the jumble of newsprint on the coffee table in front of Rycarte, pausing as she did so to refold and straighten, restoring the pile to a semblance of order. Refusing to feel cowed, he asked her, 'Where can I find a photocopier? I just found a piece here that my son would be interested in. He works for the French Green Party, in the Rhône-Alpes region.'

24

The tendering of personal details was not likely to effect any degree of thaw in Dr Clarke, it seemed. She eyed him impassively.

'Miss Kett-Symes would do that for you. She always comes in at nine thirty.'

'Oh no, no need for that. I can easily do it myself, if you just tell me where I can find a photocopier.'

Rycarte congratulated himself on spotting and successfully skirting this first small trap. He was not going to give her the opportunity of thinking he was the kind of man who expected his secretary to perform personal tasks for him – or was so elevated that he had forgotten how to work a photocopier.

'In that case, you need to sign out the card at the porter's lodge,' replied Dr Clarke smoothly, settling herself into an armchair with the *TLS*, the ice undented by this minor defeat. 'They will tell you where to find the machine.'

Thus dismissed, Rycarte tucked the *Independent* under his arm, murmured his thanks and set off as directed.

Dr Ros Clarke was a woman who knew her own mind; but as she perused the review articles the firm line of her mouth evinced even more determination than usual. She would have him out by the end of Full Easter Term.

It was not the Head Porter on duty this morning, but the younger man, Terry, whom Rycarte had encountered the day before. Terry exhibited extreme doubtfulness when asked for the photocopying card.

'Well, I don't think Miss Kett-Symes would like it if I gave you hers, sir. Dame Emily never borrowed the Mistress's office card.'

Patiently, Rycarte tried another tack.

'Well, is there perhaps a Fellows' copying card which I might borrow on this occasion?'

Terry still looked reluctant but, when Rycarte continued to smile at him in confident expectation, could do no other than hand it over, pushing with it across the counter an exercise book ruled with lines and columns, with a Biro attached by string.

'Sign here, then, sir.'

Rycarte printed his name and the date and, in the final column marked 'College/Personal', virtuously inscribed a capital P.

'When you bring it back, you write down the number of copies and sign. Personal photocopying is billed termly, along with wine from the Fellows' wine list and other sundries. The copier is in the lobby outside the tutorial office and the bursary. Across the court, C staircase.'

Rycarte's own undergraduate background was brilliant but redbrick. He was not, however, without some familiarity with the idiosyncrasies of this place. Certainly he knew that the signs flanking the lawn of First Court, enjoining visitors to keep off the grass in three European languages and Japanese, did not apply to Fellows of the college. He was therefore permitted to strike a course directly for C staircase across the hallowed turf, rather than following the flagstone path round two sides of a square. The turf was so perfectly tailored, though, its smooth surface striped regularly in two shades of green by the passing and repassing of the mower, that somehow it seemed an unwarranted liberty. Rycarte turned his feet round the perimeter, aware that by doing so he was attracting the scorn of Terry, watching from the windows of the lodge.

He was not the first to the photocopier. Bending anxiously over the tray into which was spitting a rapid stream of yellow A4 sheets was a young Fellow whom Rycarte remembered only by sight. She had not spoken at his interview to his recollection, so he had no way of placing her as friend or foe. She straightened at the sound of his approach and coloured a fetching pink.

'Oh, Mr Rycarte. You're here then. I mean, of course, um, welcome.'

'James.'

'That's right! Susie James, Admissions Tutor and Fellow in Biological Sciences. Fancy you remembering.'

The blush had deepened, now set off by a delighted sparkle in her eyes. He knew that later, as soon as he was gone, she would realise the error and cringe, but he still had not the heart to point it out. Instead he merely offered her an answering smile and extended his hand; but she held ruefully aloft fingers stained black with toner, and shook her head in apology.

'I'm sorry, I've been having such a fight with it to get it going. As soon as I switched it to double-sided it kept jamming, and some of the paper got stuck so far inside it was dreadful to get out. Only just got it working again, in fact, and I shouldn't be surprised . . .'

It was only then, apparently, that she noticed the plastic card in Rycarte's other hand and the newspaper under his arm.

'Oh, but of course, you want to use the copier! I'm ever so sorry, but it's a long run, two hundred, double-sided and collated. Programmes for the next Open Day, actually. If I cancel it now in the middle of the job it might get confused and jam again . . .'

Rycarte held up an arresting hand. 'Don't concern yourself. There must be another machine I can use?'

'Well, er, there are the ones in the photocopying room, I suppose, in the library, but those are for student use really – coin-operated, you know. This is the only staff copier. Except I think the college fax machine takes copies, too, but that's in the Bursar's secretary's office and she won't be in just yet.' Dr James nodded in the direction of the closed door behind them and to the left.

'Oh, not to worry. Mine can wait, it's nothing important. And after all, I mustn't stand in the way of the college's schools outreach activities, must I? I'm sure you are doing a great job there.'

She shot him a look of gratitude and relief, whilst

28

contriving to keep one eye on the copier tray and also take in a glance at her watch. Rycarte backed tactfully away.

As he returned once more round the immaculate turf of First Court to sign back the photocopying card, Rycarte pondered the matter. One photocopier between forty-eight Fellows and over a hundred assistant staff – college administration, finance, conferencing, maintenance, housekeeping, library and archives, not to mention all those gardeners. He was reminded of neighbours of his grandmother in Barnsley when he was a boy, with a scrubbed step and cake on a china plate in the front room, but a patched cloth and no meat on the family table.

Having returned the card to Terry – casting a wistful eye into the back of the porter's lodge where he thought he heard a kettle beginning to hum – Rycarte made for A staircase, where Dame Emily's office was situated. His own office, that is to say. It took him some time to find the right key from amongst the many, but then he was inside, and the place was very much as he remembered it from his short meeting with Dame Emily prior to his interview. It bore, fortunately, no manifestations of his predecessor's domestic tastes but was spacious and businesslike, with an understated Victorian elegance. Through an adjoining door, propped permanently open, was the anteroom to be occupied by Miss Kett-Symes from nine thirty a.m.; this formidable female had, as she had not missed

29

the opportunity of informing him on the day of his interview, filled the post of Mistress's secretary at St Radegund's for twenty-three years.

Through the doorway he could see a coffee filter machine, but a quick scout around its vicinity did not reveal any source of coffee. Sighing, Rycarte returned to his own office. He consulted his watch: eight twenty-five. Still no sustenance, and over an hour before any might be in prospect. Shelved behind his desk were two long rows of box files, neatly labelled as containing the minutes and attendant papers from meetings of the Governing Body, the College Council and various committees over the past dozen years. He pulled out the latest Governing Body file, carried it to the desk and sat down to read.

He was deeply enmeshed in the intricacies of a change to the college's Standing Orders, the previous February, to permit members of the Governing Body to vote *in absentia* upon the election of Honorary Fellows, when the door opened to admit Miss Kett-Symes. She stepped smartly forward to stand before his desk, clasping an outsize leather handbag before her like a weapon and regarding the open box file with what felt uncommonly like disapproval.

'Ah, Miss Kett-Symes,' he began in his most disarming tone, rising and holding out his hand across the pile of minutes. 'How do you do? Very glad to be here, and very much looking forward to working with you.'

His secretary nodded her acknowledgement and shook his hand briefly, but continued to survey the papers on his desk.

'Dame Emily used to come in at ten o'clock. That way I could have her schedule all ready for her. Not that she wasn't always up and working at six. But she liked to reserve the early part of the morning for her own work – her *academic* work, I mean. However, in your case, of course . . .'

Rycarte's illustrious predecessor had received her title not primarily in recognition of her services to educational administration, but rather on account of her seminal text on the royal cities of ancient Assyria. Whereas what was he? A former foreign correspondent turned television executive. Miss Kett-Symes probably didn't even own a television – just a wireless tuned permanently to Radio 4 and a Siamese cat. Rycarte absorbed the slight, but was more disposed to forgive the deliverer of it as he watched her unlock a filing cabinet and withdraw first a packet of filter papers and then a tin of ground coffee.

'Well, it is my first day, and there is so much for me to learn.'

This token of deference was recognised by a slight softening of the secretarial shoulders.

'So I thought I may as well make a start. No shortage of reading matter here for me, eh?'

So no need to worry about your not having been here before now. Clearly not the thing to say. Instead, he went for sympathy.

31

'Actually, I came into college early because I thought there might be some breakfast on offer. Haven't really got myself sorted out yet, over at the lodging. But I gather not. "Fellows' Breakfast Parlour" appears to be something of a misnomer.'

This approach seemed to produce a connection; at least it elicited a ready flow of words, none of their hostility aimed at him.

'Yes, the college kitchens have stopped serving breakfasts. They didn't break even, the Bursar said, not enough takers. Young girls today don't seem to worry, they just eat a bowl of cornflakes in their room, walking about or sitting in bed, I shouldn't wonder, or else go out without anything at all. So the Bursar said breakfast in Hall is a luxury we can no longer afford. Luxury! Breakfast is the most important meal of the day, I was always told.'

Rycarte's stomach agreed with her, luckily only silently.

'It's two years since they stopped serving it. Except during Ramadan. The Muslim girls like to get something solid inside them then, before sunrise you know, to last them through the day. Cereal and toast, maybe an egg. Not bacon, of course. I still can't quite get used to the idea, the college's catering working round the Islamic calendar. But we do have a lot of Asian students – British Asian, I suppose I should say, to be correct, because that's what they mostly are. Their families like to send them here, rather than somewhere co-residential.'

Rycarte felt a little uncomfortable with the ground they were treading, and nudged Miss Kett-Symes gently back on track.

'And what about Fellows – those that live in, I mean, the Research Fellows and so on?'

'Well, the Research Fellows are entitled to Commons as part of their stipend, and according to the college Statutes that means three meals a day. But these days they just pick up their supplies from the Fellows' pantry once a week: orange juice and bread and tea bags and suchlike.'

The coffee machine was now glugging cheerfully. Rycarte leaned against the interconnecting door between the two offices and closed his eyes for a moment, wondering idly when the holy month of Ramadan began this year. He was recalled to the present when Miss Kett-Symes opened a scarlet-bound desk diary and got down to business.

'This is where I log all your meetings and other appointments. If you have any personal engagements coming up, I will need to know so that I can enter them in the diary. Your first appointment this morning is at ten thirty with the Bursar and the Senior Tutor. They want to talk to you about student rents.'

Martha, meanwhile, had a good breakfast but nobody with whom to share it. She filled the cafetière only to half-mast, and over her muesli and plate of fresh apricots she resorted to reading

33

out the most irritating sections of the *Economist*'s leader column to her ginger tom, Maynard, who fixed her with a satirical gaze.

At eight thirty she rinsed her bowl and plate in the sink, downed the rest of her coffee, shooed Maynard off the draining board, then mounted the stairs two at a time and banged on her daughter's bedroom door.

'Lucia? Are you awake, love?'

A non-committal grunt from within indicated that she might or might not be.

'Are you getting up? Only I must get off to college.'

A short silence, then, 'Go on, then. I'll see you tonight, Mum.'

'Lucia, you are going to get out of bed, aren't you?'

Another pause.

'Is Dad up yet?'

Martha strove to ignore the clinching force of this argument.

'Can I come in, love?'

'S'pose so.'

The room was in darkness, but not enough to mask the disarray. Martha picked her way to the bed and sat down next to the hump of duvet that was her daughter. Two arms snaked out silently and curled themselves round Martha's waist, clasping her floppily. She groped for the tousled head, half hidden beneath a pillow, and ruffled it.

'There's some chicken pieces in the fridge. And

broccoli. You could cook them for lunch – I'm not sure if Dad's going to be in, you can ask him. Or have them tonight, if you'd rather. But do eat.'

Something other than bread and biscuits, preferably. She felt like her own mother: *eat your greens!*

'So you're not going to be here? For supper, I mean.'

The stab of guilt made Martha do what she had sworn she would not, and start on the perennial battle.

'What are you planning to do today?'

The arms round her waist lost their sleepy languor. Stiffened perceptibly.

'I dunno. Write, probably. If anything comes to me.'

'Look, sweetheart, writing isn't just a case of waiting for something to come. Sometimes it does feel like that, I know. You feel blocked. I get like that with my academic writing at times, so I know how frustrating it can be. But there are things you can do to help the process. Of course your writing has to come from inside, from the heart, but you can improve your technique, give yourself new ways of approaching things. Pick up fresh ideas.'

There was no response from the duvet.

'Have you looked at those websites I mentioned, the writers' message boards? Why don't you post something you've done, and see what feedback you get? Or get in touch with that student in the English Faculty who runs the creative writing group? You could even go to a few lectures.'

35

literary criticism. Critiquing other people's material is a great way to learn to look objectively at your own writing.'

Now the arms slackened again and withdrew a little way under the heat of the bedding. Lucia's voice was muffled by the pillow but the accusation it held rang through loud and clear.

'Oh yes, I see where this is heading. Just some lectures, and then it'll be a writing course, then next it'll be English A level. Look, Mum, if I wanted all that I'd have stayed at school and finished my A levels, gone to college. But it's not what I want, OK?'

'I know. You want to write and I respect that, really I do. But being a writer isn't about lying in bed all day. It's hard work. You ought to try treating it like a job.'

The hump in the bed had begun to quiver. Oh God, now she'd made her cry! It was so easy to do these days. Martha laid her arm across the part of the duvet which putatively covered her daughter's shaking shoulders. And was relieved only for a second when she realised that Lucia was not crying but laughing.

'Yeah, treat it like a job – like Dad does, you mean . . .'

Only towards the end of that first afternoon, after a day of briefing meetings with all the people who pulled the strings in his new workplace, and several others who wished they did, did Rycarte finally persuade the University's central computing service to divulge to him the details of his e-mail account. How an address which he only knew himself five minutes before could already have been targeted by so many advertisers and other assorted badgerers was a mystery to him. But amongst the long column of messages were two which drew his attention.

The first was from Kate Beasley, the Bursar, and was addressed to all members of the Hardship Fund Committee – a list which apparently included his own name, *ex officio*. As its convenor, Kate was summoning an extraordinary meeting of the committee, which was not otherwise due to meet until the end of term, in order to discuss what her e-mail described as 'an important issue of principle'. A birdcage was attached, upon which members were to indicate their availability for a number of dates over the next few days. Rycarte had no difficulty in guessing what the issue of principle might be. It had already come up in his first meeting of the morning, with Kate and Martha Pearce, the Senior Tutor. Kate had been both adamant and voluble in expressing the view that any student withholding her rent as part of a so-called 'rent strike', and thereby getting into financial difficulties when that rent fell eventually to be paid, was not to be a recipient of hardship support from the college. Martha had not voiced dissent, but Rycarte had noticed a shadow come over her soft features, and seen the glint of resistance in her mild brown eyes.

The second e-mail to catch Rycarte's eye was a circular to all members of the St Rad's Fellowship. It read as follows:

To all Fellows and College Teaching Officers –
Please would colleagues note that the news-papers and other periodicals in the Fellows' Breakfast Parlour are provided for reading in the Parlour only. They are intended to be a resource available to all, and are not to be removed for personal use.
Ros Clarke,
Fellows' Parlour Steward

Rycarte's glance was drawn to the copy of the *Independent* which still lay like an indictment, unphotocopied on his desk, with the initials FBP felt-penned blackly above the masthead. Touché – that's one to you, Dr Clarke, he acknowledged grimly. But the battle was barely joined; from now on he would be on his guard, and ready to parry anything she cared to thrust at him.

CHAPTER 4

The buzz of anticipation which always marked the arrival of the new intake of freshers was apparent to Martha well before she arrived at St Rad's on Saturday afternoon. Cycling through the city, nobody familiar with Cambridge could have failed to notice the unaccustomed density of traffic in the semi-pedestrianised streets immediately surrounding the central colleges, or the proliferation of people carriers and family estate cars, driven slowly by parents unfamiliar with the town and laden high with boxes, blocking rear-view mirrors. Every other car seemed to Martha to contain a Swiss cheese plant. The cyclists were suddenly different, too. Gone were the freewheeling posses of language students, Italian, German or Japanese, kitted out with matching Day-Glo rucksacks in the team colours of their respective language schools. In their place were young people who were quite unmistakably undergraduates, second and third years with their easy ownership of the streets, and the occasional first year, an early arrival, trying to look at home on a freshly unloaded bicycle.

For Martha the start of a new academic year always brought a thrill of excitement: a sense, shared with the newcomers, of infinite possibilities – the ideals as yet uncompromised, the hopes as yet unqualified, the brand new stationery. But it also brought with it a pang of guilt, this year sharper than ever. Somehow, she never managed to get done in the Long Vacation half the things she planned, and October came round like an annual accusation of her wasted summer freedom. Not that a Senior Tutor's responsibilities ever exactly allowed her freedom to pursue her own work uninterrupted even in vacation, but the calls on her time were nothing compared to the intensive pressures of the eight-week term ahead.

Guilt, too, about Lucia. Saturday, when they could have been doing mother–daughter things in town: trying on clothes, browsing the book shops, sitting in Starbucks. How much time would she have to see Lucia, really to talk to her, over the weeks ahead? Martha vowed, of course, that time must somehow be found. Of all the cares weighing in upon her at the start of this new term, Lucia was the most gnawing and pervasive, the one which was left to haunt her, each night, after the more pressing worries of her professional life fell away and she drifted towards sleep. Lucia. The name was chosen by Douglas, after that summer he spent in Italy 'finding his muse', while Martha was hot and heavily pregnant on her own here at home, writing up her PhD. But for Martha, though she mocked herself at the notion, it could not have proved more appropriate: Lucia, the light of her life.

Martha applied her bicycle brakes as a family group – father, mother and freshman daughter – crossed the road in front of her, absorbed in one another and unaccustomed to looking out for bikes; they heard the brakes' protesting squawk and turned as one, the woman apologetic, deprecating herself and her family, while the girl smiled in confidence of forgiveness.

Lucia had been such a vibrant child, so full of life and energy; adolescence had made her volatile but had not sapped her essential vitality. But recently her spark seemed dimmed. It was not merely her decision to drop out of her sixth form course this spring, though that had marked a crisis point. And Martha *did* nurse to herself – of course she did – the hope that Lucia might some day go back to her studies. But that was not the real cause of Martha's pain. It was what the decision represented, the utter falling away of direction or drive; it was the lack of anything to replace school, beyond this formless urge to 'write', which was productive of nothing but a few scribbled fragments and long hours on the sofa looking miserable. Lucia seemed never to be far from the edge of tears. If one of Martha's tutorial students had been in this state, with what ease would she have voiced her suspicion of depression and advised seeing a doctor; why was it then so hard in her daughter's case?

41

She was crossing the river now, away from the city centre and towards her own college. Here the streets were broader and tree-lined, Victorian rather than medieval, the fallen leaves turning to mulch in the watery gutters, splattering and slipping under her bicycle tyres.

This afternoon Martha's role was not a major one. The formal welcome would come tomorrow; for today, what was required of her was little more than to be on hand, mainly to answer any concerns of the newcomers' parents. While the freshers gathered in babbling knots, exchanging preliminary details of home town and schooling, the parents were offered refreshment before the return journeys in empty cars. Once it would have been sandwiches and cake; this year, as last, plates of assorted biscuits. The anxious ones would spot her badge (*Martha Pearce, Senior Tutor*) and would come up to her diffidently, asking about registration with a GP or the cost of college meals. She could well imagine her own apprehensions in the same situation, leaving Lucia at an unfamiliar university – but she had to face the fact that it was a position in which she might never find herself. Martha sometimes reflected how different it would be to teach in a school, where relationships with parents were a constant feature of the job. At St Rad's her dealings were exclusively with the students themselves, her young adult charges. Parents she almost never came into contact with, after today, until graduation. In most cases, that would be an occasion for mutual pleasure and satisfaction; she treasured the exchange of fond reminiscences on both sides. With those who had experienced 'tutorial problems', what she saw of the parents frequently went a long way to explaining the daughter's difficulties.

Turning into the college, dismounting and wheeling her bike towards the Fellows' bicycle shed, Martha's mind began running through the arrangements for tomorrow's Induction Day. In previous years, with previous Student Union executives, she had planned and run the event in close partnership with the undergraduates. But Karen and Deepa remained distant and uncommunicative except upon the most essential of practical questions. She hoped the tension would not be evident to the freshers, or affect the smoothness of tomorrow's events. And of course there was the matter of the rent strike itself. Even today the new arrivals, locating and emptying their pigeonholes for the first time, would be confronted with the screaming red wall of posters and would wonder, perhaps, what battleground they had happened into. It was not the start she would have wished either for them or for the college.

'Martha, hi!'

It was two of her final year economists, Lauren and Peta, coming round the corner towards her from the direction of the porter's lodge. Martha found herself quickly enveloped in a three-way bear hug and a rush of excited chatter, about respective summers spent in Prague and Indonesia and their choice of option papers for Part II. They turned to walk with her the way she went, talking still, and Martha was flooded with the recollection of why she loved her job and why each new term could still be a source of delight. Until Peta paused in the account of her proposed dissertation topic to ask, 'So what's the new Master or whatever he's called like, then, Martha? And what's all this about a rent strike?'

'The runner-up was an interesting woman, working on the epithalamium in ancient Greek culture. But we decided to award the Fellowship to Adeola Onoge. She is just waiting to be *viva*'d for her Oxford DPhil. On post-colonial literature: themes of motherhood in the African novel.'

It was Rycarte's first meeting of the College Council, on Monday afternoon in the first week of Full Term. The speaker was Professor Letitia Gladwin, a grey-haired and desiccated don of unknowable years, Vice-Mistress of St Rad's and chair of the Research Fellowships Committee.

'I believe Ms Onoge will prove an excellent addition to the Fellowship – a fine young scholar. She will be joining us in January. I have to report, however, that the field was disappointing in this year's competition – very disappointing indeed.'

Rycarte was conscious that his primary task in chairing the meeting was to keep proceedings moving expeditiously, and certainly not to hold matters up with his own novice questions. But this was something he could not allow to go by without a request for information.

'Why is that, in your opinion, Professor Gladwin? Is there anything we should be doing about it for next time?'

'On the contrary, there is nothing whatever that we can do – not whilst the Fellowship remains non-stipendiary.'

Rycarte was mystified. 'Non-stipendiary? You mean we aren't proposing to pay this person?'

'Non-stipendiary. Which means, as you astutely observe, that no stipend attaches to the appointment.'

'Then what . . . why . . . ?'

'The position of Research Fellow affords the opportunity to partake in a vibrant research community here in St Radegund's. The appointee will have the chance to gain teaching experience should she so wish. She will have the benefit of a room, meals and Commons and use of our own excellent college library, as well as membership of the University, giving access to its facilities and the intellectual life of her own faculty.'

Professor Gladwin spoke in tones of bitterness which were quite at variance with the words.

'But no stipend,' reiterated Rycarte, still at a loss.

The Vice-Mistress directed a look of pure venom at the Bursar, and was about to respond when Martha Pearce cut in with the explanation.

'Naturally the Research Fellowship in Arts and

Social Sciences traditionally carried a stipend. In Sciences, the situation is rather different, as there is a wealth of excellent young scholars engaged in externally funded post-doctoral research, for whom the offer of a non-stipendiary college Fellowship is a much coveted additional privilege. But in the arts external funding after PhD level is very hard to come by.'

'Ms Onoge holds a three-year British Academy Research Associateship,' put in Professor Gladwin with pride, sliding swiftly to something approaching disdain as she added, 'Most of the other candidates were married women with husbands to support them.'

'Moving the competition forward to September, ahead of other colleges, was an attempt to attract as wide a field as possible,' continued Martha evenly. 'However, by making the Fellowship non-stipendiary we are clearly excluding a lot of promising candidates who lack independent financial resources. It is highly regrettable to have to narrow the net in this way, but it was by no means a decision which the college took lightly. There was (if I may call it such) a good deal of soul-searching. But in the end it was a matter of economic necessity.'

Letitia Gladwin might well snort in disapproval, thought Martha, who had shared her dismay at the change – though in the end she had perhaps been more persuaded than her colleague by the weight of Kate Beasley's financial arguments.

Research Fellowships were the very lifeblood of the profession, the seedcorn for a healthy academic future. How else were young scholars to find the space to develop their own work beyond their doctorates, to build a secure foundation, to put in place the habit of research which would last them a lifetime? Where, outside the JRFs provided by Oxford and Cambridge colleges, were there pure research posts to be had in the arts? The only alternative was a junior teaching post, and twenty hours a week of contact time, repeating the same supervisions to successive groups of undergraduate students. What time did that leave for research? But these were not easy times. Savings needed to be found, and there was so little else that was expendable. They had to teach; they required books for the library; the college must be cleaned; they needed heat and light. Whereas research, although at the heart of everything the college stood for, was productive of no immediate measurable gain. And so it was research which fell to be cut.

She was recalled to business by James Rycarte, who ended a thoughtful silence with a slow 'I see', before undertaking to write and congratulate Ms Onoge and then announcing the next item for the Council's consideration. This matter – a routine report on conference bookings – was dispatched in short order, and that marked the end of the unreserved section of the agenda, at which the junior members were in attendance.

'Before we thank our student representatives and

move on to the reserved agenda,' said Rycarte, 'has anyone any other business?'

'Yes, actually, there was something we wanted to raise.'

He turned to the two undergraduates, seated at the end of the table on his left, neither of whom had uttered a word during the meeting so far. He thought they both looked ill at ease in their borrowed academic gowns – just as he felt in his own, freshly acquired from Moss Bros this morning. It was not the beautiful Indian girl who had spoken, but the other one, the blonde.

'It's about the Hardship Fund Committee. A point of information – since that is a committee on which students are denied representation.'

Kate Beasley opened her mouth to quibble with this choice of words, but the blonde girl pressed on firmly.

'We are seeking a guarantee that students suffering financial hardship will not be penalised as a result of their participation in the current rent strike.'

This time Kate was almost spluttering. Martha it was, however, who answered, and Rycarte noticed the calming hand which she laid upon Kate's forearm, under cover of the table.

'We did indeed, as I am sure you have heard, hold an extraordinary meeting of the Hardship Fund Committee on Friday. And it is perfectly true that the rent strike was discussed. What I can promise you is that the committee has agreed not to fetter its discretion. The withholding of college room rents will not rule out a student from making an application.'

At this point Kate's arm was snatched away from beneath Martha's fingers, a gesture which she made no attempt to disguise from those around the table. Martha's voice showed no sign of reaction as she continued, 'Each application will be considered on its merits, just as usual. Anyone in a situation of genuine hardship will still be assisted.'

Both undergraduate representatives appeared satisfied with this answer and rose to take their departure. Through his words of thanks to them Rycarte just caught Kate's muttered aside, '*Genuine* hardship, indeed!'

The reserved agenda items proved relatively uncontentious – staff regradings, applications for sabbatical leave, and the like – until once again 'Any Other Business' was reached. This time it was Ros Clarke who raised her voice. Rycarte steeled himself for an assault and was quite wrong-footed when the matter seemed to be wholly different from anything he had been expecting.

'I should like the Council to consider the question of refurbishment of the Mistress's Lodging. As colleagues will be aware, there has been no significant expenditure upon decoration, furniture or fixtures at the lodging since it was refitted for Dame Emily fourteen years ago.'

Dr Clarke's beatific smile circled the table,

embracing Rycarte before it settled upon Kate Beasley.

'I took the liberty of ascertaining from the Bursar in advance of today's meeting the sum which was allowed to Dame Emily for her refurbishments at that time.'

Kate nodded her confirmation. Dr Clarke consulted a note lying amongst her papers.

'To be precise, Dame Emily was allowed and spent in total £12,642, give or take a few pence.' Her smile broadened. 'Of course, costs have risen considerably in the interim. I think Council members will agree that it is only right that our new Head of House should be offered the same sum as his predecessor, along with an inflationary increase. I should like to propose that a figure of fifteen thousand pounds be approved for this purpose.'

As the nods of approval passed round the table, Rycarte's imagination drifted to the master bedroom, stripped in his mind's eye of every trace of Dame Emily's floral garlands; to the en suite bathroom, equipped with a state-of-the-art power shower. But the dream lasted only a moment. *All the kingdoms of the world, and the glory of them . . .* Of course it could not be: get thee hence, Satan. He might perhaps not yet fully understand the sacred place which the fostering of research held in the St Radegund's philosophy, but he had been here long enough to know it was important. Six days in post and he recognised that already Martha

50

Pearce had become his barometer for gauging what mattered in the college; if St Rad's had a beating heart she was it, or close to it. Martha evidently felt that the abandonment of a stipendiary Research Fellowship was a cut to the quick, and so it must be understood in those terms. The two were not directly interchangeable, of course, but the symbolism was clear: fifteen thousand pounds must be equivalent to one year's stipend for a young researcher, if one ignored the overheads. It would be political suicide to take it.

He had scarcely launched upon his short speech of gratitude and renunciation when he observed the irritation which flickered across Ros Clarke's face and knew that he had been right. He could put up with the rosebud curtains: victory was sweet.

CHAPTER 5

At five twenty-five that afternoon Rycarte heard Miss Kett-Symes in the adjoining office close down the computer upon which she had been writing up the minutes of the Council meeting and begin to gather up sundry items into that voluminous leather bag of hers. Just as the hands on the office clock ticked round to five thirty she emerged through the interconnecting door. Under one arm was gripped the bag and over it draped her raincoat; in the other hand she clutched a bunch of chrysanthemums wrapped in cellophane and pink candy-striped tissue paper.

'I'll be off now, Mr Rycarte. Don't forget to turn off all the lights when you go. And don't leave your computer on stand-by, will you?'

'Oh no, indeed; I shouldn't want to add to the burden of global warming, Miss Kett-Symes.'

She directed at him a stony stare and her reply was short.

'Power surges, I was thinking of. The wiring is rather old, and we sometimes get power surges.'

Unable to think of any suitable rejoinder to this

unlikely piece of intelligence, Rycarte opted instead for a switch of direction.

'Nice flowers. Are they for someone special?'

His secretary's mineral features cracked a little, like wet sand under a hot sun.

'Very special,' she croaked. 'I'm going to visit Dame Emily.'

'Oh, that's . . . nice. She'll be pleased to see you, I expect.'

For some reason she seemed to stiffen, and her eyes could only be described as baleful. He tried a light tone, self-mocking.

'I'm sure she'll enjoy hearing about what's been going on at the old place. What a mess the new man's making of things.'

'Mr Rycarte . . .'

She gulped noisily. Oh dear, what had he said?

'Dame Emily isn't in any position to enjoy hearing about things. She can't speak, and very probably can't hear either. She suffered a stroke at the beginning of September, and has so far recovered very little function.'

'*Oh, Christ!*'

Apparently he had spoken aloud, and it certainly had not helped matters. Why was it now for the first time that he noticed the filigree gold cross, dangling reproachfully below Miss Kett-Symes's cashmere roll-neck? *And why had nobody told him?*

'I mean, I'm dreadfully sorry. I really had no idea, or I would never have . . . Please give, er, what I mean is, please accept . . .' He made an effort to pull himself together. 'What hospital is she in? Or is she at home?'

'She's in the Beeches. It's a small hospital on the edge of town, just for chronic patients, no acute wards there any more. I try to go every day after work, except Fridays, and a lot of the other Fellows visit, too. And the staff. She was – is – dearly respected. Dearly loved.'

There seemed little more to be said on either side beyond his muttered 'Of course'; mercifully soon she was gone and Rycarte could sit down at his desk and give way to the urge to bury his face in his hands. How could he have been so stupid? And yet really, how was he to blame? How could he possibly have known if no one had seen fit to mention it? He also experienced an irrational wave of remorse towards the *grande dame* herself. It was as though they had been together for days and he had not even known she was ill.

Hauling himself out of his private mire of embarrassment, he consulted his wristwatch. Dinner was at seven thirty, the first occasion on which he was to preside at High Table; this somewhat alarming landmark was to be preceded by sherry at seven p.m. in the SCR. That left an hour or so before he needed to wash and change and re-don the Moss Bros gown, which now hung on the back of his office door as if it – and he – belonged here. He would take advantage of one of the first quiet moments all day to recommence acquainting himself with the contents of those box files.

Precious few spades in St Radegund's, he was discovering, were openly identified as such. The Development Committee, for example, whose most recent minutes he now began to peruse, turned out to mean fund-raising; its sub-committee on Alumnae Relations meant fund-raising from old members. But the record of these bodies' deliberations did not retain for long his undivided attention. Sherry before dinner. If there was one thing he was determined to change after a hundred and sixty years of tradition it was the sherry. What he fancied more than anything just then, after seven hours of parching meetings, was a nice long pint of draught bitter. Perhaps that was pushing it a bit – but wouldn't most of the Fellows be just as happy with a glass of chilled Pinot Grigio?

Dinner on the occasion of his first visit to the college was something of a blur. He had been too busy playing over everything he had said in his interview – and all the things he ought to have said and hadn't – to pay close attention to the conversation around him; but he did recall being grateful that he knew at least a little about Eric Gill, and about cultural relativism. What of this evening? He stood up and moved over to the side table, on which lay the seating plan drawn up for tonight's meal by Miss Kett-Symes. Martha Pearce, who would undoubtedly have been his first choice of conversational partner, she had located half a table away, while to his immediate right she had placed Ros Clarke. He was undecided whether to suspect

his secretary of active conspiracy or simple vindic-
tiveness. To his left was to be seated Susie James,
the Admissions Tutor and amateur photocopier
mechanic. By convention in St Rad's those dining
sat along one side of High Table only, facing the
rest of Hall. There would therefore be nobody
opposite him; any talk would necessarily be
confined to his two neighbours.

Returning to his desk, he clicked open the web
page for the Faculty of English, and searched for
the name of Dr Clarke, Reader in Modern
Literature. He allowed himself the outlet of an
audible groan; her work all bore titles including
words such as 'post-structural' and 'metalanguage'
and would clearly be incomprehensible to ordinary mortals. Jane Austen this was not. And any
subject of college interest would surely only lead
to the crossing of swords. The young biologist
might be a better bet, if she could relax and get
beyond either gushing or tongue-tied. Plants or
animals might be something he could talk about.
He looked her up – no luck. Anything she studied
could only be observed through a powerful micro-
scope and analysed with the aid of a specialised
computer program.

At this juncture, Rycarte's defensive groundwork
for the evening ahead was interrupted by a knock
at the door; he called out a welcome and it opened
to admit, to his pleasure, Martha Pearce, and,
rather less so, Letitia Gladwin. Martha, he noticed,
wore faded jeans, in contrast with Professor

56

Gladwin's sensible skirt and cardigan. He had yet to see Martha in anything else, though dinner tonight would perhaps reveal a greater breadth to her wardrobe. Very woman-of-the-people, very in-with-the-students, he had thought at first sight, but further acquaintance with her had made him adjust his position. He couldn't imagine Martha doing anything purely for effect; besides – though it might be a capital offence even to think such a thing in such a place – she did look remarkably good in them. It transpired that the dual deputation had come *ex officio*, in their respective capacities as Senior Tutor and Vice-Mistress; they had been sent here on a mission. It was Professor Gladwin who, the necessary pleasantries having been exchanged, revealed the purpose of their visit.

'The Fellows feel that we need to reach a decision about your title, Mr Rycarte.'

'James.'

This being clearly no solution, it was ignored.

'As I believe you are aware, the Governing Body was unable to reach a consensus at the time of your election as to the most appropriate title to be attached to your headship of the college. It was decided to leave the choice of nomenclature to yourself, upon your arrival. It has now become a matter of some urgency that this matter be resolved.'

Rycarte's eyes strayed towards Martha Pearce's face, as if seeking some clue.

'It certainly is rather pressing,' she said. 'I'm afraid

that, as we had no better information to give them, the University diary and network telephone directory already have you listed as "Mistress".'

There was sympathy both in the words and in the smile which accompanied them, but no indication of a route through the quicksand. At length he slowly ventured, 'So, what are the possibilities?'

The Vice-Mistress took over once more.

'The obvious equivalent of Mistress, of course, is "Master". Quite a few of us would favour that title. Others would prefer "President". There was no real support for any other contender: "Provost" is particular to King's; Robinson has a "Warden" like several of the Oxford colleges; Newnham and Homerton both have "Principals" . . .'

She tailed off with a dismissive hand gesture. Rycarte was visited by an improbable picture of her as a trackside bookmaker. A hundred to one bar these five.

'And might I be allowed to ask what arguments have principally been employed on either side?'

Professor Gladwin did not seem inclined to divulge the private views of members of the Governing Body, but Martha stepped to his aid.

'The majority of Cambridge colleges of modern foundation have a President. It is, after all, perhaps the best description of the role of Head of House: to preside over the college on formal occasions, and over its democratic machinery of governance, as well as to represent it to the outside world.'

58

She was choosing her words with care, and he had no way of discerning whether this represented her own view of the issue. Moreover, she was now looking interrogatively at the Vice-Mistress as she added, 'I believe that those amongst the Fellowship who oppose this option – Letitia, I think you are amongst them – do so on the grounds that the term "President" has too much of a . . . corporate feel to it.'

Her feelings overcoming her concern for discretion, Professor Gladwin gave this proposition her trenchant endorsement.

'Absolutely it does. It makes it sound as if we are some American-style business enterprise.'

'Letitia – and there are many who share her view – would prefer the more traditional term "Master". But again there is a grouping of Fellows for whom this title has unfortunate resonances, particularly in a women's college.'

'Ah yes, I see. They fear that I shall wish to assert mastery over them; try to be too masterful.'

Letitia Gladwin clucked her disdain for such linguistic scrupling.

'And this latter grouping, would it by any chance include Dr Clarke?' hazarded Rycarte innocently.

A further cluck from Dr Gladwin was all the answer he required; it appeared that Martha's loyalty, however, was not so easily to be swayed.

'Ros Clarke has firm principles and is never afraid to follow them,' was all he could get out of her on the subject.

'And why not "Principal"? Surely, if we are worrying about the roots of language, that term is the one which best expresses the idea of *prima inter pares*?'

This time the sound emitted by the Vice-Mistress was more vocal than a cluck and, making a wholly unnecessary adjustment to the folds of the gown which hung over her arm, she excused herself on the grounds of a dinner guest to greet and swept from the room. Martha would have followed her, but Rycarte called her attention back with the prompt, '"Principal"?'

The careful look relaxed from her eyes; her smile was suddenly warm and merry, almost conspiratorial.

'There are those who would die before they would do anything which Newnham does.'

Rycarte laughed at that, and tentatively Martha joined in with him. It was a moment of alliance, a moment he thought it prudent not to waste. He risked the direct approach.

'I can see Dr Clarke does not like me. Or rather, she does not like what I represent.'

Her look was guarded again, and he was afraid he had gone too far, too soon. Less sure of himself, he nevertheless persisted.

'Is there anything that I ought to be looking out for, from her direction? Anything I need to avoid?'

Martha was silent for some moments, apparently trying to reach some kind of decision. When at length she spoke it was with that meticulous weighing of words which Rycarte had come to recognise as characteristic of her.

'Ros Clarke makes no secret of the fact she opposed the appointment of a male Head of House at St Radegund's. She was by no means alone in so doing. I myself was against it as a matter of principle. However, your particular strengths as candidate were such as to persuade the majority of the Governing Body of the case for your appointment in spite of the powerful reservations expressed in some quarters. We are a democratic institution, and we accept the collective decision that we have taken. I myself accept it. No   that is ungracious – I embrace it. You are here, and I shall be honoured and delighted to work with you in every way I can to serve the best interests of our college. Whether Ros Clarke accepts the decision in quite the same spirit is debatable. And there may be others.'

He took a step towards her, but she dropped her eyes and turned back to the door. Then, with her hand on the door handle, she faced him again and added a personal promise.

'One thing you can be certain of: I shall never do anything disloyal to St Radegund's. To that extent, you can rely on me.'

'. . . *ut illis salubriter nutriti tibi debitum obsequium praestare valeamus, per Christum Dominum nostrum. Amen.*'

Rycarte hoped his rusty grammar school Latin

61

passed muster. But really, what an absurdity it was to be reading grace in Latin when it was almost half a millennium since the established church had gone over to the vernacular. The college Chaplain, the Reverend Joan Tilley, to whom he had been introduced over the wretched sherry, did not seem remotely High Church: an approachable, homely female, purest C of E, who would not have looked out of place as an extra in Dibley.

As they seated themselves – first Rycarte and then everybody else – he cast a regretful glance towards the distant figure of Martha Pearce, clad now in something plain but elegant and figure-hugging beneath her academic gown, before turning to his left with his most professional smile.

'So, I think this time you really can call me James, Dr James.'

She flushed scarlet, but he could tell she was pleased by his teasing: pleased that he had remembered.

'Susie.'

'Well, Susie, you don't sound like a native East Anglian, if you don't mind my commenting. Have I perhaps the pleasure of encountering a fellow northerner? Or should I say a northern Fellow?'

She dimpled pinkly. 'I'm from Sheffield.'

'Really? How wonderful! My first job in television was as a reporter on *Look North*, and Sheffield was my patch – although the main studios were in Leeds. I loved it there. I lived in lodgings with a couple in Eccleshall – used to go and watch United play on Saturdays with my landlord, Ray.'

'Oh, my goodness! How funny, because I'm a huge Blades fan. I always go and watch them with my dad whenever I make it home for a weekend.'

'Well, this was a long while ago, of course. Bramall Lane will have changed a bit since I used to go there. That was before they built the fourth stand, when it was open to the cricket pitch along one side. They used to have to have armies of ball-boys to go and fetch all the balls that went into touch. Mind you, there wasn't a lot of loose passing when Alan Woodward was playing on that wing. And that was the team that had the young Tony Currie in it, of course. I saw them win promotion to the old First Division in 1971.'

'Oh, yes, Dad talks about that side all the time—'

The colour returned to her cheeks as she realised what she had said, but Rycarte laughed. Against the odds, he was beginning to enjoy himself.

'It's all right, I know I'm as old as the Pennines. But tell me, what are they like these days under Neil Warnock?'

'Oh, they're going great guns. I'm sure promotion is on the cards this season. If Shipperley can keep sticking them away the way he has been doing recently . . .'

CHAPTER 6

D
r Darren Cotter did not hold a strong view on whether the new Head of House – who seemed like a sensible enough man and had always struck Darren as quite impressive in his television appearances – was called Master, President or anything else he cared to choose. But even had he had such a view Darren would not have been called upon to express it, for he was not a member of the Governing Body. Although statutorily debarring him by reason of his gender from holding a Fellowship, St Radegund's was more than happy to employ Darren to fulfil its teaching needs in Electrical Engineering, under the title of College Teaching Officer. In return for his twelve hours per week of college supervising he drew a stipend, received the benefit of a college room and all his meals (breakfast excepted, apart from during Ramadan) and was still left with sufficient time to pursue his own lab work, especially during the vacations. It was an arrangement which suited Darren admirably. He had no interest in college politics, and was merely relieved to be excused the additional administrative burden

which being a Fellow must necessarily have entailed. Moreover, he rather liked teaching girls, who were less prone than their male counterparts to challenge the credentials of a young and inexperienced supervisor.

Admittedly it had briefly struck Darren as odd, last winter, when he first heard that St Rad's was considering appointing a man to replace Dame Emily, but it made some sense when it had been explained to him over High Table. College Statutes expressly provided that 'all Fellows shall be female', but referred throughout to 'the Mistress and Fellows'; hence, as a matter of construction, the Mistress was not herself a Fellow, and so was not caught by the gender restriction.

Darren had been less than enthusiastic, however, when Martha Pearce had approached him during the Long Vacation and asked him if he was prepared to act as Dean. But Martha was a difficult person of whom to refuse a request. She had been very supportive of him personally when he had first arrived at the college last year – and besides, she herself appeared never to say no to anything that was asked of her. He had not been at all sure what the Dean did. He knew that the post did not at St Radegund's have a religious function, since that role was filled by Joan Tilley, the Chaplain. Martha had explained that the duties were light. Formally speaking, Dean was shorthand for Dean of Discipline, but indiscipline in St Rad's was rare and usually trifling, and what little there was of it was these days mostly dealt with by the miscreant's Tutor. The Dean's job consisted almost exclusively of approving the arrangements for, and if necessary subsequently closing down, noisy undergraduate parties. Recent tradition decreed that the post be held by a young male College Teaching Officer and the previous Dean (the confusingly named Dr Dean O'Connor) had left in the summer to take up a tenured lectureship at the University of Essex.

So, against his better judgement, Darren had said yes and was now on his way to meet the Student Union Ents Committee. This was the student abbreviation for 'Entertainments', of course – though Darren, an avid fan of all things Middle-Earth, could never quite rid his mind of the image of walking trees. He had arranged to meet them in the JCR, an untidy room adjoining the college bar, bestrewn with newspapers and piles of unread careers handbooks, and lined with vending machines for the dispensing of chocolate bars and other late-night necessities. They were already there waiting for him when he arrived, diffident at thus encroaching upon what was normally exclusive undergraduate territory. It was just the three of them: two whom he recognised as Karen and Deepa, the president and vice-president of the college Student Union, and a third, a tall girl with curly brown hair who was introduced as Julia, the ents officer.

They moved a heap of coats, bags and trailing scarves off a fourth chair around the small table at which they were seated and as Darren sat down it was Karen who spoke first.

'When Dean was the Dean, we always used to have a meeting near the beginning of each term to let him know what we had planned, so he could OK the programme. It's Julia's department, really.'

She looked towards her ents officer, who shuffled through her bag for a sheet of paper covered with a handwritten list of dates. She laid it on the table in front of Darren and leaned towards him a little as she indicated the salient entries.

'It's all similar to last year. We've lined up live bands for the bar most Tuesdays after Formal Hall; they normally play two sets between eight and eleven thirty. Film Club you don't need to worry about – that's Fridays. Nor Quiz Nights.'

'Those certainly sound peaceful enough,' Darren smiled. Julia and Deepa both giggled politely.

'We've also booked a DJ for the last Saturday night of term. Drum and bass stuff, you know.'

Darren's eyes followed Julia's finger to the words 'Luvdemsistas, 10 p.m. – 1 a.m.' Just like him she still bit her nails, he noticed.

'A one a.m. finish. Is that usual?'

Julia looked across at Karen, who sat back in her chair with just too much airy confidence not to rouse Darren's suspicion. Any minute now she was going to fold her arms. Or give an ostentatious yawn.

'Well, we're always allowed until midnight for the last big ent of term. But the DJ didn't want to start before ten p.m., so we thought ten 'til one would be OK, instead of nine 'til twelve.'

Darren did not respond straight away; though he continued to study Julia's sloping handwriting he did not miss the exchange of glances which passed between the girls. He might be new, but he wasn't that naive. He looked up, avoiding Karen's eye and focusing on Julia.

'I'll talk to the Bursar and see what she says. What about security?'

'We normally pay a couple of the porters to keep an eye on things. Their overtime is covered out of the ticket sales.'

'Fine. I'll check that with the Head Porter, too, then.'

He rose to leave, asking, 'Is it all right if I keep this copy of the schedule, Julia?'

She looked up at him, her expression unfathomable.

'Course. I wrote that one out for you. And, er . . . well, Dean usually used to come along to the bar when there was anything on. The first gig is next Tuesday: just a student band, cheesy eighties pop, but they're very danceable. I don't suppose you'd be free that night? Just to keep an eye on things, I mean.'

Darren nodded, trying not to look pleased, and departed with his sheet of paper. When he had left, Karen and Deepa both turned towards Julia, who was watching the way he had gone.

'So?' said Karen. 'What do you reckon? Feasible?'

Julia turned back to her companions with a slow smile. 'Definitely feasible. He's even quite cute, for a card-carrying computer geek.' She hesitated, the smile fading into a shadow of concern. 'But . . . I don't know, he seems so . . . I just think it's a bit harsh, that's all.'

Later the same evening, elsewhere in St Radegund's, another meeting had just broken up. In the Graduate Seminar Room a mixed audience of senior and junior members of the college had been listening to an earnest young woman from the Faculty of Law decrying the government's failure to eradicate the practice of female genital mutilation. Everyone had drifted away, still talking in scandalised gaggles, with the exception of Karen, Deepa and Dr Ros Clarke.

'Can you believe what she was saying? Over twenty years they've had the legislation, and literally not a single prosecution. Not one!'

This was Deepa, dark eyes ablaze, moved from her usual contained reserve by what she had just heard.

'Yeah, and we worry about the low conviction rates for rape,' agreed Karen. 'But this is something else again.'

Dr Clarke felt a glow of pleasure to see their outrage, their passion to see something done. It was to achieve exactly such an effect that she had conceived, nine years ago now, the idea of RadFem. (The name, with its air of retro chic, still gave her a small private glow.) The grouping brought together dons and students, graduate and undergraduate, who shared a concern with women's issues. Interdisciplinary seminars were held with speakers from all branches of gender studies, on topics of current concern in sexual politics. She had made it her mission to encourage the young women of St Rad's first to understand more clearly and then to seek to change the world and their place within it.

'If these girls were not from Sierra Leone, Somalia and Ethiopa,' she said, looking straight at Deepa, 'if they were white, you can be sure there would not be the same complacency.'

Then, casually, as if the thought had just that moment occurred to her, she added, 'Pity not to see Martha Pearce here. I know she has strong views on FGM, and last year she was such a regular.'

'She probably knew we'd be here. I don't suppose she wants to run into Deepa and me just at the moment,' replied Karen, with grim satisfaction.

Deepa raised one finely arched eyebrow, and fixed on her friend a gently ironic eye. Over the past two weeks she had watched Karen delete at least half a dozen e-mails from the Senior Tutor, as well as tossing a note from her into the mail room waste-paper bin.

'Ah yes,' said Dr Clarke, 'the rent strike. Well, I must say, it couldn't be better timed. A nice hot welcome to the college for James Rycarte. Adverse publicity already in the student press, creating an unfortunate early impression around the University. Maybe it will be picked up by the nationals – he is a media figure, and they are always interested in their own.'

Karen's eyes glittered; Dr Clarke contemplated in whose ear the hint might be leaked. Meanwhile, a word of warning to the students was required.

'You know that Martha Pearce will be trying her hardest to settle things quickly.'

It was not that Dr Clarke was insensible to the unprofessionalism, as most would view it, of speaking thus about a colleague to the under-graduates. But the stakes were too high for such niceties, the matter of too much overriding importance. On this issue, it was vital that all those within St Radegund's who were of the same view must make common cause. Besides, she told herself, didn't RadFem exist to break down the barriers between the Fellowship and the student body? Wasn't Martha herself a firm believer in that very principle?

'You need to be very wary. I dare say she will have all kinds of attractive compromises to offer you.'

In Ros Clarke's politics, as in her writing – and for her the two were hardly distinguishable – there was no room for compromise.

'You see, I rather think that Martha has sold out. That is the real reason, I suspect, why she was not here tonight. She doesn't want to appear to be in alliance with us, because she no longer shares our position on James Rycarte.'

71

'But how can she do it? How can she work with him?' burst out Karen. 'She was so dead against appointing a man!'

It was certainly true, reflected Ros. Martha, with quiet passion, had been amongst the most outspoken of opponents last winter, when James Rycarte's name had first come up (Kate bloody Beasley!) in connection with the post of Mistress. She had spoken up against the principle of a male Head of House at every meeting of the Governing Body, right down to the day of the final vote. Demonstrated the flawed logic of offering places to women students, giving them the role models of female Fellows, and then undermining the whole construct by placing a man at the apex. Deplored the replication of the pattern so often found in the world outside St Rad's – the very pattern they existed to challenge – with women in subordinate positions doing the work and a man at the top leading them. Then, after his election, everything had changed. Ros had of course at first considered resigning her Fellowship, after that last fateful electoral meeting; but she loved the college, and could not bring herself to abandon it just because it had abandoned its own principles. It was not in her nature to run from a fight; and so she had stayed, and dedicated herself to the task of driving out the colonist. Martha, in contrast, had simply capitulated: a decision which Ros could neither understand nor easily forgive.

Karen cut through her thoughts.

'Don't worry, we're not caving in on this, not for Martha or anyone else.'

Ros Clarke leaned forward and looked from one student to the other, claiming their gaze.

'The rent strike is good – it sets a tone of friction, it's an occasion for bad publicity. But we need something much more than this. Something big.'

What they needed was to force Rycarte to take a position. To find some issue on which to drive a wedge between him and the majority of the Fellowship. It was just a question of watching and waiting for the right issue to come along; it could only be a matter of time.

'Come on – I don't think there's anything more we can do just at the moment. Come to the bar and I'll stand you two impoverished students a drink.'

CHAPTER 7

O n Tuesday morning the following week, when Rycarte was taking advantage of a quiet moment to get to grips with past minutes of the Investment Committee preparatory to chairing that body's first meeting of the Michaelmas Term, the telephone rang in the adjoining room and Miss Kett-Symes announced that she was putting through a call from Italy.

'*Buongiorno, egregio Signor Rycartè.*'

By the redundant sounding of that final e he recognised at once Luigi Alvau, a television contact from his days as a BBC correspondent in Rome. Sr Alvau, director of a leading Italian network, had been of invaluable help on a number of occasions, smoothing potentially difficult situations with words in appropriate ears or the mention of vicarious favours which might be called in.

'*Ciao, Luigi. Come stai?*'

This small flourish was nothing but a gesture of *cameratismo* on Rycarte's part. Alvau's English might be heavily accented, but this was merely ostentation; after five years in London and three in Chicago as a young television executive his command of the

74

language was unerring. By contrast, living in eight different countries as a foreign correspondent had taught Rycarte woefully little of the local languages, in a world where the initials BBC still worked their magic and English speakers were always readily to be found.

'I understand that congratulations are in order, James. That you have crawled out from this media swamp of ours. Secured your own ivory tower.'

Rycarte grinned into the receiver. Alvau's delight in anglophone imagery had clearly not abated: he had always loved mixing his metaphors.

'Ah yes, the groves of academe. Though at the moment I'm often finding it hard to see the wood for the trees.'

This feeble attempt to enter the game was rewarded with a shout of laughter from the other end of the line, and Rycarte was invaded with the memory of why he had so enjoyed the Italian's company.

'Listen, my friend, I am going to be in London on Friday morning early; my business should be concluded before eleven. It would give me great pleasure to come and offer you my felicitations in person.'

And so of course Rycarte responded with an invitation to lunch in Hall, and a hearty assurance of how glad he would be to see Alvau again.

'The feeling is entirely mutual, James. And of course there will be the added enchantment of meeting the delectable ladies of St Radegund's.'

He was sending himself up, of course, acting up to the stereotype of his nationality, but he was not beyond doing so in person, too, at High Table. Rycarte half dreaded, half relished the reaction such blandishments might provoke.

'On no account are you to say anything of the sort to my esteemed new colleagues, however decorative you may find them. This invitation is strictly conditional upon good behaviour.'

After he had rung off, Rycarte fell to divining the meaning of this first phone call in almost fifteen years. It was true that to a European media magnate a fifty-five-minute train journey was like stepping across the street. But would Alvau really have contacted him simply to bestow his congratulations, or because he was attracted by the notion of lunch in a Cambridge college?

'Media magnate' was no more than a factual description of what his former contact had become: 'media mogul' would not have been overstating things. The relationship between the two men, hovering between business and friendship, had seemed an unlikely one, even back then. Alvau was a Christian Democrat and in Italian life, Rycarte had found, political allegiances were not a matter for polite apology but were worn openly as a badge of honour, cutting through every aspect of life. When Alvau took him to the Olympic Stadium it was inevitably to watch Lazio play, and not the *giallorossi* of AC Roma. This made for an uneasy fit with Rycarte's own South Yorkshire politics, tempered by

76

BBC liberalism; yet somehow as a foreigner Rycarte was off the graph, making the alliance possible. The period since their acquaintance, of course, had seen the flowering of Forza Italia. With it, rising to the surface in the wake of Silvio Berlusconi's prominent dorsal fin, had come shoals of smaller fishes; Alvau, by dint of devouring many of those around him, had become a very big fish indeed. Big enough to remain buoyant when his political mentor finally ran into the electoral dragnets last April. Smiling at the thought of how much the man himself would have enjoyed the conceit of this analogy, Rycarte was still left wondering: why was he coming? Alvau's was a world in which every transaction, whether commercial or personal, was a matter of favours curried, tendered, exchanged or repaid; for Italians of his stamp it was a way of life. The question came down to this: was he buying or selling?

Barely had Rycarte fixed his attention back upon the minutiae of Investment Committee business when the phone sounded again in the interconnecting office. Miss Kett-Symes rose from her chair, hand over the receiver, and called through, 'Apparently there is a delivery for you over at the lodging. Shall I just tell them to leave it somewhere for you? Or get one of the porters to go round and sign for it?'

Rycarte jumped up at once, feeling like a schoolboy on his birthday – though he regretted it when he saw the widening of his secretary's eyes.

'No, no, don't bother. It's no trouble; tell them

I'll be straight over myself. Investment Committee isn't until noon.'

Of course her gaze followed him in puzzled reproof as he gathered his coat and keys and made his getaway, but he did not care. It must be his new bicycle. It had been Paul, teasing him on the telephone from Lyon last week, who had decided him: Paul, the virtuous proponent of universal pedal power. If Paul could ride a bike up and down the steep *côtes* of the Rhône valley, doing battle with French lorry drivers, he himself could surely manage one on the fenland flats of the British capital city of cycling. He had barely had the Alfa out of the garage since his arrival. There was almost nowhere in the town centre where cars were allowed during daylight hours and certainly no chance of a parking permit at any of the central University sites for a mere college Head of House, with neither a disability nor toddlers in tow. Besides, all those kerbs and cobblestones would spell ruin for his tyres and suspension.

Rycarte reached the driveway of the lodging just as two men were wheeling his acquisition down the ramp from the van. A state-of-the-art mountain–tourer cross in magisterial dark red: a bicycle fit for a Master. Not that Rycarte knew anything about bikes – only that this one would have rather more gears available at the fingertips of both hands than had been usual when he had last owned a bike thirty years ago. But Paul had told him what to get so he knew it must be good.

78

He entered a squiggle on the sheet as indicated and waved off the delivery men; but as he was about to unlock the garage and wheel the bike into the space at the side of the Alfa, he changed his mind. If he had to come back over to the lodging every time he went into town he would end up walking. No point in having the machine if he didn't intend to make use of it. Adding the key of the D-lock to his oversized bunch, he took hold of the handlebars and began to push his new treasure down the drive and through the college grounds in the direction of the Fellows' bicycle shed.

Meanwhile Martha Pearce's morning had largely been taken up with two meetings with students, one scheduled and one not. The first of these she had finally succeeded in arranging with Karen and Deepa, although in the event it was Deepa alone who turned up. At this Martha found herself torn between frustration at the Student Union president's intransigence and gratitude for the opportunity of opening a channel of communication with her deputy.

Things took a hopeful course from the start when, after Martha had settled herself cross-legged on the velvet footstool, Deepa opted to sit opposite her on the floor. Martha considered the offer of coffee, but feared that this instinctive gesture of hospitality might be misinterpreted as a bribe.

'I assume Karen chose not to come because she expected me to seek to barter about rents.'

She watched Deepa consider and reject putting forward the lie which Karen had supplied as her excuse for absence. In the face of Deepa's silence, Martha carried on.

'I don't wish to do that. I have no authority to do so, indeed, since as you know the rent levels are final, having been approved by the Finance Committee. Nor do I want to try to dissuade you from continuing with your action.'

Deepa looked up hopefully, as one who might after all be spared some expected punishment. Her glance dropped back to the carpet when Martha continued, 'It does remain the case that I believe targeted and not generalised subsidy of student rents to be the only defensible way forward for the college. I shall be bringing detailed proposals for a rental bursary scheme to next week's Finance Committee.'

There was no response to this and Martha, sure of the unanswerability of her case here, pressed the point.

'I do hope I can count on the Student Union to give the scheme its backing.'

How could they not? Deepa was a reasonable person; more than that, Martha was convinced that she was a caring and community-spirited young woman, who had stood for office out of a desire to serve her fellow students. What possible ground could there be for her to refuse to back a scheme designed to assist those from less advantaged backgrounds than her own with meeting their housing costs? Martha watched with satisfaction as Deepa fiddled with a loose strand of carpet before conceding, 'Naturally we welcome any hardship scheme.'

If only she could make her meet her eye. Martha felt that a connection might be possible here, that Deepa could be made to listen, to understand. There was something about her, indeed, which reminded Martha of herself as a young student activist twenty years earlier: the quiet reflectiveness, the powerful sense of fair play. If she could only win her round, then maybe Karen could be isolated. Martha refused to believe that the majority of students were supportive of their president's line, or would be so if she could get the issues put before them clearly. Martha slid forward off her stool and on to the floor, six inches closer to Deepa, who looked up at last.

'I am also very concerned about the hardship which might result from the strike.'

Deepa's gaze flickered but Martha held it by sheer force of will.

'I'm worried about the position in which some students will find themselves . . .'

. . . when the rent strike fails.

'. . . when the present dispute is resolved. For some people, of course, it is easy enough to keep back the rent money, and just write a cheque for whatever is owing when the time comes.'

Deepa must know that she fell into this happy category; unlike Karen, she had never tried to pretend that in her family money was any object.

'But for others, where things are tighter, it will be very difficult not to dip into that money to meet living expenses. The dispute will end and there will be no money left to pay the rent.'

An acknowledging nod from Deepa gave Martha heart to go on and outline her proposal.

'What I am suggesting is that a special bank account be set up, into which anyone seeking to withhold her rent in protest at the increases can pay the sums which would normally be due. Then there is no danger that it will be spent, leading to debt and hardship later on. The money would be held in trust, with both junior and senior members as signatories. It would not go into the college's general funds unless and until the protest is settled.'

The nodding was more positive now. Martha knocked home her advantage.

'It would buffer the most vulnerable from suffering any adverse effects as a result of our current failure to reach agreement.'

'I think it's a great idea, Martha,' said Deepa as they both rose to their feet, in Martha's case with just a suggestion of stiffness. 'It seems very sensible – just a safeguard, really, as you say. Making everything official and fair.'

Martha smiled at her with real warmth, and not a little relief. No doubt Karen would find some reason to object to the suggestion, and would vituperate Deepa for an imagined capitulation. But Martha had the agreement she needed, to enable her to do the thing she cared about most in all the mess of this rent strike: to protect the poorest students from its possible ill effects. Now, she thought as she showed Deepa out, all she had to do was get the idea past Kate Beasley.

Any satisfaction at this small forward step proved short-lived, however, once Martha was alone again with her much-shelved lecture preparation and the rest of her crowding worries. This might prevent the most damaging potential fall-out from the action – no one would get into serious financial difficulties now – but she was no nearer to seeing any way to resolution of the dispute itself. And yet she felt confident that most of her student flock were reasonable women. If she could just explain it to them. Maybe once the rental bursary scheme was approved and in place for next year, once her promise on targeted subsidy bore this tangible form, then they might hold an open meeting in the JCR, speak not to the Student Union executive (and Karen, in other words) but directly to the whole undergraduate body. She was sure she could persuade them of the rightness of the college's position. If only she could keep Kate Beasley from attending – that could not fail to make things worse. No doubt Kate would insist on being there and sharing the platform.

Unless . . . it occurred to Martha to wonder what James Rycarte might be like up in front of

83

the students. If it was anything like being in front of a camera he ought to be able to handle it with consummate ease. And she thought she could trust him to stick to the college line – to 'stay on message' (she grimaced at the phrase). She had seen enough of him to judge him to be nothing if not professional. But of course it would be a huge gamble. Among the students, as amongst the Fellowship, feelings had run high last year about the appointment of a man to head St Radegund's. Placards had actually been brandished on the day of the Governing Body's final vote. To put him up there before the mob defending unpopular rent rises could spell disaster – especially as it would be impossible to keep the student press out of such a meeting. But if he were able to tame the wolves, to bring them to bay, it could be an important advance on more fronts than just the rent strike.

It was at this point that the circling possibilities were interrupted by a knock at the door and in came Martha's second, unscheduled visitor. She was a pale, freckly girl whom Martha recognised as a third year modern linguist, Sophie Ifield. Not an economist; not one of her own tutorial students; not a member of the Student Union committee. It could only be something nasty. She summoned her best senior tutorial smile.

'Hello, Sophie – come in, sit down. What can I do for you?'

Sophie went straight for the armchair before Martha had made it from desk to footstool, though she did perch rather gingerly on its edge, and she looked far from comfortable. Her opening was a defensive one.

'Dr Gallagher said to come and see you.'

Carolyn Gallagher was the college's Director of Studies in Modern and Medieval Languages.

'Yes?'

Think receptive and helpful; ignore that crawling sensation in the lower abdomen which always preceded the unfolding of some new problem.

'Well, Dr Gallagher has lined up Dr Stedman to supervise us for Italian Poetry Post-1945.'

The crawling became a stampede.

'We had him for our language classes last year and, well, to be honest, we weren't very happy with him. So we're not keen to have him again.'

'What was the problem, exactly?'

Martha hoped that her voice sounded calm, with no more than the correct amount of mild concern.

'It's not his teaching *as such*. He does know his stuff, I mean. But he was . . . well, a bit unreliable, really. Cancelled a couple of classes at short notice, nearly always turned up late. And some of our written assignments he took months to mark – I did one translation for him in March and he only gave it back a few weeks before the exam.'

'And of course you have told all this to Dr Gallagher? So that she can pass it on, have a word with him?'

'We did all that last year, yes. She says she talked to him about it, a couple of times in fact.

85

But things didn't improve. And, um, well this year if it's a literature paper we'd have him for, we're even less keen. You see, even with the language stuff he didn't always seem very clear on what was going to be required, the format of the papers and the oral and everything. But with an essay paper, detailed knowledge of the syllabus is one of the main things. *The* main thing, really, in some ways. I mean, I'm sure he knows loads about poetry, but that's not our point.'

'And what does Dr Gallagher say now?'

Martha knew exactly what Dr Gallagher would have said to Sophie and her disgruntled friends. The only thing she could possibly say in the circumstances.

'She told me to come and see you.'

And there was also only one reply which Martha could give.

'Tell Dr Gallagher she can find you another supervisor, if she knows of someone suitable. And not to worry: I will talk to Dr Stedman.'

Sophie's flow of gratitude barely registered with Martha as she showed her to the door. She was wondering whether the students knew, and if so what they thought about it. Was it just a joke to them, or did they feel embarrassment for her – or worse, sympathy? Anyway, she had promised to grasp the nettle this time, and so she would. She would talk to him today.

It was not difficult for Martha to picture how the conversation would go. She had known

Douglas Stedman for twenty-three years; they had been undergraduates together here at Cambridge, she at St Radegund's, he at King's. And she had been married to him for the last fourteen. For some reason, as Martha sat back down at her desk the picture of their wedding day came to her, though it had been a rather improvised affair, not for the two of them the life-changing rite of passage it was for many couples, less committed already. She had not thought of it in ages; and now that she did it was not Douglas she saw but the three-year-old Lucia, like the sun in sky-blue taffeta, toddling down the central aisle of the Register Office clutching the leg of her grandmother's trouser suit.

Douglas had been the brilliant one, though it was Martha, with less originality but more consistent application, who got the First. The pattern of their later lives had therefore begun at graduation. Her doctorate was fully funded; his postgraduate place was unconditional but his Upper Second was not enough to secure a studentship, and he had scrimped and patched his way through his PhD. It was hardly surprising, then, if it had taken him far more than the statutory three years to complete his thesis on D'Annunzio and the Italian War Poets. While Martha, undeterred by motherhood, had written up, submitted, received the degree and secured her teaching Fellowship, Douglas had completed his research in intermittent bursts of wild enthusiasm, interspersed with long periods of disenchantment. By the time his thesis was finally finished to his

87

satisfaction, Douglas's working habits were set into a pattern which would have made it very difficult for him to settle to a nine-to-five job. He had also in those years seen a number of his own poems published in minor anthologies; these small successes, underpinned by Martha's approbation and encouragement, had helped to allay his chronic self-doubt and keep alive the flame of his under-graduate urge to write. So writing poetry was what Douglas did, alongside the odd book review and whatever bits and pieces of teaching Martha could channel in his direction. Martha still believed passionately in the value of Douglas's poetic work, even though since those early days little of it had been published and almost none of it to any crit-ical acclaim. She knew that his time would come, and meanwhile she was happy to be supporting him, financially and in every other way she could.

Martha was possessed of enough self-awareness to recognise that Douglas's vulnerability was a major part of his hold upon her. He needed her, and Martha needed to be needed. But she still did not relish the prospect of telling him that his super-visions at St Rad's were to be cancelled; having to sack your husband is never a pleasant task.

CHAPTER 8

Having once decided upon the necessity of performing an unpleasant duty, Martha's strong preference was for getting it over with as soon as possible. It was this prompting which saw her packing up her papers and books at six o'clock, a full two hours before the time at which, guilt finally outweighing stress, she would normally have left her desk.

She even had time to pick up the peace offering of three organic fillet steaks on her cycle ride home. Lucia, like her mother, could take it or leave it but Douglas was a man: he loved steak. In spite of the unwonted earliness of her arrival – or perhaps because of it – Martha entered the house to silence. The kitchen, usual hub of any daytime family activity, was deserted, but for the cushion-like mound on the table which was Maynard. Next to him the computer screen was blank but the stand-by light winked redly; Martha resisted the temptation of clicking it on to see who had been writing and what, or of checking her college e-mails one more time. Instead, she ran a finger over Maynard's striped forehead and round behind the silk-covered cartilage of one orange ear, finding his favourite spot. He inclined his head against her hand without opening his eyes, then slowly blinked and uncoiled. His hind quarters rose first, and he arched backwards, stretching his front paws luxuriantly, his yawn ending with a snap.

'Where are they then, puss?'

Maynard stalked towards the end of the kitchen table and stared at Martha from glassy green eyes.

'Sitting room?'

He followed her, and there she found them, asleep: Douglas stretched full length on his back on the sofa, one arm flung behind him across the cushions, and Lucia curled by his legs with her arms crossed in front of her chest, face half obscured beneath a hunched shoulder. Before the rush of physical love which the sight of her sleeping daughter never failed to provoke in her, Martha had time for a moment's irritation. Not irritation that they should be asleep while she had been at work but something much harder to locate. It was somehow directed at Douglas, in relation to Lucia; perhaps a stab of jealousy at seeing them so peaceful together, so free of friction. But more than that: it was a sense of helpless frustration at his effect upon their daughter. The word she tried to block from her mind was 'corrosion'.

Just as she had caressed Maynard to wakefulness, so her hand smoothing into the tumble of Lucia's hair produced a stirring; the blue eyes opened, focused, smiled. Martha laid a finger to her lips;

cautious not to disturb her father, Lucia rose and the two women went back into the kitchen. Martha pulled her daughter into an embrace but after she had returned it briefly Lucia slid away and leaned against the worktop at a short distance, standing with one socked foot on top of the other, toes out-turned, and hands thrust deep into the pockets of her jeans. Where was the brightness in her eyes? Of course Martha silenced her own foolish anxiety – they were simply still clouded with sleep – but she still found she needed to turn away.

Putting the steaks away in the fridge and filling the kettle gave her something to do while she fought the obvious, the universal mother's question: *How was your day?* She had asked it of the three-year-old Lucia, running to her arms from the nursery school gates. She had asked it of her at seven, sitting on the bathroom scales and watching Lucia create swirling mountain peaks with the peach-scented bubbles. At thirteen she had asked her casually over her homework or while she dished up the macaroni cheese. And Lucia had always answered, always wanted to talk about the little details of her friendships, the blow-by-blow of this lesson or that conversation at break, all the small triumphs and hurts and disappointments. But now the question could not be asked without its being an accusation, nor answered without the mounting of a defensive wall. It would be interpreted as the opening salvo in a battle for which Martha, just at present, lacked the stomach.

'I bought steak. I thought we hadn't had it in ages, and you know how much Dad likes it. Shall I do it with green peppercorns, you know, the pickled ones?'

'If you like.'

It was a compromise. Lucia knew how much Martha hated the current dismissive 'Whatever', so she avoided the word but the tone was still there. Then, 'How come you are home so early?'

What had been an effort of goodwill was turned round into recrimination for all the other nights when Martha had come in tired at eight or nine o'clock.

'Well, I had just finished off a few things,' lied Martha; she followed it with the truth, but could only do so behind the protective screen of self-mockery. 'I thought it would be nice to spend some time in the bosom of my family.'

Lucia looked at her for a second before she laughed. Although it was not comfortable laughter it softened Martha's tension; and when she took two knives from the block and emptied a bag of tomatoes on to the chopping board, Lucia moved to her side and took up the second knife, accepting a swift kiss on the side of her head before she began to slice her half of the fruit.

They worked side by side, peeling and crushing garlic, tearing basil, mixing vinaigrette, without any need to speak. The salad was almost ready when Douglas appeared blearily in the doorway and echoed Lucia's reverse swipe about Martha's

92

early homecoming. This time she gave no reason for her appearance, but only passed him the corkscrew.

'Let's have a bottle of the Bardolino.'

'Lucia – shall I pour three?'

Martha knew he was daring her disapproval, and said nothing, concentrating her attention on turning over the wedges of tomato to coat them evenly in the slick dressing.

'Why not? It's not like I'm going to be doing anything tomorrow, am I, Mum?'

It felt as though all the eggshells on which Martha had so carefully been treading had sliced into her at once. It wasn't bloody fair – why was everything always her fault, even when she had said nothing?

'You know you were thinking it.'

Somehow her own transparency fuelled her fury, and Martha suddenly wanted to deflect all this unfairness on to somebody else. On to Douglas. She would tell him now about Sophie's visit, about the complaints: tell him that he was to be replaced as Italian supervisor. But the temptation was only momentary. Of course she had to wait; she would not talk to him about this in front of his daughter – in whose eyes he could do no wrong, added the bitter voice in her head. Martha took a breath and steadied herself.

'Come on, pour the wine, Douglas. And can you fetch the rest of those breadsticks, Lucia? We can finish them while I do the steaks. It might be early but I'm starving.'

'Well, you would be, wouldn't you, Mum? You've been slaving away at work all day . . .'

Alone later she would allow herself to cry, but for now Martha contented herself with dropping the steaks into the spitting oil with the peppercorns and allowing the evaporating vinegar and the smoky rising vapour to fill her stinging eyes.

That evening was live music night in St Radegund's student bar. The floor was already packed and the air dense with voices raised above the pounding bass beat when Darren Cotter edged in late, awkward in his Burton's shirt. He had not dined in Hall like most of those present but had been over at the lab, trying to iron out a glitch in one of his experimental programs. Before that, in the afternoon, he had been teaching, which accounted for his attire. Darren always wore a proper collar and tie for supervisions; he was not entirely confident in his abilities as a teacher, and if he was occasionally to flounder in his explanations he could at least disguise his uncertainty behind the external trappings of authority. Running late tonight, he had had time to ditch the tie, but not to change the shirt.

He would have been overdressed in any student gathering, but the contrast here was extreme. Most of the girls, in particular, seemed to be half naked in the sweaty crush; Darren took in a variety of strappy top halves which revealed in different combinations of arcs and triangles the bare skin of shoulders, backs and midriffs. The boys wore T-shirts like a uniform. Raising his eyes above the moving human mass on the dance floor and that clustering around the bar, Darren examined the band. 'Charlie Goes to Chorley Wood', Julia's list had billed them. Two lads on drums and electric bass and two girl vocalists, one with lead guitar, the other swinging a tambourine against her bony hip. They were at this moment executing, with more enthusiasm than finesse, a cover version of 'Relax'. If only it were that easy.

A drink would be a way of using up some time, as well as giving him a prop to occupy his hands – and a watertight excuse for not dancing. He was threading his way through the throng when he caught sight of the dark curls of Julia, the ents officer, being ruffled by the draught from an open window at the far side of the room. He changed course, abandoning the idea of beer in favour of fresh air and a familiar face. A pretty face, as well, he wasn't too professional to admit. And she was probably the only person in the room who wouldn't be wondering what he was doing there.

Julia looked up at his approach and smiled her welcome.

'Thanks for coming,' she mouthed against the barrage of noise.

'Is everything going OK?'

He was the Dean; that was why he was here. That was the sort of thing deans asked. But apparently the question did not deserve an answer. Julia merely met it with a barely perceptible shift of the shoulders – one sheathed in something clinging and sparkly black, the other all collarbone and white skin.

'What do you think of them?'

She leaned close to his ear to make herself heard, while the direction of her grey-green eyes indicated the foursome on stage. Now this was a tricky one. Clearly the group's name was ironic, as too must be this whole celebration of the escapist culture of Thatcher's narrow decade. The band had moved on to an energetic rendition of 'Walking on Sunshine' and Darren was uncomfortably aware that to the undergraduates – to Julia – this stuff was ancient history, dating from the undifferentiated block of time before they were born. Whereas he had jumped about to Katrina at primary school; his big brother had bought the single. The thing must be to laugh, so Darren laughed.

'Yeah, great . . .'

'You dancing, then?'

It occurred to him to pretend not to have heard her over the hubbub, if only to play for a few extra seconds. But Julia was already spinning away from him, wading out into the tide of bodies on the open floor, and in her cool white fingers she had hold of his hand. He wished he had had that cold bottle to hold earlier; it might have chilled the sweat from his palms. Finding a space which surely could not accommodate two people, she stopped and turned towards him. It wasn't easy to move at all, but Julia was definitely dancing. He could do nothing but follow suit, though as a general rule – in common with most of the males in his faculty – Darren did not dance.

Conversation was impossible, so Darren concentrated on trying not to bump into his neighbours or tread on his own or anybody else's feet. Being, as he knew, utterly incapable of assuming that look of rapt absorption which most of the dancers seemed to affect, he opted instead for smiling vaguely in Julia's direction from time to time in what he hoped was a friendly and collegial manner. She did not smile back, but he did catch her looking at him quite a lot. For some reason – it could be the heat – his tongue seemed oddly overlarge for his mouth.

When, after a couple more songs, Charlie and his (or her?) three friends went into a Madness number, sending the crowd on the floor into a whooping, high-stepping frenzy, Darren decided that enough was enough. Shooting a look of pleading apology at Julia, he pushed his way towards the haven of the nearest wall.

He leaned back against the cold paintwork, enjoying the shock of its smooth chill through the damp heat of his shirt, and closed his eyes. When he opened them again Julia had materialised before him, holding two bottles of Weissbier. It was not Darren's usual drink but it was mercifully, astringently cold. She hadn't brought glasses. Darren didn't generally like to see girls drinking straight from bottles or cans; watching the soft O of her mouth, however, circling the rim of the bottle, he found that his reaction was very far from disapproval. He sought to distract himself with talk.

'Do you know the band, then?'

It was pretty pathetic but she smiled and leaned near with her reply.

'No – they're from Fitzwilliam. But they're quite popular for college gigs. This stuff gets people dancing – and they're cheap!'

Somehow it didn't seem the moment to ask her about the annual ents budget, but Darren's limited small talk reserves were running out fast. He was almost relieved when Charlie and co. slowed the pace on a series of chromatically descending chords and slid into a ballad. The opening instrumental section had the comforting ring of familiarity, and it was only when the vocals began that Darren recognised it as an appallingly schmaltzy song by . . . Nik Kershaw, was it, or Rick Astley? Someone like that. The cringe, and the irritation at not remembering who the artist was, distracted Darren for just long enough to ensure that he failed to resist when Julia took hold of his arm and steered him out once more into the swaying crush. This time the space was even more confined but, in any case, the slow nature of the music dictated that Julia should raise her arms and drape them along his shoulders, and that he should politely place his hands on her lower back. Luckily, the particular design of her top did not include any unexpected gaps in that area, so that Darren's hands met only the hot stretchy fabric and not hotter skin. Though that was bad enough. And there could be no avoiding, without overt rudeness, a certain amount of contact between them.

Julia was singing along to the tune – inaudibly, but he could feel the soft rhythmic exhalations against his neck, above the now limp Burton's collar. She smelt of peppermint and something else, something more musky which Darren could not place. He was focusing all his attention on remaining as upright as he could and trying to shift his feet at appropriate intervals, when he thought he felt – no, he distinctly did feel – Julia's mouth touching his jaw. He didn't want to turn away too obviously; he couldn't exactly just shake her off like a teasing insect. But things were getting urgent; her lips were feathering across his cheek. *Oh, God.*

Darren took himself in hand. In fact he took Julia in hand, placing his fingers firmly upon her shoulders and holding her at a small distance from him. He cleared his throat determinedly.

'Look, Julia . . .'

It was hopeless: the band was too loud, and they were being bumped and elbowed left and right by intertwined couples. He indicated the far corner of the room with a tilt of the head and set off, Julia following obediently behind. It was hardly quieter, but at least breathing was possible here.

'Look, Julia. Why don't we meet somewhere we

can talk, one day? We could go for a coffee or a drink . . .'

Julia but not Darren could see, across the rippling sea of heads, the shape of Karen watching them through narrowed eyes.

The St Radegund's Tigresses met in somebody's room every other Tuesday evening. There, in company with invited male consorts, they consumed on a semi-competitive basis cocktails mixed in washing-up bowls purloined from staircase kitchens.

Karen arrived late from the college bar, having first watched Julia and Darren leaving in their separate directions, just as the band began to pack up. As she entered the room, all those nearest turned to her expectantly.

'Well?' inquired a redhead waving an electric blue drink in a beer mug.

Deepa was there, and made her way over, joining the ring that was forming round Karen.

'So? Where's Julia? Did she do it?'

Karen shook her head, a half-smile twisting her face. 'Julia won't be coming tonight, I'm afraid. She flunked the test.'

If Julia wished to join the elite ranks of the Tigresses, she must pass the test. She had already made herself eligible to be brought forward for membership, and Karen herself had proposed her. The basic qualification was either a Blue or a Half-Blue (Karen, for example, had represented

100

the University at small bore rifle shooting) or playing three Cuppers sports for the college, and Julia had at the end of last summer term added the St Rad's tennis team to her record of netball and rowing. So far so good. But she must also go through the initiation test: getting a snog off the Dean. Interest among the other Tigressess was keen. Julia was well liked, a team player in every sense. She was also the first aspiring new entrant this term and something of a guinea pig: the test had become an unknown quantity.

'What happened?' clamoured half a dozen voices.

Under the previous regime, things had been unproblematic. Dean O'Connor had always entered into the spirit of the thing with some gusto; Karen grinned warmly at the memory of her own initiation test, in the dim entranceway to Hall following the Benefactors' Dinner, the Dean's right hand straying unapologetically to the swell of her left buttock. There were rumours – doubtless unfounded – that he liked to give his disciplinary role a very personal attention. But Darren was a different kettle of fish: quiet and shy and, she rather feared, *honourable*. He was going to be much harder work.

'You're not going to believe me if I tell you.'

'What?' 'Go on.' 'Tell us!'

'Well, she got him smooching and she was trying to make her move but he wasn't having any of it.'

The circle of faces variously registered amusement, disappointment, sympathy.

101

'But then he asked her on a *date*.'

The entourage erupted in delighted, incredulous laughter. This was unprecedented; this was beyond all expectations; this was brilliant.

'So now she'll just have to get him next time . . .'

By this time Martha Pearce had been long in bed, her head upon Douglas's pillow, although she was not yet asleep. She liked to go up in good time on days, like today, when she had a nine a.m. lecture in the morning, for which she had yet to look over her notes. It would do no good to read them through now, after a glass of wine; she was too tired and in any case she knew from experience that the revolving ideas would drive away sleep. Instead she had set her alarm for six a.m.. Martha had never been able to adopt the compromise of speaking without being absolutely on top of her material; to do so would have transformed into an ordeal what for her could still be a genuine pleasure.

Lucia had followed her up not long afterwards. Martha had heard her tread on the stair, missing out by long-ingrained habit the third one from the top, the one that creaked, in order not to wake her mother. A year or two ago, at fifteen and sixteen, this had been an essential precaution. Then the battle had been against Lucia's late homecomings, the struggle to get her into bed at a reasonable time in order to be up for school in the morning; yet in those days, however late the hour of her return,

Lucia had always appeared bright and fresh at the breakfast table. Now, although she no doubt lay in bed half the morning, Lucia was always yawning as widely as Martha by ten o'clock. Where had all her energy disappeared to? Sometimes, thinking about her daughter, Martha found her mind filled with images of waterlogged limbs and wet, dragging weed. Maybe, after all, there was some organic cause; maybe it was not simply the exhaustion of inactivity but something else, something post-viral perhaps? But to suggest the doctor would be to guarantee a row.

Of Douglas, on the other hand, there was no sign. He would be lying on the sofa in the unlit sitting room as he did most nights until late, stretched out in the flickering light from the television screen, the last of the bottle of wine on the floor by his head and the perfidious Maynard curled at his feet. She should go down – go back down now and talk to him. She should have gone down as soon as Lucia went to bed. Why else had she come home early tonight? But she lacked the courage. If she went back down it would put him immediately on guard, on the defensive; whereas if she waited for him to come to bed she could tell him more naturally, as part of her day, make it less of an issue. But she must speak to him tonight; she mustn't allow herself to go to sleep.

Nevertheless Martha was shaken out of a half-doze when the door eventually opened and her husband's padded footsteps approached the bed.

He lifted the duvet and slid beneath; as she always did, Martha rolled across to the cool of her own side of the bed, leaving to him the warmth she had created with her body. He moved close to her, casting an arm across her shoulders, and she found his cold feet with her warm ones, chafing them gently.

'Hello,' she said, to indicate that she was awake and that talk would be welcomed.

In reply he grunted and pulled her head into the crook of his shoulder. She felt the roughness of his chin nudging her cheek and fought the spurt of resentment of this life of his which imposed no need to shave. Odd, too, that she had not noticed downstairs the two-day growth of stubble; she would once have seen it immediately, found it sexy. Now she raised her hand to finger his jaw and discovered that she did still enjoy the sensation, hovering between harsh and satin soft.

'That was the last bottle of the Bardolino,' he muttered. 'I thought there were two left in the rack, but it was just the one. We should get some more.'

It had certainly gone nicely with the steak. But if she was to tell him, she needed to do so at once. If he thought her abrupt, it could not be helped.

'Douglas, I'm afraid there have been some complaints to Carolyn. About your teaching. There isn't really anything I can do. I'm really sorry, but she's going to get another supervisor for the Post-1945 paper.'

There was a fractional moment of hesitation in the darkness. Then came his reply, tangential but unexpectedly upbeat.

'Well, there's one good thing – I was going to have to cancel next Wednesday's supervision anyway. I've got an interview with Valerio Magrelli, next week at the Cambridge Book Fair; he said he'd give me an hour at his hotel.'

'But that's wonderful!'

Magrelli was an idol of Douglas's. They had never met, beyond a brief greeting once at a conference; the interview was a real coup.

'I can probably sell it to more than one rag: certainly the *London Review of Books*, maybe *Poetry Review*. It's excellent timing, because he has a new collection out in Italy – really well received – and it's going to be published over here in translation in December.'

As he talked, so the glow of her vicarious delight in his success slowly faded, to be replaced by more complicated feelings. So that was it? This was all the response she was going to get from him about his firing as supervisor? On one level she was relieved – of course she was. It was over with, and more painlessly than she could have dared to hope. There had been no recriminations, no censure of her failure to stand up for him and defend him against the students' attacks. And yet she was frustrated by his evasion of the issue, his shifting of the ground from beneath her feet. She had worked herself up for a confrontation which he had sidestepped and now she felt obscurely cheated. Besides, *ought* he not to care more? How could he be so cavalier about this professional failure, this loss of even so limited a part of his livelihood? But she could not possibly bring it up again without seeming to be casting blame or expressing recriminations of her own. The usual argument would inevitably ensue, so well rehearsed that she knew his part as well as her own. Bloody St Radegund's. Her precious college, which took up so much of her time and mental energy, which took her away from them, out of their lives: his and Lucia's.

Tears were close to the surface again as Martha rubbed her face against his chest, wishing there were something to say. His arms closed around her then, quickening, restricting, leaving no more room for accusation or reproach. And when he reached down to find her mouth she met his casual insistence with an urgency of her own which could easily have shaded into desperation.

CHAPTER 9

It was very hard to focus on college investment policy when figures wearing ermine above their academical dress kept intruding in one's mind's eye. James Rycarte was trying his best to listen to the Bursar's arguments and to shut out all thought of the Colleges Committee.

'The fund managers cannot be expected to produce the most favourable return if they are hamstrung. Apart from the fact that the trustees of an educational charity are not at liberty to impose their own moral or political whims upon the portfolio at a cost to the value of the funds of which they have the stewardship. It is quite wrong.'

Kate Beasley's hackles were still high as a result of last week's Investment Committee, and the discussion of St Rad's 'ethical investment policy'. He didn't know a great deal about Kate, beyond the fact that her previous post was as Bursar of an independent girls' school in Hampshire; but he already recognised her as a woman whose hackles seldom lay smoothly horizontal. Appeasement seemed the simplest course, at least for the moment while his thoughts were straying to the meeting ahead of him at Trinity.

'Of course. Naturally we must keep in mind our fiduciary obligations as trustees of the college's endowment.'

But she was hardly listening.

'Aerospace is such a significant sector, and its predicted performance over the medium term is unmatched. To rule it out as a blanket policy is wholly indefensible. This argument of Ros Clarke's about land mines and the views of the International Red Cross – it's all misplaced bleeding-heart nonsense. What's more, I am almost sure she doesn't believe in half of it herself. She is stirring this up for some mischievous reason of her own, mark my words.'

Rycarte was not sure whether he agreed with Kate's assessment on this point. Of course he was aware that Dr Clarke might have some ulterior motive for choosing the present time to push for a more over-arching ethical stance on investment; no doubt she hoped to flush him out into the open over an issue upon which she could make his position appear unprincipled. He would have to move with circum-spection. But he had listened carefully to her impassioned account of the shocking humanitarian cost of land mines and, unlike Kate, saw evidence of true zeal. Ros Clarke believed in the justice of her cause – and that made her more dangerous, not less.

'Then there is tobacco. Yes, there have been problems in the West, but it is still a fast-growing sector, with expanding markets in developing countries. To rule out any investment in what could be a highly lucrative commodity is blinkered to the point of blind obstinacy.'

His heart sank. First it was children in Afghanistan and Cambodia with limbs missing after stepping on land mines; now it was Third World smokers choking on offloaded low-grade cigarettes. Rycarte had been a journalist: it did not take much to see the colourful political paintbox Ros Clarke had at her disposal here. It was a tightrope he would need somehow to negotiate. But he was not ready to take a position right now. It was only forty-five minutes until his meeting, and he needed time to think.

'Well, Kate, I shall certainly give it some serious thought before the next Investment Committee. I can see that we are going to have to come up with some kind of strategy which does not tie our hands too far in terms of choice of equities. Thank you so much for putting the issue before me so clearly.'

He rose and moved towards the door and Kate had no choice but to follow him. Once the door was closed behind her, Rycarte sat down at his desk and allowed the ermine-clad spectres to walk unhindered. It was to be his first experience of the Colleges Committee. After only these few short weeks he had gleaned enough from his reading and conversation to appreciate the fierceness with which the colleges making up this unique and vibrant University guarded their independence, each one treasuring and nurturing its own maverick dissimilarities.

The point at which these disparate elements collided was, it seemed, the Colleges Committee: a twice-termly meeting of the Heads of House at which could be discussed those matters of common interest which routinely divided them.

It had always been Rycarte's practice when preparing for any meeting at the BBC to study the names and backgrounds of those who would be in attendance. On this occasion the strategy had not proved encouraging; rather the opposite, in fact. The list of thirty-one heads of college to which he had referred included one Nobel prizewinner, two Fields medallists, six Fellows of the Royal Society, four peers and three knights of the realm, twenty-one professors and a former ambassador to Australia. Two, it appeared, were chosen by royal appointment upon recommendation of the Prime Minister. His fifty-six years and a challenging and largely successful career had given James Rycarte a certain confidence – though not, he trusted, an overinflated one – in his own abilities. But something about this roll of the great and the good filled him uncomfortably with a sense of his own intellectual inconsequence. The agenda which he had received was hardly more reassuring. In contrast with the wash of documentation usual in St Radegund's, it had come with no accompanying papers and the agenda itself was brief and cryptic, making no concessions for the novitiate. The items included 'supernumerary appointments', 'review of the stipend spine' and, most forbiddingly, 'University tax'.

Sliding the paper back into its brown envelope, he stowed it in his briefcase, pocketed his fountain pen and consulted his watch. Ten minutes: the perfect amount of time to reach the venue for the meeting neither conspicuously among the first arrivals nor cutting it flurriedly fine. He almost forgot – from his top drawer he took out a paper bag containing his latest essential purchase: a pair of shiny aluminium bicycle clips. They had worked for Dame Emily; let them work for him.

As he strolled down to the Fellows' bike shed, Rycarte struggled with an obscure impression of watching himself from a distance, as if he were performing a part in a play. Not terribly convincingly, he feared. But he shook off the foolish image, finding his bicycle and clipping his briefcase firmly to the rear rack. It was as he rattled through his bunch of keys to find the one to his D-lock that puzzlement struck him, followed in rapid succession by incredulity and outrage. Eight years he had lived – and driven and parked – in London, since the end of his globetrotting days. In those eight years he had never once been clamped. Yet now, in Cambridge, in his very own college, on his brand new bicycle, next to the black D-lock lay a bright yellow immobilising device. *Bicycles left here without authority will be impounded*, he read. *For release, apply to the Head Porter, St Radegund's College.*

Unclipping his briefcase resignedly, he retraced his steps round the shrubbery and back in the direction of the porter's lodge. Would people have

111

clamped his bike if he were Professor Sir James, he wondered, or Bishop James or His Excellency?

Mercifully it was not Terry on duty; he at least had the satisfaction of dealing with the Head Porter himself.

'Mr Rycarte, sir. How may I help you?'

Mr Rycarte. Already he was on the back foot. The Head Porter addressed Martha religiously as 'Senior Tutor' and Kate as 'Bursar'; he had even heard him calling little Susie James 'Admissions Tutor'. It would not surprise Rycarte in the least to hear him hail the deputy chair of the Library Committee by the title of her office. That he alone was stripped to his surname and plain 'Mr' (underlining his lack of even a basic PhD) served as an uncomfortable reminder of the titular quandary which he had still failed to resolve.

'My bike. You appear to have locked it up. Immobilised it.'

'Ah well, I'm afraid we do have instructions to impound unauthorised bicycles which we find in the Fellows' bicycle facility. Space is very limited, and there are those who take advantage.'

Rycarte bit back the obvious question of whose authorisation, exactly, needed to be obtained by the Head of House. An answer of sorts was forthcoming anyway.

'All members of the University, senior and junior, who keep a bicycle in Cambridge must be issued with a bicycle registration number, to be painted on the frame. It is a matter of longstanding agreement between the University authorities and the Cambridgeshire Constabulary. I presume that your bicycle displays no registration number, which is how this unfortunate error will have come about.'

It was clearly the nearest they were going to come to an apology.

'And where would I obtain such a registration number, if I might ask?'

'From the office of the Motor Proctor.'

'The Motor Proctor?'

Some of Rycarte's mounting sense of bewildered unreality must have showed in his voice, because the Head Porter adopted a softened tone.

'I could see to it for you if you wish, sir.'

'That would be very kind. Thank you. Now perhaps if we could go and release my poor bike, I can get along to the Colleges Committee before the tea interval.'

Neither Rycarte's attempt at matiness, nor the none too subtle mention of the elevated gathering for which he was now embarrassingly late, produced any further relaxation of the porter's stiffly formal mien. But as they stepped out of the lodge together a further nasty idea crept into Rycarte's mind.

'So, I understand that all bikes need this special registration number. But what made you check the Fellows' shed in particular? Just at the moment, I mean?'

For the first time he sensed a touch of hesitancy.

'Well, er, we do the rounds from time to time. As I say, the Fellows' bicycle shed is limited on space.

There are complaints sometimes, you know. People who can't find a vacant rack when they need one.'

Rycarte felt him beginning to give, and pressed relentlessly on.

'People, yes. But somebody in particular has mentioned it recently, haven't they? Asked you to clamp an unauthorised bicycle?'

Of course he knew exactly what the reply would be before it came.

'I believe Dr Clarke did say something the other day . . .'

Sheer craven avoidance it might be, but the Colleges Committee would have to wait for an occasion when he could make his entrance on time. Instead, Rycarte permitted himself the rare fortifying treat of lunch off site (in an agreeable little pub in Newnham village) before the afternoon's Buildings and Estates Committee. Having half an hour in hand, he took a slightly longer route back, walking along Fen Causeway and back along the river as far as Silver Street bridge.

There had been a lot of rain, on and off, in the few weeks since Rycarte's arrival in Cambridge – a wet autumn following on the heels of a wetter summer. The water meadows were flooded to a depth of several inches almost everywhere, but for small tufty islands inhabited by clans of mournful cows. Near a half-submerged bench Rycarte passed a single melancholy pony, standing up to its knees in muddy water. He wondered vaguely what bog

114

spavins were, and if they came from standing on waterlogged ground. When he reached the bridge, the waters of the millpond were swirling high against the banks in grey-green eddies. He felt a strange dragging sensation as though, instead of the river rising in flood, the city itself were slowly being reclaimed back into the fen from which it had once been raised up. What would a century more of global warming do to these ancient walls?

Although a member *ex officio* of the Buildings and Estates Committee, Rycarte was not called upon to chair its meetings, this task falling to the Bursar's lot. He frowned his way semi-distractedly through the first few matters of reported business. Elsewhere at this moment were world-changing scientists and life peers hearing details of the cost of replacement guttering in their own respective colleges?

Then came the seemingly routine item headed 'Library basement'. It was again Kate who had information to report to the committee.

'Colleagues will be aware of the ongoing problems which we have been experiencing with damp in the lower ground floor of the library. As you know, last year we had to relocate all the books that were held in storage there, for fear of deterioration. Further surveys have now been carried out, and I am sorry to have to tell you that it is a more serious problem than we had anticipated.'

The words 'serious problem' captured at once the committee's errant attention.

'According to the structural engineer instructed

by the surveyors, there are not only flaws in the tanking which must be remedied, but we also have an issue of subsidence. The Victorian foundations are inadequate to support the weight of the super-structure, and the south-west corner of the library is beginning to subside. That may in part account for the fissures which have appeared in the skin of the damp-proofing.'

'Subsidence?' said Rycarte. 'That does sound rather alarming. And do we yet have any estimate of the cost of remedial work?'

'We only have a preliminary view as to cost at present. A more detailed assessment can only be made once investigative work commences. But early indicators suggest a total cost, for under-pinning and additional damp-proofing treatment, upwards of three hundred thousand pounds.'

In BBC terms this was little more than loose change. But Rycarte was by now familiar enough with the scale of the petty economies of the college accounts to appreciate the gravity of the news. Even had he not been, the reaction of those around the table would have told him all he needed to know. Letitia Gladwin, elbow on table, pressed her knuckles into the roots of the grey hair at her temple, stretching tight the loosely wrinkled skin. Ros Clarke stared at Kate Beasley with an expression which it was clearly an effort for her to keep from aghast.

'But there is the building contingency fund. How much have we in hand?'

'Well, as you know, a decision was taken four

116

years ago to reduce all figures budgeted against contingencies, in order to meet current costs. The fund for this financial year was just over a quarter of a million. But there was the unforeseen expenditure on additional fire escapes, last May, necessitated by the new regulations. And the upgrading of student kitchens in Cloister Court this summer ran considerably over budget.'

'Tell us the worst,' prompted Rycarte.

'The amount currently standing in the building contingency fund is £78,112.'

There was a short pause while the dispiriting mathematics was digested, and Kate took her opportunity.

'Of course, there is only so far we can go in trimming the costs of our enterprise, and most of the corners which can be cut and pared have already been so. We need to approach the equation from the other end, and think further about how to maximise our available income. The college endowment can be made to work much harder for us. Our present limited strategy will never give us the yield we need and which we could so easily obtain.'

The picture of ground riddled with lethal land mines which flashed into Rycarte's head struck him as doubly appropriate. Without looking he could sense Ros Clarke making ready to spring.

'Yes, thank you, Bursar. But that is a matter for discussion in another forum. I think for the moment we need to focus our minds on what is to be done about the library. What is the optimal

117

time frame for the work? Can it be begun during term, or must we wait until the vacation?'

Kate's gaze reluctantly broke lock with Ros's as she looked down at the papers before her.

'Exploratory work can start at once without causing too much disturbance to readers on the floors above. There will be a certain amount of noise and dust, naturally, but we can work around it. Then, depending upon what is found, the major structural work may be able to be undertaken during the Easter vacation or it may have to wait until the summer, after exams are over.'

'If it starts at Easter, what about exams?' asked Deepa Dasgupta, the student representative, timid but tenacious. 'There won't be any noisy work going on when we are trying to revise, will there?'

Small-scale quarrelling then broke out over the best way to accomplish such work as might prove necessary with the least disruptive effect upon the academic life of the college. Rycarte stepped back from the fray, leaving the field to those with more knowledge or more appetite for the fight. The image of surging waters re-entered his mind. It might not be true that the whole of Cambridge was sinking back into the fens, but in the case of St Radegund's, it seemed, the illusion was becoming reality.

CHAPTER 10

When the call came from the porter's lodge on Friday to say that Sr Alvau had arrived, Rycarte hoped that it was formality or even a sudden reticence rather than ostentation which made him send Miss Kett-Symes to meet his visitor and bring him to his office. As soon as Alvau entered the room, however, any awkwardness fell away at once, as the big Italian first pumped his hand and then clapped him resoundingly on the back, a great grin bisecting his features.

'Well, my friend, and so you are the master of all this fair citadel?'

Rycarte pulled a face and tried to ignore the disapproval emanating from Miss Kett-Symes's back as she retreated into her side office. The decade and a half since they had last met had been generous to Alvau, Rycarte noted. The deepening of the lines around his mouth served only to underscore his decisiveness and those around his eyes his bonhomie; he had ceased blackening his hair, which had reverted to iron grey but seemed thicker and more resilient than ever, especially in contrast with Rycarte's own impoverished situation. Why didn't

Italian men lose their hair? Had it perhaps, he speculated, something to do with olive oil?

Master. It would have to be Master, he now all at once determined; he would send round an e-mail to all members of the college later. Ros Clarke he would just have to deal with.

'Come down to the SCR for a drink before lunch. The natives hereabouts have a nasty habit of drinking sherry, but I have taken the precaution of ordering a few bottles of prosecco in honour of your visit.'

If nothing else, Rycarte's time in Rome had taught him the necessity of lubricating the machinery of Italian negotiation. And, as it was to transpire in this instance, Italian generosity. Not that it was Alvau's way to cut straight to the chase. Whether begging alms or offering largesse he would have regarded it as equally bad manners to give any indication of the fact before having played his part as grateful guest to the utmost of his ability.

Also in the SCR before lunch were Susie James, entertaining a brace of visiting head teachers, and the Chaplain, the Revd Tilley. All four ladies were soon prevailed upon by a persuasive Sr Alvau to exchange their small dry sherries for generous glasses of prosecco. Susie, Rycarte noticed with amusement, could not resist putting her nose to the bubbles and inhaling, causing it to twitch like a rabbit's. Rycarte did his duty and started in on the headmistresses, leaving his own guest to work his charm on the two dons.

'I am *so* delighted to meet you, Mr Rycarte.'

This was the younger and plumper of the two teachers, from the Midlands by her accent and the maintained sector by her general manner.

'Media Studies is one of my teaching areas, in the sixth form you know – or was when I still had time to do even a few timetabled hours.'

Rycarte had always had some difficulty in picturing exactly what a Media Studies course would look like from the inside, but did not think now to be the moment to reveal his ignorance. Not when she was looking at him with a star-struck expression such as he had not encountered once since his arrival in Cambridge, and which gave him, childish though he knew it to be, a certain pleasant buzz. Smiling at her with unfeigned warmth, he then turned to her companion, and inquired, 'And what is your subject – or what was it when time permitted?'

This one's demeanour could hardly have been more different. He had her down at once as head-mistress of an independent school. Probably single sex, probably expensive. And the penetrating look he was receiving was telling him with no want of candour that this was not a question it befitted him to ask when he manifestly had no subject of his own.

'I am an historian,' she informed him loftily. 'I had the privilege of visiting the college once before, five years ago.' It was said with the air of one stating a prior claim. 'That was when Dame Emily was Mistress, of course.' A much-lamented, golden

121

bygone era. 'I heard that the dear lady has been unwell. I wonder if I might inquire how she is?'

Feeling unaccountably uneasy that he didn't have a more specific answer to give her on this point, Rycarte made suitably grave and non-committal noises and then decided the time had come to escape into a more general conversation. He widened the two groups into one in time to catch Alvau directing his full force at the Chaplain.

'It is my one regret about the Roman Church – of which I am a fallen and reprobate member – that it has not followed the example of its Anglican sister and added infinitely to the ornamentation of its offices by the ordination of women. Beauty is always an edifying spectacle; to be in its presence is to be spiritually uplifted.'

How did he get away with such nonsense? Yet Joan Tilley, though she rebuked him in no uncertain terms for his foolishness, was clearly delighted by him. And while Rycarte had not heard what Alvau had been saying to Susie, he had never seen her pinker; you could bet they had not been discussing Sheffield United's midfield line-up.

It now approaching one o'clock, Rycarte assumed his role as host and bade the party drink up and come through into Hall. At lunch there was no pre-determined seating plan for High Table, although the central chair was always left vacant in case Rycarte should be present. He was therefore extremely glad to see Martha Pearce among the small group heading through the double doors and up towards the dais. Intercepting her and effecting introductions, he was able to seat Alvau at his right hand with Martha beyond him, placing Susie to his left between her two headmistresses. He was more pleased still with the felicity of this arrangement when he noticed Ros Clarke arriving, a little late and looking none too sunny. Grace was said (the abridged version, it being merely luncheon), the Fellowship and guests seated themselves, and the meal began.

While Rycarte supplemented the Media Studies curriculum by telling the Midlands schoolteacher selected anecdotes from his days in the field as a foreign correspondent, Alvau turned the greater part of his attention upon Martha.

'How can you have reached such an elevated and illustrious position when you are evidently so young, Dr Pearce? I would have taken you for one of the graduate students.'

Certainly not original, thought Rycarte from Alvau's other side, but guaranteed a good reception from most women for all that.

'And what was it like in the Gulf?' his head teacher was asking him. 'Weren't you reporting from Kuwait during the Iraqi invasion in – when was it – 1990?'

'Yes. The hotel in which most of the press and media were staying was close to the Emir's palace, so we heard all the shooting. But then of course we were detained for some time and we had no way of knowing what was going on. The hotel had

123

CNN, so we watched Desert Storm on TV like the rest of you.'

All attempts at self-deprecation merely stoked her admiration. He could have enjoyed the rare indulgence of basking in it for a while, had he not been listening all the time with half an ear to the conversation on his right.

'Clever women always have such a particular brilliance about them, in my experience. It has never been more apparent than now as I look about me at St Radegund's . . .'

Rycarte was curious to note that while Martha was as engagingly polite to the Italian as was her invariable habit, she yet maintained about her an ironic distance. There was no sign of her coming under Alvau's spell; indeed, as Rycarte glanced her way he was almost certain that he caught her meeting his eye to share a wry amusement at his friend's verbal antics. Not for the first time Rycarte was both surprised and impressed. There was something admirable about such apparent immunity to male flattery. He, on the other hand, was a shameless slave to the least sign of adulation from the opposite sex.

'But it must have been very dangerous. You could have been used as a human shield. Or caught in the crossfire when the Allies reinvaded.'

'Oh no, we were never much at risk. The bombing was far worse in Baghdad. And my colleagues in Jerusalem had to live in daily fear of Scud missile attack, never knowing if the Iraqis

124

had nuclear or biological capability. Though of course we have since discovered that was not the case – discovered it at quite a cost.'

The headmistress was nodding in vehement approbation at this throwaway piece of liberal sentiment. It had been a pretty safe hunch, with a state school head. Alvau, meanwhile, was having markedly less success.

'A daughter of seventeen? How can it be possible? And, may I say, if she resembles her mother in any respect, you must have a hard task to keep her at her books and away from the attentions of amorous young men.'

It was not that Martha's response was frosty – that was not a word that Rycarte could imagine ever applied to her – but there was a decided reduction in the level of her warmth. A fleeting shadow crossed her features; it was like a momentary withdrawal. Then she was smiling again, but with something else behind it. Bitterness? Grief?

'Lucia is beautiful. She is also nothing like her mother.'

From his far left, past Susie, Rycarte caught the words 'Dame Emily'. It was the other head teacher, the one from the private school. And from beyond her drifted snatches of Letitia Gladwin's reply.

'No improvement . . . tragic situation . . . dreadful to see that unmatched spirit so reduced . . .'

Presently, as their dessert plates were cleared away and coffee brought, Alvau turned towards

Rycarte and then back to Martha, commanding their attention.

'Well, now that I have the two central pillars of this gilded edifice here with me and your most excellent lunch inside me, I think it would not be inapt for me to tell you the reason for my visit.'

He sat back comfortably in his chair and embraced them both with a satisfied smile.

'My friends, I have been blessed in life. Though I count it the least among my riches, considerable worldly wealth has fallen to my portion and I wish to share my good fortune.'

The pause for effect was scarcely necessary in the circumstances.

'I have already lent my support to a number of causes at home in Italy. But as well as a good Italian I like to think myself a good European. I am looking further afield, beyond my native shores.'

He raised both hands with fingers spread wide and cast his eyes round the high, moulded ceilings of Hall.

'This: this is the crucible of all our futures. Education is my crusade; education is where I hope to leave my mark, to make my humble difference. And where better to invest in the future of Europe than at one of our continent's finest and most ancient universities?'

Where indeed? Rycarte maintained his expression of serious attentiveness and allowed Alvau to enjoy the stage.

'When I heard that my good friend James had begun his association with this esteemed institution, it seemed like serendipity. And so it is to St Radegund's that I have come to offer what modest contribution I may.'

With this final flourish he laid his hands open upon the table before him, palms uppermost, a gesture more of supplication than of charity. Rycarte knew enough of the man and his background to appreciate that a modest contribution in Alvau's terms was likely to prove a very large one indeed in St Radegund's: sufficient, in all probability, to fund any number of stipendiary Research Fellowships, any quantity of concrete injected into the library foundations. He was just rounding off a suitably fulsome speech in reply when, from beyond Alvau, Martha attracted his eye.

'If I may . . . ?'

Both men deferred to her, Rycarte with a nod and Alvau with what could almost have qualified as a bow.

'If it's not an intrusion to ask, Sr Alvau, how long do we have you with us here today? When do you fly back to Italy?'

'My flight leaves Heathrow at ten p.m.. I am quite at your disposal for the afternoon, most honoured lady.'

It was a clever trick, really: to employ phrases which sounded as if they were translated from some polite formula in the Italian. But he could swear Alvau made half of them up. Maybe he should call his friend's bluff and get a phrase book. *Ingratiating Italian for Business and Pleasure.*

'In that case,' Martha was continuing, 'I wonder whether we might be able to discuss with you some suggestions regarding how best to put your most generous proposal into action. We could perhaps indicate some areas in which the college could make good use of any benefaction – place before you a menu, so to speak.'

She was a shrewd woman; she was clearly aware that they were not talking here about a few hundred pounds for books. Evidently she was also a closer.

'I am certain that we could assemble sufficient members of the Development Committee from those present in college this afternoon to hold an informal meeting, to talk further. The committee, as indeed the whole college, will be so delighted to hear of your kindness. They will be honoured to meet you in person and to discuss possible ways for us to move forward together.'

It was beautifully done: Alvau appeared merely to be flattered at being given the opportunity of exhibiting his liberality before a wider audience. Coffee being finished, Rycarte rose to say the closing grace before showing Alvau out in the direction of the Fellows' Breakfast Parlour and a waiting bottle of single malt. He wondered whether Alvau still smoked those evil Swiss-manufactured cigarettes, and whether the Fellows' Parlour Steward enforced a no-smoking policy. He had better open a window or he would be receiving an admonitory e-mail later. Martha, meanwhile, begged leave to go and make her phone calls to the members of the Development Committee.

At three thirty a suitably senior quorum was assembled, consisting of Rycarte and Martha, Kate Beasley, Letitia Gladwin and Ros Clarke. After Rycarte had laid the situation before the committee with appropriate words of gratitude it was the Vice-Mistress who took the floor, in her capacity as chair of the Research Fellowships Committee.

'These junior research posts are a vital spring-board, from which any number of stellar academic careers have been launched. If, as you say, education is the future of society, then Research Fellowships are the future of higher education. To withdraw the stipend has been a disastrous move—'

Here she aimed a look of undisguised animosity at the Bursar.

'—having the effect of disbarring many deserving candidates, the very people who might have been the leading thinkers of the next generation. The application of a sum to endow one or more Research Fellowships in perpetuity would be an unequalled contribution to the academic life of the college and of the wider academic community.'

Kate Beasley took her turn next, with a plea for the library basement.

'If you would like to see your bounty take a more tangible form, of course, then there are several areas in which expenditure upon the fabric of our buildings could bring enormous benefits to St Rad's.'

Professor Gladwin was clearly restraining her desire to cluck as a concession to the presence of their prospective benefactor, but her expression was eloquent.

'And what building better epitomises the educational function of the college than its library? After all, you cannot put a plaque on a Fellowship – but I think the Alvau Library has rather a distinguished ring to it.'

Her tone was light, but nobody in the room made the mistake of thinking this a jest. Rycarte told himself that he should not have been so surprised, next, to find Martha and Ros Clarke on much the same side: the side of the students.

'We are ever anxious to find new ways of increasing access to St Radegund's for students from poorer backgrounds,' Martha began, 'and to ensure that, once here, none has to drop out of her course, or suffer any other hardship, as a result of her financial circumstances.'

'A relatively modest sum would make a very significant difference,' chipped in Dr Clarke, 'in terms of funding scholarships and busaries, or hardship grants for those in need.'

'Bursaries could be general – a contribution towards fees and maintenance – or they could be more specifically directed,' pursued Martha. 'We have proposals on the table at present, for example, for rental bursaries to subsidise the cost of living in college accommodation.'

His colleagues were certainly not shy about putting forward their demands, reflected Rycarte, but figures were politely not being mentioned. Evidently the menu at this stage came without prices attached. However, Alvau was a businessman. He must have a good idea of the scale of cost of the items being enumerated. And he had not blenched; indeed, he had been greeting each successive appeal to his munificence with smiling equanimity. None of this, it seemed, was out of his ballpark. Rycarte allowed himself to begin tentative estimates in his head. Half a million? A million? More than that? But now Alvau was speaking again, after having for the most part listened in silence to the views of the committee.

'This is all most instructional and, if I may say so, most satisfactory. I shall give all your ideas serious thought and be in touch with Sr Rycartè again very shortly. There is only one small other matter which I should perhaps mention. I have explained that I take a general interest in education. But I may claim, perhaps, an especial interest in the education of women.'

For some reason, Rycarte felt the shower of ice hitting his stomach even before guessing the reason for it.

'Dr Pearce here has a seventeen-year-old daughter: the lovely Lucia. I, too, have a daughter of that age.

Paola is just completing her schooling and is looking to spread her wings through university education. Languages and literature: Italian and French.'

Again, the devil taketh him up into an exceeding high mountain . . .

'Her imagination has been captured by the idea of studying abroad – and what better place for her than here at St Radegund's?'

. . . and saith unto him, All these things will I give thee, if thou wilt fall down and worship me. But in this case, wasn't the temptation worth braving the consequences?

Martha Pearce came very close, later that afternoon, to nipping the whole dilemma in the bud.

Coming to find Rycarte in his office shortly after he had seen Alvau into his taxi at the porter's lodge, she sat down looking less comfortable than he remembered seeing her before. She had the look of one steeling herself to carry out some unpleasant task: no doubt to tell him all the reasons why they could not take his friend's money at the expense of compromising the college's integrity over admissions. Of course she would take that view; how could she not? And finding himself thus presumptively at odds with her was a more unpleasant sensation than he could logically account for. But he had mistaken the nature of Martha's mission.

'I don't think this problem is necessarily insurmountable, if we tread carefully. In the case of existing donors, things are trickier, but Sr Alvau

132

has not yet given any money to the college. His name is known only to those of us who attended this afternoon's meeting. We must construct some Chinese walls.'

She bit her lower her lip and moved forward a little on her chair.

'Admissions decisions in Modern Languages are made by the Director of Studies in that subject, Dr Gallagher, together with Dr James as Admissions Tutor. Neither of them, so far, knows anything about this prospective benefaction. What we need to do is make sure that they do not hear anything about it, not until after they have interviewed Signorina Alvau and decided whether or not to offer her a place.'

Rycarte looked at her intently, hesitating. But he couldn't let the assumption stand: the question needed to be asked.

'And if the decision that they come to is not to make her an offer?'

Her teeth were indenting her lip so that it appeared lividly red.

'Well then,' came her carefully measured reply, 'that will mean that Signorina Alvau does not have the intellectual capacity necessary for the course. In such circumstances it would be a favour neither to the candidate nor to her father to admit her to St Radegund's.'

And we will have thrown away a million pounds. Martha was on her feet now, moving to leave.

'But we will need to act quickly if we are to

ensure that this is managed effectively. We must make clear to the Development Committee the imperative need to preserve confidentiality.'

'All right. I'll get on to it straight away.' He escorted her to the door. 'And thank you.'

As soon she was gone, he opened his e-mail to draft a note to the members of the afternoon's committee. But a new message highlighted in his inbox halted him in his tracks. It announced itself as being from Dr Ros Clarke. With a sinking heart he opened it.

> *To all Senior Members of the College –*
> *I wish to draw to the early attention of all colleagues an item of business which I propose to put forward for discussion at the next meeting of the Governing Body. The matter raises fundamental issues of principle. It concerns a potential large financial donation to St Radegund's, which it is suggested might be linked to the admission of the donor's daughter as an undergraduate member of the college . . .*

Rycarte read no further. But even when he had pressed 'close', 'delete' and 'expunge' in quick succession he found that the words still danced tauntingly in front of his eyes.

CHAPTER 11

If James Rycarte had been any other new arrival with whom she would be working so closely Martha would have taken him out for a drink in the first week of term. If he had been a new junior colleague in Economics, for example, he would probably have been round at her house sharing pasta at the kitchen table by now. As it was, it took her until after the division of term to decide that she must ask him. 'Division of Term' was a Cambridge phrase which had always appealed to Martha; she pictured it as a physical watershed, like a mountain col to which she struggled upwards for the first half of each term, before the slithering descent down the scree-strewn slope towards Christmas or Easter. Being Head of House must be a lonely business, she reflected. It was not something which had ever really occurred to her during Dame Emily's time. Then the Mistress's Lodging had been a hub of activity, with coffee constantly being dispensed and matters archaeological and universal discussed round the kitchen table. But Dame Emily had been in the department, though not

135

at St Radegund's itself, for twenty-five years before her appointment as Mistress. For Rycarte, an outsider, it was quite a different matter. It was more than a mere technicality of College Statutes that the Head of House was not a member of the Fellowship. Members of the teaching staff were hardly likely to drop round to the lodging on a casual basis. Should they do so, indeed, it would soon be known to all and their motives would be immediately suspected. He was in a very tangible sense outside the fellowship of the college. As Senior Tutor she alone, perhaps, might make overtures of friendship, and now she regretted not having done so sooner.

'I'm going for a drink with James Rycarte.'

She had tried the words out on Douglas and Lucia last night, experimentally, gauging their reaction. But there was none – why should there be, to something so unremarkable? She had taken drinks with him before, of course, many times: pre-dinner sherry, and that dry white from the Veneto he had introduced as a welcome alternative, sipped in claustrophobic groups, making college small talk. But never a real drink – a normal drink, purchased from a normal, crowded bar and consumed at a normal, smeary table.

Avoiding the city centre pubs where there might be a danger of running into colleagues or students made Martha feel strangely furtive, but she told herself that the object of the exercise would be defeated if they didn't find somewhere quiet where

136

they could talk properly. Not that she had much idea what they would talk *about*, she realised, as she cycled through a tight maze of brick-terraced streets to the pub near the railway which was to be their rendezvous. The Alvau donation intruded whenever she tried to think of college topics, and she did not want to be drawn into a bitter exchange which could do nothing but damage the tentative respect and trust which was building between them. She was certain that Rycarte wanted to take the girl and the money – and equally certain that it was impossible. But not to talk of it would lead to an uncomfortable restraint, and what else could possibly engage them? Asking about his family would have been feasible, if it had not meant he would ask about hers; that was a subject she wished to avoid just at present. Her own professional future was ever present in her mind. She would have liked to seek advice from this cool-minded, impartial outsider. But how to do so without appearing to beg for crumbs from the St Rad's table?

He was there before she was, standing at the bar, and turned with a warm smile as she entered. Rycarte was certainly an attractive man for his years, and had an ease of physical movement which drew and held the eye. He was a man you would always listen to if he was talking. 'Magnetism' was a devalued word, but in his case it seemed to be almost literally apposite. Martha was all at once reminded of how he had once been branded by a broadsheet journalist: the Des Lynam of TV politics. It was true that in recent years he was more notable for well-received appearances on *Have I Got News For You* than for having grasped any organisational nettles at the BBC, but Martha remembered his reports from Kuwait, the West Bank and Rwanda: sharp edged, intelligent and hard hitting. If Ros Clarke thought him all smooth surface and no substance beneath, she was wrong; if she sought to make an opponent of him, she had chosen a formidable one.

'What are you drinking?'

'Thanks, but that hardly seems fair when it was I who invited *you*!'

It was her innate sense of hospitality speaking and she hoped very much that he would not take it (the idea only occurring to her after the words were out) as some prickly gendered point. If the thought occurred to him, too, then he was far too well trained to show it, replacing his wallet in his inside pocket: the impeccably gracious twenty-first-century gentleman. They moved with unspoken accord towards the corner table furthest from the door, and took seats facing each other – like lovers, thought Martha distractedly, or chess-players. She it was who had invited him; the onus was on her to commence play. But obligation, for once, failed to overcome uncertainty and in the end it was Rycarte who spoke first. And with a far from conventional opening.

'You're very young.'

He spoke appraisingly, but not in a way which embarrassed or threatened her. She laughed.

'You could always look at our files, you know, if you're curious.'

He grimaced in reply. 'When Miss Kett-Symes is out of the office, you mean?'

They shared a smile. Defensiveness was not in Martha's nature, however; coyness still less so. She supplied seriously the information he sought.

'I'm forty-one.'

'Not too old, then, surely, to secure a post in the University?'

But it was too old. Too old to contest next term's faculty lectureships with men and women fifteen years her junior; on a strict publications-to-age ratio they would beat her hands down. And in these days when all appointments had to be made with a weather eye to the next Research Assessment Exercise, publications were the only measure of value. A decade of unstinting service to her college would count for nothing – as if the colleges and the University had no connection with one another. But how to explain any of this to a man who was still, after barely five weeks, an outsider? A man whose background, indeed, would ensure that in Cambridge terms he would still be an outsider after five years.

'It's not that easy.'

'Well then, the college must come up with something for you.'

Martha sighed, even while her smile acknowledged

this sign of his appreciation. Yes, forty-one was too old; but it was also too young. Too young simply to be put out to grass like other former senior tutors who had come to the end of their term of service. Her predecessor as Senior Tutor of St Radegund's, a quietly spoken scholar of Roman Law by the name of Isabella Chawton, having completed her tour of duty at the age of fifty-nine, had been taken on to the college payroll as a teaching officer, seeing out the short months until she began to draw her pension instructing wool-gathering first year students on the Institutes of Justinian. But for Martha things were different. Nine years ago she had, at thirty-two, been the youngest senior tutor in Cambridge; now that distinction had become a millstone round her neck. She still had twenty or twenty-five years of active working life before her, and nobody to foot the bill. Even had her pride allowed her to throw herself upon the charity of her colleagues at St Rad's in the hope of the wooden spoon of a college teaching appointment – even were the college in a financial position to make this a possibility, what-ever Rycarte's view of the case – is it what she would want? Such appointments – untenured and hand-to-mouth, unconnected to any formal University position and paid on a scale consider-ably below her present stipend – were really intended to be short term, offering young academics a springboard into a permanent University post. Good enough to see Dr Chawton

140

through to her retirement, but hardly the back paddock in which to spend the remaining three-fifths of an academic career.

Martha became aware that she was staring down into her half-pint in a manner which might be perceived as moody. Worse, she had not answered his implied question; had said nothing at all, in fact, since his generous assertion of the college's obligation towards her. She sighed once more, dragging her mind back to the problem of what to say to him, how to make him understand. Really, she must pull herself together; she had asked the poor man to the pub, she reminded herself again, and now all she could do was ignore his consideration and brood silently into her beer. But the knot of her future – which as things stood was a broken thread as from 1 October next year – had been coiling and recoiling itself beneath her consciousness for many months. Nobody else had asked her about it, she realised; not even Douglas or Lucia, even though it was their bread and butter. Now all it took was James Rycarte's kindly concern and the irresolubility of the thing came rearing up to the surface, tightening her chest and actually leaving her close to tears.

Kindness was only a part of it, though. Maybe she had forgotten that politics had been his métier, that it would have given him an eye for the subtext.

'Perhaps a fixed term appointment? Academic rather than administrative, but with only very limited teaching duties attaching to it. To give you a chance to kick-start your research again. Put you in a position to apply for a tenured lectureship – here, or elsewhere if necessary.'

Her gratitude was sharp, her warm gaze wholly inadequate to convey it.

'A sabbatical, even? You must surely be due at least a term or two of study leave after ten years running the shop?'

Martha shook her head, the smile around her eyes fading back into habitual lines of worry.

'Terms of service as a college administrative officer do not carry entitlement to sabbatical leave.'

It had been thrashed out at length last year, when Kate Beasley had wanted to do a term's course on investment management at the London Business School.

'It's a question of finance, really. The cost of covering the person's duties.'

Everything was a question of finance at St Rad's.

'But you will have completed your duties. There will be a new Senior Tutor doing the job. What you need is research time.'

'My needs and the college's needs may not coincide.'

And your job is to promote the latter, not the former.

'But if we were to appoint you to a college teaching post, that would carry with it a leave entitlement, wouldn't it?'

'Yes. But only after six terms of teaching. "Six days shalt thou labour"; only on the seventh are you due a sabbath.'

St Radegund's appointed its limited slate of college teaching officers strictly in order to cover unmet teaching needs; research, while necessary for the advancement of the individual post-holder, was of secondary importance to the college. Its pound of flesh must be exacted first.

'But haven't you been teaching for the college while you are Senior Tutor?'

'That's true. But my appointment is nevertheless an administrative and not an academic one.'

They both supped their beer, letting the arcane Cambridge distinction settle between them without comment.

Rycarte reaching the bottom of his pint very much as Martha drained her half, he rose and made to take his turn at the bar, this time without occasioning demur. He did not need to glance back to be aware that she was circling her empty glass slowly on the edge of its base, the look of absorbed tension back upon her face. In a moment, perhaps, she might raise her fingers to rub the skin at either side of her nose, between her eyes, a gesture he had frequently observed in her and found obscurely touching. Maybe he shouldn't have raised the issue of her job. Maybe it was crass of him, the moment ill judged. The poor woman had invited him for a friendly drink, and he had come over as the officious employer. Not that he was her employer – except in a collective sense – any more than she was his. Her mentor, perhaps (a notion which attracted him); yet, in spite of the disparity in their ages, it might equally be said to be the other way round, in many vital respects.

As he walked back to the corner table, indeed, he was on the verge of seeking her advice on the subject which was constantly uppermost in his mind: Alvau, his daughter and his million. They might well be divided on the matter, but it would be instructive to hear his opponents' case from the most reasonable among their number. Instead, as he reseated himself, he surprised them both with a completely different question.

'What was Dame Emily like?'

Immediately he regretted that 'was'. Martha surveyed her replenished glass levelly and volunteered nothing, so he hastened on in the present tense.

'I mean, I'm sleeping in her bed, so to speak, but I hardly know her.'

A Mona Lisa of a half-smile, still down at the beer.

'She was . . . like a mother to us all, really. Sorry, I know that sounds corny. She could be difficult, stubborn, volatile, sometimes unapproachably prickly, but you could always rely on her to tell it how it was. And she would die for St Radegund's.'

The choice of words, as always with Martha, appeared to Rycarte to be deliberate. An affirmation that the former Mistress still had a life to offer for her cause. He paused, then spoke as lightly as he could.

'Which of us is going to be the first to say it? "A hard act to follow".'

The smile spread and was raised in his direction.

'Don't try,' was her simple advice. 'Be your own act.'

It was a moment of connection, and he seized it. Raised, finally, the topic they had both been skirting since they arrived.

'What will happen if I push to take Alvau's money?'

The answer was unhesitating; not said with challenge or belligerence, merely presented as a statement of fact.

'You will lose the support of the majority of the Fellowship.'

He thought he knew most of the early steps in the argument, but chose to adopt the academic habit and begin from first principles. Let her walk him through the proof.

'And that would be because . . . ?'

She accepted the disputation on his terms.

'Because his daughter is a candidate for admission at the college.'

'And if we are able to ensure an unbiased assessment of her application? If she is good enough to secure a place on her own merits?'

'It is not merely a question of justice being done but also of its seeming to be done.'

'Meaning . . . ?'

'Meaning that for decades – centuries, even – it was the case that money was sufficient to secure admission to Cambridge. Who your father was, where you went to school, links with the college, benefactions. Places could be bought.

Fellowships, too, if you go far enough back, like livings in the church. Patronage was everything, scholarship and personal attainment merely incidental.'

The image which came to Rycarte was of the independent school headmistress Susie James had entertained to lunch: her proprietorial attitude, the unshakeable assumption of insider status.

'All right. Let's accept for a moment that the world will refuse to believe we took Signorina Alvau on academic merit. Let's brave their disapproval and ask another question. You said, when we discussed this once before, that if she were not assessed as being good enough for a place, we would be doing her no favours by admitting her. But is that true? When you select students, what is your aim? Is it, for example, to take only those that you feel capable of attaining a First?'

This produced for the first time a momentary hesitation.

'No. I suppose we would be looking for those who we feel are likely to achieve at least an upper second class degree. Or who have, in our judgement, the raw ability to attain that level at least by Part II.'

'Understood. So those among the undergraduate number who make up the Lower Seconds and Thirds on the class list, they are what? Admissions mistakes? Tutorial problems? Girls who have devoted their time to the boat club or Footlights rather than to study?'

146

Now she was smiling again. 'All of those things, yes.'

'And if there were one more name in the lower second class, a student who had suffered no personal trauma, who had worked hard and neither rowed nor acted? Would it be so terrible?'

She inclined her head in acknowledgement of the debating point, but her gaze was unwavering.

'She would still be taking a place from a candidate with a greater chance of academic fulfilment – one who could, at least potentially, make better use of that place.'

Rycarte took a long pull at his second pint, wishing he had bought crisps, though in his mind Martha and bar snacks did not quite mesh. Altogether too frivolous – even plain ready salted. Though the way her eyes skipped with fun sometimes, frivolity could be in her nature; he would love to see her being frivolous. He shifted the argument sideways a step.

'What if she were not to take the place of another candidate? What if she were admitted in addition to our usual numbers?'

He knew there would be an answer to this one, and there was, the numbers admitted annually being dictated by the limits of St Radegund's capacity to house and teach each new intake, as well as by mysterious governmentally dictated maxima which Martha referred to as MASNs. It seemed inescapable: one more Paola meant one fewer deserving other. But how to measure desert? Who was to say that the young Italian was any less deserving of opportunity than one who might fritter away putatively greater talent by preferring the college bar to the library? He kept coming back to the host of variables which made up the final class list.

'But there are so many things, are there not, which go into the mix, determining academic success or failure? Not just brains, but motivation and character, as well as the unknowables, the unforeseen circumstance. How can all of that be measured with any confidence? What I am getting at, I think, is this. That you seem very certain of your assessment of applicants' abilities. Are you certain enough to turn down financial salvation on the strength of it?'

It sounded rather more confrontational than he had intended; the pronoun had a ring of the singular and personal when he meant to signify the college in general. But Martha was too well steeped in scholarly detachment to take an abstract argument to heart. Her answer came with careful deliberation.

'Of course we cannot be sure that we always select the best students. But the point is that we try. We do the best job we can, on the basis of all the information available to us.'

It was the sincerity in her eyes, finally, which forced Rycarte's glance back down to his beer.

'If we abandon the attempt, even modify it by

148

the smallest degree, then we forfeit our academic integrity. After that, everything is up for grabs.'

While the two principal officers of St Radegund's were drinking beer together in a side-street pub near the railway, the college's Dean and under-graduate entertainments officer were doing much the same half a mile across town in a pub near the bus station. It was Julia who had suggested the venue for their meeting (a word which felt much safer to Darren Cotter than the alarming and unlikely 'date'). It was off the commonly beaten student track, for which Darren's relieved grati-tude outweighed any suspicion of embarrassment on her part.

The evening had got off to an awkward start when Julia had arrived – late and flustered and lovely – and greeted him as 'Dr Cotter'. If Karen had used his title it would have been with irony if not outright antagonism, but in Julia's case it seemed merely to be a mistake, judging by the way her cheeks flushed to a deeper shade of breathless pink. The selection and purchase of beverages – Weissbier for her, Pilsner for him – and their installation at an appropriate table had got them through another couple of minutes without too much pain, but then it became imper-ative to talk and Darren could think of nothing whatever to say. Several topics which might have interested or even amused her had suggested themselves to him during his day at the lab, and

149

he had gone so far as to jot down a note of one or two of them on a yellow Post-it from his desk drawer, before tossing it in the bin in a fit of self-mockery. So Darren took refuge in drinking the first half of his lager rather more quickly than he would normally have done, and it was Julia who spoke.

'What do you do, then, when you're not on your computer?'

That she was sending him up just a little, he knew; but that it was partly, at least, to cover her own nervousness, he also sensed. He therefore considered the question at face value. What *did* he do? Well, he was Dean, but she already knew that. He was put in mind of the question on the form he had had to fill in for the German exchange, at school, when he was fifteen. *What are your hobbies?* The word conjured up short-trousered schoolboys of the 1950s and, perhaps by mental association, all that the panicking Darren had been able to think of was 'stamp-collecting', even though he had not so much as looked at a first-day cover since he was eight. Against the odds he and Emmett (who had no trace of an album either) had hit it off very well. But he could hardly talk to Julia about either philately or his German penfriend.

'I like music.'

This was no good either – who didn't? He needed to be more specific, but being specific was difficult without straying further and faster on to

150

personal territory than Darren had intended. No other ideas occurred to him, however, so he found himself wading in deep.

'I make music, is what I mean. Not just listening to it, but making my own. Just for me.'

'Oh, really? What kind of thing?'

She looked at him with pleased interest, fuelling his courage to press ahead.

'Well, I don't know what you'd call it exactly. It's computer-generated stuff, you know. Not much structure.'

'All retro like Jean-Michel Jarre or something? Or new agey? The music of the spheres and all that?'

Not at all sure that he wanted to identify with these references – whether, indeed, he could identify them at all – Darren waved a non-committal hand. Unfortunately in doing so he caught the rim of Julia's half-full beer bottle, sending an effervescent stream of wheat beer across the polished surface of the table and down into her lap. For no other reason than to distract them both from the disaster as he righted the bottle and attempted ineffectually to swab the pool on the table with his sleeve, he said, 'Maybe I could play you a bit some time? It's on the computer at the lab.'

A minute later, while Julia mopped herself up in the Ladies and Darren queued for a replacement beer, he marvelled at his own stupidity. They had been here less than quarter of an hour and already he had thrown beer at her and, worse, had actually invited her to his lab. Get a grip, he told himself. Ask her about herself.

That went a little better. Julia, once talking, was seemingly able to do so without causing embarrassment to either of them and happily also with little need of prompting from Darren, leaving him at liberty to admire the way her brown curls bobbed with the animation of her words, and the long, pale shape of her fingers, cradling her glass – curiously graceful despite the ragged nails. Two drinks later, Darren had almost forgotten himself so far as to begin to relax and join in the conversation; one more after that, and as Julia licked the froth of her beer from glistening lips and looked at him with dancing eyes he forgot himself entirely. Without conscious thought he leaned towards her, watching her mouth; saw her eyes, above, darken with awareness before the veiling lashes flickered down; felt momentarily the warm yeastiness of her breath on his chin – until she turned away. The dismissal was clearly recognisable to Darren, who was not unfamiliar with the experience. Strange, therefore, the slight sag of her shoulders, mirroring his own – a slackening which seemed to suggest disappointment.

Strange, too, that after the almost-kissing incident Julia, unlike previous women caught in the same predicament with Darren, did not grab her coat at the first opportunity, nor withdraw into huffy silence, nor yet (worse still) assume a sympathetically bashful playfulness. Teasing was always the worst. Instead she resumed, with very little pause, her flow of warmly engaging chatter: almost as if nothing had happened, almost as if she liked him, almost as if she regretted her rebuff. And in the darkness of the side alley outside the pub it was Julia who reminded him of his invitation to come and hear his digital compositions, she who pinned him to a time (eight p.m. the following Tuesday), and she whose fingers slid down his wrist and entwined themselves briefly with his as they were parting.

Girls were definitely confusing. But it was only eleven o'clock; plenty of empty lab time ahead to get on with reworking his latest program while things were quiet. There was nothing quite like a touch of parametric time delay modelling to soothe a troubled heart.

Making counterproductive efforts to be quiet as she opened her front door, Martha was aware of having had rather more to drink than she did when out at college functions – rather more, in fact, than she had had in a long time. Four halves of bitter, and after that, how many Glenfiddichs? The house was in darkness. Lucia would be in bed, of course, but the low patter of American voices from the television told her that Douglas was still downstairs, behind the half-closed sitting-room door. She approached the door, hesitated, retreated. She needed some coffee first. She would fill a cafetière and take it through for both of them.

The kitchen felt cold. It would surely have been warmer if the oven had been on tonight, heating up the casserole she had left; they had probably eaten it cold, or given it a cursory blast in the microwave. Martha shuddered; after putting on the kettle she went over to the radiator, racking the thermostatic control up to maximum, rubbing her calves to and fro against the ridged metal as it gurgled and the heat began to spread slowly upwards. The computer was not on stand-by but had been closed down and even unplugged. Relinquishing the radiator to take the foil packet of coffee from the fridge door, Martha emptied the last of it into the cafetière. Barely enough, and there was no more in the cupboard; it wouldn't be as strong as Douglas liked it, but there was more chance they would sleep. The bin, when she opened it to deposit the empty coffee packet, was full of paper, the discarded evidence at least of work's having been done. Feeling disproportionately guilty, she removed the top few crumpled sheets and smoothed them out, taking them over to the table and laying them down next to the waiting cafetière and mugs. Heavily, filled of a sudden with weariness, she sat down.

The first two sheets both bore lines, heavily over-laid with insertions and crossings out, in Douglas's spiky hand. Martha could make out most of the words but little of the sense. The incongruity struck her, as it had not done for years: that Douglas, who hailed from Dagenham, should write his poetry exclusively in Italian.

154

. . . il tempo perduto . . . sembrava indifferente . . .

Her belief in his unappreciated talent lay, immutable, at the heart of their relationship, like her belief in their surviving love. But, just sometimes, it was hard to keep away the intruding doubt, the disloyal fear. Was it all a chimera? Was he, in fact, Casaubon? Was she Dorothea? Had the emperor, after all, nothing on?

The kitchen door swung silently open, pushed by a ginger head, and Maynard sauntered in, his everyday presence mocking her foolish and self-dramatising thoughts. He walked with precision, each foot placed perfectly in front of the last, as if he were navigating the top of the garden fence and not merely crossing the kitchen tiles. After curving his body briefly round her ankles, he looked up, tensed for a moment and then sprang, landing by the coffee mugs with a single short mew. Martha absent-mindedly ruffled his Seville orange fur, before pushing him away a little to free from under his front paws the final sheet of paper which she had retrieved from the bin. It was Lucia's writing: uneven and crowded, still retaining a childlike roundness.

It was a fragment of prose – a children's story in the first person, or more likely an adult story told in a child's voice. The child was in the bath, waiting in the cooling water for an unnamed parent to come. There was a close-up description, which Martha found moved her profoundly, of lifted toes breaking the surface and of the scum, formed of soap and dirt, beginning to adhere to the sides of the tub.

There the narrative broke off and a short way further down the page were two more lines.

My father is a poet and always in his head. My mother is busy and always in her college. Where am I?

Below this the word 'I' was repeated over and over, becoming more indistinct and erratic until it amounted to nothing more than a series of vertical jabs, scoring the paper, leaving deep indentations. Martha stared at it unblinking until her eyes stung and she lowered her head, burying her face in Maynard's dusty warmth, hating herself because no tears would come.

CHAPTER 12

St Radegund's, in common with a majority of the larger Cambridge colleges, had adopted a system of cabinet government. The daily running of operations being delegated to the College Council, the Governing Body, of which all Fellows were members, met only three times a year: in November, March and June. For Rycarte, the November meeting – held, as always, in the fifth week of the Michaelmas Term and the 492nd since the college's foundation – would be the first time he had faced the Governing Body *en masse* since his interview. Now, of course, he would be in the chair rather than in the hot seat, but he found that he relished the prospect almost as little as on the last occasion.

A committee with too many members and not enough to do is a dangerous thing. Council took care of all needful business, merely tossing to Governing Body for picking over such small policy bones as it chose. The latter's agendas were therefore confined largely to issues not requiring an immediate decision – matters of general, theoretical or purely social concern. Ordinances also

157

provided for items to be raised for discussion at Governing Body at the prior written request of any Fellow, a procedure which opened the door to the hijacking of its meetings by mavericks: the knife-wielding, the aggrieved and the merely boring. The only redeeming feature of the meetings, in fact, was the manner in which debate was conducted. There was no tradition in St Rad's of the formal set-piece speeches which had driven many of the former men's colleges to appoint a council in order to get anything done at all. Instead, Fellows spoke off the cuff and, as often as not, from the heart.

The first item on the agenda for the 492nd meeting fell distinctly into the time-filling cate-gory. It was only the five weeks' learning curve behind him, indeed, which moderated Rycarte's incredulity that the entire academic staff of a Cambridge college could gather together in order to discuss the colour of the SCR curtains. The choice of material for the much-needed new curtains had become ensnared in the St Rad's committee structure and the Governing Body was being called upon to exercise a tie-breaking role. Opinion was divided between a traditional William Morris print (forwarded mainly by Kate Beasley: in period with the college's foundation and, what's more, available at high street prices from John Lewis) and a more geometric Mondrian-style pattern in primary reds and yellows, obtainable only via special order on the internet and pressed for most vocally by Ros Clarke.

'The Pictures, Plate and Furniture Sub-Committee considered this matter at its October meeting,' the Bursar was saying. 'It is all settled. Swatches were circulated; a vote was taken. The minutes, indeed, have subsequently been approved by the Buildings and Estates Committee. The order is all prepared. The Morris – floor-length and fully lined. The committee felt the cost to be most reasonable, even including making up. We need not trouble the college seamstress.'

'These are not just curtains for students' rooms, Master, or even for the administrative offices,' countered Dr Clarke. Since Rycarte's recent announcement of his chosen job title she had enjoyed using it on all occasions, inflected with exaggerated precision. 'This is not a question to be settled by Buildings and Estates. It concerns the Fellowship directly. The Fellows' Parlour Committee is strongly in favour of the Mondrian.'

Less a divergence in artistic taste, it seemed, and more a demarcation dispute. The Vice-Mistress joined the fray.

'Dr Clarke is perfectly right. The Fellowship must of course be consulted in this matter. The Senior Combination Room is our domain.'

Rycarte would have had Letitia Gladwin down as a William Morris woman, if not indeed Laura Ashley. But personal preference was clearly of little moment when it came to defending her power base against bursarial encroachment.

'The Fellows' Parlour Committee is convened by myself and does not report to the Buildings and Estates Committee but directly to College Council and thence to this Governing Body. It cannot be overruled by a vote in Buildings and Estates.'

Kate was beginning to show signs of impatience. 'But the curtains aren't for the Parlour, they are for the SCR.'

It seemed a not unreasonable point to Rycarte, but from the reaction of most of the dons seated round the long table it was clear that it was viewed as so self-evidently flawed as to suggest clutching at straws. It fell to Ros Clarke, Fellows' Parlour Steward, to point out the obvious.

'The Parlour is more than simply a geographical location; it is a much larger concept. It represents the social side of Fellowship: all the day-to-day incidents of our coming together.'

The newspapers and the coffee – and in this case the curtains. It did make sense, in a Cambridge kind of way. Rycarte allowed discussion to flow back and forth for a few minutes more before deciding that the time had come for some proactive chairing.

'Perhaps, colleagues, since we are agreed that this issue is of concern to the whole Fellowship, and being all now conveniently gathered in one place, we might take a vote upon it? That is, if it is within the power of the Governing Body to decide the question.'

There were general murmurs of assent and, as a show of hands approved William Morris by a narrow majority, Rycarte congratulated himself on having brought an amicable neutrality to bear and thus resolved a potentially tricky situation. He was about to move on to the next agenda item (concerning the amalgamation of two categories of the dining rights granted to external supervisors) when Letitia Gladwin brought him back.

'So what exactly are we minuting about the curtains?'

Rycarte glanced at Miss Kett-Symes, seated with the minute book at his left hand, but her impassive face and obediently poised fountain pen afforded him no clue. Hers only to serve and not to reason why. At the opposite end of the table Martha Pearce met his inquiring look with sympathy but remained silent, as she had throughout proceedings so far.

'Well, er, that we have chosen the Morris print. Should we also record the number of votes cast? Is that the usual procedure?'

Professor Gladwin clucked and waved away the suggestion with one of her repertoire of bookie's hand signals.

'I would like it formally noted that furnishing and decoration of the SCR fall within the exclusive purview of the Fellows' Parlour Committee.'

Half an hour and several heated exchanges later, a form of words acceptable to all was found and recorded in Miss Kett-Symes's fine italic hand.

Twenty minutes more were devoted to discussion of dining rights, categories 3B and 3C. The heavy sense of time wasted began to weigh upon Rycarte, more irked now than diverted, and his furtive glances at the brass clock on the mantelpiece became more frequent – that is, until an end was reached to the items of formal business referred from College Council. This was the point in the agenda at which business tabled by individual Fellows came up for debate: the moment at which the devil, in the shape of Dr Ros Clarke, made work for idle hands.

Her written notification, received in Rycarte's office the statutory twenty-four hours in advance of the meeting, had simply requested a discussion of the guest list for the Advent Feast. He should have known, of course, that the sting would be in the supplementaries.

'I wonder whether the Master could tell us whom he plans to invite to the forthcoming Feast?'

Would the Prime Minister please list his engagements for the day?

'I shall be returning the hospitality of the Master of Corpus Christi and his wife. I have also invited Janet Greerson, a former colleague at the BBC, currently Head of Foreign News—'

There must be no hesitation, no hint of a change in tone.

'—and a colleague from Italian television, Sr Luigi Alvau.'

The gauntlet had been cast down and Rycarte

162

had no choice but to pick it up. Battle lines were drawn; an expectant hush settled round the table. Dr Clarke's first move was a formal one, establishing the ground.

'Am I correct in understanding that Sr Alvau is a potential parent? That is to say, that an application for admission to the college has been received from his daughter?'

Rycarte bowed his head in assent. He could hardly deny the fact, nor his knowledge of it. The deadline for undergraduate applications had passed two weeks before, and he had not seen any point in seeking to preserve an ignorance which would, quite rightly, be regarded by all as a charade. Seeing no reason to place Susie James in an awkward position, he had called into the admissions office at a time when the lecture list informed him that she would be teaching in her faculty and been shown the file by the administrative assistant. Paola Rosetta Alvau was seeking admission to read for the Modern and Medieval Languages Tripos, specifically Italian and French. A curious ambition: to come from Rome in order to read Dante and Anna Maria Ortese in the flatlands of East Anglia. A sudden venom rose in Rycarte against *la principessa* Paola: were none of Italy's universities good enough for her?

'There is no question, then, of any possible financial gift to the college from the girl's father?'

In spite of the interrogative form, Dr Clarke's words clearly did not constitute a question. His

163

reply, directed to the room in general as much as to his immediate opponent, more genuinely solicited information.

'Why is it so certain that there should be no question of it?'

It was the Vice-Mistress, rather to his surprise, who volunteered the first answer, a variant of the one Martha Pearce had outlined for him in the pub.

'It is vital that our admissions procedure should be above reproach. The independence of Directors of Studies; their unqualified right, in consultation with the Admissions Tutor' – she crinkled her already deeply creased eyes in the direction of Dr James – 'to select those candidates showing most promise in their subject, these are fundamental principles. It is a question of academic freedom. Already, in the laboratories of this University, the direction of research is too often dictated by the needs of industry, and increasingly even in the libraries by commissioning government departments. Our conclusions remain our own but, more and more, the field of our endeavour is determined by outside paymasters.'

The word 'libraries', Rycarte noted, was spoken in a tone of devout respect which did not belong to 'laboratories'. He doubted, however, whether the tyranny of external research funding had made many inroads into Professor Gladwin's own small citadel in the Department of Anglo-Saxon, Norse and Celtic.

'We do still decide what and how we teach – at least, with the exception of some of the professional subjects.'

Which were already soiled in Professor Gladwin's eyes, he speculated, by their potential usefulness.

'This is despite the depredations of the Higher Education Funding Council, which seeks to measure teaching excellence by sitting directors of Marks & Spencer in the back of lectures on quantum mechanics or institutionist theories of moral epistemology. What is left to us, then, which is still within our exclusive control? Very little, except for the selection and admission of our students. This remaining bulkhead we must surely defend to the last. This, at least, must surely be kept free of money's taint.'

The virulent look which accompanied this final phrase was directed, much to his relief, not at Rycarte but at the unfortunate Kate Beasley. Next to speak was Carolyn Gallagher, Director of Studies in Modern Languages. Reserved and thoughtful, lacking that delight in the sound of her own voice which can be a failing of the professional lecturer, to Rycarte's knowledge Dr Gallagher never spoke in committee unless she had something to say.

'I must express serious concern, Master, at the suggestion that a place to read for my subject might be used as coin in any fund-raising barter. It cannot fail to have a damaging effect upon the morale of all my students, if their places at the college are seen to be devalued in this way.'

'As upon the morale of the whole student body.' Ros Clarke now re-joined the assault. 'I agree with Dr Gallagher: how will any of them feel, if their hard-won places are now to be made available to the highest bidder?'

That this was not exactly what Dr Gallagher had said was apparent to all without her needing to point it out; she cocked one eyebrow and remained silent. But Dr Clarke was in her stride.

'Many of our intake, Master, come from ordinary backgrounds: state educated, the first generation in their families to go on to higher education. Our statistics in this respect, I am proud to say, compare favourably with those of almost every other college. We must consider the question from the viewpoint of these young women. To come here at all they have had to battle every step of the way. There have been no extra resources at school to prepare them for interview or to coach them to the needful A grades. Large teaching groups; no money for books beyond the bare essentials. Sometimes little support at home, either, or at least no knowledgeable support. Is it right that they should be forced to rub shoulders with another student who has not had to work for her place at all – who is here not on her own merit but simply because her father is in a position to make a significant financial donation to the college?'

Rycarte had not intended to be drawn into exchange of fire over matters of detail, but the immoderate sweeps of Ros Clarke's confrontational rhetoric were so difficult to let lie. Deliberate as he knew the provocation to be, he found it impossible not to rise to it.

'I feel certain that we can rely upon Dr Gallagher to give full consideration to the merits of any candidate for admission.'

'Oh, I dare say your benefactor's daughter will have no trouble in convincing us of her merits, Master.' Dr Clarke's voice was now dripping with ironic syrup. 'How could we be blind to her merits, with a million pounds to help open our eyes?'

For the first time that evening, Martha Pearce intervened, with an admonitory glance at Dr Clarke.

'It sounds as though you are implying Carolyn can be bought, Ros. But I think the point is that it would place any Director of Studies or Admissions Tutor in an extremely invidious position, to know that a negative judgement on a particular candidate could cost the college a large sum of money. The pressure is a wholly unfair one.'

Ros Clarke was unabashed by the reprimand.

'The point is that if even we know the decision would be an impossible one, then what is the rest of the world to think? Our students and our potential future students? "Of course they took her," people will say, "how could they do anything else?"

And our reputation for fair process in admissions – all our hard work over widening access – will be shot to pieces.'

This was the territory of Susie James, who had been listening to the debate so far with quiet concentration, two small frown lines nestling between her soft brown eyebrows.

'Um, I think Ros is right, actually, up to a point.'

She must spend a large portion of her life speaking before groups of schoolteachers and sixth formers, reflected Rycarte, yet pink rose in her cheeks at thus addressing the Governing Body – or perhaps it was strength of feeling, given what was to follow.

'I came to St Radegund's from a comprehensive in Sheffield, where none of the teachers had any experience of or connection with Oxbridge. Nobody had ever applied there before. Mum and Dad knew nothing about it either; they'd both left school at sixteen. The college gave me a chance, and I shall never cease to be grateful for it. Thirty years earlier, it would have been impossible for somebody like me to get to Cambridge. I am proud of the way things have changed, and of my part in helping to continue to ensure the broader access which benefited me. To broaden it still further, if we can. This feels like a huge step backwards, if you don't mind my saying so, Mr Rycarte, er, James, I mean Master.'

He gave a smiling wince in sympathy.

'People like me, like I was, I mean – people like

the kids I talk to – what are they going to think?'
She was even pinker and more earnest now. 'There
are already so many barriers, not just financial
and social and educational, but the self-imposed
ones, too, I'm talking about, where people think
that Oxbridge will be full of snobs and rich kids
and isn't for people like them. This is just going
to confirm all their prejudices, isn't it?'

'Get it wrong just once,' put in Ros Clarke, 'and
you undo a decade of getting it consistently right.'

Rycarte looked round the table, overtaken by a
sudden feeling of helplessness. He seemed to have
achieved what he would have thought impossible:
united all of St Radegund's disparate and frequently
warring factions. Letitia Gladwin, traditional blue-
stocking of the old school, product of a fee-paying
or at very least a grammar school education, ardent
meritocrat and believer in academic independence
and intellectual integrity; the twin poles of
RadFem, represented on the one hand by Ros
Clarke's unashamed social engineering, hating
privilege and the money which buys it, and on the
other by Martha Pearce's more measured liberalism;
even the passionate personal zeal of mild-mannered
Susie James – he had succeeded in unifying them
all against him. All, no doubt, except for Kate
Beasley, and on this issue he did not regard her
as a comfortable bedfellow. And yet it was all
nonsensical! What in this room appeared to be a
broad spectrum of opinion aligned behind the
inevitable, unanswerable truth would, he was sure,

169

appear to the world beyond these walls as the extreme of blinkered purism: as self-defeating idealism, devoid of rational common sense. Their words were high-sounding, but ultimately hollow. Were they really to turn down a donation, freely made and from what seemed to be an unimpeachable, independent source – a donation which would ease the college's immediate financial worries and could even secure its medium-term future – and all for the sake of appearances? Surely academics were the last people to care for the world's opinion, if they knew their own actions to be justified? Surely they could interview the girl, make an assessment and, if she was up to it, let her in and take the money? But of course academics were also those most conditioned to go to the stake for an abstract idea, to reject muddy pragmatism in favour of an hypothesised absolute. Tired of their impractical logic, he experienced an urge to react the other way. It would have been nice to yell and bang heads together.

Time had marched on towards the hour at which (in the absence of a motion to suspend Standing Orders) the meeting must be wound up, and Rycarte became aware that all eyes were turned in his direction. He sighed, and decided to give it one shot before bringing the argument to a close – for now, because he was not prepared to be beaten on something where he felt that the demands of good stewardship were so strongly on his side.

'As you know, I am new to the conventions under

which you are all so used to working. I hope I shall be forgiven, therefore, if I ask a question.'

He was torn between amusement and irritation to see Ros Clarke assume the right to dip her head in assent. Say what you like, the woman had balls.

'Is it college policy never to accept any donation from the parent of one of your students, past or present? Or from the students themselves?'

It was the impatient voice of the Bursar which replied.

'Of course not. Quite the reverse is true. The alumnae and their parents constitute one of our primary fund-raising bases. They are a major source of financial support for St Radegund's. All the colleges are the same in this respect.'

'And what about current students, as opposed to alumnae? Would the fact that a student was still *in statu pupillari* prohibit us from accepting a gift from that student or her parent?'

'Not at all,' said Kate. 'It is very common for parents to show their gratitude in small ways while their daughter is still here with us: supporting an appeal, giving small sums for books for the library. In fact, forms for the making of tax-efficient covenanted donations to the college are routinely included with mailings sent out to the parents of final year students – when we invite them to graduation, you know. That is a time when they are often feeling particularly moved to generosity.'

Rycarte allowed this information to be digested – though it was already well known to all.

'So what is our particular problem here? Merely one of relative timings, it appears. If we admit the girl, then afterwards there is nothing to prevent us from accepting her father's money.'

Ros Clarke was bound to have an answer to this, and she did.

'None of those parents to whom the Bursar is referring had any contact with the college before their daughter's admission – except, perhaps, to inquire about room rents, term dates or whether it is advisable to bring a kettle. It is not the date on Sr Alvau's cheque which will be the problem.'

He saw where it was going just before she reached the punchline.

'Rather, it is the elements of patronage which have already taken place. You have entertained him for lunch in college; he has met with the Development Committee. And he is on the guest list for the Advent Feast.'

And so they came full circle – a circle which Rycarte pictured closing round him like a noose.

Ros Clarke tidied her Governing Body papers into her bag with the satisfaction of a job well done. She had found it: the wedge to drive between James Rycarte and the Fellowship. And so far he was showing every sign of taking the bait beautifully.

CHAPTER 13

Martha always forgot how slow walking was. Used to cycling everywhere, all her mental measurements were based on travelling, even on her trusty upright three-speed, at a conservative eight miles per hour. Waterstone's to home she had down as fifteen minutes. Moving on foot at no more than three to four miles per hour, she found the distance seemed abnormally elongated.

Sometimes the change of pace could be a source of delight. Living a life where it was constantly necessary to get from A to B in the shortest possible time (which in Cambridge meant going by bike), walking could be an indulgence; like when she and Douglas used to take a stroll by the river on Sunday evenings – though they had not done so of late. She ought to be enjoying it now, walking shoulder to shoulder with Lucia after a rare evening's outing together, but she wasn't. Instead she found herself fighting an impatience to be home, an impulse to walk more briskly rather than keep step with her daughter's trailing pace. Once they would have biked to the book event together, taking just one chain to lock together both rear wheels against the railings; but Lucia refused to use her bicycle, had been doing so now for many months. It had been discarded along with any other items associated with the University – the trappings of potential studentdom – and stood idle in the garage, a thick layer of dust melding with the oil on all its moving parts, the tyres growing flaccid.

The real reason for Martha's impatience, she knew, was not the speed at which they were progressing but the fact that tonight was the night she had decided she must present Lucia with her ultimatum. Before they reached the lamp-post in the middle of Parker's Piece, she promised herself, she would bring it up. Not just yet, though.

'She was interesting, wasn't she? Especially about where her plots come from: beginning with setting and a central scene – an argument, some-times just a conversation – and working outwards from there. Often not even knowing who did it and why until she's halfway through, and some-times not even the identity of the victim. And it was lovely to get a signed copy of her latest. Not that I've got time to read it just now, the pile by my bed is already precarious. But maybe you—'

Stupid, she berated herself. Why did she always seem to stumble into these invidious references? And breaking off like that just drew attention to it. Lucia, however, did not take advantage of the opening for any kind of dig, but continued to plod along in dragging silence. Martha tried again.

174

'She was your absolute favourite, wasn't she, a year or two ago? I think you must have read *A Quiet Death* about fourteen times. I remember your gran thinking it was funny, because she never knew anyone to reread a detective story before. "What's the point, when you know the ending?" she said. But I explained it's different when you want to be a writer; you are looking for so much more.'

They were just reaching the edge of Parker's Piece now, and circling nearer to the subject which was occupying Martha's mind – though in truth there was never a moment when it was far from the surface between them. Lucia, perhaps scenting the impending assault, was raising the barricades.

'I've gone off the idea of crime fiction, Mum. I told you.'

'A lot of what she was saying would be true of any fiction writing, though, don't you think, love?

'What would I know? You tell me, Mum.'

Like you always do. Martha knew without glancing down that Lucia's hands were balled into tight fists at her sides. She felt exasperation at the pig-headedness which shut her out, felt she would like to take those fingers in her own and gently force them to uncurl, as she had when Lucia was a toddler, refusing to relinquish some stolen treasure. A sweet, dusty from the pavement, perhaps – Lucia always used to pick up sweets. They were almost at the lamp: the place where the four diagonal paths intersected, where they

175

would turn their feet right towards home. There was no point in delaying: it had to be now.

'There's a course. Only six days, but it's residential, so it will be pretty intensive, evenings as well. Novel writing. Beginners and intermediate – it's only for unpublished authors.'

'Look, Mum, I—'

'It's at the Arvon Foundation, at their house in Devon.' Martha laboured on. 'One of Dad's colleagues has run poetry courses there, they have a really good reputation. Non-profit-making, you know. They believe in total immersion. No internet, no e-mail, no mobile phones, no distractions at all, just writing and thinking and talking about writing.'

'But I don't—'

'The idea is that by living for a week with others in the same boat you form a kind of supportive community, learn from one another as well as from the course tutors, who are all experienced, established writers. I think it would be the ideal kick-start for you. Just the input you need to get your inspiration going, get you remotivated.'

Finally Martha paused. Lucia's attempted dissention had stopped, to be replaced by a silence which was far worse.

'Your dad and I are going to pay. We've booked you in.'

Why did she hide behind Douglas? Lucia must know this was coming entirely from her.

'January the sixteenth – Monday to Saturday.'

Why did Martha feel as if she were committing

her daughter against her will to some kind of institution? In another existence this might have been fun – an opportunity to relish.

'I'm not going.'

The words were not said in challenge. Martha would almost have welcomed the defiant jut of the chin which had been so characteristic of Lucia in her mid-teens; instead, there was just this simple, flat stonewalling. Though she quailed inwardly, Martha stuck to her prepared script and delivered her terms.

'January the sixteenth. Seven months is more than long enough to sit at home doing nothing. Your father and I are very happy to support your ambition to write, but you have to show us that you mean it. And that means going to Devon. Otherwise, well, I'm afraid you are going to have to get a job.'

She tried to prevent the apologetic note from creeping into her voice as she added, 'It's what most writers have to do, after all. For years, in most cases, before they can make any kind of a living. They can't all be J. K. Rowling.'

There was no reply, and the two women continued to walk abreast, both unturning, eyes fixed on the path ahead. It would have been so much easier, thought Martha, to have been comfortably side by side on the settee, or even facing each other across the breakfast table, where she could more naturally have taken hold of Lucia's hand. But of course it wouldn't have been easier; if she could have touched her daughter, could have taken her in her arms, then she would have backed down, as she had so many times in the past few months. This was the only way.

In the hall they parted with a sigh on Martha's side and a grunt on Lucia's. Lucia made for her bedroom while her mother drifted into the kitchen, craving creature comforts. These she found in the form of Maynard, who rose from the table and stretched archingly against her extended hand, and carbohydrates: bread from the crock, cut thickly and slathered with raspberry jam. Through the half-open sitting-room door she had glimpsed the settee, occupied by her husband's horizontal form; the corkscrew on the table still speared a cork, its end reddened and crystalline. She did not need to lift it to her nose to know it was the good Rioja: the last bottle, or was it the next to last? It almost certainly would not go too well with jam. Nevertheless, she reached up to the shelf and lifted down a second wine glass, the one from next to the empty space. Would Douglas have eaten? She sliced and jammed a second wedge of granary just in case before she went through. Any brief sense of satisfaction she had felt earlier at having confronted the problem of Lucia's future had now evaporated – to be replaced only by a gnawing sense of how little she had yet faced up to the problem of either Douglas's or her own.

A senior police officer whom he had once met at a press conference had told James Rycarte that the speed-gauging technology available in a tracking patrol car (unlike that of fixed speed cameras) is accurate only to within ten per cent. Ever since, he had regarded the national speed limit as being in effect seventy-seven miles per hour, preferring not to entertain the possibility that the direction of error might not be in his favour.

It was therefore with the needle steady on seventy-seven that he kept the Alfa in the west-bound fast lane of the A14 with his fingertips resting on the lowest point of the wheel. Meanwhile Susie James in the passenger seat next to him was enthusing about a vital away win.

'Shipperley's goal was class, wasn't it? What a finish! The way he's just seen the keeper off his line and chipped him from the edge of the box.'

It was fascinating the way a young woman with more education than ninety-eight per cent of the population – a woman with a Cambridge PhD – could not help but slip into the vernacular when describing events on a football pitch. A very particular football vernacular, too, with its own unique usage. The commentator's present perfect tense: *he's beaten his man; he's rounded the goalie; he's stuck it away!*

'That puts us, what, two points clear?'

The first person plural was a concession to Susie's enthusiasm and to their shared geographical roots; Rycarte could make no real claim to be a fan. It had been partly a flight of nostalgia and partly a friendly gesture towards a Fellow whom he genuinely liked when he phoned for tickets for the promotion clash between table-topping Sheffield United and Ipswich Town, who were settling already into their perennial position just below the play-off places. Ipswich was not much over fifty miles from Cambridge, and it was dual all the way – little more than an hour door-to-door in the Alfa, or an hour and a half if there were queues to get away from the ground. Of course, she could have gone anyway. But Susie, he knew, had no car, and although there was a direct rail link between the two neighbouring county towns, from what Rycarte had seen of the timetable the service scheduled a stop at every barn and haystack along the route. She would have had to leave before the final whistle to catch the last train, and would still have been lucky to be home much before midnight.

'Three points, actually, but Preston play tomorrow night so it's a bit of a false position.'

She could have been the manager, urging perspective in the post-match dressing-room interview. *We've got to keep our feet on the ground, take each game as it comes.* (What was that Big Ronism, possibly apocryphal? *Early doors*.) But at the same time it could have been Paul sitting there next to him, as a teenager, coming back from one of their occasional father–son trips to Highbury or White Hart Lane. Susie had even insisted on hanging her red and white scarf out of the car window, one end knotted for security, the other snapping in victorious salute to the other home-bound United fans. Not that Paul ever had a scarf – his club loyalties were never that fixed; nor, probably, would Rycarte have allowed him to trail it from the car if he had.

By Bury St Edmunds their analysis of the game and of resultant league positions was pretty much exhausted. The traffic was thinning as the Ipswich fans turned off towards their various Suffolk village homes, and Rycarte drove for some time in silence, enjoying the darkness between head-lights and the undemanding curves of the emptying road. Gradually his thoughts disengaged from the fixture they were leaving behind and drifted towards their destination: Cambridge and St Radegund's. Susie sat unstirring in the seat beside him and he wondered if she was dozing; but it seemed not, and indeed that her reflections were tending in a similar direction to his own.

'Are you really planning on accepting the dona-tion from your Italian friend?'

'Well, I can't, can I? Not without the support of the Development Committee – which seems most unlikely to be forthcoming.'

He wished this had not come out sounding just a tiny bit petulant.

'And, in fact, the backing of the Fellowship as a whole. It would be very foolhardy on my part, not to mention undemocratic and unprincipled, if I were to seek to go ahead on something so appar-ently controversial against the feeling of the college.'

There was a pause. Rycarte glanced across at his passenger but her face was angled away from him, watching the black outlines of hedges speed away backwards towards Ipswich.

'But you want to?'

Her question was tentative, her voice free of accusation. Her openness, and the lingering conviviality of the away end, invited equal candour on his part.

'I do, yes. I find it difficult to ignore all the very tangible benefits which a sizeable gift could bring to the college.'

She was facing forward again and nodding slowly. All at once Rycarte wanted to persuade her, to make her understand his point of view. She was intelligent; she was young and diffident; she gave every appearance of an open mind – it must be possible to make her see things his way.

'You said at the Governing Body meeting how grateful you are to St Radegund's for giving you the chance of a Cambridge education.'

He could not see her pinken, of course, in the unlit car.

'And now you are doing a great deal to repay that perceived debt,' he reassured her, 'in your role as Admissions Tutor and through all your liaison and publicity work with the schools. We count ourselves very lucky to have you.'

Now he could almost fancy that he felt the glow from her burning cheeks. She muttered something incoherent in protest, which he brushed through.

'I imagine that many other students who come to the college from similar backgrounds probably feel the same. These kids you go out and talk to at comprehensive schools – if we offer them a place, I bet they are often the ones who feel the strongest sense of allegiance to St Rad's, and often a desire to give something back. Their parents, too, perhaps?'

'Oh yes, that's absolutely right.' Her voice was breathlessly eager. 'Ever so many of our comprehensive intake covenant a regular gift back to the college when they leave, and their parents are hugely generous, too. They often give as much or more than the richer families, when we have an appeal or something, however hard it is for them to afford it. It's really brilliant – quite touching, you know.'

He let a short silence establish itself before very gently producing his point.

'And those people who have so generously contributed their hard-earned cash, what do you think they would say if they knew we had turned down the sort of money they can only dream of, money which could have solved many of the college's financial problems overnight? And, moreover, that we had done so in pursuit of some kind of abstract principle?'

Susie was grave, not leaping to an immediate reply. Then, 'Um, well, I don't think you should assume . . . With respect—'

Was she about to call him 'Master'?

'—I don't think it's true that just because people come from ordinary, non-academic backgrounds they are incapable of comprehending an important idea, like integrity or independence.'

He nodded with a gravity to match her own, gaze fixed on the twin streams of cat's eyes racing towards him.

'Granted. But if they knew that the girl had won a place on merit? And that the donation had been refused merely in order to maintain an *appearance* of integrity? An appearance which we seek to uphold for the putative benefit of people like them, so as not to put them off from applying. Do you really think they would still understand and have sympathy with our position? Or do you think they would tell us – if you will excuse the expression – to get over ourselves and take the bloody money?'

This time the silence stretched out like the A14. Eventually Susie's reply came, sounding so unhappy that he almost regretted this first, small victory.

'You may be right. Quite a few of them would probably think we should take the money.'

Julia the ents officer was tucked up in her narrow college bed before Rycarte's Alfa Romeo passed Newmarket – and certainly well before she would have wished. Her second date with Darren Cotter had been just as frustrating as the first. Hardly a date at all, in fact, since all they had done was

184

stand awkwardly around in his laboratory, hoping that his bearded colleague (who introduced himself briefly as Jefferson as he left the room) would not come back, leaning against the long steel desks and listening to that weird, soaring music of his which embarrassed and disturbed her and could hardly have been further from the limp epithet she offered him: 'Nice.'

It wasn't what she had imagined, either, when he had talked about his lab. Julia was a Social Anthropology student; she had given up all the science subjects after GCSE. But her idea of a lab comprised taller wooden benches, the kind you stand at or sit alongside on those high stools, not standard height desks like in the Archaeology and Anthropology library. Bunsen burners were perhaps too much to expect in a university electrical engineering department, but surely there should have been some kind of specialised scientific equipment, or larger computers with aircraft-style control panels, not just these rows of ordinary-looking terminals? She had tried to convey some part of this to Darren, who had embarked upon a long excursus about how the processing capability of a computer the size of the whole floor of NASA headquarters a couple of decades ago would now fit inside a wristwatch.

'Probably be quite an expensive watch, though,' she had said; he had laughed generously at her feeble attempted joke and she had felt a quiet surge of warmth towards him. Even more than last time, in the pub, she found herself noticing the clear grey-green of his eyes, behind the frequently bemused surface of which she recognised an acute and sympathetic intelligence. She also liked his forearms, fully visible tonight below rolled-up shirtsleeves, finding their breadth and finely haired muscularity anything but geeky.

There were any number of moments when she might have let him kiss her tonight, if he had tried – and she felt certain he would have tried, had she given him the encouragement. His best opening would have been when they were leaning together over the coffee dispenser trying to work out how to unwedge the jammed water container. She could smell the heated tang of his skin, could see the individual emergent spikes which made up the shade of stubble on his jaw. But he had not taken the chance and, although she had made up her mind that they should not kiss, she nevertheless felt a wash of disappointment.

It was no good. There seemed no solution to her quandary. If Darren kissed her she would have earned her stripes and could become a Tigress – but gone would be her excuse to see him again. And seeing Darren again, she had to admit to herself, was what she increasingly wanted to do.

CHAPTER 14

It wasn't that Martha had ever exactly stopped attending the meetings of RadFem. It was nothing as positive as a boycott, nor even simple cowardice, though admittedly she had no desire to spend her Thursday evenings listening to Ros Clarke and her disciples still fulminating against James Rycarte's appointment. Martha was not a woman to use personal discomfiture as a reason to avoid something which she felt she ought to do – something to which, in the past at least, she had felt committed. But she could hardly be blamed if, for the first few meetings of that Michaelmas Term, she gave precedence to other, competing obligations which she found required her presence elsewhere.

This week, though, the duty was an irremissible one. Every third year since RadFem's inception (allowing each time for a complete cohort of students to come and go), Martha had addressed the membership on the issue of the gender pay gap, drawing upon her own research in the field. Tonight's talk was a depressingly similar one to the previous three: labour market segmentation, lack of state nursery provision, the glass ceiling. Her notes from nine years ago quoted women's average earnings hovering just below eighty per cent of that of men; the current figure hovered just above eighty per cent.

The talk went smoothly enough. There was a decent turnout, at least. Both Ros Clarke and Karen were near the back and said nothing, but Deepa wasn't sitting with Karen, for once, and Martha was gratified to see her two third year economists, Lauren and Peta, in the audience. Neither was a self-identified feminist and RadFem was not their usual territory, but they were both taking the Labour paper this year, and Martha could not help also seeing their presence as an act of support for herself and feeling touched. At the end of her allotted forty minutes there was time for questions; there were a respectable number of these, including one each from the loyal Lauren and Peta, and the ensuing discussion of part-time and flexible working could almost be described as lively. It was not easy, Martha remembered thinking before as well, to engage an audience of high-achieving eighteen to twenty-one year olds in barriers to career progression which would affect them, if at all, only when they took on family responsibilities. To most young female under-graduates children were a world away.

As she smiled her recognition of the polite stutter of applause which greeted her winding-up flourish, picking up as she did so the notes at which she had barely needed to glance, Martha should have felt at least a modicum of satisfaction. Instead she experienced only weariness, remembering the stack of urgent paperwork on her desk which still demanded her attention before she could go home. And at the door of the Graduate Seminar Room she could not help being aware of the emptying seats behind her: all, that is, except those occupied by Ros, Karen and Deepa. Martha's stomach constricted. Evidently the real business of the evening was about to be conducted without her.

As soon as she was gone, in fact, the three conspirators rose and moved together to a cushioned window seat. Dr Clarke closed the leaded window which she had opened beforehand to ventilate the roomful of November-clad women – the students in their fleeces, the sprinkle of dons, or at least the older ones, in their cardigans and lumpy sweaters. It was getting late now, and there was a chill in the empty room; Kate Beasley had the heating set to switch off in all the public areas at ten p.m.. If the effect of the economy were to discourage cabals such as this one, reflected Ros, Kate would probably count it an incidental blessing.

Karen got down to business at once.

'It's difficult to get a decent picture of how the rent strike is going. How many people haven't paid, I mean, and what impact it is having on the college.'

She fixed a frankly interrogatory eye upon Ros. When there was no immediate response, she added bluntly, 'You were there at Finance Committee on Monday. There was nothing in unreserved business, of course, but I bet the Bursar had something to report once we had left, hadn't she?'

Deepa, seated beyond Karen, shifted uncomfortably.

'Karen, I really don't think . . . Look, there's a reason why things are put under reserved business, isn't there? Dr Clarke can't just tell us what was said, it's got to be confidential or something.'

All three of them knew that they were thinking the same thing. About how, after the recent Governing Body meeting, Dr Clarke had divulged to them the outline of the proposed Alvau donation – even though the Governing Body, uniquely amongst St Radegund's many committees, met entirely without student representation. Ros's slow smile slid from Deepa back to Karen.

'Naturally I could not reveal the details of any student's individual financial circumstances.' She paused, but barely for a second. 'Kate Beasley did give us the global figures as well, however. Her spin, as one would expect, was that there is no cause for alarm. But the figures were quite promising, actually – from our point of view, I mean. Around thirty-five per cent non-payers in the second and third years and as many as sixty per cent in the first year.'

Karen contrived to grin and whistle at the same time, while Ros went on speaking.

'Kate puts the high first year figure down to late arrival of student loans. Although college bills are due for payment at the beginning of each term, freshers are often late with their first cheque. She claimed we would normally expect twenty per cent of first year accounts to be outstanding at this stage. But that still means forty per cent withholding payment, as far as I can make out.'

'But this is fantastic.' Karen's glee was unconcealed. 'Well over a third of the student body refusing to pay! That's got to be having some kind of effect. Focusing some minds.' Then her tone dropped, became more winning. 'It would be great to be able to let people know how strong the strike is. Think how it would encourage people to know that lots of others are standing firm alongside them.'

Deepa protested at once.

'Oh no, Karen, how can we possibly let out the figures? Because then it will be obvious that there has been a leak.' She shot an anxious glance at Ros. 'That sounds awful, but what I mean is that they'll know somebody has said something to us, won't they? We don't want Dr Clarke to get into trouble.'

Ros Clarke laughed. 'I don't think you need worry too much on my account, Deepa. But, you know, there are other ways of accessing the information, without its having come through the Bursar or the Finance Committee at all.'

191

Both girls looked at her, Deepa doubtfully, Karen with eagerness.

'Have a poll, a referendum – call it what you like. Ballot all the students. Ask them: are you currently withholding your rent? We know the figures are good; this way you can confirm them quite legitimately.'

'Yes,' said Karen, 'of course.' Her eyes were dancing in anticipation of this new means of fuelling the fight.

'And while you are about it . . .' Ros had their complete attention again. 'I wonder whether it might be timely for the Student Union to take further soundings. Find out student opinion on a matter of current concern. Ask another question.'

She was rewarded with a broadly spreading grin from Karen and a look of dawning shock from Deepa.

'Perhaps – and of course this is only a suggestion – something about their views on accepting donations tied to admissions.'

CHAPTER 15

'**I**'ll be off then, Master. Don't forget, will you? The lights and the computer.'

Those power surges: he was most unlikely to forget. Miss Kett-Symes's departing monition was as unvarying as the cry of the kittiwake – or the starlings in the limes by the porter's lodge. Rycarte glanced up to see a bunch of hothouse freesias tucked within his secretary's arm and was surprised, it being a Friday. He nodded towards them appreciatively.

'Lovely. For Dame Emily?'

She halted in the process of checking through her handbag, conducting the ritual inventory of keys, comb and purse. (Miss Kett-Symes saw no need to own a mobile telephone.) Her eyes as she looked up suggested wounded devotion.

'I know I don't normally visit on a Friday, but it is very nearly five thirty and the queue for the bus is always longer at the end of the week, though I've no idea why that should be. I've finished off here. And I've put out the sherry and sherry glasses for your guests when they arrive.'

He smiled his thanks, judging it fruitless to tell

her that he had no intention either of entertaining his guests in his office or of offering them college sherry. There were two bottles of prosecco and some Calabrian olives cooling in the catering-sized fridge over at the lodging.

'As I say, I don't normally go on Fridays but I've missed two visits this week. Not that I mind staying late now and again when you have additional things for me to do.'

She sounded very much as though she did mind, though, and Rycarte experienced mild puzzlement; he knew for a fact she had not stayed past a quarter to six any day this week. Maybe visiting hours at the Beeches were tight but, perhaps ungenerously, he doubted it.

'And how is Dame Emily? What I mean is, has there been any sign of improvement?'

An alarming twitch was affecting Miss Kett-Symes's lips; Rycarte wondered if it was the beginnings of a snarl or whether – heaven forfend! – she was about to cry.

'No change, I'm afraid. She can breathe without a ventilator, but they are still feeding her through a tube. She seems to be aware of her surroundings – I'm sure her eyes flicker when she hears me come in. But there's no speech, nor any movement below the neck. And the muscles in the left side of her face are still frozen.'

Rycarte was appalled. He had had no idea things were so bad. How had he watched his secretary leaving with her flowers at the end of so many days in the office together and never actually asked, never taken the trouble to find out what it was she was going to. Men and hospital bedsides, yes – but it was really no excuse. Somehow he had always pictured Dame Emily sitting up: perhaps making clumsy attempts to feed herself with a spoon, but eyes bright as a blackbird's. And reading – was she at least able to read? Three months without the sustenance of reading would be an unimaginable hardship for one whose life had been books. Books and the secrets which lay hidden in the Assyrian dust.

'Can she . . . ?'

But Miss Kett-Symes was busily rechecking the contents of her bag, the brief sortie into confidence apparently over. Perhaps he should visit, if he wanted to know the answer. Perhaps he could find some of those books on tape and take them in. If indeed the former Mistress's mind was sufficiently unaffected to take advantage of this means of imparting information. Several boxes of her personal books were still in the library at the lodging. He could take a look through to see what direction her tastes took. Dorothy L. Sayers, he hazarded; perhaps Barbara Pym. Or biography. He thought of the rosebuds: maybe Gertrude Jekyll.

His secretary's peremptory goodbye brought him back to more immediate concerns. He had the room to himself and half an hour before he needed to go back to the lodging to wash and change in time for his guests' arrival for tonight's

Advent Feast. The banks of box files behind his desk were now tolerably familiar and it did not take him long to locate the one he wanted. It was the file containing proceedings of the College Council from the Lent Term nine and a half years ago, the last time a senior tutorial election had been held in St Radegund's. Closer to ten years, in fact, because January was when discussions had begun on that occasion, although the choice of Martha Pearce to take over the role from October had evidently not been a difficult or divisive one. He took down, too, his copy of the Statutes and Ordinances of the college, turned to the section headed 'Appointments to Major College Offices' and began to read.

It was some twenty minutes later, deep in thought, that the Master left his office, first dutifully switching off and unplugging all electrical appliances, and wandered out in the direction of the porter's lodge. He wanted to pick up his mail. It was one of the quirks of Miss Kett-Symes that she collected his post and brought it to his office only once a day, at nine thirty a.m., on the dot (as presumably she had done for Dame Emily before him), unmoved from her punctilious adherence to routine by the fact that the Royal Mail had for the past year been delivering to the college only once a day as well, and that shortly after noon. It was therefore his habit to collect his own letters on his way back to the lodging in the early evening. He wondered whether it ever occurred to his secretary to be surprised that he appeared only ever to receive internal mail and the occasional delivery by Parcelforce or Amtrak.

He was greeted at the lodge not by the Head Porter but by Terry. Or rather he was not greeted, because Terry was bent intently over one of a bank of small screens, watching the CCTV image from the back gate of the college. Two undergraduates, who despite the grainy picture quality could be identified as both definitely female, were saying either hello or goodbye in a markedly amorous manner. At length the girls broke their clinch and Terry looked up, the leer sidling from his face when he saw Rycarte.

'Hello, Terry. I wonder if I could have my mail, please?'

He received something between a grunt and a huff in reply, as the junior porter shuffled to the Fellows' pigeonholes and stuck his hand in the end one, still clearly labelled 'Mistress'. On top of the pile of assorted envelopes which he prepared to hand to Rycarte was a hand-scribbled note. Terry studied his own writing like the face of a distant relative.

'Oh yes, I forgot, sir. The Master of Corpus phoned. His wife is going to be running late – coming back from London or something – so they won't be coming over to the lodging. They'll meet you in the SCR for the official sherry at seven fifteen.'

It was going to be Gavi di Gavi at his own

insistence, but Rycarte supposed if they were talking officially then Terry was right – sherry in Cambridge being not so much a wine as an occasion. He nodded his thanks.

'Where's the Head Porter tonight?'

'Gone to see the Mistress – Dame Emily, I should say. He generally goes on a Friday afternoon. He'll be back on duty before the guests start to arrive for the feast.'

If Rycarte was at all surprised by this intelligence he did nothing to show it, merely nodding again.

'Thanks then, Terry.'

Back to the lodging, next, to take a bath before Janet Greerson and Luigi Alvau arrived at six thirty. *Back home*. He tried the phrase out experimentally in his head, but could not yet make it fit. But then, there had been very many places which had provided a base for Rycarte in the last forty years and very few which he had managed to think of as home. He still mentally identified it as the lodging; dropping the qualifier 'Mistress's' in his mind had taken some time and he was nowhere near adding 'Master's' to the title.

Three weeks of November had taken their toll upon the trim, bright greens through which Rycarte had walked between the central college buildings and the lodging on his first arrival, leaving in their wake a patchwork of dull greys and leafless umbers. The tidiness of early winter no longer suggested expensively careful husbandry; rather, the denuded branches now seemed to form a better match with the threadbare college interior. The Advent Feast, though, was the one occasion in the year when budgetary constraints were forgotten and St Radegund's permitted itself to be lavish. It was an annual occasion for conspicuous consumption – albeit on a more modest scale than might be encountered in some of Cambridge's more famous and ancient foundations – at the expense of past benefactors who, reckless as to the educational future of the college, had chosen to earmark their bequests specifically for the wining and dining of the Fellows and their guests. There would be a fish course, and a sorbet before the entrée was served; after the pudding and a break to walk around First Court, which twenty years ago would have been for smoking but now succeeded mainly in getting everybody chilled in their evening attire, dessert would be laid out in the Breakfast Parlour. This was one of the many terms which had a different meaning here from elsewhere in the world; 'dessert' was not a second sweet course but a medley of cheese, fruit and petits fours to accompany the coffee, port, claret and Sauternes. Paul would no doubt have pointed out that, strictly speaking, the Cambridge usage was more correct. *Desservir*, to clear away: the diners were moved to another room to continue drinking and talking while the college staff moved in to clear the tables in Hall.

Even the Advent Feast itself was misnamed. He had received a lively disquisition on the subject from Joan Tilley at lunch a few days previously. Advent was apparently fixed as beginning on the Sunday closest to St Andrew's Day on the thirtieth of November, and so could not possibly be under way before the last few days of the month – although in former days the church calendar had designated Advent as beginning one week earlier on the Feast of Christ the King and according to some sources the festival had once comprised six weeks instead of four. This perhaps explained the anomaly of the dates, though Rycarte preferred to put it down as just one more idiosyncrasy of a university where May Week traditionally falls in the middle of June.

Forty minutes later he was scoured and dinner jacketed and seated among the floral garlands of what was now his main reception room. You couldn't call it a lounge – it was altogether too primped for such a slovenly activity – and it was on too large a scale for a sitting room. He supposed it could only be a drawing room, and thought for the first time how quietly impressed his parents would have been to see him possessed of something which went by that name. In his drawing room with him, looking remarkably at home at either end of a profoundly uncomfortable, over-stuffed sofa, were his two former media colleagues, talking shop. To be more precise Alvau, who knew that the first law of conversation with a lady is to move it on to her home ground, was encouraging Janet Greerson to talk shop.

'My present position means that I have a very largely editorial function, but I still have to show my face in the field from time to time for the morale of the troops. Keeping my reporters on their toes, you know. I've just recently returned from a flying visit to Lebanon, in fact.'

'Ah yes, Beirut, the beleaguered jewel of the Middle East.' Alvau brought his fingertips together in what could have been hand-washing or prayer. 'Is there much of her former beauty still in evidence?'

Janet regarded the Italian coolly. 'Well, you know, I was hardly there as a tourist. I didn't have a lot of time for sightseeing.'

He smiled and bowed his head, one hand tracing in the air a gracious *mi dispiace*.

'Of course not, my dear lady. I was merely curious to hear at first hand – and from the lips of a renowned expert – about the effect of the recent bombardments from over the southern border.'

'From Israel.' Janet had made her name as a foreign correspondent by straight talking. 'Well, the damage is considerable, of course. Night after night of aerial strikes cannot but leave its mark.'

Rycarte nudged the bowl of olives towards them across the coffee table and wondered if he should intervene. The formal BBC line was sceptical, if not openly critical, of Israeli military intervention in southern Lebanon in retaliation against Hezbollah attacks on their own population, but

Janet Greerson (née Liebman) had a complicated personal take on Middle Eastern politics. He himself had once stumbled into the lion's maw over the subject of clemency for a cancer-riddled Nazi war criminal, and had lived to regret it. But Alvau was a consummate politician, and he had evidently done his homework.

'The world will judge Israel, as the world always does. The United Nations; our confrères in the international press.'

He sat back and opened his hands expansively. As he did so Janet sat correspondingly forward at her end of the sofa, helping herself to an attentive olive. *Magnetism*, thought Rycarte, almost physically manifested.

'Let us imagine,' said Alvau, 'that a terrorist organisation is operating from just over the French border in the Vanoise. That its forces are regularly shelling Italian towns and cities and carrying out suicide attacks on the Italian civilian population. Let us say that this has gone on for years – decades – and that thousands of Italians have lost their lives. And that the French government merely says, "*Bof* "' – he gave an eloquent Gallic shrug – '"these people are not under our control. *Naturellement* we greatly regret their activities but there is nothing we can do about it."'

Janet was already smiling, enjoying the conceit.

'Now, if the government in Rome were finally to say that enough is enough, were to launch rocket attacks upon the terrorists' Alpine emplacements, were even to send tanks up to their mountain camps, do you suppose the world would deem it an over-reaction? Would Italy's response be condemned unanimously by the international community?' He shook his head, slow as a cobra. 'But Italy, of course, is not the whipping-boy of the Arab-fearing world.'

Rycarte eyed his friend narrowly even though he, too, was smiling at the analogy. Only one thing was certain, he decided: that there could be no way of knowing for sure what Alvau thought about this or any issue. He decided to call him out a little, mainly for curiosity's sake.

'And what if the French *terroristes* were not in lonely mountain hideouts but embedded amongst the civilian population of Albertville or Briançon: in apartment blocks, close to hospitals and primary schools?'

Alvau smiled his affable, impenetrable smile. 'Then we would have to make the argument that it was by the action of the guerrillas that civilians became targets and not that of the Italian state.'

Janet toyed with another olive, rolling it between finger and thumb like a bullet. 'But a quarter of the world – the Islamic quarter – is not ready to hear Israel make that argument. All they see is bleeding and bruised Arab children, grieving Arab mothers: the images my cameramen have no choice but to record and I have no choice but to broadcast.'

Finally Alvau gave a shout of mirth, and Rycarte felt the tension in the room shatter; like Janet he joined in the laughter before he knew why.

'Whereas of course the world would only stand by and applaud if it were the French who took a beating!'

Rycarte's inexplicable francophile tendencies had always been a source of merriment as far as his Italian friend was concerned. They were laughing properly together now – but a small part of Rycarte nevertheless wished he had served a crémant de Bourgogne instead of the prosecco.

It was nearly ten past seven; Rycarte drained his glass and laid it on the table. His other guests would be arriving imminently in the SCR and he wanted to be there to greet them. Though one of the most amiable of the other Heads of House – and neither titled nor a Nobel laureate – the Master of Corpus Christi College was nevertheless not a man to be kept waiting, and his good lady wife was frankly rather terrifying. She was the sort of woman who, he imagined, would stand no nonsense from staff, dogs or horses. The fact that the seating plan placed her on Alvau's right hand lent a pleasant anticipation to the evening ahead: it would be an encounter worth witnessing. Rycarte and Janet gathered up keys and handbag respectively and shouldered their gowns. (Janet, as a graduate of the University, was required to wear one; Alvau had studied at Bologna – an institution a century more venerable – and was not.)

Outside the damp air hung heavy like a tarpaulin, deadening even the sound of their footfalls on the stone-flagged path, sludgy with leaves.

They passed along the western side of the library, the shafts of light from each of its high windows illuminating a swath of suspended droplets, seemingly immobile, confounding physics.

'. . . although the modern season of Advent never begins before the last few days of November.'

Rycarte's words dropped heavily into the shadows which encased the lower portions of the library wall, and as they approached the flawed south-west corner he tried to dispel the image of those walls shifting in the darkness, sliding down into the saturated ground. It was not until, three abreast, they rounded the end of the library into Second Court that another sound penetrated the water-laden gloom. Rhythmic, not immediately discernible as human, it reminded Rycarte at first of the distant pound of cannon fire or perhaps the stamp of marching feet. This last impression was not far from the reality, which was the clapping of two dozen pairs of hands, the noise muted by the damp and by the solid bulk of Hall which stood between the Master and his companions and the unseen hand-clappers. The accompanying voices could be heard only at the last second, as Rycarte and the others cut through the covered passage into First Court and the front of Hall, far too late to keep the chanted words from reaching Luigi Alvau's ears.

'No cash for admissions, no cash for admissions . . .'

The gaggle of girls, one or two at the front clutching limp paper banners clearly run off a PC in 150 point Times New Roman, all tried hard not to react as the Master and the potential giver of the tainted cash walked past in the direction of the SCR. All failed equally badly; Rycarte let his eyes drift over the faces and picked out Karen, the Student Union president, chanting with exaggerated defiance at a point two feet above his head and Deepa, her deputy, looking toe-shufflingly self-conscious. At least the faces were all young: there were no senior members in the protest group, which was a small source of solace. Rycarte glanced neither at Alvau nor at Janet Greerson; nor did any of them speak until the chanting voices were behind them and a double door took them through into the sanctuary of the corridor leading to the SCR. Then it was the primary target of the demonstration who broke the embarrassed silence, his voice as unruffled as always.

'It seems that I am leading you into dangerous currents, my old friend. Causing ripples in these peaceful waters of yours. I should be sorry to bring a storm to this sylvan pool.'

Situated in the groves of academe again, presumably. Rycarte ignored the note of warning which lay behind the words and warmed to the Italian's flight of metaphor, using the easy ritual of their wordplay as a screen against the intrusion of anything less comfortable. His smile as he reached for the handle of the door to the Senior Combination Room came almost naturally.

'Then I shall just have to find some suitable oil to pour upon the troubled surface, shan't I? Never fear, the dispensing of healing salves is something they teach you on day one at the BBC, isn't it, Janet?'

Thus all three of them were laughing as they stepped across the threshold of the SCR. Rycarte took two glasses of Gavi di Gavi from the tray offered to him by the college butler at the door and passed them to Janet and Alvau. His momentary buoyancy was somewhat deflated by the sight of the Master of Corpus and his wife bearing down upon him from inside the room, glasses already in hand, even though his watch still showed 7:14. The bubble was exploded completely when, over the formidable shoulder of the Master's wife, his eye was caught by the complacent gaze of Ros Clarke, raising both her glass and one eyebrow to him in mock salute.

While the Advent feasters were enjoying their repast, the flow of the wine gradually raising the hum of conversation until it drowned out evidence of the protest beyond the windows, the mist outside grew denser, soon coalescing into a positive fen fog. By half past eight those inside Hall were scraping the last of the Atholl brose from their crystal dessert goblets and laying down their spoons, while the remaining stragglers of protesters, demoralised by the chill and diminishing visibility, headed for the warmth of the college bar.

At about the same time Darren Cotter and Julia were wandering back towards college from another discreetly outlying public house, where they had been sitting over one neglected drink since seven o'clock when Darren finished work. They were talking about the fog. Or rather Darren was talking and Julia was listening, half amazed at her own absorption. His subject, in particular, was the very phenomenon which Rycarte had observed in the beams from the library windows: namely, the failure of the suspended water droplets to fall.

'Water particles are heavier than air, and gravity ought to mean that the droplets in mist or fog should fall to earth, as raindrops do. Think about clouds. The fact that clouds stay in the sky is one of the mysteries of physics. They aren't just made up of water vapour, as some people think; they are air filled with millions of droplets of liquid water. See how wet your scarf is.'

He dragged his forefinger along the top of the band of scarlet wool round her neck, tracing the line where it met the soft, dark curls above. It came away wet, and they both halted their steps for a moment to watch as the drop of water clinging to his fingertip slowly lengthened, detached itself and fell.

'It isn't condensation that is making you wet. Water vapour condenses on cold surfaces, but your scarf is warm. Look, even your hair is damp, and your hair is really warm, because it's part of you and you are alive.'

Her eyelashes, too, glistened with tiny, trapped globes of moisture. Manfully, Darren fought down the desire to repeat the experiment by touching those. To reach out and feel for himself just how warm and alive her hair was.

'It's just that the fog is full of water suspended in liquid form which, when it hits you, makes you wet.'

He hoped she would think it was the fog which was making his voice sound oddly distorted. And maybe it was, because hers sounded much the same as, turning to walk on, she ventured a question.

'But aren't the drops of water in a cloud or fog really small? Much smaller than rain, anyway? I always thought that meant they are lighter and that's why they stay up in the air.'

'That is a popular misconception.'

He cringed inwardly at how pompous and textbookish that sounded. To lessen the effect he slid his hand under her arm, into the warmed space between her coat sleeve and the side of her body, but keeping his grip carefully low, close to the elbow and away from those areas where his knuckles might be in danger of running up against any suggestion of swell at the side of her breast.

'The water droplets are smaller than raindrops, but still up to a thousand times heavier than the surrounding air. A cloud still consists of many tons of liquid water, floating hundreds of metres above the ground.'

'So why is it, then? Does anyone really know?'

Her tone held enchantment and he wanted to say no, that it was just a miracle of nature, but both the scientist and the teacher in him got in the way.

'One possibility is heated air between the droplets. When water condenses out of vapour it releases thermal energy so that the air in between the droplets is warmer and less dense, making it rise and counteracting the greater density of the droplets themselves.'

'So a cloud is a bit like a hot air balloon, except wetter inside?'

He hid his smile from her, fearful that delight would be mistaken for derision.

'That's one way of putting it.'

'And what about the other theories, then?'

'Well, one is to do with electrical charges and polarisation. When it condenses in a cloud, a water molecule has an average electric dipole moment forty per cent greater than a gaseous water vapour molecule. The water molecule rotates to align itself with the electric field. The tops of clouds are positively charged, which appears to create an anti-gravitational tension similar to the Biefield-Brown effect . . .'

Of course he had lost her, but when he turned to glance across at her face her eyes had taken on a dreamy look.

'I was so disappointed the first time I went up in an aeroplane, as a kid. Mum had told me that we would go up through the clouds, and I was really excited because I would get to see what the inside of a cloud looked like. From below they looked so warm and white and cotton-woolly; I imagined them being like that inside, too.'

She raised her arm to pull her scarf tighter round her throat. As she did so Darren's hand slipped up along her sleeve so that when she replaced her arm at her side his hand was tucked higher, nestling in tight against the lower curve of her breast, its weight unmistakable even through the sturdy twill of her coat.

'Then when we went up there, the inside was just cold and damp like any old boring fog you would get down on the ground. But then—'

She stopped and turned towards him, eyes shining eagerly between the shimmering wet lashes. His physics did not run to explaining why the tiny curls around her brow tightened into closer coils when they grew moist. He let his hand drop to her waist but did not withdraw it.

'—then there's that moment when you emerge out of the cloud and up into the sunshine.'

'Yes,' he agreed, all science forgotten, 'and below you the clouds look fleecy and white again, the way they do from underneath – only even brighter and better, like snow in the morning that's waiting to be walked on.'

They had reached the back gate of St Rad's, and although the blanketing fog hid them from human eyes, it did not inhibit the electronic scrutiny of the college's wall-mounted security camera. Snug in the porter's lodge, Terry idly observed the pair of them, the Dean and one of the undergraduates, as they turned towards each other and moved close. It looked like he was going to kiss her but she wasn't up for it, it seemed, which was curious because her body language up to that point had been all melting and lovey-dovey. Seemed this dean was as bad as the last one, then – except rather less successful at it, thought Terry with a vindictive grin.

CHAPTER 16

'Well, I've done what you wanted, Mum.' Something about the martyred triumph in her daughter's voice told Martha that, whatever Lucia had done, it would be anything but. Still, she was prepared to begin by giving her the benefit of the doubt.

'The Arvon writing course? You've filled in that form they sent, asking about your work in progress?'

That merited only a fractional raising of the eyebrows, barely enough to indicate pity.

'I've got a job.'

Martha could not even find the voice to ask the follow-up. She merely waited.

'At Qwikmart.'

All the air seemed to press upwards out of Martha's lungs and compact itself like a solid buffer in her throat. Lucia had had jobs before, of course. Saturday jobs, holiday jobs: fruit-picking, waitressing and indeed in Qwikmart. But this was different. There was no school on Monday morning, no return to sixth form college when the new term began. This was her future – all that lay in the blank in front of her. She was seventeen!

Martha managed to stabilise her breathing.

'If you have decided to get a job, why not let me help? Something in one of the University libraries, maybe? At least you'd be around books. Or something administrative in a faculty or a college, something where you'd pick up some useful skills. Get experience of some computer systems. Improve your typing speed – it will help you get your thoughts down quick enough when you are in the flow.'

Not that Martha's own ideas had outpaced her three-fingered typing for longer than she could remember. Lucia laughed: a jarring sound.

'Well, I'll be getting invaluable experience of shelf-stacking, won't I?'

Martha wanted to slap her, a thing she had not done since Lucia was an independently willed three year old. And only rarely then – once when she had broken free of Martha's hand and almost run out into the traffic; another time when caught with a filched aspirin on the way to her mouth. How had she managed to twist her own rejection of academia and all it stood for into the belief that working in a budget supermarket was what Martha wanted for her?

'I'm starting straight away; they've had a couple of vacancies for a while. It's only three pounds fifty an hour because of my age, but that's still over the minimum wage; it'll have to go up to four pounds twenty-five when I'm eighteen. But I don't need to tell you that, do I? I expect you lecture on it. You know all about the realities of life, from studying the data.'

Martha wished she could laugh, so they could pretend this was meant as a joke.

'I'm doing two early shifts and two late shifts a week; on the late days I finish at ten o'clock.'

'When will you eat? Do they give you a break to have something or shall I keep your supper for when you get home?'

It was easy to take refuge in the practicalities of motherhood; she had, after all, planned and prepared almost every meal Lucia had eaten for seventeen years – even if too often recently she had not been there to serve and share it. Lucia laughed again and this time there was a spark of warmth there.

'It's OK, Mum. I'm a big girl now.'

But she wasn't, thought Martha. She was eight years old, sulking upstairs when she couldn't go on a birthday sleepover because Martha had a conference, tearing up the birthday card she had made for the friend in question, spiting herself and redoubling her mother's guilt. Nevertheless Martha felt grateful for the slight thaw and went across to the kettle, back carefully turned to Lucia as she asked, 'Coffee?'

She was answered by the sound of her daughter scraping back a chair and sitting down, shooing Maynard off the *Times Literary Supplement* with the soft raspberry to the top of the head which always sent him stalking off, too proud to admit that he loved it. Afraid to shatter the fragile harmony, Martha did not ask Lucia to get down the mugs but moved around the kitchen doing everything herself.

'Was Dad's review in this week?' asked Lucia, turning pages until she reached the poetry section. 'That one he was doing about the collection by what's-his-name, Magrelli?'

'I don't think so, not yet.'

Which was not entirely ingenuous, since Martha had checked as soon as the paper came on Thursday, this being so much the more comfortable route than asking Douglas about it. To be honest she was not sure that he had sent it off, perhaps not even completed it, but entrenched habits of defensive loyalty meant keeping such doubts from her daughter. When Lucia began to read out colourfully scathing phrases from another review she felt a ripple of relief.

It was not long-lived, however. Martha brought over the cafetière and mugs and joined her daughter at the table. Her eye fell upon the piece Lucia was reading and she spoke without thinking.

'Oh, it's Jack – Professor Bailey. You remember him; you used to play on the rope swing in his garden. He moved to a chair at Warwick.'

Lucia's shoulders tensed. Martha and Douglas always knew people and it was one of the things which, in her present mood, served to inflame the itch: a reminder of their cosy academic world. Provoked, she came back out on the attack.

'The woman at Qwikmart said they rotate, so everybody gets to do a bit of everything. Pricing up the stuff, refreshing the displays, as well as being on the till. So no one gets bored, she says.'

Best to let this go by, Martha decided.

'And they seem like a nice bunch, the other staff. I met a couple of people. Marcie, she's worked there fifteen years; and Carleen – she's my age – maybe we'll go out for a drink after work sometimes.'

It was said with defiance: daring her mother to comment, attempting to goad her into revealing a glimpse of snobbery. Still Martha determinedly kept her own counsel. She cast about for a safe question, something an unimpeachable mother might ask.

'What about Christmas? Will you be getting much time off?'

'They are closed on Christmas Day but open again on Boxing Day, so I'll have to do my share, I expect. No nice long University vacations.'

This was quite unfair, since most of Martha's Christmas holidays were taken up, between the seasonal shopping and cooking, with admissions interviewing, a heavy portion of which fell to the Senior Tutor's lot. Once or twice, indeed, she had been up in her study on New Year's Eve reading files from the inter-collegiate pool when she ought to have been downstairs playing Pictionary or making up half-joking resolutions with her husband and daughter.

Her coffee finished, Lucia rose from the table, leaving her empty mug on the open *TLS*, surrounded by a drying ring of brown. At the kitchen door she turned casually, speaking almost over her shoulder.

'Anyway, so on three pounds fifty an hour I'm only going to be bringing home a hundred and forty pounds a week. I'll be able to pay for my own food and of course you can stop paying my allowance, but I won't have anything much left to contribute in the way of rent. I hope that's all right.'

Then she was gone, leaving a dozen unspoken accusations behind her. But if Lucia blamed Martha, it was nothing to the weight of blame which Martha cast upon herself.

Martha delved under the *TLS* and three days' worth of the *Guardian* until she found the current *Times Higher Education Supplement*. Reading through the jobs advertised in the *Higher* was a sobering and unproductive exercise which she had been putting herself through weekly since the summer, always undertaken self-consciously and alone: the opposite of a guilty pleasure.

Senior Lecturer in Economics at Birkbeck, University of London. Dream on! Her neglected research record would unfit her for a post at any other decent school of economics just as it did at Cambridge. Or more so: her liberal Keynesianism had been thrown out longer ago at almost every other institution than it had here in the city where the great man had worked

218

from his Bursar's office in King's. Number-crunching, not political economy, was the order of the day and had been so for two decades or more at most British universities. Perhaps there might be other, more rough and ready establishments where aspirations as regards the Research Assessment Exercise were limited and where her Cambridge pedigree and sixteen years' teaching experience might count for something. *Lecturer, Department of Economics, Business and Management, Edge Hill University.* But what did she know of the business world? If economics meant glorified accounting then she would have nothing to offer. Besides, there was the intractable difficulty, which she constantly pushed just beyond the place where she would need to confront it, of how Douglas and Lucia would react if she were to ask them to move to Ormskirk.

Without enthusiasm her eye slid to the section detailing administrative vacancies. If her economics was rusty and did not fit the current mould then perhaps she might make some capital out of her ten years in a senior management position at St Radegund's. *Learning Services Manager, University of Bangor.* The notion of life as a full-time higher education administrator did not light Martha up inside as her subject had once done, and as teaching still could do; but might she not find a little time on the side, possibly, to pursue her scholarship – perhaps even to help out with coverage of the economics curriculum? But a 'learning services manager' turned out upon closer inspection to be something between a librarian and a computer officer, neither of which Martha could conceivably hold herself out as being. The role of *Deputy Director of Administration, Brunel University* sounded rather more promising, involving support and advice to deans of faculties and acting as line manager for the human resources, student administration and conference sections. But further down the advert came the depressing tidings that the appointee 'must be a qualified member of the Chartered Institute of Personnel and Development (CIPD)'.

Martha grimaced. It was exactly the same here in Cambridge. The University's central administrative offices, collectively known as the Old Schools after the buildings which still housed the core of their activities, had over the past decade or two shed the traditional amateurism which had once seen them live up to their name. Instead they were becoming increasingly professionalised, peopled by qualified and certificated accountants and personnel officers, the skill set required of their staff further and further removed from that of an ordinary, jobbing academic. As a college Senior Tutor grateful to be able to rely upon an improved service, Martha had supported the general trend of the development, but at the same time it had closed to her what had once been a back-door route into a second career for those who found themselves in an academic cul-de-sac.

Frustrated, as of course she had known she would be, she carefully refolded the *Higher*, jobs pages innermost, to a likely-looking article on the unionisation of temporary research staff and replaced it under the layer of *Guardian*s, before picking up her cold, half-full coffee cup together with Lucia's empty one and ferrying them to the sink.

'Oh, and about Christmas, Dad.'

It was not wholly unprecedented for Paul Rycarte to telephone his father during the day at a weekend, but sufficiently unusual to raise the expectation of something at least passably momentous. James was therefore not fooled for a moment by his son's studiedly casual tone. There had been nothing at all to justify the peak rate tariff in the first ten minutes of the call. Just the usual dispatches from the environmental front line: the prevention of a housing development which would have sealed in concrete the natural flood plain on a tributary of the Rhône, exacerbating the risk of catastrophic flooding downstream; a small victory for domestic solar panel owners wishing to sell their surpluses back to the regional grid; a new campaign to oblige fruit-growers to label their produce with the names of all pesticides and fungicides used during its cultivation. None of this could be it. But Christmas – aha!

'Look, Paul, if you're too busy, I quite understand. I know how committed you are to that job, and if there's something that needs you to be there, that's no problem. It's all hands on deck with these shoestring operations, I'm sure. Besides, I'm not exactly on my own these days, you know. It's like living in a commune, here – or a long-stay psychiatric institution. I can always have all the college's waifs and strays round to the lodging for Christmas dinner. Overseas students who can't afford the air fare home; the estranged, the orphaned and the rootless. I have a feeling that might be what my predecessor used to do.'

'No, Dad, I do want to come, that's not it. I mean, we are busy, it's always busy here, but I can manage to get away all right. I went to Mum's for nearly a week last year, didn't I? Even though there was that big anti-nuclear protest going on, down at Pierlatte. Those Russian green groups had come over, you remember, and we were publicising the dumping of radioactive waste in the former Soviet republics.'

Even across six hundred miles, Rycarte could tell when his son was prevaricating.

'So, this year?'

A crackle on the line, not quite masking the hesitation at the other end.

'I wondered if it would be OK if I bring someone.'

'A girl, you mean?'

He grinned inwardly to think what Ros Clarke would make of this unreconstructed piece of usage. Paul, comfortably into his thirties, had not been out with a 'girl' for approaching fifteen years. Actually, it was quite some time since he'd been out with anybody much at all, or at least anybody worthy of mention to his father.

'Her name's Marie-Laure.'

No need to ask her nationality, then. Rycarte wondered whether she spoke English, or whether he would be obliged to resurrect his schoolboy French, last practised on assignment in Yaoundé in the early 1990s. When he visited Paul he deferred to his son's near-native facility and allowed himself to be ordered for in restaurants; or else they stayed in and Paul talked nineteen to the dozen in the mother tongue which he didn't get the chance of using nearly often enough any more.

'She works at the *ecomusée* at Grésy-sur-Isère.'

Rycarte had a vague recollection of a visit there with Paul: tumbledown stone sheds filled with rusting agricultural implements, the former use of which could only be guessed at; a breathtaking setting, beneath the *massif* of the Bauges.

'I remember the place.'

'She's been really involved with a campaign we've been running to preserve the mountain habitats. Extending the Parc Régional – stopping the spread of the ski resorts, you know.'

Language would be no problem, then. Eco-tourism and activism: two good reasons why Marie-Laure would be sure to have impeccable English.

'Of course, bring her by all means. It will be lovely to meet her.' He paused for barely a second.

'I had been wondering about having Christmas here anyway, though. Even if I don't need to resort to the waifs and strays for company. They're not compulsory – let them microwave their own turkey roll, I say.'

He blanked out his eminent predecessor's disapproving image. Dame Emily didn't have an expatriate son with a new girlfriend.

'The thing is, I have to be here pretty much until Christmas Eve, so the London flat will have been closed up. Here we can be sure of a cheery blaze upon the hearth. It even gets swept out and relaid for me while I'm out. And maybe Marie-Laure would enjoy seeing our quaint British heritage. There's plenty in Cambridge to rival all her Alpine grass hooks. Hardly the time of year for punting, I admit, but we might take her to a choral even-song at King's or St John's. Very comfort-and-joy, very God-bless-us-every-one.'

'Sounds great, Dad.'

The sound of Paul's stifled laughter made him want to burst into a Stanford Magnificat himself.

'By the way, Dad, have you been riding that bike of yours much?'

Rycarte's soaring spirits took an immediate nosedive. If truth be told, he had scarcely thought about his beautiful bicycle, much less taken it out and ridden it, since freeing it from the clutches of the porters' wheel-clamp. It rested, still obstin-ately lacking an official bicycle registration number, in his garage at the lodging, alongside the equally neglected Alfa. In Cambridge everything seemed to happen on the spot, or at least never very far from the spot. The neighbourhood pub where he had supped beer with Martha Pearce was about the furthest he had ventured from the portals of St Radegund's since the beginning of term. After half a lifetime spent on planes, trains and automobiles he had become a habitual pedestrian.

'Er, not very much, no. I'm a little afraid that if I leave it anywhere unattended it will be impounded by the Motor Proctor and sent to the Department of Mechanical Engineering to be scrapped for parts.'

Paul, who had read Biological Sciences at Oxford, laughed at what they both recognised was not quite a joke.

'Well, Marie-Laure is a big cyclist, too. We've been up and down half the mountain roads of Isère together at weekends.'

It would be easier if he lived over there, Rycarte mused. The climbs might be steeper but he would be in more convivial company: those unashamed Sunday cyclists of a certain age, to be seen individually and in posses, clad in Neoprene as tight as their sun-leathered skin and bearing garish advertisments for sports clothing manufacturers along their thighs. He could hardly cycle up the A10 to Waterbeach and back looking like that.

'Why don't we bring our bikes on the train, so the three of us can go out together?'

Certainly – or at least almost certainly – he was being mocked.

'You two can pedal all the way up from Folkestone if you wish. I think I'll stick to choral evensong.'

When the front door banged Martha assumed that it announced her daughter's departure rather than the return of her husband, so was caught unawares when he came up behind her and slipped his arms round her waist, causing her hands to jerk out of the washing-up water and fling suds as far as her hair – and over the breakfast things which stood, already rinsed, on the draining board.

'I've been to Intatravel.'

She turned round to see the brandished tickets in his hand.

'Where . . . ?' she began, attempting to match his smile. 'You know I can't . . .'

Still two weeks of term, then the busy admissions season; another article to get written, if she could, over the vacation, in between the Christmas preparations. Shopping, cooking – and Mum. To say nothing of Lucia's new job. But Douglas was waving away her objections with the ticket. Because of course it wasn't a bunch of three, or even a romantic two, but one solo ticket. Why was her relief spiked with disappointment?

'Florence. The Uffizi.'

She tried not to think about the time they had gone together, as backpacking students, lingering hand in hand in front of the *Birth of Venus*, awed to silence in spite of the desensitising preparation of a thousand 30p postcards.

'I'm planning some new poems – possibly a whole cycle – on "the Renaissance gaze". Looking into the past, the past looking back at us. I want to go and submerge myself in the Botticellis and the Uccellos and the della Francescas. Just stand and respond, you know.'

His eyes contained a gleam she hadn't seen in months, so that a rush of affection and delight crowded out the more ambiguous feelings aroused by that apologetic final sentence. Standing and responding, he had made clear, was now an exclusively one-person activity.

'I want all of the poems to be linked by a central strand of antithesis. The sacred and the secular, the viewer and the viewed. I've begun one, last night. *Madonna allo specchio.*'

He brought his hands up to her waist, fingers curling through the belt loops of her jeans – as if he might lift and shake her, she suddenly fancied, the way he used to with Lucia when she was small.

'I shan't be away long. Only two weeks. I'm flying out on the thirteenth.'

Thirteen plus fourteen made twenty-seven. She hoped her dismay wouldn't sound too much like censure.

'But that includes Christmas!'

'Yes.'

There was no hint of defensiveness in his

manner; he sounded merely vague, as if she were raising irrelevancies. Frustration flared – anger, even.

'What about Mum? You know she's coming for the whole of Christmas and New Year this time, and she's going to need a lot of running round after. She's still far from right after that fall last week. She might even be better coming here sooner; I don't like to think of her going home and being on her own as soon as they discharge her. I'll be here most of the time, but I can't do everything. I will have to go into college now and then, just to keep an eye on things. There'll be the tying up of admissions to see to, and liaising in preparation for the pool.'

So what if she was beginning to scold? Even while she hated the complaining note which crept into her voice, she resented him more for putting her into the position. None of this should really need pointing out, should it?

'And what about Lucia, and family Christmas? This might be one of her last ones at home with us. You know we always do her stocking together on Christmas Eve.'

The pleading note was worse, if anything. Failing to conceal the real issue: *what about me? What about us?* But he merely grinned at her with maddening complacency.

'You'll do it fine. It's always you who gets the bits and pieces for it, anyway, isn't it? You always manage to find funny stuff. I always just forget.'

She wanted to join in, tease him, enjoy his appreciation of her contrivances. *Do you remember last year, the hippo paper clips?* But last Christmas seemed immeasurably far away: Lucia still at school and needing paper clips, her own job secure, everything . . . unquestioned. In the face of her unbending he tried again.

'Your mother will be fine mooching round here on her own while you go to work. She'll empty half the bookshelf on to the bedside table in the spare room and spend every afternoon up there working through all the bits of Trollope or Eliot or Gaskell she somehow missed out on. *Felix Holt, the Radical*: I refuse to believe anybody has ever read that one.'

She half smiled then, but her waist was still stiff with tension as he rocked her gently by the belt loops. *Felix* was an old friend – could he really not know that?

'It was only a twisted ankle and a few sore ribs. I can't see it holding her back for long.'

But he hadn't seen Mum, the way she was in the hospital on Friday night. Naturally, Martha had dropped everything and driven down there as soon as she heard, missing the Advent Feast (and Ros Clarke's mischievously factious demonstration) in the process. It wasn't the injuries, or the fall itself, so much as her mother's complete inability to account for it – even, except in the haziest outline, to recall its happening. The visit had been a distressing experience. Hospitals are

229

always disorientating places, but the extent of her mum's bewilderment had shaken them both. Martha raised her fingers to pinch the bridge of her nose, closing her eyes against the memory. Douglas released his hold on her jeans and slid his hands up her arms. The warmth of his touch gave some comfort but already his mind had pulled away. He was talking again, back on the excitement of the Florence trip and his new writing project, and Martha was left trying to listen and to share his conviction that this time it would come to something.

Ten minutes later, alone again and replenishing the tepid water in the bowl with a fresh burst of hot, Martha remembered: she hadn't told Douglas about Lucia's job.

CHAPTER 17

'Dame Emily always used to—'
Susie James broke off and looked towards James Rycarte's office curtains in confusion, then back at the owner of them with a quick, flushed smile.

'I expect you get really fed up with hearing that, don't you?'

Both of them resisted an involuntary glance towards the adjoining office, where Miss Kett-Symes was humming something which could well have been 'Abide With Me', punctuated by percussive slaps of the stapler into the sets of papers for the next meeting of the Finance Committee.

Rycarte returned her smile but merely answered gravely, 'Go on.'

'Well, it's just that she always used to do a big chunk of the tutorial interviewing. All our applicants have a general, tutorial interview as well as one with a subject specialist, you see. Of course I know it's my job really, but what with all the paperwork as well, running the office, you know, making sure all the arrangements go smoothly, there just wouldn't be time to interview everyone myself.'

He murmured something understanding about efficiency under fire and she carried on, somewhat reassured.

'So anyway, what we've done in the past is that the Senior Tutor did a quarter and the Mistress did a quarter, leaving me with just half the candidates to see.'

It still sounded an awfully onerous task.

'How many are we talking about?'

'I did just over four hundred last year. Altogether we interviewed 814 applicants.'

A sympathetic whistle seemed the only appropriate response. That, and stepping up, of course.

'I'll be more than happy to do my share, if it will reduce the burden on you and Martha. Not that I have any experience of this sort of thing.'

Not that he hadn't sat on plenty of interview panels, but even junior television executives were hardly the same thing as seventeen-year-old schoolchildren. The clouds of doubt were shading Susie's brow again: a frequently prevailing meteorological condition with her, he had observed.

'Well, there are training courses. Run centrally by the University, for first-time interviewers, you know. But it's mainly for young – what I'm trying to say is, it's mainly for newly appointed staff. I mean, I suppose you are newly appointed, too, but you're not exactly . . .'

Rapidly he stepped in to dig her out.

'Maybe you could just run me through the essentials in some more private place. We don't want

St Rad's exposed to ridicule through my evident ham-fistedness as a trainee interviewer, do we?'

The rescue mission seemed to have misfired; the clouds were massing threateningly and the blush was back in her cheeks.

'Oh, goodness, that's not what I . . . I really didn't mean . . .'

'Of course not. But don't worry: I am sure that an informal chat with you or Martha will put me on the right track.'

She smiled gratefully and began to rummage in her bag. Although strictly speaking, Rycarte noticed with amusement, it was not so much a bag as a school satchel of the kind which he himself had carried on his back in the 1960s. It was presumably, in Susie's case, assumed as a post-modern statement, a piece of ironic retro chic – but he couldn't help feeling that, actually, it suited her perfectly and wondering whether she was aware of the fact, turning the joke on its head. Somehow he doubted it – perceptions of youth are notoriously relative. Finding what she was looking for, she flourished a sheaf of papers, the typed lists completed in a rounded schoolgirl hand to match the satchel.

'I don't know if you have any strong preferences as to subject? Dame Emily always—'

They laughed together this time.

'I mean, I wonder how you would feel about doing Economics, Land Economy, Geography and Social and Political Sciences?'

'They all sound like things I've already had to learn about since being in this job. In which case maybe you should give me Philosophy as well.' He grinned at the tidy parallel. 'And just to be on the safe side, perhaps Theology?'

When she had filled in his name in the appropriate spaces and departed with the sun back in her countenance, Rycarte walked over to the window and tried to remember what sixth formers were like. Not that Paul was, in all probability, a representative sample, even if one could make the assumption that seventeen year olds were unchanged in essentials over the intervening two decades. He'd spent more time out clearing canal banks and coppicing hedgerows than he had watching unsuitable television or pushing the boundaries on alcohol, smoking and girls. Had he been found lying in a ditch late at night, it would more likely have been in pursuit of a badger or a nightjar than owing to the after-effect of recreational substances. That he had not been easy to talk to, though, at that age, Rycarte did recall; he hoped his prospective interview victims would be rather more loquacious. Girls were different, though, weren't they? He followed with his eyes an arm-linked threesome skirting the darkening court below, perforating the air with staccato jets of laughing breath. None of them seemed to have any trouble talking once they got here, at least.

Closing the curtains, and giving a wide berth to his desk where the agenda for the next Colleges

Committee sat accusingly unread, he wandered to the connecting doorway. Miss Kett-Symes, the Finance Committee papers stacked, folded and ready to dispatch, was now shuffling correspondence into the filing cabinet with the practised hand of the card sharp. Rycarte gave a well-bred cough. He opened his mouth with the intention of asking whether the latest structural engineer's report on the library subsidence had yet had come in, and was taken by surprise when something very different came out.

'Will Dame Emily be in hospital over Christmas?'

The shuttling hands slowed, then stilled. He thought he detected in the left one, clutching the sheaf of letters remaining to be filed, a slight suspicion of a wobble.

'I'm afraid so, Master. Not that there hasn't been some improvement. There has. She can sit up now, and is taking food by mouth. But she's still not able to be out of bed. There's very little function in her hands – she couldn't manage dressing or washing, let alone cooking. Of course, there's Meals on Wheels, but she still really needs more or less twenty-four-hour care. And unless you've got a fortune, that means being in hospital – or, later on, a nursing home.'

Stuck for a response, he found himself nodding, a gesture rendered even more inadequate by the fact that Miss Kett-Symes had not turned round from the filing cabinet.

'It's the speech, too.'

Not only the hand but the voice was now definitely showing a wholly unwonted wobble.

'She can't speak, and it wouldn't be safe, would it? If you can't even make a phone call, then you can't be by yourself.'

He wasn't sure where the next question came from.

'Where would home be? If she were— when she's well enough.'

He couldn't quite imagine Dame Emily rooted anywhere except the pinkly beflowered surroundings of the lodging.

'She had bought herself a place out of town for her retirement. A cottage, over at Landbeach.'

Real roses, perhaps, round the door. His secretary turned at last, leaning back against the filing cabinet and snapping the drawer closed with her tweeded rear.

'I'd been helping her with orders for curtains and cushions and so on. Choosing colour schemes. But she never got the chance to move in.'

The thought ricocheted between them: *perhaps she never will.* Once more he shook his head – redundantly again, for her eyes were on her suede boots. Oddly fanciful ones, he noticed, in a kind of elfin green.

'So, Christmas. She'll be there on her own? Does she have any family?'

'A sister in Canada, I believe. Been too elderly to face the flight for a few years now. She usually sends a scarf or a brooch, something light for the

236

postage, you know. Air mail is such a price these days. Dame Emily generally sends a paperback. The sister is a fan of Josephine Cox; I used to pick up the latest one in Heffers. I put it through the franking machine for her, but she always used to put the money in petty cash. She was a stickler for those things.'

The stack of pads for logging personal phone calls smote Rycarte's conscience from on top of the filing cabinet – but it wasn't as if France were Australia, after all. And he had taken to depositing his own copy of the *New Internationalist* in the Fellows' Breakfast Parlour (in its physical rather than conceptual manifestation) after he had finished with it.

'I'll be visiting, of course. The Beeches do a Christmas lunch and family and friends are welcome. A sit-down affair, for those who are mobile enough, but we'll be having ours in Dame Emily's room. Colin is going to be there as well.'

Colin?

'Friday is normally his day, although we have bumped into each other there on the occasional Tuesday, too, just of late. We thought it would be nice if we both went on such a special day. Try to make a cheerful event of it.'

So by Colin she meant . . . ? It could only be the Head Porter. That he should have a given name at all was hard enough to take on board, let alone such a workaday, shirtsleeves kind of name as Colin. If this were possible then perhaps, unthinkably, Miss Kett-Symes also had a Christian name. Or did he address her as 'Master's Secretary' across Dame Emily's hospital blankets?

'Colin's sister has to do an early shift that day; they ballot for it up at Addenbrooke's and she drew the short straw this year. They are going to have their Christmas dinner in the evening, so he's free to come out and have a bite with us at lunchtime.'

That the man could share a house with a nurse and eat turkey with a paper hat on like other people also took some absorbing. But the revelations seemed to have come to an end, along with any further unburdening. Miss Kett-Symes moved over to her desk and sat down with a show of purpose. Fantastical scenarios pressed themselves upon Rycarte's mind. Paul and Marie-Laure dispatched on a long cycle ride to build up their appetites for a three o'clock lunch; himself, his secretary and the Head Porter solemnly pulling crackers while Dame Emily smiled benign approval with half of her face. A final shake of the head set the images to flight. Be sensible: back to business.

'Have we had in the engineer's report on the library foundations yet?'

If the emphatic click of Kate Beasley's heels approaching along the corridor suggested a high degree of some suppressed emotion, her tightness of lip confirmed it.

238

'My office. Two minutes.'

Martha raised an eyebrow even while nodding her assent. The Bursar managed to make the invitation sound less like a request for a confidential conference than a headmistress's summons. And why the subterfuge of the two-minute wait? Could the Senior Tutor and Bursar not be seen to enter the latter's office together at half past four on a Thursday afternoon? Perhaps the request was less conspiratorial than it appeared, though: Martha had a hunch that the large cream sherry Kate was pouring herself as the door opened was not her first.

'Martha. Sherry?'

Kate barely allowed Martha time for a brief shake of the head before the dam burst.

'I know who put them up to it. She can't think we don't all know what she's about. It's that wretched Clarke woman, that's who. Her fingerprints are all over it.'

She took a savage gulp of sherry, jerking the sheet of paper in her other hand so vehemently that it snapped like a sail.

'And that Karen person – she's nothing but trouble, I knew it as soon as she was elected. Pure poison. Absolutely no sense of the responsibility of her position, or the interests of the wider institution. Just wants to make a name for herself by picking a fight.'

Martha waited patiently for the worst of the torrent to subside before reaching mutely for the piece of paper. It looked harmless enough at first glance: a sheet of figures detailing the results of a recent poll of undergraduate opinion undertaken by the St Radegund's College Student Union. The first set of statistics was of a purely factual nature, but Martha's eye was arrested instantly. Factual, perhaps – but with huge incendiary potential.

Students who have paid their rent for
  Michaelmas Term: 45%
Students still withholding rent for Michaelmas
  Term: 44%
No response: 11%

She could already see the red poster headlines which Karen was no doubt at this moment preparing to emblazon across the mail-room noticeboard. RENT STRIKE: HALF OF STUDENTS STILL STAND FIRM. The figures were skewed in favour of the rent strikers, who had naturally been most eager to participate in the poll – but not, it must be said, by any great margin. And in any case, how to point out the sampling error without revealing the true, and dispiriting, picture? Barely a week until the Christmas vacation and a sizeable portion of the undergraduate body in open revolt against the college authorities: it was hardly what Martha would have wished for her final year as Senior Tutor. She tried to but could not avoid, also, an irking sense of the injustice of it. She had striven so hard to build bridges: was her legacy to be division and discord?

Right now, however, there was no time for self-indulgent maunderings; her priority was to bring Kate down from her indignant high horse and head off any precipitate and inflammatory action on her part.

'We can defuse this: put out a letter undermining these percentages; explain the position with first years whose loan payments have been slow to come through; differentiate the can't-pays from the minority of hardened won't-pays. Perhaps offer some incentive if people pay up by the end of term.'

Kate snorted. 'I'd give them an incentive all right! Like allow them back into residence in January to carry on with their degree.'

Concealing her wince as best she could, Martha cast around for some suitably placatory words, but Kate was off again.

'Anyway, it's not *that* I'm talking about – though it's bad enough, I'm sure. It's the next part. How they dare to presume an interest in matters which are no concern of theirs, matters of trusteeship, matters of expert financial management . . .'

She stabbed an accusatory forefinger into the back of the sheet of paper in Martha's hands. Martha read on to the next set of poll results.

Students in favour of an ethical investment
policy for the college endowment: 77%

241

Kate had drained her glass and was in full flood again. Martha tried hard to listen to arguments which had the weary familiarity of frequent bursarial repetition.

'Ros Clarke brought this up in Investment Committee earlier in the term; we had seen it off. Her attempt to tie the fund managers' hands, to rule out whole industries, whole sectors – it was all voted down. And now to stir things up again she has gone running to the students. It's underhand, it's despicable, it's juvenile, it's . . .'

'Undemocratic?'

Martha could not resist this small piece of irony, though there was no sign of appreciation of it by Kate, who had frequently been heard to fulminate against the college's unwieldy committee structure, stifling of managerial freedom.

'The undergraduates are ephemeral; they stay their three years and go. But the college's endowed funds have to be preserved in perpetuity to keep an income stream flowing for the students of the future. Why should they believe that their little fads and fancies should be allowed to impact upon the long-term financial security of the institution . . .?'

The battle was lost, however: Martha had ceased to give the diatribe her attention. It was drawn instead to the third and final set of figures on the sheet in her hand. Third, final and most dangerous of all: this was a bomb which was live and ticking and Martha was at a loss as to how it might possibly be defused. Her eyes were tired after working at the opening of her new article on screen for most of the afternoon; as she stared the words formed and re-formed themselves but still the message was the same.

Students in favour of allowing the admission to the college of the daughters of donors: 3%
Students against allowing such admissions: 91%
No response: 6%

CHAPTER 18

The Michaelmas Term ended, as always in Cambridge, in a whirl of prematurely seasonal gaiety, with undergraduates, high on wine and the scent of freedom, tucking into turkey, Brussels sprouts and plum pudding before December had seen out its first week. In shopping streets, of course, such untimeliness is now universal; the winking lights in King's Parade are no earlier than those in any other town centre in Britain, though perhaps a trifle more discreet.

Martha Pearce attended the college carol service, lending her clear alto voice freely to the old familiar tunes and smiling inwardly at James Rycarte, immediately to her right, whose obviously fine baritone he kept monkishly modulated, presumably embarrassed to let it ring out beneath the female generality. They were both greeted at the chapel door with a two-handed grasp from Joan Tilley, elated to have a congregation which for once in the year rose above the usual hard core of eleven.

There had been a time, a very recent time in fact, when Martha relished the opportunity to enter into Christmas festivities with her young charges and see them off to their homes with three weeks' clear respite to come before repeating the exercise at home with her family. It was not so much an extended celebration as two separate ones, with time between for replenishing reserves of good cheer. This year, though, the early jollity merely had the effect, like almost everything these days, of concentrating her mind upon how much she had to do and how little time to do it – and upon there now being one fewer term between herself and who-knows-what. And anyway, Christmas didn't hold its usual warm sparkle of promise for her this year, what with worries about Mum, Lucia expected to be out at work half the time and – she still found it hard to imagine – no Douglas.

There was no time to think about the Christmas shopping yet, or when she would go and fetch Mum, or reviewing the supervision reports to pick up any students who might be experiencing difficulties, let alone getting her head round the latest Labour Force Survey statistics for her article – no time for anything, indeed, in the week following the end of term, except for the admissions interviews. She had the economists to see, of course, in her capacity as Director of Studies, and then her usual share of the tutorial interviewing. Except that it was somewhat more than her usual share, in fact; she had tinkered with Susie James's list to give James Rycarte a rather lighter load in his first interview season. And instead of the historians she had this year given herself the modern linguists, relieving Susie of the burden of

245

making an impossible decision, and exposure to attack by Ros Clarke and her hordes as well as the ravages of her own conscience. Martha, with a resigned heart and no more concerted strategy in view than the immediate imperative of doing justice to the candidate, was nevertheless determined: she would interview Paola Alvau herself.

Rycarte kept his gaze firmly on the china-blue eyes of the sixth former on the chair in front of him and resolved to say nothing. It was his first day of interviewing and so far, he thought, it had been going rather well. Better than he had feared, at least. There had been no tears, no candidate so frozen with fear that she was unable to speak, and nor had the conversation dried up yet in any of the sessions – although he had come to realise that there was a fine line between the kind of expansive chit-chat which helps the interviewee to relax and do her best and getting to the end of the allotted twenty minutes to find that one has discovered nothing, having done all the talking oneself.

This girl was the first one who had given him any serious qualms. She was not the only applicant for a place to read Social and Political Sciences to arrive clad in a sari. There had been one other such in the morning, plus two so far this afternoon wearing a head-covering more suggestive of ancestry in the north-western section of the sub-continent. But this girl was white. Not merely white, but a palely freckled strawberry blonde, and the small triangle of skin which showed between her cropped choli and the gold-braided edge of the draped scarlet sari was so pallid that exposure even to the watery winter sun of England seemed a rash step.

While he gave his introductory patter his mind was reeling somewhat, but he thought it best to stick to his script. Tutorial interview, Susie James had said: get them talking about what they've read. In this case it was easier than sometimes, as the girl was studying English Literature for A level. Begin with the set texts.

'You mention in your application form that you are studying *Mansfield Park*. I wonder, could you tell me whether you enjoyed the book, and a little about why?'

'If you really want to know, I think it's crap.'

Neither the short northern vowels nor the no-holds-barred opinion seemed quite to go with her English rose complexion and sweetly retroussé nose, though they fitted better with the Oldham comprehensive.

'Racist, colonial rubbish, that's what it is.'

Rycarte suppressed a sigh. Why couldn't she dislike the book on the usual grounds for a girl her age: because Aunts Norris and Bertram were evil old crows or Fanny Price was a prissy madam and deserved to be slapped?

'Oh?'

Here we go.

'Edward Said argues in *Culture and Imperialism* that Austen is deeply implicated in the slave-based economy and a supremacist world view. By point-edly ignoring the questionable morality of the source of Sir Thomas Bertram's Caribbean wealth . . .'

Did they teach her this stuff at school, he wondered? It hardly seemed likely to be material you could use in a standard A level English essay, and he doubted whether it featured on her Government and Politics syllabus either. Briefly he entertained the notion that it might be aimed at himself – a sideswipe at the latter-day imperialism of the BBC foreign correspondent – but dismissed the idea almost at once. She couldn't have known he was interviewing her until she arrived in college, and this speech was nothing if not prepared.

He let her talk until her oratory had run its course, before asking, 'And do you think any this would – or should – have occurred to Jane Austen?'

A dismissive sweep of her pale arm set twenty *jhumka* bangles tinkling; the gesture was purest Bollywood.

'Frankly, I don't care whether it did or not. The point is, it occurs to me, and it occurs to all my friends, too, when we read it together in class. It's inescapable. It's how things are.'

Aha: her friends. Presumably, he was to take it, members of Oldham's various minority ethnic communities. He would no doubt hear all about it if he mentioned the sari, but he was still determined not to rise to the bait. Change the subject. What about Shakespeare? They still always did some Shakespeare, didn't they? But knowing his luck it would probably be *Othello* or *The Merchant of Venice*. If he wanted to find out anything about whether or not this young woman could think, he needed to get her away from her rehearsed polemics. He scanned her form again. Hobbies; work experience.

'I see you did a two-week placement at Marks & Spencer in year eleven. I wonder if you could tell me something about that? What you feel you gained from it, if anything?'

He defied her to treat pre-packed sandwiches and sensible trousers as part of her world view – then instantly regretted it.

'The managers were all white, every one. Of those in supervisory grades, only nine per cent were Asian, I counted them up. And that's in a town with close to a fifty per cent BME population.'

'Yes? And what were you doing, exactly? Did they put you in a particular department? Were you able to gain any interesting impressions of the retail trade? Whether it would grab you as a possible career, for example?'

Only ask one question at once, Susie had advised, you don't want to confuse them. But with this candidate he was beginning to feel himself sinking beneath the barrage. Flinging out several questions might just increase the chances of her picking one and actually talking to him about it. It did not succeed.

'I was in women's clothing, in purchasing, shadowing one of the buyers. A white woman, needless to say. It's outrageous, the narrowness of their approach. Manchester is full of brilliant wholesale outlets for ethnic clothes and fabrics, ethnic jewellery, everything.' The bangles were jingling theatrically again. 'But does any of it ever get near a major high street chain? Of course not! They say their purchasing policies are determined at head office. Of course they are – by people who work in a posh office in west London and live in white ghettos in the suburbs. And then they impose the policy on stores in Oldham and Blackburn where there is a fifty per cent—'

'Quite. Um, so what about your spare time? What sorts of things do you do to relax?' Though he found it hard to imagine that she ever did.

'Well, cookery is my latest thing, actually.'

'Cookery?'

That sounded very normal.

'Yes. I have begun a course in the cuisine of Kashmir and Himachal Pradesh . . .'

Ushering her out of the door five minutes later Rycarte – who had spent some months once in Hyderabad and who, though no linguist, was hot on the social niceties – resisted the urge to bid her '*khuda hafiz*'. He gave a mental shrug. Impossible to tell whether she had an original brain, but you could hardly fault her on 'motivation for proposed course of study'. If only the Director of Studies in Social and Political Sciences could dissuade her from relating every essay to race relations in the north-west of England.

Later that week, Martha was also closing her office door behind a candidate for admission – the last of her day and the final applicant for Modern and Medieval Languages. She subsided into her armchair and wrote up her notes on the girl who had just left, detailing the direction of their discussion and comments on what had impressed and failed to impress her. At the bottom right hand of the interview report form was a bold black box in which to record her overall assessment of the candidate. After a minute's frowning reflection she entered '5' for 'probably not worth an offer'. Then she carefully replaced the lid of her pen and gathered up the girl's form with the sheets for the other aspirant modern linguists: twenty-nine of them, competing for seven places. She leaned forward and tapped them on the coffee table to straighten them, then changed her mind and fanned them out again, leafing through for the one which was eating at her conscience. Paola Rosetta Alvau.

There was really no good way that this could end. If they didn't make the girl an offer they would lose the money – money which would have propped up the library and with it the whole college. Sr Alvau had made it very clear to James Rycarte: if not St Rad's then his daughter would be attending some other educational institution, no doubt equally needful of an injection of benefactory cash. On the other hand if they did admit her they would probably end up losing the money anyway, but it would be much bloodier. Either they would fail to secure the support of the majority of the Fellowship for the acceptance of the gift, or at the very least the unseemly wrangle over whether or not to do so would drive away the donor; both eventualities would leave the college bitterly riven and its new Master irreparably damaged. The only thing to do, therefore, was to be fair to the candidate. To do what Martha always did, in fact; to do what she had been trained to do: to apply her professional judgement in a measured and dispassionate manner to the facts before her.

And what were the facts about Paola Alvau's interview? That she should be polished and confident was no surprise given the milieu in which she had grown up. Her English was also excellent: not only grammatically flawless beneath the musical Roman accent but idiomatic and easy. She had described plausibly and articulately her reasons for making the unusual decision of studying Italian literature outside her native land, speaking of the gaining of distance and of new perspectives rather than simply singing the praises of Cambridge as so many others did. She had done her homework – or her father had done it for her – citing the names of individual Petrarch and Ariosto scholars in the faculty with whom she was looking forward to working. Martha's eyes had narrowed only a fraction when Paola spoke of this expectation in the future and not the conditional tense; perhaps, after all, it was an issue of language and not of presumption. Signorina Alvau had been perhaps rather less assured when it came to more analytical questions. She had been reading an English newspaper in the coach from the airport, and when Martha asked her to outline the substance of the *Telegraph*'s leader column on the need for tighter anti-terror legislation, and then to advance possible counter-arguments, her response was no more than average. All in all, Martha had her down as a bright enough girl, undoubtedly well educated and trained to apply her critical faculties. Whether she had that incisive intellectual edge, that thirst for deeper inquiry, which marks out the really promising student, seemed far less certain. There was also room in Martha's mind for just a seed of doubt as to how motivated she would be for hard graft once she arrived in the madness of Cambridge's frenetic eight-week terms.

Although she knew the categories off by heart – having herself been on an inter-collegiate committee of senior tutors which had revamped the common interview report form three years ago – Martha let her eye wander down the column of numbers. '6' for 'possibly worth an offer'; '7' for 'probably worth an offer'; '8' for definitely worth an offer; '9' for 'outstanding candidate'. She picked up her pen once more, removed the cap and stared at Paola Alvau's form. The main section had already been completed with three paragraphs of assessment in Martha's compact, even hand; only the box in the bottom corner remained blank. She pushed up her spectacles and pressed with finger and thumb at the marks they had left after a long day with application forms open on her lap. Then she shook her head to dispel the blurred beginnings of a headache that was gathering behind her eyes, and made her decision. She wrote the number boldly: Paola was a 7.

'Paola Alvau was an 8 for me,' said Carolyn Gallagher.

Martha glanced across at her colleague, whose eyes were intent on her page of notes, yielding no clues. It was half past six the same evening, and they were gathered in the admissions office, the three of them, to discuss the modern languages applicants: Susie James, chairing the meeting in her role as Admission Tutor, Carolyn, who had conducted the specialist subject interviews, and Martha. Carolyn had no nonsense about her. There was no question of her not appreciating the political ramifications of the decision to be taken, but evidently she saw that as no reason for unusual fuss and bother. It was for reasons only of alphabetical priority, no doubt, that she opened the meeting with consideration of Paola's case.

'She wasn't in my top two, but she fell clearly within the next rank of candidates. We talked about Dante's *Inferno*, especially the first ten cantos which she has been studying at school – and Shakespeare, too, oddly enough. She'd recently seen a production of *Coriolanus* in translation.'

Tapping her pen against the margin of her interview notes, she looked up at Martha and Susie, neutral, unsmiling.

'We didn't get terribly far with problems of textual translation, despite her fluency in both

254

languages, because she isn't sufficiently familiar with the original version – though she had at least been interested enough to read it in English, which reflects to her credit, I think. And she had some fascinating things to say about the particular challenges of staging the piece before a modern Roman audience, as well as about Shakespearean notions of the outsider, of banishment and so on. Pretty impressive, considering she hasn't studied the piece at school – though of course she may have discussed the points with her father.'

Even this was said with no change of inflection, no hint of an agenda.

'There was no need to test her Italian, of course, as a native speaker, but she's chosen French for her subsidiary language, so I conducted a part of the interview in French. We discussed Voltaire and I must say she showed a surprising facility for a third language, including a well-developed critical vocabulary. Again, her ideas about *Candide* were interesting – far from the usual crib note standbys. She didn't strike me as stellar, but it was a highly competent performance all round.'

'Thank you, Carolyn,' said Susie, also succeeding in maintaining an outward neutrality, although the creeping infusion of pink in her cheeks was suggestive of a degree of consciousness. 'Martha?'

With Paola's score of 8 on the subject interview, she was as good as in. Even with the whole of the rest of the list to go through, there were most unlikely to be as many as seven more candidates with a mark of 8 or above. Unless Martha's own tutorial assessment were really damning – say 4 or below – it was almost certain that she would be offered a place. Unless . . . On the other hand, if an offer were a *fait accompli*, might it not make sense to put the matter beyond doubt? To head off any suggestion that the girl had scraped in, or that borderlines had been fudged in order to admit her? If she were to be spending the next six months or more defending the decision to make the offer, wouldn't it be much easier if she herself had given a decisive mark, rather than one which publicly proclaimed her opinion to have been that Paola was '*probably* worth an offer'. Why make life difficult when it would be so easy to give her a 9, or even an 8, and kill the questions.

'Martha?' repeated Susie, a crinkle of concern smudging her forehead.

Drawing a deep breath, Martha took the only course she knew how.

'For me she was a 7 . . .'

CHAPTER 19

Martha stared at the cup of tasteless coffee in front of her and contemplated her mother's bladder. It took her back to travelling with Lucia when she was little. Extreme youth and the onset of old age: two reasons for needing to break a car journey of even two hours with what the Americans call a 'comfort stop'. She didn't think she'd been in a Little Chef since Lucia was small enough to need a high chair and demand the children's All Day Breakfast. The wetly wiped plastic tabletop, the tinsel and the piped sound of Bob B Soxx and the Blue Jeans announcing the arrival of Santa Claus: it was all unfamiliar territory these days. She herself had always been blessed with more than adequate bladder capacity, except during her pregnancy – and afterwards, until she regained the muscle tone. Besides, Douglas would always have driven through the night without food or water before stopping at a motorway service area; those times she had watched Lucia swizzling her hash browns in the yellow sun of her egg yolk, now that she came to think about it, she had generally done so alone.

Where had Mum got to? It was fully ten minutes since she had left her tea to go cold while she went off to the Ladies. Martha pressed the back of one hand to her mother's cup and the other to the one-person sized teapot. Neither had been exactly scalding to begin with, and the cup at least was now barely tepid. She was determined not to be impatient, not to think of all the things she ought to have been doing, at home and at college, not to begrudge the four hours she had already invested in making the round trip to pick Mum up. That ankle still wasn't up to the train journey, that's what she and Mum had agreed on the telephone, but they both knew it was not the only reason. As a distraction from looking at her watch again she topped up her own cooling cup from the cafetière. She watched the grey dregs swirl and resettle in the transparent liquid. There seemed to be almost as much coffee above the plunge-down filter as below; did they empty, wash and refill the jugs each time, she wondered, or merely pour fresh hot water on to the old grouts? Fifteen minutes. It was the Ronettes now, with sleigh bells ring-tingle-tingling. Beginning to acknowledge the anxiety that was invading her, Martha pushed back her chair and walked towards the women's lavatory.

'Mum? You OK in there?' she called as she pushed open the outer swing door.

A teenager looked up from the basin closest to her, blankly incurious, and then back at the mirror, in which Martha watched her smooth a purple-nailed fingertip over the heavy lines of kohl beneath her eyes. She banished the sad face, and thoughts of Lucia, and stepped further inside. Round the corner at the hot-air hand dryer stood her mother, hands held horizontal under the flow of air. Martha moved beside her, reached out and took hold of the nearer hand: the hot, bone-dry skin was looser than she remembered.

'Come on, Mum. Let's go.'

'Downstairs? Why? Have they come already?'

Martha's panic lasted no longer than the single pulse for which it was visible also in her mother's eyes. Then both women were brisk again, practical. Her mother took a comb from her handbag and checked her hair; Martha filled the silence with normality.

'Coffee's appalling in these places. Wouldn't be any good if you needed a cup to fight off tiredness.'

'The tea's not much better either, love, I can tell you.'

'Shall we get going, then? It would be good to be off the M25 before the traffic starts to thicken up. With a bit of luck we'll be home by five. Would you mind if we just nipped into Tesco's on the way and picked up a few bits for supper?'

As they emerged from the toilets and headed back to their table to collect their coats, Martha lending her arm for support, the speakers were pumping out Slade. Across the decades Noddy Holder urged Martha to look to the future. Part of that future she found she had no desire to face just at the moment. And she feared he was right: it really had only just begun.

Apparently Paul had not been joking about the bikes. It meant Rycarte could not even do the minimum kindness of picking them up from the railway station, since the Alfa was not equipped with a bicycle roof rack. In any case it would only have exposed him to an early volley of the inevitable jokes about his car, which Paul regarded as a fuel-guzzling surrender to ageing male vanity. So it was through his drawing-room window that he caught his first glimpse of the new French girl-friend, pink with cold and exercise, laughing up at Paul as they wheeled their bikes up the gravel drive of the lodging. She was wearing a scarlet beret, lodged jauntily askew on her dark hair, and, in combination with the bicycle, the image made Rycarte want to shout with laughter; he wondered if it were done with conscious irony.

He opened the door, letting them in along with a billow of frosty air, and kisses were exchanged, French-style, one on each cheek. He touched skin chilled on the surface and heated beneath: two cheeks bristled and unshaven, two velvet.

'I'll put the bikes in the garage later. They'll be OK against the wall there for a bit. No one ever comes into the garden. The awe due to authority, perhaps.'

Paul's grin had not altered a jot since he was ten.

'Come on, Dad. You know full well that Cambridge is the world capital of bicycle theft. Or are you going to tell me that women are creatures of a higher moral order?'

'Oh, we're quite a civilised community here, you'll find – at least for the most part. Besides, we don't want to scare Marie-Laure with your tales of pillage and lawlessness. Come on in and let's have some tea. That's what we English do, isn't it? Shouldn't want to disappoint our guest.'

They both laughed at that, and while Paul went to unhitch the panniers with a remark about not pushing his luck with the local hoodlums, Marie-Laure followed Rycarte through to the kitchen.

'Good journey?' he asked as he clicked on the overspecified stainless-steel kettle. It was good to be needing enough water to cover the element for a change; his was not a position which encouraged people to drop round for a cuppa.

'Yes, very easy, thank you. We had booked seats as far as Waterloo, so it was only on the Cambridge train that we were obliged to stand.'

She had a light and pleasant voice, with a soft French accent which was easy on the ear, and a personal warmth sounded through the rather correct formality of the words.

'Paul talks about you very often.'

She laughed again, at herself now, shoulders eloquently hunched and open palms spread wide.

'I know this is what people always say at this

moment. But I assure you it is quite true in this case.'

He smiled back at her and wished that he could have returned the polite formula with equal honesty.

'Do you think you could reach me down the mugs, please? They are there in the cupboard just behind you.'

The invitation to familiarity would be taken as such, he hoped, and not as simple masculine expectation on his part.

'Do you want this teapot also?'

'Thanks.'

He had been going to put teabags in the mugs, but why not do the thing properly? Where was that tray with the handles?

'We'll take it through into the drawing room. I've got a fire going. If you reach down the small blue jug, I'll put the milk in that.'

'That's right, Dad, set her to work straight away.' Paul had re-emerged in the doorway. He heaved the saddlebags on to the table. 'Perhaps it was a mistake getting you those cast-iron firedogs for Christmas.'

Marie-Laure giggled, looking suddenly nearer fifteen than thirty. 'I told you we should have bought him the feather pillar.'

Rycarte could have hugged her then, and Paul did so, wrinkling his nose in sympathy as he corrected, 'Pillow.'

The blaze in the other room looked like being

neglected a little longer, because Paul sat down at the kitchen table and unbuckled a saddlebag. Loosening the drawstring inside he drew out a package in a white plastic bag bearing the name and crest of some French retailer. He opened the mouth of the bag a little, raised it to his face and drew an appreciative breath.

'We brought you cheese. Slightly to the chagrin of the other passengers on the train up from King's Cross, I have to say. It was crowded, and the heating seemed to be stuck on maximum.'

From beneath the cheese he lifted out a small bottle of marc de Bourgogne and two jars of different pâtés, no doubt made by some local artisan, probably heavily laced with marc themselves. The aroma of the cowshed began to insinuate itself into the warm kitchen.

'Better get this into the fridge quick, I reckon,' said Paul. 'Blimey, Laure, what did you buy?'

'St Félicien. I asked for one that is ready immediately.' She leaned over him and sniffed the sniff of the *connaisseuse*. Then looked up at Rycarte. '*Bon*. Would you like to try?'

So he fetched a knife from the drawer and wondered whether he had any crackers in the house, but she did not appear to require such fripperies. She had unwrapped the cheese, milkily orange-rinded in its balsa wood tray, and was cutting out a generous wedge. The reason for the tray rapidly emerged, as the wedge did not remain so for long but began to elongate as gravity exerted its pull upon the buttery yellow centre. Rycarte took it hastily from her fingers and put it in his mouth in one lump, scarcely needing to chew but letting it dissolve, coating his tongue with creamy richness and, at its heart, a nutty farmyard bite. He nodded and smiled, unable as yet to open his mouth for words.

'Mmm.'

'Good, yes?'

But it was really a statement, dressed as a question for mere politeness' sake. She had cut a similar piece for Paul, who was making noises of enjoyment which struck his father as peculiarly Gallic.

'It's *lait cru*, I suppose?' he observed as soon as the power of speech returned. 'You always buy the *lait cru*. Considering that he was a countryman of yours, you do seem to have a very low opinion of Louis Pasteur.'

Her mouth formed a dismissive moue; Rycarte hoped for an instant that she might actually say 'Bof'. Instead she began to scoop out a third portion from the molten contents of the tray.

'Laure—'

Her fingertips went into her mouth with the cheese, which would now barely hold its shape on the knife for a moment. The finger and thumb of her available hand formed an expressive circle in the air.

'Parfait.'

Just for a second Rycarte thought he caught a shadow in his son's face: a look, something

264

telegraphed between them, something that seemed oddly like hurt or disapproval. But it was over at once, and Paul was laughing again.

'I think I need a spoon. Come on, Dad, won't you join me? You need energy if we are going to get you out on that bike tomorrow.'

So Rycarte fetched spoons and between them father and son demolished the remainder of the small cheese while Marie-Laure looked on and half smiled.

As things worked out they didn't make it into the drawing room until the fire had burned down to embers, talking and drinking tea, and then eating Rycarte's chicken casserole and then talking again over coffee and marc, all at the kitchen table. The potentially ticklish problem of bedrooms was happily circumvented in this instance by the fact that the beds were, as always, made up and ready in every room. He just left the two of them to take up the bags and choose a room or rooms while he refilled the coffee cups and took them through to the little side table by the fire, which he stirred back to a passable show of life with judicious use of the poker. This was at least one skill, he reflected, which had been well honed since arriving in the damp autumn fens; the London flat had log-effect gas – less atmospheric but Clean Air Act compliant.

After a few minutes Paul came back down, alone.

'Marie-Laure is knackered. She's turning in, if that's OK. She says to wish you good night.'

Rycarte rose from the hearth on slightly complaining knees and waved a hand at the coffee cups. Paul took one with a nod and the two men stood side by side staring at the struggling knot of flame.

'She's always knackered at the moment, actually.'

It was sufficient of an opening, and Rycarte accepted it. The admonishing glance across the St Félicien; the marc which had barely wet her lips.

'Would I be correct in surmising . . . ?'

Again the swift schoolboy grin. 'Due in late May.'

Their hug was heartfelt, for all its awkwardness. Rycarte experienced a mindless urge to bellow and punch the air like a sports fan.

'So, you are going to be a dad. I can't quite believe it.'

It was all a bit sudden – he had not even heard of Marie-Laure a month ago.

'So, you are going to be a granddad. I can believe it completely!'

He cuffed his son lightly on the arm. 'It's brilliant news. The best. Are you going to—' He broke off.

'Are we going to what? Get married?' Paul was laughing.

Yes, get married.

'Not that, of course not, not if . . . But you'll need a bigger flat, won't you? I can help. You know I will.'

The smile was still there but Paul's eyes met his seriously now.

'Marie-Laure doesn't want to leave her job. The

ecomusée – she loves it, it's her life. Plus she's from round there. It's where all her family are: parents, sisters, even a ninety-year-old grandmother.'

'But—'

Be careful, he warned himself: this is dangerous territory. It's his decision – support him in it. But, move to Grésy-sur-Isère? Halfway up a mountain in the middle of nowhere?

'What will you do? I mean, will there be work there for you?'

What was he going to do – herd goats? But Paul merely laughed again.

'Oh, I'm not moving to Savoie. I feel the same about my work, my life in Lyon, as Laure does about hers.'

Something of Rycarte's dismay must have shown in his face in spite of himself, because Paul instantly dropped his bantering tone.

'Look, Dad, it's not as though I shan't be involved. I'll be up there most weekends. I'm not . . . this isn't just some casual event for me.'

A log fell apart with a pop, making them both start. Paul pushed a glowing splinter back towards the pile of white ash with the toe of his trainer, staring as it winked back at him, orange and black.

'It's the way we both want things, at least for the moment. We've only been seeing each other a few months. We don't want to rush into anything we might regret, just because of this.'

Just? But remember: careful – say nothing *you* might regret.

'We're not kids. I'm thirty-two, Laure is twenty-nine.'

At thirty-two, Rycarte had been married for a decade with an already eight-year-old Paul. It felt like another lifetime.

'Things change,' continued Paul.

Had he read his thoughts? But his son's reflections were on an entirely different track.

'I've got a father who lives sixty miles from my mother. You're going to have a son who lives a similar distance from your grandson or granddaughter.'

Another son might have said it with resentment or been sparring for a fight, but Paul was barely regretful. He was simply describing facts. Although he knew he was not accused, Rycarte felt the consciousness of guilt so that, in soft voices, they both spoke the same words at the same time.

'I'm sorry.'

'Maynard! Maynard!'

Martha stopped rattling the tin-opener on the doorstep like a deranged short order chef and closed the back door. Back in the enveloping warmth of the kitchen she gave a delayed shiver and tried not to make too bitterly the obvious connection about absent gadabout males.

'Where can that dratted cat have got to?' she asked the room at large.

Her mother looked up unperturbedly from the

268

Observer 'Books for Christmas' supplement – which Martha had been meaning to throw away, for fear of seeing things more appropriate or exciting than the presents which now lay wrapped, for better or worse, around the tree in the sitting room.

'I shouldn't worry, dear, he'll be back. Don't you remember how Tufty used to disappear off for days on end? It was getting on for two weeks one time, but he always turned up again.'

Martha knew her smile was coming out on the wan side.

'But we lived in a village, Mum. In the 1970s. Not near the centre of a city with far more cars than are good for it – most of them, just at the moment, driven by young men who went for Christmas drinks at lunchtime.'

Lucia, leaning at the work surface, laughed, or at least came as close as possible to a laugh with her mouth crammed with the brick of bread and peanut butter that was to sustain her through her evening's half-shift at Qwikmart.

'Honestly, Mum,' she said when she had swallowed, 'you always used to say the same things about me when I was eleven and first allowed out on my bike by myself. I swear if I was ten minutes late you used to call A and E before you phoned round my friends.'

That raised a proper smile, because her daughter was not far from the truth, and Martha made a concerted effort to banish her swarm of petty anxieties. Be a sunny mother, a sunny daughter.

'Cup of tea, at least, before you go?'

'Get something hot inside me, you mean?' teased Lucia. Then, relenting, 'Go on then.'

'Mum? D'you fancy one too?'

'Why not?'

So Martha made a pot of Earl Grey and, as she cleared away the strewn newspapers to make space on the table for the cups, she uncovered the book which her mum had been reading while she was out at college.

'Marge Piercy?' she queried.

'Yes, I found it on the shelf, hope you don't mind. I don't think I've read any of hers since *Woman on the Edge of Time*. Must be thirty years ago, nearly. I didn't know she was still writing, to be honest.'

'Course it's fine. It's not that, it's just – I thought it was *Our Mutual Friend* you'd borrowed?'

'Oh, well, yes, I was going to reread it but I just couldn't get into it this time, somehow.'

She rubbed distractedly at the strapping on her ankle, elevated on a cushioned stool which Martha had found for her in Lucia's old playroom.

'All those dozens of fiddly people, you know. I kept losing track.'

'God yes, Gran. I couldn't stand it when we did it at school.'

Martha forced herself to be sensible. Just because her mother had abandoned Dickens for *Sex Wars* most categorically did not mean the onset of Alzheimer's. Didn't she always say herself that the great man always had far too many minor characters?

She slid in a stray Christmas card to mark her mother's page, closed the book and poured the tea, while Lucia began to entertain them with tales of supermarket life. Putting on a show for her grandmother, thought Martha – just like when she was seven and used to dress up and act out scenes from Goldilocks with her teddy bears. But she had not seen her daughter this forthcoming in weeks; she resolved to enjoy it and squash down the sense of its brittle artificiality.

'There's this man comes in nearly every night, an old Geordie guy, don't know if he's permanently pickled or just not quite all there, but he always buys one bap and a packet of Polos and then hangs about. We call him Breadroll. He is sort of doughy-looking.'

'Oh dear, I hope he doesn't make a nuisance of himself?' asked her grandmother, sparing Martha the need to say the same thing.

'No. He doesn't even try to chat to us or anything, and I'm certain he's not trying to lift stuff. He stands there looking vaguely at the magazines sometimes, or sometimes he just stands. We reckon he fancies Marcie. Carleen winds her up about it all the time – yesterday she slipped a bread bap into her handbag as a joke, and there was a hell of a cat fight.'

Martha, who never swore in front of her mother or her daughter, often wondered how they managed to do so to each other with such apparent unconcern on both sides.

'And do you think he really does like this Marcie lady? Maybe she likes him, too, and that's why she's so prickly about being teased? We always used to say it was a sure sign.'

'What, and you think he's not really a drunk or a nutcase, Gran, just moon-faced because he's in love?'

They were giggling like fourteen year olds, the pair of them, and although Martha laughed too she felt suddenly old and world-weary.

'This Breadroll does sound to be harmless enough, but I do worry about you, especially with the off-licence trade at nights. What happens if someone comes in and starts threatening you?'

Her subconscious mind had conjured the scenario many times. A large man, inebriated and belligerent, in need of more whisky but lacking the funds. First shouting, then a throw of fists; shattering glass, screaming, the warm well of blood.

'Honestly, Mum, I've told you. I'm never on my own, and we have the phone right there behind the counter. Allan, the manager, lives two doors down and we've got him on speed dial.'

She had to go then, and as she pulled her arms into her old Puffa jacket she kissed the top of Martha's head: just the lightest of touches.

'Really, I can look after myself, you know.'

Maybe she could, thought Martha. Maybe they

all could – Lucia, Mum, Maynard, Douglas – and she should stop trying to hold everything together for them and concentrate on her own worries.

The front door had banged shut behind Lucia and Martha was collecting up the empty cups when her mother said, 'You really shouldn't be letting her work there, you know.'

'Oh, I'm sure she's right, it's not really risky. This Allan sounds a sensible man, and it's in a busy street, always lots of people about. It's not as if it's one of those all-night places or anything. She never works past ten o'clock; the pubs aren't even turning out yet when she's coming home.'

It was a mantra she repeated to herself nightly when Lucia was on the late shift. But it did not seem to appease her mum, who waved it away impatiently.

'That's not what I'm talking about. I mean the job – working in a supermarket, for goodness' sake. I dare say you'll think I'm interfering, and probably I am and it's none of my business. But I really don't think you should ever have let her drop out of school, Martha.'

Oh, God. Well, she had been expecting this, ever since it happened. Mum had been remarkably buttoned up about it, on the phone, at the time and since, whenever Martha mentioned it. But it was inevitable that they were going to have to talk about it. At heart, of course, she wanted to agree with her – of course Lucia should not be on a till in Qwikmart. But some contrary instinct made her leap to Lucia's defence, and to her own. She swilled water into the teapot so emphatically that it splashed up her sleeves.

'It's not really a case of letting or not letting her, Mum. She's seventeen, she's entitled to leave school if she wants. What am I to do, chain her to her desk?'

'Seventeen – she's a child! She's certainly acting like a child, taking this job. What is it, some kind of mind game she's playing with you? Are you going to lie down and let her make a decision at her age which will ruin her life?'

Hearing voiced all the things Martha had been lashing herself with for the past few months somehow drove her further back on the defensive.

'She wants to write.'

'She wants to do anything which isn't studying so that she ends up going to Oxbridge. It's crystal clear. Though if she wants to rebel, I don't see why she couldn't stay at school and just stick two fingers up by applying to Durham or Bristol like anybody else.'

There was much truth in this, and Martha felt her hands unclenching a little round the handle of the teapot. With care she laid it next to the cups in the sink and reached for the washing-up liquid. There certainly *was* truth in it, and it was enticing to think of her daughter as simply a teenager in revolt against parental expectation. But there was more to it than that, more than was visible to her mum, to anyone who didn't live with Lucia every day. To anyone at all, perhaps, except Martha herself. She saw again the recurrent mental picture: tangled underwater legs enshrouded in clinging, wet weed.

'What do you want for her,' her mother was continuing, 'now, in a year, in five years? To be the checkout girl with the best GCSE results in Cambridge? Lucia is bright – she's talented, she's brilliant. Maybe you lose sight of it, working where you do, but the rest of the world would see she's got a brain that it's a crime to waste, to throw away like this.'

It was a crime – but it would also be a mistake, she was certain, to put too much pressure upon the miscreant just now. Move forward delicately, that was the way; see her through this trough, which must surely only be temporary. When Lucia's light rekindled, then she would begin to write again, study again, make plans for a real future – wouldn't she? What use meanwhile to drive her away, deeper inside her own darkness? Rinsing the last cup and placing it on the draining board she turned back to face her mother.

'Look, I'm sure you are right, but it's a case of how to get there. In the end I want all the same things for her that you do.'

But more than anything I want her back again as she once was: my buoyant, vivid child. Her mother nodded but it was clearly no more than an agreement to differ. Just for a moment Martha experienced a pang of self-doubt. She sincerely hoped that it was because of Lucia's demons that she was treading so gingerly with her, and not on account of her own.

At least it was good to be able to have an argument with Mum. There wasn't much wrong with her ability to analyse everyone else's problems for them, anyway.

It was after six o'clock now – seven in Italy – and the Uffizi would be closed. Douglas had only rung once since his arrival; now might be a good time to try him at the hotel, before he headed back out in search of dinner. The phone rang for several minutes before being answered by a girl with a Florentine accent and a supremely unhurried manner. No, she did not know whether Dottore Stedman was in his room. Ah, yes, she could see that his key was on the hook. Possibly *il dottore* had gone out to eat. Would the signora care to leave any message? Martha thanked her in her best formal tourist Italian and replaced the receiver with a sigh. Why did her husband stubbornly insist on being the last remaining person in East Anglia without a mobile?

There were two salmon steaks for her mother and herself for supper, and evidently even the thought of whether to pan-fry them or put them under the grill was sufficient to alert Maynard's fish-loving antennae. Before the fridge door was open the cat flap clicked and in he strolled, tail tall and whiskers twitching in anticipation. Martha cupped her hand to receive the butt of his head as he raised his front paws from the ground for a greeting rub. Maybe she would warm the skin for him in a little milk, the way he liked it.

Although she told herself firmly that it was nothing, the shine was nevertheless taken off the prodigal's return when, looking up from the pages of Marge Piercy, her mother tossed her a satisfied smile.

'Ah, there's Tufty. I knew he'd be back before too long.'

CHAPTER 20

The new year fell on a Sunday that year, which meant that Monday, 2 January was a bank holiday.

'So, you have one additional day of *détente*,' Marie-Laure had said, knowing that the word had come into English usage but unaware of its rather different connotation on this side of the Channel. Probably she was close to the truth, reflected Rycarte: one more day before the redrawing of St Radegund's battle lines.

He had seen them off first thing in the morning, her and Paul, pedalling off in the direction of the station, their presents to him replaced in their saddlebags by his to them – Paul with covert solicitude having ensured that his was the heavier load. Without them the lodging was cavernously empty, resuming the air of unhomely formality that he had not noticed had been dispelled while they were with him. May as well go across to the porter's lodge to put in a word of encouragement, he decided, and then perhaps catch up on some of the neglected paperwork in his office.

Outside it was bitingly cold and he wished he

had thought to put on his gloves even for the short walk across the college grounds. He found the Head Porter on duty alone, as indeed he had been for much of the holiday period. The lodge was kept open 363 days a year, the only exceptions being Christmas Day and Boxing Day, but Terry and the other junior porters liked time off for revelry and its aftermath at this time of year, and it generally fell to the senior man to hold the fort.

'Morning, Master.'

'Morning. A very happy new year to you.'

'Thank you – and the same to you, sir, if I may.'

Even without his bowler hat, and wearing a chunky knit sweater over his collar and college tie in deference to the season, he still looked to Rycarte very little like a Colin. Idly, he wondered whether the jumper had been a present and, if so, from whom. He was no expert, but he thought it could even have been hand-knitted.

'Keeping warm enough in there?'

'Very cosy, thank you, sir.'

He indicated beneath the counter near his feet and, leaning over, Rycarte saw a portable electric heater of the kind last manufactured in the 1960s, which certainly breached every fire regulation in the book and would constitute who knows what hazard were they to experience one of Miss Kett-Symes's famous power surges.

'Aren't the radiators working?'

The Head Porter shook his head, one marginally

elevated eyebrow indicating surprise at the ignorance on this subject of his Head of House.

'The Bursar has had all the heating switched off since Christmas Eve. Except in the lodging, of course, and the end staircase of Cloister Court where she's put the overseas students who have stayed up. It's a step up in the economy drive.'

So Kate Beasley had loosed the first shot of the new year. Just as Napoleon was driven back from Moscow by the snow, so Kate was apparently determined to freeze out the forces arrayed against her. If opponents of the Alvau donation wished to stand firm upon their high moral ground, it seemed, they could do so in the cold.

'It's gone back on this morning, of course, Master, but it takes a few days to get back to full heat, especially with the weather outside being what it is.'

Nevertheless, Rycarte feared for Ros Clarke's hot-water pipes over the bitter months ahead.

As he left the lodge he handed across a box of *marrons glacés*. These had been an indirect gift from Marie-Laure's parents: those other grandparents-to-be, blessed in the knowledge that they would be seeing the new arrival on a daily basis. The porters had already been in receipt of one of a number of bottles of whisky and cognac which he had distributed to key college functionaries on Christmas Eve, but if he kept the *marrons glacés* in the lodging he would eat the lot before Twelfth Night, at a cost to his already slightly enlarged waistline. His position in St Radegund's occasioned far more wining and dining than was good for his health and Christmas had taken an additional toll. Paul could always trough like a weaner and stay lean, while Marie-Laure was a Frenchwoman, and eating for two into the bargain; politeness as host had dictated that he should keep pace with them. Maybe he should get out on that bike after all.

Arriving at his own office, he inserted the key in the lock and was surprised to encounter no resistance as he turned it. He surely hadn't left it unlocked since before Christmas, had he? Miss Kett-Symes would have his scalp for boot leather if she found out. But as he pushed open the door he heard the familiar sound of stapling from the adjoining office. The lady herself: that explained the door – but why on earth was she here on a public holiday?

Calling out at once his new year's greeting for fear of not being anticipated and making her start, he moved straight to the doorway between the two rooms. She was sitting at her desk behind four neat stacks of minutes which she was deftly protecting from the riffling updraught of an electric fan heater by her feet. He saw that her usual ensemble of tweedy browns was relieved not only by the suede pixie boots but also now by a Fair Isle sweater in a complementary shade of green, laced with buttercup yellow. Another present? Had the entire college been given new jumpers for Christmas?

'I hope you had an enjoyable Christmas, Miss Kett-Symes?'

He was rewarded with a rare, warm smile.

281

'Surprisingly festive, yes, thank you, Master.'

'And what brings you to work when you should be putting your feet up, or in the Grafton Centre looking for bargains?'

'Oh, a person can have enough of sitting down at home, don't you think? And I'm not one for all the crowds, at the sales. Nice to be getting on with things, isn't it? New year, fresh start.'

Her manner was characteristically brisk, but something of that smile still lingered around the corners of her mouth. Also – was that lipstick?

'Well, in that case,' he said, 'I am extremely grateful for your example of industriousness, and I had better be following it.'

Returning to his own office he investigated the radiator, to find that it had reached only a degree or two above the glacial; nor did it seem possible to ask to share his secretary's whirring column of hot air. There was nothing for it but to sit in his cold chair and pull his in tray towards him. However, he was not to be allowed to get very far forward with his reading of the papers for the first Buildings and Estates Committee of term. The city's retailers must be having a lean time of it out there if the crowded corridors of St Radegund's this bank holiday were anything to go by. His first visitor was the Vice-Mistress, Professor Gladwin.

'Letitia. Come in, sit down.'

'Master.'

A light remark about her presence in college on a day of rest died upon his lips; he could imagine

Professor Gladwin relaxing in front of the television still less than he could his secretary. He did not have much time, at least, to speculate as to the reason for her visit. She did not even wait to take the proffered chair.

'I hear that you have offered a place to Paola Alvau.'

And so it begins . . .

'Of course, I would not for one moment question the integrity of my colleagues who were responsible for assessing her application. In the instant case, I naturally accept their judgement: if they have made an offer, she must have been worthy of a place at the college.'

Ros Clarke might have said the same thing insinuatingly, suggesting the opposite; but sarcasm, or indeed anything besides honest scholarly analysis, was alien to the Vice-Mistress's nature.

'However, I made my view clear, I hope, at last term's Governing Body meeting, and I should just like to say that it has not changed. Having taken the girl, I do not in conscience see how we can accept the man's money.'

There was no clucking today and no waving of the arms; she merely stood before him, grey cardigan huddled tightly about her and her face grooved stone, and stated her position.

'Above all else Cambridge is, and must remain, a meritocracy. We must be free to take the best students without fear of any consequence, whether financial or otherwise. Academic freedom in terms of admissions is all-important, and in this regard justice must not only be done, it must be seen to be done.'

An echo of the words Martha Pearce had spoken in the pub that night in November. Yet neither woman, it seemed to him, had any high regard for appearances.

'The integrity of the admissions process requires that strict separation must be maintained. The Alvau donation was already on the table last term; now we have admitted the daughter. I am afraid, Master, that I shall not be able to support any motion to accept the gift. Should it arise.'

The final three words were separated by a small hesitation. Except that you could not really call it a hesitation, being deliberate rather than hesitant. Not exactly a warning, and certainly not a threat. She was simply raising for him the possibility; laying open before him all lines of approach, all possible conclusions, in true academic manner. In the same spirit he thanked his Vice-Mistress (though perhaps she was now technically a Vice-Master?) and accompanied her to the door.

Barely had he sat down again to his chilly committee documents when there was another knock and this time the door opened to admit the Senior Tutor.

'Martha, happy new year. Very good to see you.'

The pleasure, he found, was not a mere formula; his spirits rose to see her bright eyes and the way the red woollen scarf which she was wisely keeping on indoors lent colour to her cheeks. It would have been nice to have kissed her to mark the start of the year – a temptation which had not arisen with the Head Porter, Miss Kett-Symes or Professor Gladwin – but not much kissing of the fraternal variety went on round here. There had not been a great deal of kissing at the BBC, either, but there was still less in Cambridge (though kissing of the other variety, he assumed, went on behind closed doors here just as much as everywhere else in the world). It was a pity . . . but anyway, he reminded himself sternly, her presence could herald nothing good. It was odds on she had come on a similar mission to his previous caller's. Unlike Professor Gladwin, she did at least tentatively accept the seat he offered her, but her opening was almost equally abrupt.

'I've come about Paola Alvau. Or rather, about Sr Alvau's intended donation.'

It was no good feeling all '*et tu, Brute*' about it. She had never concealed from him her opinion of the matter.

'I fear it is going to be a major uphill struggle to convince the Fellowship of the legitimacy of accepting the gift, now that we have taken the decision of admitting his daughter.'

That the decision was in part her own seemed not to enter into it: she spoke as if it were an externality which was simply being fed into the equation.

'You interviewed the girl. You supported the making of an offer.'

He didn't wish to sound accusing, only to understand her viewpoint. Her reply was simple.

285

'I thought she was a 7; Dr Gallagher marked her as an 8. That meant she was in.'

Of course: for her it really was that simple. No difficult political decision to be negotiated but a straightforward exercise of academic judgement. For a short while she said nothing more, so he tried to make it easier for her.

'And now you have come to warn me off, is that it? Drop the whole thing for the good of college harmony – even if it means we sink harmoniously into the mud? Morally the high ground, physically the mire?'

He was slightly shocked by how caustically this came out, and perhaps she was, too, because something flitted across her eyes which might have been puzzled hurt. Or maybe it was merely surprise, because it seemed he had her all wrong.

'No – no. It's just . . . it's more . . .'

Why this uncertainty, which he had rarely encountered in her before?

'He is your contact, your friend. I suppose that you may think of it therefore as "your" donation. Of course I don't mean,' she rushed on, 'to suggest that you would feel proprietorial about the money, certainly not for a moment act in that way. But, inevitably, it's how the world will see it. A major, transformative donation – a new building, a rebuilt library – these things are the outward legacy of a Mastership.'

Unsure of her direction, he nodded and held his silence.

'What I am trying to say is, I shouldn't want you to think that I wanted to direct – which of course in a democratic institution is impossible – but to influence, if I may say, the way in which any donation might be applied.'

He was still fumbling to get a footing on her ground. A donation they were unlikely to persuade the Fellows to accept, a donation she herself opposed – and she was this worried about how to spend it?

'Go on.'

'Well . . .' She leaned forward a little in her chair. 'I know that the Buildings and Estates Committee see the library foundations as the most urgent priority. Kate Beasley certainly does; Letitia Gladwin has come to see it as such, much as she would love to re-establish the stipendiary Research Fellowship. And they are right – it is imperative. The money for the work must be found from somewhere, and quickly.'

'But Dr Gladwin's concern to see the library shored up is not sufficient to persuade her to take a million pounds when it's being offered to her.'

This time he successfully kept the bitterness out of his voice; he was merely stating facts.

'Right. Now, once we have secured the gift ways can always be found of rerouting funds. Not all sums in the budget are hypothecated. Money from one source can be used to free up money from somewhere else to pay for essential repair work. Kate is at it all the time: just look carefully in the accounts.'

Once we have secured the gift. But what about the daughter? What about the sanctity of the admissions process – not simply freedom from the sway of wealth and influence but also the appearance of it?

'Of course in substance a portion of the donated money will be needed to pay for the work on the library – probably around a quarter of a million if we factor in the building contingency fund. But that still leaves three quarters of the cash available for other purposes, and we can make it look more by reassigning funds from other accounts. What we need to do is to find some use for the bulk of the donation against which it is impossible to argue. To find a use which trumps on its own merits the argument of our opponents. Their contention is, at heart, one about breadth of access in admissions. Let us use the money for that purpose.'

Stronger than his curiosity to hear what she was going to suggest, stronger even than his surprise at her uncharacteristic apparent capitulation upon a principle, was the overwhelming sweetness of that 'we', that 'they'. Martha Pearce on his side, by his side; like the college's sainted patroness, he felt ready to slay dragons.

'Entrance scholarships,' she said. 'Not just a few hundred pounds to pay for textbooks, to help undergraduates from poorer backgrounds to eke out their student loan. Proper full-funding entrance scholarships, to cover fees and maintenance: more like graduate studentships than the present Cambridge model of an undergraduate scholarship.'

Her fingers went up briefly to where her reading glasses would have been. It was only the third time he had seen her without them.

'That is what the colleges' scholarships here used to be, decades ago, before the advent of state funding and the student grant: they met all the costs of poor grammar school boys – and boys it almost always was, in those days – whose families could not otherwise afford to send them here.'

He offered her a rueful smile. 'And here we are, come full circle.'

She nodded emphatically. 'Loan funding, and families who have no experience of higher education fearful of taking on that level of debt.'

'And what would be the cost of a full-funding entrance scholarship?'

'Well, we would have to work out exact figures, of course, but something in the region of a hundred thousand apiece would provide the capital to set them up in perpetuity.'

'So eight hundred thousand pounds would provide eight fully funded places at St Radegund's for kids who couldn't otherwise afford to come here.'

It was hard to see how to argue with it. How could Ros Clarke bleat about openness in admissions, and turn down the money that would let in eight students a year from inner city backgrounds? He thought about Susie James and her concern for the kids at those comprehensives she visited, pictured her able to give eight of them the promise of free places to come to

289

Cambridge. The Pearce Peace Plan was un-answerable.

'Or maybe,' he said, eager now, 'if we only offered, say, six or seven entrance scholarships we might have the funds also to cover that student rent support scheme of yours as well. Twenty or thirty Alvau Rental Bursaries to cushion next year's increases for the least affluent students.'

He was almost laughing, but nevertheless conscious of a flutter of diffidence as he tried out, experimentally, a return of her use of the plural possessive pronoun.

'That will be tricky for our opponents to rebuff, given their public support for the students on the present rent issue.'

His reward was a smile and he allowed himself the delight of a brief bask in its glow, before the monotone chanting of Ros Clarke's placard-wavers hammered itself back to mind. 'Opponents', he had said, as had she; both of them knew, though, that there was only one person, in the end, who mattered – one voice raised against them which needed, above all, to be silenced. And here, perhaps, was the means to achieve it.

He found himself unequal to asking Martha the reason for her change of heart, but as soon as she had taken her leave he quizzed himself comprehensively on the matter. The peace plan was brilliant, but why was it she who was the broker? She could not really have been persuaded of the moral and political case for accepting the

290

bequest, of that he was convinced. Everything he had seen of her suggested that such a deeply held conviction would not be so readily adjusted. Yet, full of sound sense as he knew her to be, the notion that she should be acting out of pure pragmatism and against her conscience seemed even more unthinkable. What was it she had said to him once, shortly after his arrival? *I shall never do anything disloyal to St Radegund's. To that extent, you can rely on me.* That seemed to provide at least a partial answer: more than anything she must wish to avoid having to watch her beloved college descending into internecine strife. But why was taking his side the best way to achieve this, when it seemed that everyone (with the possible exception of Kate Beasley) was united against him? In the end, he could only suppose that his fate as Master must seem to her to be inextricably bound up with that of the college. They had voted him in and must stand by their decision; ignominious reversal for the new Master must be experienced as a reverse for the whole community, in its own eyes and that of the world. That had to be it: she was supporting him because he stood at the head of the institution she loved. But having reached his conclusion, he found himself still naggingly dissatisfied. It couldn't be, could it, anything so absurdly, so irrelevantly personal as the wish that she were supporting him, even just a little bit, for himself?

CHAPTER 21

'almost half of us still on rent strike and there's no sign of movement from the college authorities. If they refuse to listen to our views, then we are going to have to find other ways of making ourselves heard.'

Making herself heard was rarely a problem for Karen. It was not that she had an especially loud or carrying voice, but it held a quality of conviction which made people – even a JCR full of female undergraduates freshly released from the mellowing embrace of Hall – stop and take notice.

'They have got to realise that they cannot just blithely take the decision to move college rents closer to market rents without any consequences. OK, so maybe in a few years some of us are going to be doing all right, some of us might be in the City and earning six-figure sums – but so what? Students aren't the same thing as recent graduates. We don't have salaries and nice fat bonuses at the moment, we don't even have a basic wage. We live on loans and handouts and whatever our parents have scraped together to put us through university. We can't afford market rents!'

There was a good deal of murmuring and head-nodding around the room at this, both from those whose parents had needed to scrape and from those whose parents had not. Karen played her pause to perfection and then pressed on.

'If rents here are to be much the same as private sector rents, then why should students choose to live in college at all? The ballot for next year's rooms takes place towards the end of this term. What if nobody put in their names? What if we all went and found our own accommodation, since it won't be any more expensive? Then what would the college authorities do, with no room rents at all coming in? They'd have to pay attention to us then.'

This line of argument did not meet with so much approval from her audience. They had already been press-ganged into attending an extraordinary meeting of the Student Union after supper when the adjacent bar or the unfinished essay was a more powerful draw. It was one thing to be told that you are paying too much in rent – even asked to stop paying it at all – but quite another suddenly to be confronted with the possibility of having to trudge the streets and lettings agencies in search of a bedsit within less than a half-hour cycle ride of lectures. College was comfortable; college was near all your friends; college was easy.

'Too much trouble,' called out a voice from the back near the chocolate vending machine.

'Places in town are all so grotty,' agreed another.

'My friend at Christ's lived out last year and it was really noisy. She never got any decent sleep.'

There were even mutterings from those in Karen's own circle of acquaintance who knew that she already lived out, and knew what that meant: that her parents footed a rent bill which had continued through the Christmas vacation while they themselves had gone home to live rent free for five weeks with their families. But Karen was a politician and could read the popular will. If they didn't respond to Plan A, then never mind: Plan B was a certain winner.

'What we need is a protest. Not a demonstration, I don't mean – a proper protest event. Something that will disrupt the college so seriously that they have to take notice.'

She had the room back now. All whisperings of dissent had ceased.

'What we need is a sit-in.'

It was not that the idea had exactly been Ros Clarke's. Dr Clarke may have sown the seed of a suggestion but Karen, certainly, had come to believe that the plan was entirely of her own devising.

'A proper, old-fashioned sit-in,' she continued, 'like they used to have in the sixties and seventies. Non-violent direct action.'

This time the buzz which had sprung up again was of a different colour. Diverted, intrigued – excited.

'Like Gandhi,' said a historian near the front.

294

'Or the Greenham women, lying down in the road,' suggested a social anthropologist.

'Or that bloke in Tiananmen Square who stood in front of the tank.'

Karen's oratorical SU president face softened to admit the sketch of a grin.

'Let's take over Hall. Barricade ourselves in, block the entrances. We can operate in shifts; it would only take a dozen or so at a time to hold the lines – maybe even fewer; there are only the two doorways. And they're not exactly going to risk a violent confrontation, are they? I mean, this is College, it's not the Metropolitan Police. They've got their precious reputation to think of.'

There were some assenting nods at this, and one or two giggles.

'An event like this is meat and drink to the student press,' continued Karen. '*Varsity* will cover it, and we'd probably get the *Evening News*, too – perhaps even the nationals. Maybe local TV – anything's a story for *Look East*.'

This, as she knew, was her trump card. There was not a girl in the room who was wholly immune to the magical promise of television, and it gave Karen all the more satisfaction to feel that she was taking a tilt at James Rycarte with the lure of his own seductive medium.

Shortly after this the main meeting broke up. While the bulk of the undergraduates drifted away in twos and threes still thrilling at the prospect of being glimpsed amongst a crowd by teatime viewers in the eastern region, a hard core, more hungry than the rest for the adrenaline of conflict, remained behind to form an *ad hoc* war cabinet. The most obvious impediment to the sit-in plan was dealt with first: namely the choice of venue and its impact upon the student body.

'If we put Hall out of action, then what about meals? Where are we going to eat?'

This was waved away by Karen as a self-serving irrelevancy, a mere mote, an irritating speck in her vision of the greater struggle.

'There are gas rings on every staircase, aren't there? Pizza Antonio's deliver, don't they? We can live on Rice Krispies in our rooms for a few weeks if we have to – what is this, a men's college, where they don't know how to boil an egg?'

Deepa, who strongly suspected that Karen had never boiled an egg in her life, silently wondered whether her friend knew that Marks & Spencer's ready meals were beyond the purse of the majority of students.

'The point is that it will hit *them*, won't it? They'll have nowhere to entertain their cronies. How will they impress their influential friends, persuade them to hand over their cash to the college, if they don't have Hall to wine and dine them in?'

The thought of Rycarte feeding that Italian millionaire of his on toast and Marmite over at the lodging filled Karen with malevolent glee.

'What's the worst they can do to us?' asked one

Due dente
27/11/13

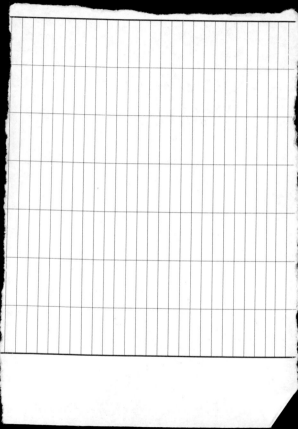

pragmatist. It was not a rhetorical question: she was reading Law.

'Exactly – what can they do?' said Karen in wilful misunderstanding. 'The press interest will stop them trying anything heavy-handed; they won't be able to discipline us if we are peaceful about it, and especially if we rotate, so that there are always different individuals involved. The Bursar might cut off the heating, but we can get sleeping bags and blankets and hot-water bottles.'

'Like Guide camp – except with more drink, hopefully.'

'Floor will be bloody hard. Wonder if we could smuggle in some mattresses – the housekeeper'd have a fit!'

'Can we draft in reinforcements from other colleges, do you think?'

'What, you mean so you can have Simon from Christ's to keep you warm?'

Karen allowed their imaginings to range, an indulgent smile shading across her lips.

'Martha Pearce isn't going to do anything, is she? We can handle her all right. Anyway, at the drop of a hat she'd probably be in there joining the protest. A good sit-in would be just her sort of thing.'

Joining in the sniggers which greeted this image, Deepa nevertheless felt the stab of guilt. Nor did she intend a jest when she asked, 'What about the Dean?'

Karen led the general mirth and then spoke through it, laughter still fracturing her voice.

'Oh, I'm so scared. Darren Cotter, man of discipline. The limp fist in the polyester cotton glove.'

'What's he going to do?' cried one physical scientist in delight. 'Throw us in Markov chains? Stretch us on an indecomposable rack? Apply the Archimedean thumbscrew?'

And so an outline plan was laid for the occupation of Hall to begin on Saturday night after supper, with the first detachment of sitters-in primed to remain *in situ* after their meal and to barricade the doors once the last of the waiting staff had departed. Nikki, the welfare officer, who had had a thing with Guido from the kitchens last term, was confident that those clearing away could be brought on side, at least to the extent of making a timely exit. Karen looked at her watch: almost ten to nine. It was time for her and her fellow Tigresses to depart. There would be alcohol awaiting them – and boys.

Needless to say, Julia had not seen fit to mention to anyone her second and subsequent meetings with the Dean. As these had so far been marked by a continued absence of kissing, she rationalised, it could really be of no concern to them. To the Tigresses' start of term cocktails, therefore, she was not entitled to an invitation. They met, as last term, without her; without, in fact, the presence of any new members. Since the beginning of the academic year, no eligible St Radegundian had succeeded in completing the initiation test. The new Dean was proving a tough nut to crack.

'He's got to be gay,' opined Karen, dipping a borrowed ladle into a fizzy vermilion concoction with the approximate specific gravity of neat ethanol. 'What other explanation can there be?'

Deepa eyed her sceptically across the rim of her coffee mug.

'Oh, come on. Couldn't he just be shy?'

She was never quite sure why she had joined the Tigresses. A tidy squash player, she had been a Half-Blue since her first year and Karen had persuaded her to take advantage of her entry qualification. As she did not drink, it had occurred to her many times since to wonder whether it had been worth letting Dr Dean O'Connor slide his distasteful tongue between her lips for the dubious privilege of watching fellow sportswomen get legless once a fortnight. She had almost stopped attending, and was only doing so tonight because they were meeting in her room.

'Shy!' squealed a women's football Blue, semi-entwined with a men's football Blue and wagging her empty glass at Deepa as though at an erring referee. 'It takes more than just being shy not to want to kiss *us*. Doesn't it, Josh?' she added to her companion, whose mouth was now pretty well enclosing her ear.

'Julia is really cute; she even went out with him but she still couldn't get him to come on to her,' said Karen.

'Certainly is. I wouldn't say no,' said Josh, lips sliding down towards the collarbone of the female footballer.

'Katie Parker,' said a basketball-playing blonde. 'She's eligible since she got her Half-Blue for trampolining last term. She got him to walk her back to her room by saying she thought she'd seen a prowler. There they were, checking behind the bushes together, and she's all trembling and vulnerable and in need of manly comfort. Result – absolutely zilch.'

'Laura Graham,' volunteered the University's netball goal shooter. 'She's in the team this term at wing attack, and she's really hot. Jeez, I'd snog her myself if she asked me. But he wasn't into the idea at all. Just advised her to drink plenty of water before she went to sleep.'

'Don't forget Anna Axelsson,' said a boy, in the manner of one stating a clinching argument. 'She's Swedish.'

Karen grinned round at the other Tigresses.

'So it's incontrovertible, I'd say. Definitely gay – or else sodding well married.'

It was Deepa who made the suggestion; her motives for doing so were entirely humanitarian, and she could hardly be blamed if the idea backfired.

'Well, maybe we need to have a different initiation test.'

Something indefinable ignited in Karen's eyes. Carefully refilling her glass with the ladle, she cast Deepa a smile of which a real tigress might have been proud.

'Yes, of course. If we can't get him to kiss any

300

of us, then we'll find out who it is he does like to do it with. That can be the new challenge.'

She prised her 3G mobile out of the pocket of her jeans.

'Photographic evidence. If anyone can get a picture of the dean snogging his boyfriend, then she's in.'

'Ciao, esimio Signor Rycartè.'

The smoothly teasing voice when he picked up the telephone that evening in the lodging brought a smile to James Rycarte's face, and it was with real warmth that he tendered his greetings in return.

'Hello there, Luigi. *Felice anno nuovo, amico mio.'*

If he could have sat down he would have, anticipating the pleasure of his friend's conversation, but Dame Emily had seen the need for only the one instrument, and that located in the chairless and draughty hallway. Doubtless she preferred to do her chatting standing up, lest it detain her too long from her books. A moment later, though, he was glad that he was standing.

'For myself and Paola, as you must know, it is the best of new years. I want to thank you, my friend. We have received the letter with your most generous offer, which we shall be delighted and honoured to accept.'

Rycarte itched with impatience at the Italian's attitude. The easy, arrogant assumption – as if the offer of a place to study at the college were no

301

different from an invitation to the Advent Feast. He kept his voice in perfectly calibrated neutral.

'Well, you know, it isn't me that you have to thank, of course. I did not interview your daughter myself.'

'And never fear, James, those who have been instrumental in this kindness shall not remain unaware of how greatly I am beholden to them.'

This actually provoked a wince, as Rycarte tried hard not to picture either Carolyn Gallagher or Martha Pearce in receipt of flowers, or worse, from the grateful father.

'You must understand, these are not personal decisions, Luigi. All such matters come under the aegis of the Admissions Committee.'

'Then the committee members shall receive my thanks.'

There seemed no way out of this line of discussion, so instead Rycarte sought to deflect the conversation on to less precarious ground.

'Are you going to be in England again any time soon? It would be very nice to see you here in Cambridge again, if so – or we could have lunch in London if that is easier for you.'

The simple motion of friendship, however, Alvau chose to interpret as a move towards closure of the transaction.

'Ah yes, of course. We must meet very soon, as you say, and talk in detail. We must get down to real figures at last.'

Not for the first time since lifting the receiver,

Rycarte felt devoutly glad to be alone. The way in which the two issues were being run together by his friend made him distinctly uncomfortable. He had no reason to feel this way, he insisted to himself; Paola's admission had been by the book, and he had no reservations now about accepting any money which her father might care to lay on the table. But still – it was difficult not to begin to see things as others in this place, he knew, would see them. He coughed.

'Well, if you would like to do so, then it goes without saying that we shall be very grateful to listen to your proposals.'

His own slight hesitation, perhaps inexpertly masked, produced an answering one in Rome.

'Unless, of course . . . I do hope that my intended gesture of comradely aid does not threaten to create awkwardness for you, my friend.'

No cash for admissions, no cash for admissions. Rycarte hoped, though he could not safely believe, that the echoing voices were sounding in his own head only.

'I know that you English swear never to look a gift horse in the mouth, but it may be that on this occasion you should be circumspect, dear James. I should certainly not wish you to take delivery of my horse should it prove to be full of Greeks wielding spears.'

At that, Rycarte was able to laugh, and offer a creditably plausible reassurance.

'No, no. Rest assured that things will only be better in Troy for your kindness.'

'Well then, I shall indeed come soon. And perhaps I may bring Paola this time, with your permission? She did not have very long to wander within your esteemed walls when she flew over for the interview.'

An echo of something he had heard Susie James saying came to Rycarte's lips.

'If you think it a good idea, certainly. But we do not generally advise students holding an offer to spend too much time in the college. For fear of pinning their hopes too much on the possibility, you know, while the offer is still a conditional one. Might a visit not be better after she has her *Diploma di Maturità*?'

Alvau dismissed this suggestion with an audible expulsion of air from the lips, which Rycarte fervently hoped was a sign only of his daughter's certainty of success in her state examinations and not of any other, more misplaced source of confidence.

'We thought it might be possible for her to select a room.'

'I'm sorry?' Rycarte was genuinely at a loss.

'A suitable room, for her to live and study in, when she arrives in October.'

Oh. Naturally, Alvau would know nothing of the annual room draw.

'I'm afraid it would not be that simple. There is a ballot for rooms conducted amongst those going into their second and third years; students drawn out highest have first choice of the available accommodation. A block of rooms is kept aside for the new first year intake, of course. As I understand it, questionnaires are issued about preferences as to size, cost, location and so on before the ballot. Perhaps I might pass on any particular wishes that Paola may have.'

It made him start when this explanation was met with an explosion of laughter down the line from Rome.

'Ah, James, my old friend. But this is beyond words. You English are always so incurably democratic, are you not?'

He continued to guffaw; with luck this should mean that he accepted the situation as to choice of a room – or lack of. Rycarte found space to wonder slightly at himself, and his absorption of the rituals and values of this place. When and how had the sanctity of the room draw, for heaven's sake, become for him an article of faith?

'Well, I shall come very soon, James, and I shall bring Paola with me, and she will look round the college and its facilities – though only in very general terms at the student accommodation. Let her name go into the hat together with those of her English comrades. Penthouse or garret, she will be equally serene, I am quite certain of it. And you and I shall sit down together over a glass of your port wine, along with those of your fair colleagues who are empowered to decide such things, and we will see how my poor portion may best be employed to further the scholarly work of St Radegund's College.'

After they had said their goodbyes, Rycarte walked back towards the kitchen, where his *Times Higher Education Supplement* was still spread open on the table. *Further funding cuts expected over five years* read the headline. *Higher top-up fees the only solution, say VCs.* He was not in the wrong; he remained as convinced as ever that it was not wrong to be seeking to take the Italian's donation. But everything about the telephone call had left him feeling not just uneasy but actually – though he mocked himself for thinking of the word – sullied. Thank God Ros Clarke could not have overheard the conversation he had just had with Luigi Alvau; she would have had a field day. Strangely, however, it was not the fear of what his enemies might think which was the worst, but the imagined reaction of a new-found ally. More than anything else, he found he was relieved that Martha Pearce had not been party to the contents of that phone call.

Julia may not have attended the Tigresses' drinks, nor therefore did she know about the new initiation test, but as ents officer she had certainly been present at the earlier extraordinary meeting and also, though she did not speak and hung largely on the periphery, at the campaign strategy session which followed. She had heard the detailed battle plan for the sit-in and, more important, she

306

had heard their cruel laughter about Darren Cotter. Although she had not felt able to say anything to Karen and the others at the time, their taunting had the effect of filling her with resolution. Maybe she couldn't defend him publicly, but she could jolly well go and find Darren and be nice to him.

She tracked him down without difficulty at his lab, it being still some way before eleven p.m.. When she pressed the security buzzer downstairs at the outer door she was relieved to hear Darren's voice answering and not that of the other man, Jefferson, the one who worked at the next desk. Julia was nervous of that type of American, especially ones with beards, because she never could tell if they were joking or not; nor was she sure whether to call him 'Dr Jefferson' or whether that was his first name, which made things awkward.

'Um, it's me. Julia.'

'I'll buzz you up.'

For some reason the Star Trek resonance of this set her giggling, so that it was with a smile playing across her face that, halfway up the stairs, she met Darren coming down towards her.

From the angle at which he saw her she seemed to him all merry eyes and dark unruly curls, spangled with moisture from the ubiquitous soft drizzle which in Cambridge could make January or June alike seem like November.

'Are you coming up, or am I coming down?'

Why did she always make him say stupid things? Manifestly they were both doing both.

'What I mean is, I'm on my own up here, Jefferson's gone home, and the coffee dispenser is working for once. But if you'd rather go out? A drink or whatever.'

'I think we might have missed last orders.'

Now he was an idiot who couldn't even tell the time. But she had stopped at the step below his, and the smile she cast up at him was innocent of any mockery.

'Let's just walk.'

So they headed first back up, to close down the computer and switch off the lights, and then down again and out into the thin night rain. Without any consultation they both turned their feet towards college the long way round by the cinder path that led along the river. Darren's bike was in the rack at the rear entrance to the lab but he left it there, even though it would mean walking again in the morning, and a ten minute earlier start. Wheeling it now would have given him something to do with his hands, it was true, but would have taken away the possibility, however remote, of holding hers. As it was, they walked close together without touching and from the shelter of his kagoul he wondered how wet she was getting inside that coat she always wore, which smelt gloriously of damp Julia but had nothing about it to keep out the rain except the time it took for water to permeate the thickness of its dense fibres. Wool was so dreadfully hygroscopic; it must absorb, what, about thirty-five per cent of its dry mass at one hundred per cent humidity? He wondered if it felt heavy on her.

Moving experimentally even closer, he saw that where their arms brushed together, the Gore-tex of his kagoul came away blotched with moisture.

'Are you getting wet?'

She only shook her head, impatiently he thought, and moved a fraction away from him. Was she upset with him for some reason? Her usual pattern was to welcome closeness provided it stopped short of kissing. Or maybe she just had something on her mind, because twice she seemed about to speak and then changed her mind.

'You OK?'

That seemed to do the trick, anyway. She stopped abruptly, turned to face him, even seized two handfuls of lightweight waterproof where his lapels would be if he were wearing a proper jacket.

'They are going to have a sit-in.'

Who was? When? Where? What had this to do with them? And why did her curling fingers, tightening his clothing across his chest, feel so deliciously distracting?

'I shouldn't be telling you, of course. They'll kill me if they find out. Please don't say anything, will you? About who told you, I mean.'

Having Julia not only holding on to him but actually pleading gave him a rush so heady he could have shouted aloud. Instead he put his arms awkwardly round her shoulders and gave her what she wanted, even though he still had very little clear idea what he was promising or why.

'Of course not. I won't say a word. You know you can trust me.'

At this her lips, already enticingly wet with rain and anxious chewing, gave a very slight quiver and it was all he could do not to ruin everything there and then, as he had done on several previous occasions.

'I know,' she whispered and for a mad moment it seemed as though she might even be the one to kiss him, but then she had turned again and they were walking on as before.

'It's starting on Saturday night, after supper. They're going to take over Hall. Stay put, camp out, not let anybody in. The idea is to put a stop to the serving of any meals.'

'Why?'

The food in college could certainly be pretty execrable at times, but this seemed a rather extreme response.

'It's a protest about the rent rises.'

'Oh.'

There was not a great deal more he could say. Being debarred by his sex from service on college committees he tended to take little interest in the internal affairs of St Rad's, beyond doing his teaching, paying his own modest rent for the small Fellow's flat which he occupied and emptying his pigeonhole regularly. Now that she mentioned it, though, he did hazily recall having seen posters up about a student rent strike, and Kate Beasley had certainly been banging on about it at lunch more than once, if he had been bothered to listen.

'Um, are they putting them up a lot, then?'

'I don't know, really. Twelve per cent over two years or something, I think it is. Karen did say but I've forgotten.'

Evidently he was missing the point. He tried again.

'So, er, a sit-in. That sounds serious.'

She nodded, looking sideways at him with a curious sympathy lighting her eyes.

'What do you think you'll do?'

Do? What would *he* do? It was only then that he remembered. He was the Dean: nominally responsible not only for the conduct of ents and other late-night revelries but also for the general discipline of the college – including, no doubt, sit-ins, occupations, bra-burnings and the rest. His heart plummeted.

'Well, I suppose I'll talk to Martha Pearce.'

How weedy that must sound; the slightest hint of trouble and he went trotting off to the Senior Tutor.

'Just for advice, I mean. About how I should handle things. Find out exactly what powers I have, you know.'

This apparently did not hit quite the right note either, because Julia convulsed into giggles; he had a horrible suspicion that she was picturing him as Superman, with his underpants over a pair of tights. Even so, her laughter warmed him, and on impulse he grabbed her hand, finding it hotter than his despite the damp and cold. Where had all his saliva disappeared to?

'Thank you, Julia,' he croaked. 'For warning me about it, I mean.'

'Oh, that's OK.'

Her eyes were averted, focused somewhere in the knotted bark of the willow tree behind his shoulder. Her mouth sounded dry, too. Maybe they should have had that coffee before their walk.

'I wanted to warn you. They said . . . they were being . . . I wanted you to know, that's all.'

He was still trying to work out what it was she was not saying when she turned her eyes back to him and he abandoned the attempt. Abandoned everything, in fact, at the sudden close-up vision of her tilted face, including caution and even self-consciousness. And this time, at last, when their lips met she did not pull away but sighed and rubbed her chin shyly against his for the sweetest of instants before her mouth came alive beneath his, wet and slippery and mobile.

Coming up for air some dark, mindless time later, he heard her murmur against his throat what sounded through his pumping blood like, 'I don't want to be a tigress.' This he could only interpret, in the befuddled second before resuming their kiss, as indicating her intention of being gentle with him; he really was not sure whether this came more as a relief or a disappointment.

CHAPTER 22

It was just as she was winding up her final supervision of the day that the knock came on Martha's office door. They had more or less tied up the loose ends of their discussion of human capital theory and she was handing out the reading list and essay title for next week: *How important has institutional change been to the rise in wage inequality?* She continued talking as she opened the door, outlining key aspects of the new topic and giving pointers as to the most crucial of the set readings.

'The Fortin and Lemieux article from 1997 still gives an excellent overview of—'

That was as far as she got: her thoughts on the article were left dangling in mid-sentence. Outside in the corridor, like an undergraduate expected for the next class, stood James Rycarte.

'Anyway, you've got the book list, I'm sure you can go and get on with it without any more blather from me. Well done this week – you've all worked hard. And that was a much improved essay from you this time, Peta.'

She showed them out, shouldering bags and

rucksacks and winding on scarves, their chatter momentarily silenced by curiosity at encountering the Master of St Rad's waiting outside the Senior Tutor's door.

'Master,' she said; then, safely inside and the door pulled to, 'James.'

As his eye roamed with interest over the furnishings, books and photographs in this room which he had not seen inside before, she intercepted his glance with an apologetic smile.

'You could have called; I'd have come to your office.'

But then she saw that he was laughing at her for this small sign of consciousness of the proprieties of status.

'Oh, I think I may come and see you just as well as you may come and see me, don't you? Besides, I see that you have your own kettle, which is an indulgence Miss Kett-Symes will certainly not allow me.'

That should have relaxed her, at least by giving her something to do, but as she topped it up from the bottle of water on her desk and switched it on she still felt an unaccountable embarrassment. Probably it was the mess of empty mugs scattered on the coffee table on top of the papers and open textbooks: three consecutive supervision groups this afternoon, making nine dirty mugs in addition to her own. He picked up the one nearest to him and inspected it as he subsided into an armchair. It bore the crest of

314

St Radegund's: the dragon with mouth aflame coiled around the impaling spear. (All in a day's work, apparently, for an abbess in the sixth century.)

'Patriotic as well as hospitable, I see.'

'I'm afraid I've only got instant, or there's tea,' she said, reaching to the back of the shelf for the last remaining unused mug.

'Tea would be perfect. Thanks.'

She wished she had a teapot, feeling slightly ashamed of her box of supermarket tea bags, as well as the fact that she was forced to reuse her unwashed mug. But the choice of seat was at least unproblematic; she could hardly take the footstool without risking further teasing for her earlier deference to his rank. She sat down next to him democratically in the other armchair and they both took a first tentative sip of tea.

'Actually, I came to seek your advice, Martha.'

Placing his mug down among the debris on the coffee table, he drew a sheet of paper from the inside pocket of his jacket. He unfolded it, shook it flat and frowned at it for a moment before handing it across mutely. It was a single sheet of notepaper bearing the college crest above the name of the Vice-Mistress, and contained just one short, typed paragraph.

Dear Master,
I am writing to you, and for the attention of the College Council, to nominate Dr Rosalind

Clarke for the position of Senior Tutor with effect from 1 October next.
  Nominator: Professor Letitia Gladwin
  Seconder: Dr Isabella Chawton

Well, it had always been on the cards. Ros had her readership but a chair seemed out of the question in the immediate term; the college was her most natural forum for seeking to extend her power and influence. Rycarte's most vociferous opponent from the first moment his name had been mentioned, she would see the Senior Tutorship as the perfect platform from which to neutralise and frustrate him. Martha spoke guardedly, withholding from her voice the wave of sympathy she felt go out towards him.

'I suppose it was to be expected that she would apply.'

'Yes.'

But from the flatness of his tone it appeared that he had not expected it – or perhaps had hoped that he could wish it away.

'I was rather surprised to see Dr Chawton's name on the nomination.'

Martha remembered introducing him to her predecessor at High Table one evening last term. Certainly the grave lawyer, always so measured in her reactions, was poles apart from Ros Clarke's abrasive style.

'Ros commands a great deal of respect. She has high principles, and she knows how to get things

316

done. She would be a Senior Tutor to reckon with.'

But of course it would be Rycarte who would face the reckoning. It seemed, however, that his query was of a more procedural nature.

'What I meant was, I was surprised because I thought Dr Chawton is retired.'

Was this what he had wanted her advice about?

'That's right, she retired eight years ago, not long after I took over from her as Senior Tutor. But with thirty years of service she automatically became a Life Fellow, and while no longer entitled to active participation in routine college governance, Life Fellows retain certain privileges. Rights of nomination to major college offices, voting rights on certain matters, such as the election of Honorary Fellows – and new Masters.'

His trademark grin came back at that.

'Oh yes, that's right.'

Though really, there was no reason why he should recall every detail of his interview before the Fellowship, and the quietly searching questions put from the back by the former Senior Tutor.

'Don't worry, I wasn't looking to challenge the nomination on a technicality. I'm not calling my lawyers – this isn't a US presidential election. I just wanted to know how these things worked.'

He picked up his tea again and there was silence for a short spell as they both drank. She tried to remember whether the flattened packet on the table contained any chocolate digestives which had escaped the ravages of the students; if so, they would probably be the broken ones at the end, and she did not feel she could offer him those.

'It's an impressive slate of nominators, though, isn't it?' he mused presently. 'A former Senior Tutor and a Vice-Mistress. It certainly places the weight of seniority behind her claims.'

When she merely nodded he went on, 'Frankly I was a bit surprised by this coming from Professor Gladwin, too. In so many ways she and Dr Clarke are chalk and cheese, aren't they?'

Except . . . It was not she who would be the one to voice it. He sighed.

'Except that I have managed to unite them in their opposition to the Alvau donation.'

Then he appeared to shake himself out of his brooding.

'Anyway, since we have one nomination in, it seems that the race has begun. Or the runners are cantering down to the starting line, at the very least. That's why I had hoped you might be able to advise me. Who else is there who might come forward?' The swift grin again. 'Failing which, whose arm might I twist?'

Martha laughed with him but her mind was scanning seriously through the possibilities – and finding that she must reject them all. Susie James would make a fabulous Senior Tutor next time or the time after, but not now. Carolyn Gallagher was a fair-minded woman and devoted to her students, an efficient Graduate Tutor, but she lacked a wider educational vision for the college – no, that was unjust, she was simply too caught up in the concerns of her own department, where she was director of the troubled MPhil programme. Warsha Ramachandra, the pharmacologist; Maggie Trent, the geologist – both far too busy with their research. She realised that she was gazing down at her empty mug and biting her lip; raising her head, she caught the amusement in his eye.

'It's all right, I'm not asking you to come up with somebody who will support me over the Alvau money. I don't expect miracles: I know the score. Just anyone sensible, anyone reasonable to work with.'

Anyone who isn't Ros Clarke.

'That wasn't why I was hesitating. I know you wouldn't seek the appointment of a yes-woman, even if such a creature existed.'

'In St Radegund's? I hardly think so!'

She felt her shoulders relax and leaned forward earnestly – even while a small, traitorous voice in her head asked how often, as a journalist, he must have benefited from this gift for putting people at ease.

'The thing is, it's difficult to think who might be persuaded to stand at all – besides Ros, I mean.'

'To be Senior Tutor? I had imagined it would be a singular honour.'

She shook her head, shrugging off the suggestion along with any sense of her own distinction.

'For somebody, perhaps, at the right moment in her career. As it may now be right for Ros.'

319

And as it had been utterly wrong for herself ten years ago.

'But for most, the pursuit of research is the only route to tenure, and thereafter to advancement, to academic recognition and reward.'

'Ah yes, the infamous Research Assessment Exercise. The bane of every academic's existence.'

'You may joke about it – we all do, I know – but its pressures are very real. The need to be turning out publications has never been more acute. Funding depends upon it. For scientists, in particular, it can be the difference between having the equipment they need and not having it, simply being unable to operate. College offices which were once taken on out of a spirit of community, knowing that the job needed to be done, are getting harder and harder to fill.'

'People are not as collegially minded as you.'

He spoke softly, and she knew it was not a question.

'And then there's the job itself,' she went on. 'It has changed beyond all recognition during my ten years in post. The amount of paperwork generated by government consultations and reviews, by HEFCE inspections, seems to increase exponentially: aims and objectives, student feedback on teaching and tutorial services, top-up fees and increased hardship support. It used to be a job a person could do alongside a full lecturing load in her faculty and still maintain an active research profile. Not any more.'

His eyes looked into hers questioningly until she shifted her gaze.

'I've hardly written anything in years.' She hoped it didn't sound as though she were making excuses when she added, 'Really, it's more or less a full-time job now.'

Without needing to look up again she knew that he was still watching her face; his voice was cool and deliberate.

'What the college really needs, of course, is another someone like you. Somebody with a commitment like yours, somebody whom we can exploit, bleed dry for ten years and then abandon at the wayside, as we are about to do to you.'

She did raise her eyes then, smiling ruefully in acknowledgement of the truth of it.

'But I'm afraid you won't find any such person.'

'No.'

He spoke the syllable so quietly that she could not be sure she had really heard it at all.

Although she had to be back in college later for a meeting of the St Rad's Economics Society, Martha was determined to get home and cook supper first. The evening's speaker was a former student of hers, now working in the government economic service and invited back as a small counterbalance to the dozens of careers events staged around the university by city banks and accountancy firms, and really she would have liked to take her into Hall and catch up on her news before the talk. Good manners, indeed, would have made it a necessity, had not her government economist indicated that it would be a rush for her to get to Cambridge from work even in time for the post-dinner meeting. This, though a disappointment, was also a great relief, because not once since term began had Martha made it back for supper, such had been the clutter of essential appointments, meetings and dinner obligations which had crowded the past week. Douglas had returned from Florence in buoyant mood, with two poems complete and several more under way; Mum was back at home and sounding chipper on the telephone; Lucia had an early shift today and would be home in time to eat with them. It was with a pleasurable sliding away of strain, therefore, even if not of guilt, that Martha wheeled her bike out of the Fellows' bicycle shed at six forty-five, with three fresh tuna steaks in her bag and a clear ninety minutes before she needed to be back in the Graduate Seminar Room to introduce her guest speaker.

For once the traffic through the town was light. It had not been raining in the morning at the time when Cambridge's citizens were setting off for work, so more of them had chosen the bicycle over the car than during the rest of that cold and drizzly week. Every set of lights seemed to be with her, and it was not yet seven o'clock when she turned into her own drive. The security light mounted on the side of the house, detecting her arrival, blazed her path into light, enabling her to manoeuvre her bike along the narrow passage between wall and fence and round to the back door – and she was grateful for it, because otherwise the house appeared to be in complete darkness. She needed to unclip her front bike light in order to see to insert her key into the Yale. The sudden, noiseless presence of Maynard, wrapping his sinuous warmth around her legs, made her start but she was grateful for his welcome as she entered the silent kitchen. She went round switching on lights, kettle and fan oven, enjoying the companionship of the electrical clicks and whirrs as well as the flood of warmth and light.

Only after she had glazed the tuna with olive oil and a squeeze of fresh lime and placed the baking tray in the oven did she spot the note. A sheet torn from an old school exercise book of Lucia's which they were using up for shopping lists and phone messages.

Mum, Not back for supper tonight, gone for drink with Carleen. L xx

And added underneath, bringing a smile to Martha's face in spite of herself, *Don't worry, I will eat!*

Oh well, the third steak would keep; cooked tuna was always useful to have in the fridge. It was good to see Lucia going out with anybody at all. Somewhere along the way her old friends, with their chatter of A level coursework and university applications, had been jettisoned along with the rest of her rejected life. Cold tuna . . . maybe she could make a *salade niçoise* at the weekend if she had time to buy some green beans at the market. Tonight, though, she would keep things simple because time was tight. Some boiled potatoes, a basic green salad. She rinsed and cut up the potatoes now, covering them with hot water from the kettle, salting the saucepan, bringing it back to the boil and then turning it down to simmer before she left it to look for her husband.

The sitting room was in darkness. She did not switch on the light for fear of jolting him awake if he were dozing on the sofa but stood in the doorway, her eyes adjusting to the darkness, until she could make out the empty space between the cushions. Then she returned to the hall and mounted the stairs, carefully missing out the creaking step third from the top as if it were midnight and not ten past seven. Just as she gained the landing, however, the phone rang in the kitchen downstairs, so she retraced her steps, omitting the same stair, and reached for the receiver.

'Hello?'

'Um, hello. Is that Miss Pearce?'

Well, more or less, she supposed, though nobody called her that. Perhaps it was a sales call, early evening was a prime time for them, but the voice was not bored enough. Far too engaged – even anxious.

'Yes, speaking.'

'I'm Mrs MacDonald. Mrs Pearce's— your mother's cleaning lady. Her twice-weekly daily, she calls me. It's our little joke.'

She was gushing: nerves, probably.

'Been doing her Tuesdays and Fridays for must be five years now, not that she makes much mess, if it weren't for all those books, but I think she enjoys the company. "What would I do without you, Mrs Mac?" she always says.'

'I'm certain you're invaluable to her, Mrs MacDonald.'

'Well, I say the place is never a mess, and that was true until recently. I'd come in on a Friday and it looked like nothing had been touched since the Tuesday, all I had to do was flick round with a duster. But these last few months, she's been different. Not every time, but quite often I'll come in and things have been moved, not just the piles of books, but other things, odd things. Left about in the wrong places, you know.'

Despite the heat of the tuna-scented kitchen and the twist of Maynard's silken warmth around her ankles Martha felt an encroaching chill.

'I don't mind the extra tidying, of course, it's not that. You should see the houses of some of the people I do for, the ones with kids, mainly. But it's the change in her, you know. Not like herself. And sometimes it's things that bother me, like one time I found a lamb chop on the bathroom windowsill, still in its polythene bag, been there a few days by the looks. And last week her hair-curler left switched on – just on the side in the kitchen, but still, it was ever so hot and had left a bit of a mark on the Formica.'

There was a lurching inevitability about this recital, a plunge of recognition, so why did Martha's voice sound out so calmly, reassured and reassuring?

'Oh, I know. She is getting a bit scatty these days, isn't she? Kept putting things down, when she was here for Christmas, and then forgetting where she'd left them. I know the feeling, I do it myself. Car keys in the fridge, butter in the handbag, that sort of thing.'

She tried a laugh, but couldn't quite manage it. Down along the line she felt Mrs Mac's uncertainty, tempted to seize hold of the soothing words and regard her duty as done, yet still irresolute, fearing to ring off and reshoulder the responsibility alone. Pull yourself together, Martha told herself; you aren't being fair to the woman.

'Look, I do know how she is; I mean, I've noticed things myself, and it's very good of you to telephone. I'm glad you've got my number.'

There was an awkward cough at the other end. Of course the call would be without her mother's knowledge; Mrs Mac had no doubt found her address book and looked for the name of the daughter Mum would have talked about, Martha the big-shot Cambridge don.

'It's OK, I won't say anything to Mum. But if you are ever worried, if there is ever anything . . . well, anything at all that seems worrying, you can just call me, and I can always come down. I was going to pop over one weekend soon anyway, just to check how she's getting on. You know, I am so very grateful that she has you coming in, Mrs MacDonald, to keep an eye on her.'

This seemed to be sufficient to mollify her caller, who after a few comfortable nothings about old age and it coming to us all brushed off Martha's thanks, said her goodbyes and put down the phone.

It was now seven twenty-five; she had only half an hour left before she ought really to set off back to college, and the tuna would be overdone, no longer melting pink in the centre as Douglas preferred it. She took the baking tray from the oven and drained the potatoes, which were also beginning to fall to pieces, leaving a floury sludge in the water that she poured away. Just as she was about to head out into the hall again to find her husband he appeared in the kitchen doorway, clothes bearing the dishevelment of daytime sleep, and asked, 'Why didn't you wake me?'

Martha surveyed him through the rising steam from the potato pan and her smile failed her. Anger kicked inside her ribs. He had been asleep and she felt stupidly, irrationally resentful; resentful that he should snooze through her exhausting afternoon, snooze through her fear and guilt about Mum; resentful of his three brothers and the parents in Dagenham he rarely bothered to call. In place of a greeting she answered his accusation with one of her own.

'The tuna's spoiled.'

Without speaking he circled the table and approached the hob where the offending steaks lay, inspected them coolly and then turned towards her with a shrug. Really wanting to throw things, she attempted to soften her face, yet feared that if she did so she might cry. There were still times, though, when he chose to notice, that Douglas could read her like a book. He gave a short, wry laugh and crossed over to her, removing the saucepan from her hands and pulling her against his chest.

'Hey, look, it's OK. I'm sorry.'

It was only a thing to say, she knew that; he had no idea what he had to apologise for – if indeed he had anything – but the words nevertheless made her feel better.

'Come on, it still looks good and I'm starving. Lucia's out, is she? I must have missed her when I was upstairs. Does that mean I can have two?'

She could smile then, feeling the tension ebb, writing off her *salade niçoise*.

'You'll have to fight Maynard for it, then.'

The activity of gathering together plates and cutlery, tearing lettuce and turning the overcooked potatoes into a buttery mash soothed her, and by the time they sat down to eat she felt ready to tell him about Mrs Mac's telephone call.

'I don't know, it's so difficult, isn't it? I'm here and she's there, and I can't keep calling her every few minutes. But Wiltshire didn't seem half so far away when Dad was alive, somehow.'

'That's mainly because of the speed he used to drive at,' said Douglas, sawing with unfeeling relish into his tuna.

'And when I do call, I can't exactly ask, can I? Have you nearly set the house on fire today, Mum? Are you absolutely sure you've turned the gas off?'

'Perhaps if you listen really hard you'll be able to hear it hissing.'

'And I know she isn't going to say, either. She's so bloody proud, she's going to insist everything's fine, just like she did at Christmas.'

Though wouldn't she herself be just the same if it were her? Her mother's daughter: guarding her independence, not wanting to create worry where there was no power to help. He was chewing ruminatively and looking at her with exasperation, probably thinking the same thing. She sighed.

'Maybe I should have said something while she was here, something more direct, I mean. It would have been easier than over the phone. Or perhaps I should go there sooner than I'd planned, maybe this weekend? Have a proper talk to her.'

'And say what, exactly?'

It was a good question; her mind had shied away from thinking that far.

'Well, for a start, maybe she should see a doctor.'

Douglas laid down his knife and fork and sat forward in his chair, taking hold of her wrist.

'Look, Martha, will you please stop torturing yourself about this? It's what you always do and it does nobody any damn good. Going to a doctor

329

wouldn't help, if you think it's Alzheimer's. You know they can't cure it. All it would do is get her down, and label her so she can't get her driving licence renewed, like happened to that poor sod Normanby in Linguistics.'

Very gently retracting her hand, she saw that it was shaking. Everything was so easy for Douglas, and even when it wasn't easy it was at least black and white. He seemed immune to the muddy uncertainties which afflicted her.

'But aren't there drugs which slow down its progression? And they could help her to manage the symptoms, couldn't they? Talk to her about modifying the house, making it safer. Because of being on her own.'

He shook his head.

'Everyone's on their own some time. If it was you or I, we'd still be on our own when the other one was out at the shops. It only takes a second to go blank and do something stupid.'

The tuna and mash she had swallowed felt leaden in her stomach.

'But if someone were coming home, it would be different. If there were someone there to talk to . . .'

As if the power of conversation, of daily intellectual connection, could somehow keep the synapses of her mother's brain sparking and delay the degeneration of her cognitive powers.

'For God's sake, Martha! You've got to accept that not everything is within your power to solve. Not everything is your fault.'

He grabbed her hand again, forcing her to look at him.

'It's not your fault that your dad died, nor that your mum is sick.'

He must be right, she told herself with determination: all this self-blame got her nowhere, and it couldn't be much fun to live with. But even as she was depositing her plate in the sink and pulling on her coat with a glance up at the kitchen clock, leaving him to share the remains of his meal with Maynard, she wished he could have been gentler, maybe taken her in his arms again: less casually right and more understanding.

And as she pedalled back through the quiet mid-evening streets towards St Rad's and the Economics Society, the words which kept repeating themselves inside her head were the very ones she knew she ought to banish. *I should be there; I should be there with her.*

Two hours later, James Rycarte was waiting outside a door for Martha Pearce for the second time that day. This time it was the door of the Graduate Seminar Room, and he found himself wondering whether he ought not, in fact, to have lent his presence to the Economics Society meeting which was taking place within. Not for the first time he felt his own lack of a subject specialism, which would have enabled another Head of House – had no doubt enabled Dame Emily – to slot into an appropriate niche within the academic life of the college. He had occasionally turned up at random to grace with his attendance various graduate research seminars, guest lectures and subject-based social gatherings, but had often felt out on a limb, unable to contribute and unsure of his credentials for being there. The University of Cambridge, of course, offered no degree course in anything as worldly as Journalism or even the more theoretically respectable Media and Communication, and a few years in the boardroom at Broadcasting House could hardly be thought to qualify him as an expert in Management Studies. Yet somehow he was certain that had he gone along to her meeting tonight, Martha would have made him welcome.

At last he heard the sound of muffled applause followed by a scraping of chairs and the trill of student chatter. He stood back against the wall and allowed them to stream by, waiting until he could hear only Martha's voice left in the room, laughing with her speaker as she thanked her. Then he moved forward, gave a token knock at the open door and stepped inside.

'Good evening, Dr Pearce. Excellent turnout, I see.'

She looked genuinely pleased to see him – her face was positively glowing, and he could not help noticing that the russet shade of the silk shirt she had changed into as a compromise above the inevitable jeans was perfect with her colouring – and, he was glad to say, less taken aback than she had been this afternoon by his unexpected appearance.

'Oh, they all come all right, if they know which side their bread is buttered,' she said with a grin. 'I employ some of the larger third years as whippers-in. Not that they wouldn't all have rushed along anyway to hear tonight's speaker.'

The trouser-suited young woman at her side returned her smile amiably.

'It's OK, Martha, I remember what it's like. The government economic service was never exactly sexy.'

Martha formally effected the introduction which they all knew must be unnecessary on one side.

'James, this is Claire Newbold, old Radegundian and now an analytical wizard at the DTI. Claire, this is James Rycarte, Master of the college.'

Claire, very soon, was consulting her watch, refusing all offers of refreshment or entertainment and insisting on getting a cab to the station and home. Left alone together, Rycarte turned to Martha.

'Would you regard an invitation to the lodging as more fitting than this afternoon's improper visit?'

She nodded her assent gravely, but he did not miss the smothered smile which twitched her lips. As they walked he began to talk.

'I have been thinking a great deal about what you were saying earlier. About the nature of the senior tutorship and the difficulty of securing applicants for the post.'

'Yes?'

'You say that it has become pretty well a full-time job.'

'Definitely it is heading that way, yes. I suppose I have managed to continue to combine it with my academic position mainly because I have been doing both for a long time, and have learned to cut corners. Been forced to cut corners, perhaps, all too often.'

He felt sure this was not true, at least not as far as her college functions were concerned, but let it pass. She was not angling for a compliment and he did not wish it to appear that he thought she was.

'So then why not treat it as such? Advertise the post as a full-time appointment. Free-standing, not merely an office to be held in conjunction with a university or college lectureship.'

She glanced at him, then back to the path in front of them.

'It's certainly something some other colleges have done in recent years,' she conceded. 'To do so might attract a certain kind of person; somebody who has reached a point where academic preferment is not coming their way, perhaps a scientist on soft money whose research grant is coming to an end. Or an older person who is seeking a change of direction, a switch from research and teaching and into a more administrative role.'

It was his turn to nod now, while she went on considering aloud.

'We could advertise in the *Reporter*. It would open the field to those outside St Radegund's. We might find somebody from elsewhere in the University, or even from Oxford. But, you know . . .'

Even in the darkness he could tell that she would be chewing the left-hand side of her lower lip.

'Go on. Of what must I beware?'

This made her laugh and he knew that he had hit the mark.

'Well, if the only internal contender is Ros Clarke and you end up pushing for an external candidate, there may well be a rallying behind her of those who want the job kept in house. It will be easy for Ros to portray your actions in a negative light.'

An outsider, supported by another outsider.

'Oh, I think I was prepared for the fight to be dirty. I hadn't imagined that Dr Clarke would pull any punches. But in any case, an applicant from outside the college is not necessarily what I had in mind.'

They had reached the porticoed doorway of the lodging, and she stopped and turned towards him in the light from the Victorian lantern, like a nocturnal visitor to Sherlock Holmes.

'But even making it a full-time appointment – perhaps especially so – I find it hard to think who in college might be interested in the post. Everyone seems to be at full tilt pursuing their research and their faculty interests.'

He found his key on the extravagant bunch,

which had distorted the pockets of all his jackets and still made him feel like a gaoler. As he pushed open the door and moved aside, she stepped into the hall and groped for the light switch. There was a moment of awkwardness as he found it for her, their hands making contact in the darkness. But she seemed not to notice, intent on the conundrum of finding her successor.

'What you need is someone like me, who has reached an impasse with teaching and research and might be tempted to move across into administration. Not that everyone who is a failed academic,' she added with a self-mocking smile, 'is necessarily going to be any use as an administrator either.'

Instead of returning the smile he looked at her with sudden directness.

'The person I want as my Senior Tutor isn't just someone like you, Martha. It *is* you.'

Her mouth opened at once. 'But—'

He held up his hand and halted her. 'Don't say anything. Wait until you've heard the rest. Tea again? Coffee? Or I've got beers in the fridge?'

Rather to his surprise she accepted a beer; he hoped she wasn't humouring him or hoping to soften a blow. He didn't pour it but handed her the bottle and a glass, and they sat down opposite each other at the kitchen table. There was a silence while they both concentrated on angling the amber stream so as not to raise a head. Her success was markedly greater than his and he set down his bottle with an exaggerated grimace, making her laugh.

'I used to work in a bar when I was a grad student,' she explained.

'OK,' he began, 'so this is how I see it. We need to make a fundamental change in the way we view the job of Senior Tutor. No longer is it simply a "college office", consisting of limited duties to be performed in a few snatched hours each week in between teaching and conducting research, like being Fellows' Parlour Steward or Praelector – or even Vice-Mistress. The better model would surely be the Bursarship. Kate's was an external, full-time appointment, wasn't it?'

She licked a cream of bubbles from her upper lip and nodded.

'Yes. The day of the amateur, academic Bursar has passed. No one is ever going to do a John Maynard Keynes again, transforming the college finances in his time off from revolutionising economic thought. To get the skills they need, the colleges have had to pay qualified professionals, hired from the outside world – at outside world salaries.'

'And what are the terms of Kate's contract?'

He knew already, having spent the afternoon in careful study. It was a habit ingrained from his days as a journalist: always make sure you know the answers to the questions before you ask them.

'Well, just as you say really, that it's a full-time post, not including any teaching or other academic duties.'

'And the term of her appointment?'

Her brow contracted a fraction.

'It isn't a fixed term contract, if that's what you mean. There was a probationary period when she first took up the job, of course, but now she just holds the job until retirement, assuming that she wishes to stay that long.'

'Right.'

He raised his eyebrows inquiringly, waiting to see whether she rose to the bait; but her brow only furrowed more deeply, and she shook her head dubiously.

'But the Senior Tutorship is quite different. College Statutes specify a maximum term of three periods of office, each of three years: a total of nine years in all.'

'Granted. But that related to the old model of the post. A short-term office, once perhaps hardly more than a sinecure, more recently an increasingly bothersome set of duties to be rotated amongst the Fellowship every three, six, or nine years so that nobody's research is held up for too long. But the job has got out of the box; it has run away with us. What we need is a full-time Senior Tutor, and for that we need to make it a viable career option. That means a full-time salary and a permanent contract.'

'But – what about Statutes? We can't just ignore them.'

He lifted his beer glass almost to his mouth, then laid it down again untouched.

'A statutory maximum of *nine* years, you say? But I thought this was your tenth year in the job?'

She was still shaking her head at him, but now with the suggestion of a smile.

'"Normally". That's what the Statutes say. The appointment shall normally be for a maximum of nine years. My third and final period of service was, exceptionally, extended by one further year to enable me to see in your arrival. It was thought undesirable to have a new Head of House and a new Senior Tutor at the same time.'

'Of course,' he replied gravely. 'Heaven knows what disasters I might have stumbled into had it not been for your steadying influence.'

They drank in companionable silence for a minute. Then he tried again.

'OK, so it's going to be tricky to swing a permanent appointment through under the current Statutes, even given the existence of a helpful "normally". So let's amend the Statutes.'

Her beer went back on the table and she sat looking at him with an expression he could not decipher. Shock, amusement, sympathy – or a blend of all three?

'Changing the College Statutes isn't that simple. It requires the consent of the Privy Council.'

The Privy Council? And yet it would have to be something like that, wouldn't it? Cambridge would not be Cambridge without it. Well, if there existed a procedure, however arcane, then why shouldn't they use it? He was filled with a sudden determination not to be beaten. Leaning forward across the stretch of table that lay between them he seized and held her gaze.

'Let's do it! Let's change the Statutes. It's going to take more than the Privy Council, or the Queen in bloody Parliament for that matter, to stop me getting the Senior Tutor St Radegund's needs. It's you we need, Martha, and I'm going to make sure we get you.'

CHAPTER 23

Having a job, Martha had assumed, would at least get Lucia out of bed in the mornings. Routine, she had reasoned with herself, and a structure to her daughter's day, ought to break the pattern of passivity and lassitude. In fact it appeared if anything to have the opposite effect – or at least to provide the latest in a long series of excuses for inaction.

There had been a period when Lucia was seven years old – it probably only lasted a few months all told, though at the time it seemed an eternity – when she had refused to eat regular meals. A sandwich in the car, an apple at break-time at school, biscuits any time and anywhere, but never a proper tea at teatime, and never, never breakfast. Day after day Martha had been obliged to send her daughter in at the school gates without any food inside her at all, or else risk parting there instead from a child rigid with fury and red-eyed from crying. Some days she had given in and let Lucia eat a shortbread finger or a gypsy cream; at least that way she would have a fizzle of energy, however short-lived. It was then that she had had the idea

341

of the bedroom picnics. She would bring her own breakfast upstairs to Lucia's room and they would eat together cross-legged on the bedspread, sharing their Coco Pops with Pandy, Ted, Old Ted and Stripy Ted. (Lucia had been a very literal child.)

This morning Martha decided to revive the tradition. Having sat in James Rycarte's kitchen until after midnight, and having no fixed appointment before her ten a.m. lecture, she had planned on catching up with some reading over a leisurely breakfast. There were some new topics on the Industry syllabus this year and, by force of the pressure upon her, she had committed the unwise time-trimmer's sin of preparing the supervision handouts before she had herself had time to read the articles in question. She must do so now, or face the ignominious prospect of skulking round the library in two weeks' time working through her own reading list at the same time as the students. When she had cut two slices of wholemeal bread and switched the grill on to heat up, they looked lonely in the middle of the broad grill pan, so she cut two more pieces and shuffled them up to make room. Coco Pops were no longer an item on the family grocery list, had not been so for some years, but Martha was sorry not to be able to make that nostalgic gesture – although the chocolaty milk had not been to her taste, even then. Lucia had always been fond of lemon curd, the expensive kind made with eggs and real lemons, and she had a jar of that somewhere in the cupboard. Toast, lemon curd, and instant coffee made with hot milk, mixed in the mugs straight from the microwave just as her daughter liked it; and would it be too much to dig out from the bottom of the drawer the old checked linen tablecloth that used to serve them as a picnic rug?

All this meant a tray, and she was almost tripped on the stairs by an eager Maynard who approved strongly of any food that was not served at a table. Did he remember the breakfast picnics too? It seemed unlikely – it must be nearly ten years, and he had been little more than a kitten, jumping on the bed and tipping milk everywhere.

She couldn't risk putting down the tray to knock with the cat in attendance so she called out her daughter's name and pushed open the door with her hip.

'Whatimesit?' mumbled the groggy mound in the bed.

'Nearly a quarter to nine.'

The news was greeted with a less than joyful grunt; evidently Lucia had hoped not to surface until the hour was safely in double figures.

'I've brought breakfast.'

Martha heard her voice as her daughter must hear it: bright, overloud and artificially cheery. She set down her tray on the empty desktop, out of reach of Maynard unless he chose to take a leap. The duvet edged back a few centimetres just as Martha was unfolding and shaking out the squared tablecloth.

'What's this?' said a more human voice than before, and the duvet flipped back properly.

'Bedroom picnic. I thought we hadn't had one for ages.'

There was just a moment when it could have gone either way and Martha pictured her sentimental gesture ending in an uncomfortable retreat. Lucia eyed the tray.

'What, no Coco Pops?'

It was enough to seal the deal: she remembered; she would play along.

Martha laid out the two plates and passed Lucia a mug. Neither of them sat cross-legged; Lucia reclined on her pillows with the duvet pulled up to her chest while Martha perched on the side of the bed, still wary of her welcome. Stripy Ted, though, who still sat propped against the wall at the foot of the bed, watched the scene with button-eyed approval.

'Great lemon curd, Mum. You're the best,' enthused Lucia in a buttery spray of crumbs and Martha's heart lifted as it had not done in weeks.

'Why are you still here, anyway?' was her daughter's next comment, as she started on her second slice of toast. 'Still home at nine o'clock with us slackers.'

For once there was no edge of resentment there, real or even imagined. Martha laughed.

'Ten o'clock lecture, but nothing 'til then. So I'm starting slowly for once.'

'Late night, was it?' Again, there was no accusation in the words – merely a teasing relish. 'You weren't back when I went to bed. And Dad was being rude – reckoned you were getting pissed

344

with your students. Setting all sorts of bad examples, he said.'

'He's right, I was at a student meeting, but then afterwards I went over to the Master's Lodging for a drink.'

Lucia swigged her cooling coffee.

'What's he like, in real life, James Rycarte? You've never really said. He's very sexy on the telly, but a bit, I don't know . . . a bit too smooth for his own good, I've always thought. Can't imagine him let loose in a college full of women. Doesn't everyone swoon at his feet?'

Martha's laugh was one of surprise at the truth of this – and also at the way it wasn't true. He was a very charismatic man and could be highly persuasive; she thought it a testament to the Fellows of St Radegund's how little they had fallen under the spell of his masculine charm. The respect he had gained he had had to work for; there had been a decided absence of swooning.

'Oh, we are a tough old lot, you know. It takes more than a few male blandishments to make us cave. Anyway, how about you? You were out with Carleen, you said. What's she like?'

Was there a very slight retraction of confidence? There was certainly a shrug.

'She's funny. Makes me laugh.'

'Where did you go?'

'The Anchor. But it was full of students, so we didn't stay long.'

The recurrent rebuff: your world, which is not my

world. The toast all gone, Maynard now appeared on the bed, treading weightlessly between plates and mugs to inspect for crumbs. Martha had not meant to push, not today; her intention had not gone beyond the picnic. But she could not help just one light question.

'And today?'

'Late shift again, like yesterday,' replied Lucia, the misunderstanding undoubtedly wilful. Her attitude irked Martha, made her want to drag her daughter's stubborn head out of the sand.

'But before that, I meant. This morning?'

The duvet hoicked defensively higher round her shoulders, Lucia's jaw jutted.

'I did a long shift yesterday, one 'til ten; I'm doing the same today. I'm knackered, all right?'

'You went to bed before I did – you said so yourself.'

I worked a sixteen-hour day yesterday, thought Martha, and it wasn't even exceptional. But that avenue was blocked by a big, red 'no entry' sign. *Clever you, with your high-powered job. Is that why you are never here for me?*

'You're awake now. You've got a whole morning before you need to go to work. Why not try to do some writing?'

'Because I'm knackered. As I just said.'

Maybe it was Qwikmart. Martha had done boring jobs; she hadn't sat at a checkout but she had poured drinks and taken money, and she'd spent one summer as a teenager packing components into boxes. She knew enough to recognise the crippling inertia which is bred out of boredom. Especially when Lucia was permanently tired to start with. But would a job with more stimulation – the job that Martha would have found her had she been allowed – in fact have made any difference? The lethargy seemed too deeply ingrained, its stranglehold too close.

She tried another approach. What she herself would do: an escape.

'Sometimes when a task is monotonous and doesn't take all your brain, you can use the time to think.'

The framework of several of her best economic arguments had been formulated while sitting at traffic lights, the tightest analytical knots ironed out along with the creases in Douglas's shirts.

'Have you ever thought about writing while you are at work? In your head, I mean.'

Lucia's expression, which had been truculently set, gradually softened and then melted into laughter. It might be sour, ironic laughter but it was something.

'Can you imagine? I stand there like a moon-faced idiot while people have to ask three times for twenty Lambert & Butler. "Oh, don't mind about her, she's writing her novel . . ." Well, I suppose it would be an original reason for getting the sack.'

In earnest despite her smile, Martha assured her, 'I'm certain you wouldn't be the first person to write a book in a supermarket.'

347

'War and Frozen Peas,' suggested Lucia and began to giggle. 'Harry Potter and the Half-Price Mince. Tesco of the D'Urbervilles.'

'The Darling Buds of Mace,' chipped in Martha, glad to put the fight on hold; more glad still to have her sparky daughter back, even for a moment.

'The Famous Five-Items-or-Less. Love by the Cold Cabinet.'

Mother and daughter exchanged grins as they exclaimed more or less in unison, 'The Da Vinci Barcode.'

Applying for the Senior Tutorship on a permanent basis was quite out of the question. James Rycarte had been so kind, the mark of his confidence in her so appreciated, that Martha had not liked to turn down the proposition flat, there with his beer in her hand and sitting at his kitchen table. She could at least do him the courtesy of allowing him to believe her to have slept on it. In fact, she had barely given it a thought, either last night cycling home for the second time to a dark and silent house, or in bed next to the unstirring Douglas, where she had fallen asleep at once – a sure sign that there was no difficult decision to be made. This morning Lucia's picnic had chased away other thoughts, and then on her bike on the way to the Economics Faculty she had been wholly absorbed by a mental run-through of her lecture, even to the extent of forgetfulness of the cars and bicycles that surged around her. Only back in the sanctuary of her office did she take the issue out and examine it – and, whichever way she looked at it, the sole problem she came back to was how to tell him.

It was not that she disagreed with the strategy of advertising the post full-time; it might create division, it might even be perceived as a direct attack on Ros Clarke's candidacy, but the case could certainly be made and he would no doubt make it with persuasive verve. She could even see the argument for amending Statutes to make the appointment permanent, although experience suggested that doing so within the time frame necessary would be a tall order. Where she could not go along with him was simply in relation to her own situation.

As had become second nature for Martha, her first thought was for the college. In this she was in tune with the founding draftswomen, who had without doubt had the interests of the institution and not of the individual incumbent in mind when laying down ('normally') that nine-year maximum. After that long, an individual, however efficient in the performance of her duties, must necessarily begin to become stale; an injection of new blood and new ideas at the top must then be beneficial. The same was just as true, if not more so, with Heads of House, whose service was to the retiring age; but theirs was an eminent office to which elevation much before the mid to late fifties was unlikely, so that the march of time could generally be relied upon to bring about a natural end. Indeed, James Rycarte at fifty-six had been a comparatively youthful choice by recent Cambridge standards, with colleges increasingly showing a defensive tendency towards the sexagenarian, fearful of being saddled for too long with the fruits of a misguided appointment. But senior tutors, taking up the post in their forties or even, like Martha, in their thirties, might have a tendency to loiter. The college needed an exit strategy and Statutes had provided it.

And for the office holder? For Martha herself? Nine years – ten in her own case – represented a quarter of an academic lifetime. It was enough. She had done most of the things which she had set out to achieve in St Radegund's, reformed most of what she had identified a decade ago as ripe for reform. Or worse, to her increasing frustration, she had watched the alterations she had wrought proving to be ephemeral: all that she had worked for in terms of closer cooperation with the Student Union, for example, laid waste by one term of Karen's presidency. As year by year the same battles came round to be refought, she endured a sinking sense of Cambridge's innate and stubborn immutability, weathered into its stones: of the futility of hoping to effect any lasting change. This was no mindset with which to be facing the fray. It must be time for somebody else to gird up her loins.

There was more to it, besides; there was a question of the hubris. Even if James Rycarte persuaded the Fellowship of the need to seek a permanent, full-time Senior Tutor, she found that she hated the idea of her colleagues linking this to the idea that it should be her. Job security, a post which represented an attractive career move, these things she could justify as an inducement to help secure the right candidate. But permanence for herself, after having already had ten years in the post? The image which kept returning to her mind was that of a Central American president, claiming the support of the popular will to cancel future elections and continue in power flanked by uniformed guards. Martha had humility enough to know that she was not irreplaceable; she therefore had a horror of appearing to hold herself out as being so.

More than anything, there was simply a feeling of having reached the brick wall at the end of the street. Maybe James Rycarte could perform the miracle and dismantle the wall brick by brick, but she was no longer convinced that this was the road she wanted to travel. A fresh direction, a new start: these were the things she sensed she needed – though, as things stood, she had to admit she had absolutely no idea how or where to find them.

The telephone on her desk stared at her uncompromisingly. She must call him, make an appointment to see him; after his generous gesture it would be churlish in the extreme not to tell him her decision face to face. Not that it was fair to him to call it generosity; she knew it was only her own perversity which was tempted to cast it as charity. He genuinely valued her, and that gave her a sweetly treasured fillip, even while making it harder to pick up the phone. Twice she extended her hand determinedly towards the instrument. The second time her fingers actually alighted on the receiver before she was thwarted – or saved – by a knock at her office door.

At her call to enter, the door was pushed open by Darren Cotter, the Dean.

'Er, hello. Are you busy, or have you got time for a quick word?'

She was round her desk before he was properly inside the room, smiling and motioning towards an armchair.

'Of course, Darren. What can I do for you?'

She took the footstool.

'Well, there's something I think I ought to tell you. What I mean is, I want to tell you. It's something you need to know.'

When nothing further followed she tried a gentle prompting, almost subconsciously picking up his diffident pattern of speech, a thing she sometimes found herself doing with nervous students.

'So why don't you? Tell me, I mean.'

'I would do. I do want to. But the way I know about it is— that is, the person who told me doesn't want . . .'

So that was it: he was anxious to protect an informant. She found it obscurely touching. Stifling a laugh which might be mistaken for mockery, she contented herself with an understanding smile.

'Don't worry, Darren, I will be discreet. I'm neither a High Court judge nor the editor of a national newspaper; you have no need to reveal your sources.'

He laughed uncertainly, turning it into a cough. Martha waited. Finally, just as she was wondering how to open the way for him, he blurted it out baldly.

'The students are planning a sit-in over the rents. On Saturday. They are going to blockade Hall after dinner and just stay there.'

'Ah.'

Her first response, intrudingly, was a spurt of anger that she would not now be able to go to Mum's this weekend after all. Why could they not play their petty games some other time? The second, quite opposite to the first and equally inapt, was a grudging admiration for this sign of readiness to take a stand. She recognised the adrenaline rush of protest, even if she now stood on the side of authority: the protested against and no longer a co-protester. Dismissing both feelings, she focused on the problem at hand. Which was, most immediately, Darren perched anxiously in her armchair.

'OK, thank you very much for letting me know. Don't worry, I'll handle it. And of course I won't mention to anybody how I found out.'

She rose, still smiling, from her position at a level with his feet; he rose also, his burden lifted and cheerfulness returning – with it even coming a modicum of confidence.

'If you'd like me to do anything, you know, help sort it out on Saturday . . . ?'

'No, it's all right, Darren, really. You've done your bit by letting me know. I'll take it from here.'

The relief in his face was palpable; it struck her as wholly out of scale with the news that his services as Dean would not be required on the night. As she showed him to the door and watched him walk away along the corridor, it occurred to her that his lightness of tread might have something to do with having safeguarded the mysterious source of his information.

With a prospective occupation of Hall to head off, Martha had more than sufficient to engage her thoughts for the rest of the morning at least. The phone call to James Rycarte would have to wait a little longer.

'Just you and me as usual, puss,' said Martha, arriving home late again two nights later, this time following a cello recital given at the University Music School by one of her second year economists. Strains of Paul Hindemith were still swirling around her head – although it wasn't the kind of stuff you could exactly hum. She had rather wished it had been the Dvořák. Maynard leapt on to the kitchen work surface from a standing start, there the better to greet her with lowered head and back arched like a sprung bow. With one hand she idly flattened his ears, feeling the purring vibrate his skull, while the other reached across to flick the switch on the kettle. As she moved round to find mug and coffee jar it hit her quite suddenly, the banked-up exhaustion of too many working evenings, too much truncated sleep; perhaps the music had released it, freeing her brain from surface activity and letting in tiredness.

The red light was blinking on the computer. Lucia, she supposed; Douglas most often worked either in his study or else recumbent on the settee with eyes half-lidded, but her daughter shared her own preference for the warm kitchen over a lonely desk. How many times, though, had she nagged her not to leave the computer on stand-by? Weren't the young supposed to be the ones who were passionate about global warming and saving the planet? Going over to the keyboard, she touched the space bar to bring the screen to life, intending to select 'shut down', but was greeted by an open file of text. Not one of her own, and being prose – and in English – it was unlikely to be Douglas's. Lucia – writing at last? Her heart rose and skittered in her chest; as she began to read, she felt as though breathing had ceased to have its imperative force.

I am lying on my back and overtaken by an overwhelming lethargy; if only I could close my eyes and sleep. I could sleep here, like this, for ever. But my eyes are open, and the world above me is insubstantial and shifting, as if isolated in its own medium; concentric circles move apart and widen. And it comes to me: it is just as if everything I am seeing is under water, as if I have been watching ripples on the surface

*of a pool, spreading from where I have tossed
in a stone. But how can I be lying down and
looking up at water? It makes no sense. Unless
. . . Understanding comes over me, chokingly,
like a blanket. It is I that am under the water,
looking out at the world of light above – I that
am trapped, frozen into my looking-glass
prison. The cold laps round my body. I am
marble inside and out; only my lungs are on
fire, burning with the need to find a pocket of
life-giving oxygen. But I cannot move, cannot
raise myself towards the sunlight, up towards
the warming, breathing air. I can't. I can't I
can't I can't I can't. It's all shit. All of it. It's
shit. Shit shit shit shit
shit
shit
shit
shit*

Martha closed the file and shut down the
computer; for a moment of disequilibrium she was
half unsure whose were the tears which she felt
wet upon her cheeks.

CHAPTER 24

There was an unusually good turnout at dinner on Saturday night. Mostly, on that day of the week more than any other, students chose not to dine in Hall but to eat later, perhaps pizza or a curry, at one of the town centre's many bars and restaurants. That should have been especially the case this early in the term, before lack of funds drove them back into the subsidised arms of the St Radegund's kitchens. Karen was there, of course, with Deepa and the majority of the Student Union committee. Julia was not particularly conspicuous by her absence; she had been missing more and more frequently over the first couple of weeks of the new term. Karen looked up and down the long tables which stretched the length of Hall, taking some satisfaction in the noisy crush but wondering at the same time how many of those gathered had come in order to sit in and how many simply out of a sense of occasion.

Seated between the Chaplain and the presiding Vice-Mistress at High Table, Martha wondered the same thing. In contrast with the student tables to which it sat perpendicular along the dais at the end of the room, High Table was all but empty, leaving her with an uneasy feeling of being exposed. Very few St Rad's Fellows dined on Saturdays; it came, no doubt, of being a women's college and lacking the monastic tradition of some of the older, men's colleges. People had kids to feed and get to bed and at the weekend, she reflected with a self-conscious lurch, family responsibilities tended to come first. But she had no choice in the matter tonight: she had a sit-in to prevent.

Not that she had any finely honed plan of action in mind. In fact, her strategic forethought had stretched no further than simple inaction. The protesters were presumably intending to stay put at the end of their meal, and bar the doors once the Fellows had withdrawn and the serving staff departed. The thing to do seemed to be to stay put too. They could hardly put up the barricades with her inside, could they?

Pudding was served and eaten. Letitia Gladwin stood and spoke the short closing grace and she and the smattering of other Fellows retired to the breakfast Parlour where the coffee urn would be waiting, leaving only Martha and Joan Tilley. The latter was in the middle of a rather involved story about the post of Organ Scholar at another college.

'The Chaplain went back to the original Statutes of 1642 which were in the college archive.

Apparently it was stipulated that the honorarium be two shillings per annum, but it also said that the Scholar should be entitled to "rooms and Commons in all charitye" . . .'

If necessary, thought Martha, she would stay here all night, and the next day if she had to. In some ways, this might be seen to defeat the object, but it could not really count as an occupation if she were here with them, could it? They weren't about to unfurl their banners and start singing 'We Shall Overcome' with the enemy sitting peacefully in their midst – it would rather take away the spice.

'There is a set of rooms in Front Court which have always been allocated to the Organ Scholar and modern practice has been to charge for them at the usual student rate. But somehow the lad who holds the post this year has found out what the Statutes say and is demanding to live there rent free.'

'Goodness. I should imagine their Bursar would have a few things to say about that?'

'Well, actually they're having to get the University Draftsman involved, to give a view on the meaning of "charitye". Of course the college is contending that it did not by any means suggest a free hand-out as in the modern usage. It was probably mere surplusage.'

Listening to Joan with half an ear, Martha cast her eye over the student tables. The crowds had thinned now, leaving only a dozen or so under-graduates, presumably the would-be demonstrators, who were slowly converging at the table closest to the entrance. They all seemed to have come equipped; most carried bulky bags and all had coats and scarves. Finally the tale of the Organ Scholar came to an end and the Revd Tilley drained her water glass.

'We'd better be cutting along or there will be no coffee left for us. Are you coming?'

'Not just at the moment, thank you, Joan. I think I'll stay here a bit longer if that's all right.'

The Chaplain eyed her curiously as she scraped back her chair and stood up.

'I just want to think for a bit,' offered Martha, unable to come up with any more convincing explanation for her conduct.

A beatific smile broke across her colleague's face.

'Ah, yes. A moment of silent communion. I'll leave you to it, then,' she said and suited her action to the words, leaving Martha alone at the deserted High Table.

Martha hated conflict. It was certainly not that she was afraid of standing her ground, of fighting her corner when she had to; however, over her career and personal life to date she had come to the firm opinion that the best way to resolve conflict in most cases was not to confront things head on but to steer a course designed to avoid collision, allowing all parties wherever possible to leave the battleground with dignity intact. Face-saving was all: it left open the door to compromise. If she had stood up and asked the students to leave the room they would have been forced to refuse; she in turn would have been forced to take some action to back up her demand. The stakes would have risen, positions become entrenched. Equally, if she announced her intention of staying, they might be tempted to try to force her to leave, or to blockade the doors anyway, with herself inside – and then what? No: better simply to watch and wait. She took out her detective novel and began to read.

Without looking up she could tell that the would-be protesters were wrong-footed. Through Adam Dalgliesh's latest investigation intruded the sound of restless movement at the student table, followed by anxious whispering. She resisted the temptation to raise her head, forcing her mind back to the commander's carefully constructed questioning, while at the same time mentally sizing up her opponent. Uncertainty about Karen was her main cause for concern. She was certainly strong-willed, she appeared to enjoy drama and she had an unpredictable reckless streak; maybe she would be the one to force things to a head. But there was no sign of it yet, at least. Nobody approached her table, and indeed after a few more pages of Baroness James things seemed quieter at the other end of the room. The shuffling and the whispering had subsided to a more settled hum. She risked a glance. One or two had adopted her example and taken out books or folders of notes. Some were chatting in groups round the table, one foursome playing cards. Karen and Deepa were bent in a huddle with another committee member, deep in conference.

Martha went back to her book. So far, then, so good. The doors remained unobstructed, no furniture had been moved, no placards raised at the windows. This really did not have the full appearance of a student occupation – it looked more like a dozen or so undergraduates lingering informally to chat or study after their meal. The ball was in their court and she was happy to leave it there. She could sit here and read all night if she had to. If she finished the P. D. James she had a new collection of industrial relations essays in her bag which had received excellent reviews. Time was on her side, because it occurred to her that if they were all still here when the catering staff arrived and began to serve Sunday lunch, normality would wash back in around them and the attempted sit-in would surely dissolve completely. (What a pity it was not Ramadan, or the same thing would have happened at break-fast.) Karen had until then to take some kind of action; Martha tried to think through the possible moves her adversary might make. The bottom line, she supposed, was that the entrance needed to be barred before the kitchen staff came to lay the tables, or else the students were not in control of the room and their presumptive object of putting Hall out of use would have failed. Whichever way you looked at it, Karen had until approximately eleven forty-five the next morning to make Martha her prisoner.

At eleven thirty p.m. the Head Porter, making his evening security round of the College precincts, was surprised to see lights still blazing from Hall at a time when normally all would have been washed up, locked up and deserted. Sharing Martha's preference for the low-key approach, he extinguished his flashlight, stood quietly in the darkness outside the double doors and looked inside. By eleven fifty he had completed his beat and was returning to the porter's lodge, deep in thought. It was just past midnight when he picked up the telephone and put a call through to the Master's Lodging.

James Rycarte had been cleaning his teeth when the phone rang. He spat hastily and descended the stairs at a trot. Really, he must have another extension or two installed soon. The intelligence which the Head Porter had to impart was unexpected, to say the least, and it was more slowly and thoughtfully that he returned upstairs to rinse the toothpaste from his chin and exchange his striped pyjamas for his suit trousers and two warm sweaters. As an afterthought he picked up a family-size packet of Murray mints which were lying on the kitchen work surface.

There was a decided lack of sound coming from the brightly lit Hall as he approached. He was not sure what he had expected: perhaps some

363

chanting, as at the anti-Alvau demonstration outside the Advent Feast. Even as he drew close to the entrance, he could only just make out a low buzz of conversation; no raised voices, no angry arguing. Gently and unobtrusively he gave the closer of the two heavy doors a nudge, just enough to feel the give and know that it was neither locked nor barred. Carefully he peered through the panel of glass which, some time in the late twentieth century, had been placed across the decorative wrought-iron grille in the upper half of the door to cut down on draughts and heating bills. Inside, at the nearest table to the immediate left of the door, sat ten or fifteen undergraduates clad for the outdoors, reading or talking quietly, and having every appearance of orderly normality were it not for the lateness of the hour. And there at the far end of the room, alone at High Table and the very picture of peaceful contemplation, sat Martha Pearce with a book.

For a moment Rycarte stepped back again into the shadow of the court, making up his mind; then he took hold of the iron door handle again and pushed determinedly. All eyes turned to him as he walked in.

'Hello there. Very sorry to barge in, but I heard a rumour that the Senior Tutor was being held hostage in Hall!'

Almost at once he regretted the attempt at humorous bravado. As he moved up the centre of the room towards High Table there was a ripple of nervous giggling from behind him at the student table; Martha rose from her seat and came forward quickly, a look of anxiety tightening her face.

'James.' Her clear voice rang, as his had done, with conspicuous resonance round the high-ceilinged room. 'I think everything is all right. I mean, I am certainly free to leave, if that was your concern. But these students seem determined to remain in Hall tonight and if they are to stay then I feel there should be a senior member here with them.'

There was no giggling this time; he felt more than heard an uncomfortable shifting behind him. Instinctively he knew that he had forced her already to show her hand more than she would have wished. If he could not discern exactly what her strategy was, he felt a sufficient access of sympathy to appreciate that he ought not to interfere any further in whatever delicate stasis had been achieved.

'Murray mint?' he offered, taking the bag from his pocket.

Much of the tension slid from her features as she took a sweet with a smile. He took one himself, and she graciously indicated the seat opposite hers at High Table as if she were about to serve him supper. They both sat, and he picked up her novel from where it lay splayed upside down in her place.

'Her latest? Haven't read it yet. Any good?'

'So far, yes. Right up to the usual standard. I didn't know you liked crime fiction.'

He cocked his head with a grin. 'Nor I you.'

'It's a sit-in.' She did not drop her voice conspiratorially, merely continuing in the same quiet, matter-of-fact tone as before. 'Or at least that was their plan.'

A pause, so he probed gently, 'Is there anything I can do to help?'

She shook her head with a slow smile. 'It's hard for them to do anything decisive with me here.'

It was neat, he thought. Unless and until the students were prepared to take some more drastic action, a stand-off was achieved. He wished he had thought to bring a book, too.

'Right, then. It will be even harder with the Master sitting here, too.'

For a while they chewed their mints in sociable silence.

'It's a long time since I sat up all night,' he said presently. 'Perhaps we should suggest some party games to pass the time. Do you think kids these days still know how to play charades?'

She laughed with him, but her lower lip was caught in her teeth.

'Actually . . .'

'Yes?'

'Well, since you're here, would you mind holding the fort for a few minutes while I just nip to the loo?' She laughed in embarrassment. 'I shouldn't have had any water with dinner.'

So she departed, without let or hindrance from Karen and her lieutenants. As she left he had risen to his feet and followed her a short distance down towards the doors in a vague gesture towards defensive chivalry should there be any move to bar her exit. He ought then, he supposed, to have returned to his station at High Table to continue to watch and wait. But James Rycarte was not Martha Pearce and besides, he had no detective novel to read. So instead he carried on walking, until he arrived at a level with the table around which the protesters were gathered.

'Do you know what Dr Pearce's proudest boast to me has been about this college?' he began without any introduction, purposely not addressing Karen but sweeping the table at large with his eye. 'And this bearing in mind how proud she is of almost everything, where St Radegund's and its students are concerned?'

He allowed only a fleeting pause before going on, determined to hold the floor.

'The thing which pleases her most of all is that no undergraduate has ever had to drop out of St Rad's due to financial hardship. Nobody could be a firmer believer in the "access" cause than Dr Pearce. She, along with Dr James and others, has worked tirelessly to bring to the college young women of brains and talent regardless of means or background. And having got them here, she is determined to keep them.'

They were listening: reluctantly and even with a show of hammed scepticism in some cases, but at least they were listening.

'We are not a rich college – certainly no Trinity or St John's – but what resources we have, Dr Pearce has been proud to tell me, have always been applied for the benefit of all, and especially those in greatest need.'

Access; financial hardship; greatest need. It was the first lesson of the foreign correspondent seeking a way in: maybe he hadn't learned much Swahili or Italian but he knew how to speak to people in a language they understood.

'But now the library is sinking.'

Not so much as a titter. They weren't an easy audience but at least curiosity about what was coming kept them attentive.

'It's going to cost three hundred and fifty thousand pounds to sort out. The estimates are on my desk. And it needs doing sooner rather than later, before the problem gets worse – this coming summer would be best, to minimise disruption to your studies. But there is no money for it in the budget.'

Looking round at their faces, it occurred to him how little direct contact he had actually had with the students since arriving at St Rad's, apart from within the formal confines of committees. He would have been hard pressed to put a name to any of them apart from Karen and the pretty Indian girl, Deepa. He must give a few more parties.

'You probably know better than I do how the Bursar has pared and scraped away at everything which is in the least expendable. Every surplus paper clip has already been identified and done away with. There is nothing left to cut.'

He was standing at the head of the students' table like a barrister delivering a plea for the defence; all eyes were turned to him so that he was the only one to see Martha coming quietly back into Hall. He chose not to acknowledge her with any visible sign but he felt the reconnection and also just the mildest hint of surprise to find him thus addressing the mob.

'Where is the money to come from? We already make you vacate your rooms the moment term is over so that we can pack in the conference guests, when you would rather have another week of partying or catching up on missed work; we can hardly throw you out in term time as well, can we? We can fund-raise, of course. But Dr Pearce would be able to tell you all about the gender pay gap. If we appeal to our alumnae for the library renovations, where are the women who are in a position to write a cheque for fifty thousand pounds? It is much more likely to be tens and twenties, perhaps the odd fifty. We could ask your parents to give, but again the sums would be small – and those ill afforded in some cases.'

He braved a glance at Karen and saw that her face was set and hard, but around her a few nods were beginning to break out.

'We gaily assume that the ship will always stay afloat – but will it? And if we are to remain above water, what will have to be tossed overboard? The inessentials. And what counts as inessential in bottom-line bursarial terms may include some of things which Dr Pearce – and you and I – currently regard as absolutely key, as sacrosanct. Such as Dr James's admissions outreach work in schools with no Oxbridge tradition. And hardship funds to assist poorer students when they arrive.'

Martha, who had been standing motionless just inside the entrance, took a few steps forward but still nobody seemed to notice her presence. He returned to his main theme.

'Why is it that we have never lost an under-graduate to financial problems? Because although not particularly well off by Cambridge standards we have at least been solvent. Some might even call it privilege. Do you imagine that at many of the newer universities they have funds to bail out students who sink into debt, who cannot make ends meet? In most places the students get a part-time job or else they simply go under.'

He ran a glance round the table and found that few could meet his eye, so he pressed his point home.

'Some of your peers in less ivied institutions might well look at you and say, "Get real!" We simply cannot any longer afford to subsidise the rent levels of students across the board. And the sooner we face that uncomfortable truth, the more chance we have of being able to continue to offer assistance to those who need it most.'

Finally, one of them plucked up courage to speak – though whether what had hitherto deterred them was awe of himself or of Karen he could not be sure. The intervention came from a diminutive ginger-haired girl in an enormous synthetic fur coat.

'But if we give way on the general subsidy, what guarantee is there that the hardship funds are going to continue to be available? How do we know that won't be the next thing cut? Thin end of the wedge, sort of thing.'

It was a fair question. While he was contemplating his answer, one came from behind his left shoulder in Martha's quiet voice, as she stepped closer, saying, 'There can never be an absolute guarantee, Leanne. None of us can predict what the future holds financially for higher education – it would be dishonest to suggest otherwise. But I can promise you that for me, certainly, and for a large majority of the Fellows' – drawing level with Rycarte, she shot him a questioning look – 'ensuring a safety net for students in need is a fundamental priority.'

He nodded firmly, including himself in her pledge.

'And we have plans for specific bursaries set aside to go towards the rents of those who can least afford to pay, don't we?' he said, smiling at Martha, who picked up her cue and began to outline the Alvau Rental Bursary scheme, shortly followed by the Alvau Entrance Scholarship

371

scheme – though naturally attaching the potential sponsor's name to neither.

'And would they be advertised beforehand, do you mean, these scholarships? Not just handed out after people arrive?' inquired a serious, bespectacled student of Chinese heritage.

'That's right, Suyin. An open competition, but with a means-tested qualifying requirement.'

There were further questions, then, and soon a lively debate was under way, incorporating almost all of those assembled with the exception of a taciturn Karen, who by now bore the disgruntled look of one thoroughly upstaged.

At around one thirty a.m. the discussion had broadened sufficiently from the issue of rents and hardship support to embrace in more general terms the college's finances and Rycarte, judging the moment ripe, raised the subject of their controversial would-be benefactor. By this time he and Martha were seated side by side amongst the debaters, elbows on the table, while Karen sat silent with her chair pushed back and her jacket clutched closely about her. As he spoke he looked studiedly in every direction but hers.

'I know how dear to many of your hearts is the principle of open admissions. And what more tangible way to contribute to that end than to offer these proposed entrance scholarships? Eight, maybe ten young woman a year would be enabled to come to St Rad's who otherwise would be prevented from enjoying that opportunity by lack

372

of means and fear of debt. Now, if we are offered the wherewithal to achieve that aim – to establish those scholarships and give those students the chance to come here – wouldn't it be cutting off our nose to spite our face if we were to turn it down in the name of open access?'

So disputation raged again, but without the immediate knee-jerk negativity with which he would hitherto have expected mention of the Alvau donation to be greeted. And by the time the Hall clock had slipped round to quarter to three, more were with him than against. At length, glancing at his watch with a luxuriant yawn, he rose and said, 'I know three a.m. is probably early for you lot, but I am not accustomed to the student lifestyle. I need my sleep, or I'll be next to useless in Work and Stipends Committee on Monday morning. We are reviewing the structure of the college's pension contributions in the case of part-time staff, and I fear I'd have been finding it hard enough to stay awake as it was. You can take a nap in your lectures, I dare say, but it doesn't look good when you are meant to be chairing the meeting.'

Several of them were actually smiling with him now; one or two began to pack up their books and files. He turned to Martha.

'I'd offer you a nightcap but it would be setting a poor example to these young people. Perhaps a cocoa would not go amiss?'

Although she answered his smile the uncertainty showed round her eyes.

'Come on,' he urged, and she turned obediently and went over to High Table to collect her book and bag.

It was an extremely testing task to walk out of the double doors together – like Orpheus and Lot's wife, thought Rycarte incongruously – and to cross the court without looking back. However, they were both equal to it. Had they not been they would have observed, following them out of Hall in a straggling trickle, all but one of the dozen students who had been at the table with them, bleary-eyed and stamping the pins and needles out of their cold feet. Had they lingered another ten minutes until these had said their goodnights and gone their separate ways, leaving the quadrangle in silent emptiness, they would finally have seen the SU president coming out alone and slinking away from the site of her ruined plans.

CHAPTER 25

'Miss Kett-Symes, could you possibly dig me out a copy of the correspondence with the Old Schools about—'

The end of the request evaporated, along with everything else in James Rycarte's mind apart from the floating image on the screen in front of him. A quadrant of light like the downbeam from some small alien spacecraft illuminated two connected shapes, one round, the other slightly more ovoid, curling up and round at the end to form a plump comma. There was little definition within the circumference of the shapes, although tantalising craters of dark and light appeared, such as can be seen on the surface of the moon when viewed through a telescope. And, clearly visible in profile at the top of the more circular shape was a tiny triangular nub. His grandson's nose.

When breath returned along with awareness of his surroundings he realised that his secretary was standing at his shoulder, presumably called there by his sudden frozen silence. He still could not wrest his eyes from the screen but addressed her without turning, the words coming only with difficulty.

'My son's baby. His girlfriend, that is, Marie-Laure, she's expecting.'

My grandson. Trying the words out again in his head made them no more real, no less astonishing.

'They've just had the twenty-week scan. It's a boy, apparently.'

He peered at the pocked surface of the larger blob, searching for the clue which would confirm this reputed fact, but could make out nothing to satisfy him. The idea that Miss Kett-Symes might be looking for the same thing brought him back to self-consciousness and he swivelled in his seat and glanced back at her with a sideways smile.

'Sorry. Not that interesting to anyone else. I'm afraid you just caught me off guard there in a moment of fond foolishness.'

But she was not looking at him, she was still staring raptly at the ultrasound image on the screen.

'He's beautiful.'

He coughed; she remembered herself and coughed, too, and he clicked back on to the text of Paul's e-mail. It was very difficult to associate Miss Kett-Symes with maternal longings – still less the more earthy longings which are the normal precursor to maternity. He wondered for the first time how old she might be. Certainly younger than himself; possibly not a great deal older than Martha Pearce, implausible though that might seem. Meanwhile she had backed politely away so as not to be able to see the content of his private correspondence.

'And this is your first grandchild?'

'Yes. There's only Paul, and he hasn't been with Marie-Laure for very long.'

Not long enough, he thought with a fierce possessiveness: not long enough to guarantee that this child would be properly Paul's, properly his. Though of course he knew this to be illogical; there were never any guarantees.

'And they live in France, I believe you said? I expect that seems a very long way away just at the moment.'

It was such a human thing to say. He felt rather moved by her concern, yet pushed the feeling away with a comment which sounded lighter than it really was.

'Oh, in the line of work I had I've grown used to distance from family. Occupational hazard, you know.'

He had too often been too far away from one child; now he was to be too far from another. But France was only a short plane hop away, he reminded himself – Stansted to Lyon in seventy-five minutes. Plenty of people saw their grandchildren only every few months, even when they lived half an hour down the road. Regret about Paul (not to mention the death of his marriage) should not be allowed to cloud his pleasure in this new baby.

'And is there going to be a wedding? I hear the French do marvellous wedding receptions.'

The vision came to him unbidden. Long trestle

tables out in the sun with the mountains as backdrop; female relatives bustling from the kitchen with steaming tureens of *potage* and groaning platters of meats; Marie-Laure's father bringing out bottle after bottle of the wines he had saved for his daughter's special day. Spring, perhaps, with the higher slopes still white above them and the tang of snowmelt lingering behind the warmth of the day; Marie-Laure resplendent in white to match both the snow and the cherry blossom in the orchards clustering around the old stone house, with one of her hands and one of Paul's resting intertwined on her ripe, round belly. The picture was hard to relinquish.

'Er, no, they don't have any immediate plans in that direction. You know how kids are these days. The baby is the priority at the moment.'

She nodded, tutted sympathetically and excused herself, heading back to her own side of the interconnecting door and leaving him to reread Paul's message. Everything was as it should be, everything developing normally, and no problems had shown up. The baby was reportedly of good size – which Paul attributed mainly to the quantities of cheese which Marie-Laure had been consuming.

I have managed to steer her away from the unpasteurised ones a bit better, though, Dad. It's been all Emmental and Beaufort. She has also developed the traditional cravings, mainly

378

one for Chivers Oxford marmalade, after
demolishing that jar you sent us back with.

It was pure Paul and it made him smile throughout but it did not touch upon the one subject which really mattered: the distance not between Cambridge and Lyon but between Lyon and Grésy-sur-Isère.

After reading the e-mail through one last time, he moved it carefully to the saved-messages box. The only printer in the office sat on Miss Kett-Symes's desk; he would wait to print out that magical image in the attachment later, at home. He found he had also lost interest in correspondence with the Old Schools. A more pressing matter demanded his attention this afternoon: that of persuading the Fellowship of the merits of the Alvau donation.

His unexpected success in selling the Pearce Peace Plan to the rebellious junior members in Hall on Saturday night had given him hope that he might be able to convince at least some of their equally rebellious senior counterparts. Whether he could convince a sufficient number to carry the day was another matter. The timetable for his task of persuasion was to some extent an immovable one. Final D-day was the 493rd Governing Body meeting on 4 March and before that, in only just over a week's time on 25 January, he first had to get the principle past the Development Committee. It was the box file containing proceedings of the latter which he lifted down now.

One of Rycarte's guiding principles when it came to corporate governance – first recommended to him by a former director-general of the BBC – was that if there was an argument to be won it was always better to win it before the board meeting began than at the meeting itself. Pick the members off individually in advance rather than risk attempting persuasion in the public forum, where reactions are harder to predict and control. Opening the file, he ran his eye one more time over the membership list for the Development Committee, even though he already had it by heart.

Kate Beasley (already on side: the only Fellow to support the donation by natural inclination); together with Martha and himself that made three bankers. Letitia Gladwin and Ros Clarke: two whom it would be almost impossible to win over. That left Joan Tilley, Maggie Trent and Susie James. Joan was something of an unknown quantity. Her notion of fund-raising was probably the hunger lunch and the bring-and-buy and although there were no doubt principles upon which she would stand and fight, he did not envisage academic purity's necessarily being amongst them. Maggie, the geologist, he had down as a possible. He had spoken to her at High Table both about rocks and about higher education funding; her science and her opinions seemed equally firmly rooted on *terra firma*. But the key to it all, the person who could tip the balance of the committee his way, was surely young Dr James. In an argument about the integrity of admissions, who better to have speaking up from within his camp than the Admissions Tutor – herself also a relatively recent beneficiary of St Radegund's admirable access policies? Since their night out at Portman Road they had not talked about the issue directly again but he sensed her to be at least halfway to being convinced. It was therefore Susie whose knock he was expecting any moment at his office door.

She was late in fact, he realised as he glanced at his watch. Three o'clock, they had arranged, and it was already almost quarter past. There was a limit to how many times he could reconfigure and recalculate the committee maths and when the hurried knock finally came at three twenty-five he was on his feet and at the door with a smile of relief.

'Susie, come in. Good to see you.'

'I'm so sorry,' she began at once, almost cutting through his welcome. 'Really I am – I can't believe I've kept you waiting, only I was over at the Beeches and the chain came off my bike and it took me ages to fix it, but leaving it there and walking or wheeling it back would have taken even longer and I didn't have enough cash for a taxi.'

'Bikes can be as bad as photocopiers, can't they?' he said, solemnly passing her a sympathetic handkerchief with which to mop the worst of the oil from her hands.

She smiled at the shared recollection even while the pink in her cheeks grew pinker. He took one of his armchairs and waved at Susie to take the other; she did so, taking care not to touch any part of it with her hands or arms, which were streaked blackly almost to the elbow. While she resumed her wiping, he queried, 'The Beeches?'

Glancing up and nodding, she launched into a reprise of her earlier apology.

'It's such a long way – right across town – without fixing the bike it would have taken forty-five minutes.'

'Oh, no need to worry about being a little late; not your fault at all. It was just that I didn't know – that is, do you often go and visit Dame Emily?'

The blackened oil did not seem to be shifting despite her best efforts. His predecessor, he felt sure, would have had Vaseline to offer, if not indeed Swarfega – she probably cleaned her trowels with it – whereas his own linen handkerchief, however large and masculine, seemed wholly inadequate for the job.

'Not as often as I always intend – I've been quite bad recently. At the beginning, after it happened I mean, I used to go once a week.'

He hoped the surprise did not register – the ill-matched pairing of the young, northern microbiologist and the venerable Assyrian expert – but perhaps he had not hidden it as well as he intended because she paused in her rubbing.

'Dame Emily was ever so kind to me. Supportive,

you know. When I first arrived, and then when I took over the admissions.'

Martha Pearce's words came back to him: *like a mother to us all* – or perhaps a grandmother in Susie's case, because now she said rather abruptly, 'My nana had a stroke last year, too, a few months before she died.'

Realising what she had said she flushed again and her brow rucked unhappily.

'Not that Dame Emily . . . I don't mean to suggest . . .'

'I know.'

He leaned across and took the handkerchief gently back from her fingers, where she was turning it over and over.

'Sorry, I'm afraid that's not going to come clean now. I think I've ruined it.'

'Forget it. Was she from Sheffield, your grandmother?'

'Yes.'

'Blades fan, like her granddaughter?'

That succeeded in raising the shadows a little from her face.

'She hated football! Hated it with a vengeance. Grandpa used to go, right until he was in his eighties, and Dad and Uncle Geoff as well, and she couldn't stand the way everything in the family had to be fitted round the fixture list. Holidays, trips out, even weddings. Uncle Geoff and Auntie Barbara's reception had to be moved forward because United got through to the FA

Cup semi-final and Nana never let anyone live it down.'

'Under Dave Bassett? In 1993?'

'That's right. Uncle Geoff met Auntie Barbara through a personal ad; they were both in their forties. Nana was furious because she had boiled a ham, a proper one on the bone, and then in the end they just had a brunch and moved to the pub so they could watch the match live from Wembley on the big screen.'

He sighed reminiscently. 'Alan Cork's goal took it to extra time, but United still lost. I watched it in a bar in Rome, and there were one or two United fans in there, and a family of Wednesdayites, too. I don't suppose the result put anybody in a great mood at your uncle's wedding?'

'Well, half of Auntie Barbara's lot turned out to be Owls fans anyway, so there was going to be trouble whatever happened.'

There was a shared moment of insider's laughter.

'And they're still married?

She nodded with a disbelieving shrug. 'Remarkably, in the circumstances.'

Pushing the soiled wreck of his handkerchief into the recesses of his trouser pocket, he judged it time to get down to business.

'Have you any school visits coming up this term?'

'A few, yes. It's the mid-season lull, really. This year's round of applications and interviews dealt with and next year's closing date still ten months away. But we try to keep up the publicity and the communication twelve months a year if we can.'

It was interesting how her diffidence fell away when she began to speak about admissions; her countenance lifted and even the pinkness lessened. He wondered if talking about biology had the same effect.

'I am doing some stuff at the moment targeting younger ones, mainly year elevens. It's all about persuading them to aim high. I'm going to Huddersfield next Thursday to work with some science students; a master class we call it, giving them an idea of what doing science at university will be like.'

It was easy to picture her with the kids, forgetful of herself in her enthusiasm for her subject and her college.

'Then the following week I'm in London, talking at a tertiary college in Hackney. It's an evening thing, with mums and dads as well as the sixth formers themselves.'

'Parents? Is that usual?'

'It's something new I'm trying.' A small crinkle of earnestness appeared above her nose. 'I suppose that with students from traditional Oxbridge backgrounds, parental support is something we have always taken for granted. But with some families, in some areas, you've got to convince the parents as much as the kids that university is a good idea.'

He nodded; waited just long enough before he asked his question, voice neutrally light.

'And I suppose you get questions about cost? From the parents, I mean.'

'Oh, all the time. In fact, I prefer it when they do ask because otherwise I just know they are thinking it anyway. "It's not for us, we can't afford it." At least if they raise the issue I can give them some kind of reassurance. You know, about the little pots we've got where we can find money to help those who run into difficulties.'

Again he made sure not to rush in too quickly, allowing a space to open before he spoke.

'And do you think it would make a difference at these events to be able to say that we have free places to offer at St Radegund's?'

'Well, yes, of course that would be amazing, wouldn't it? Such a fantastic incentive for the kids and such a gesture of good—'

Only then did she break off and look across at him properly, cheeks colouring again and mouth frozen open in mid-word, a caricature of the double-take. The glimpse of rather crooked front teeth, he decided, did not detract from her charm.

'Say, six or eight fully funded places – fees and maintenance.'

She came back to earth sufficiently to close her mouth but she was still staring at him.

'The Alvau money?'

A nod, an interrogative smile – wait for her to do the speaking now. And indeed he had to wait a while, watching sunshine and cloud chase each other across her face. At last she shook her head slowly, so that for a second he feared defeat before he met the beam of soft gratitude in her eyes.

'I think it would make all the difference in the world.'

It was with a step which was almost jaunty that he made his way out of college ten minutes later, taking the path across the Backs and into town, there to purchase half a dozen jars of Chivers original Oxford marmalade, a large quantity of bubble wrap and a roll of brown paper.

Cycling home that evening, Martha was upbraiding herself for having once again failed to find the opportunity of telling James Rycarte that she wouldn't be his Senior Tutor. Mind you, in the light of Saturday night's performance in Hall, he didn't appear to require one at all. Knowing herself, she recognised that the greater his assurance in his position, the less he could rely on what would always be a winning card with her: that of being needed. And yet, the more she saw the new Master in action, the more she had to admit to a feeling that it would be good to be staying and working with him, at least for a little while longer.

For a change the house was already brightly lit as she braked and scooted to a halt on the crumbling concrete of the driveway; the security light did not even trigger at her approach, tripped into daytime mode by the blaze from the front windows. At the back door Maynard burst out

387

through the cat flap only for as long as it took to complete one tight circuit of her ankles before preceding her back inside, leaving the flap banging – a sure sign that warmth and companionship, perhaps even food, awaited within.

'Hello, back already?' Douglas greeted her, without looking up from the paperback he was reading at the kitchen table.

It was in fact almost half past seven, and she saw – or perhaps smelled – that she had been over-optimistic about the food. Yet his words implied neither apology for this fact nor backhanded criticism of her lateness; his mind had evidently just been, as so often, absorbed. She walked across to him and ran one hand up his arm and along the bony ridge of his shoulder, letting her fingers rest there as she bent to see the cause of his distraction. Andrea Camilleri, and not in translation, either. Why did he have to read even detective fiction in Italian, she thought in momentary frustration? Did he imagine it made his idleness somehow more intellectually acceptable?

Withdrawing her hand she went over to the fridge and peered inside; there had been no time to shop since the weekend, however, and she could find nothing there to kindle her creative interest. Carrots needed to be with something; eggs sitting stolidly in their box were just eggs.

'Shall I phone for a takeaway?' she asked.

He looked up without enthusiasm, pressing his lips together and slightly forward in a way she had seen Luigi Alvau doing – surely he couldn't have got that from a book?

'I suppose if there's nothing else . . .'

She concentrated hard on not wishing she had stayed to dine in Hall. 'Indian or pizza?'

'I'm happy either way, but you know Lucia prefers pizza.'

'Lucia?'

Surely she was at work. It was her late shift today.

'Upstairs asleep.'

He jerked his chin towards the hallway and the foot of the stairs.

'What do you mean, asleep? She was meant to be at work five hours ago, wasn't she? Why didn't you wake her?' Then, her puzzlement and irritation pushed out by leaping concern, 'Or is she ill? Is she all right, Douglas? What's happened – what's the matter?'

Finally, with infinite patience, he laid down the Camilleri.

'She's fine, Martha. Stop panicking, OK? She just didn't feel like going in today.'

She opened her mouth to say something, changed her mind, stood gazing at him with hands on hips.

'But she can't just decide not to turn up.'

'Don't worry, she called in sick.'

How could Lucia – how could Douglas – be so cavalier about it? It was a job, not a casual lunch date.

'She'll get the sack if she cries off when she isn't even ill.'

'Oh, relax. What if she does get fired? It won't be the end of the world. It's Qwikmart, for goodness' sake, not the Regius Professorship of Retail Studies.'

Did he think she didn't know that? She struggled to keep her voice from rising, striving to match his blithe composure.

'I know it's hardly the job either of us would have chosen for her.' But it was a job; it was a commitment, a piece of stability, however flimsy. 'She needs . . .'

What did she need? Structure to her life: a raft, perhaps. *A pocket of life-giving oxygen . . . up towards the warming, breathing air.*

'She doesn't know yet what she needs,' he said. 'She's taking the time and space to try to work it out. And she's sure as hell not going to find it out in Qwikmart.'

Maybe he was right; maybe she was placing too much store upon Lucia's having a job. She hovered uncertainly for a moment and then came and took the chair next to her husband's at the table, rubbing wearily at the bridge of her nose.

'Come on,' he said more gently, 'take your coat off, at least. Do you think we'll manage with two large ones between three, if we go for deep pan?'

For some reason, that made the earlier certainty surge back. Lucia was asleep upstairs. Thursday evening at half past seven, and her physically fit seventeen-year-old daughter had slept the afternoon away instead of going to work. She clutched her coat around herself defiantly.

'She might not know what she wants long term, but for now she needs something to get her moving, to get her out of the house. There's no point in sitting staring at a blank computer screen all day.'

'She could read. Reading is the best fuel for a writer.'

Sit and read detective stories like her father, perhaps? Had that fuelled his poetry today, she wondered bitterly, or only served to kill the time before she came home to feed him – like Maynard dreaming his life away beside him on the other chair cushion?

'Yes, she could read; she does read. But without some focus, all the drive dissolves.'

She told her students the same, when they had an essay block: go out to a lecture or even for a walk; you'll be twice as productive when you come back.

'Having a job gives shape to her day.'

But what was the use? They had had this argument twenty times before, round and round with no progress towards resolution. Or she had argued, and he had evaded. He said nothing now, merely surveyed her with an unreadable face. How strange that it had never occurred to her before to wonder, as she did now, whether when they talked like this about Lucia he ever thought she might also be talking about him.

Then his expression softened a little.

'You know, she really didn't feel up to it, not today.'

If this was meant to soothe, it had quite the opposite effect.

'You mean she *is* ill?'

She was back on her feet at once and halfway to the hall before he called her back.

'Not ill exactly . . .'

As his words tailed off she met his eye and the possibility of talking about it – really talking about it properly for once – was tangibly there, palpable in the air between them; she could have reached out and grasped it if she could only make herself say the words. Words which were so easy to use at work, with the students. *Depression*; *diagnosis*; *medication*. But it was too hard. Instead, she saw an easier route; rising and moving over to the computer she booted it up and waited for the working screen to appear and with it the hard disk icon. She was already clicking on it as she called Douglas over.

'Have you read what she has written? Come and see.'

Feeling him arrive at her shoulder, she did not glance round but continued to scroll down and up again through the accumulated files: her own, work and home, neatly sorted and labelled; Douglas's with their cryptic, one-word Italian headings. And nothing else – nothing of Lucia's at all. It was not there.

'I don't understand it. There was something here earlier. A piece she'd written last week, about . . . well, about how she was feeling. If you could have read it you would see. But it seems to have gone.'

She sensed him nodding.

'This afternoon. She deleted all her files before she went up to bed.'

He said it so matter-of-factly, he sounded almost offhand, but she was not entirely deceived. As the screen blurred into the unfocus of tears, she felt the tremor in the hand which settled on her nape, and she recognised the tightness in his voice as he promised her, 'She'll be fine. Now why don't you ring for that pizza?'

'There's got to be a mole,' said Karen.

That evening's meeting of RadFem – attendance at which Martha had considered for barely a moment before pedalling home – had broken up early, when the representative from the English Collective of Prostitutes, invited to speak to the title 'Sex Workers and the Law: Protection or Predation?', had called at the last minute to say that she had a rush on with work and would not be able to make it after all. Karen, Deepa and Ros Clarke were gathered round a small table in the corner of the college bar and conducting an autopsy over the abortive sit-in.

'It's the only explanation. Martha Pearce must have known about our plans in advance, I'm certain of it. Somebody must have tipped her off.'

Deepa eyed her friend doubtfully.

'Well, you know we did look a bit conspicuous with all our stuff. Suyin brought her sleeping bag in just rolled up, not in a bag, not even a bin liner round it or anything, even after what we'd told people. Who takes their sleeping bag with them on a Saturday night out?'

'Martha is a woman of many talents, I'm sure,' replied Karen dryly, 'but I'm not prepared to attribute to her supernatural powers of deduction. From one sleeping bag and a few rucksacks to an occupation of the building – I just don't see it. Besides, she had a book with her.'

'She's an academic!' retorted Deepa. 'They all have books with them all the time. I saw what's-her-name, the Vice-Mistress – Professor Gladwin, you know – reading a commentary on Bede in the checkout queue at Sainsbury's the other day.'

Karen indulged her deputy with a smile but shook her head nevertheless.

'No. I still say we have a mole.'

Ros Clarke, who had been sipping her brandy and dry ginger in thoughtful silence, now threw in her penn'orth.

'I hadn't heard any whispers. Which does rather suggest that nobody on the Fellowship knew – apart from Martha, that is. I normally have my ear pretty close to the ground.'

'Right,' said Karen, rounding on her in triumph. 'So we know that Martha has a tame student informant. And it's got to be somebody close to the Student Union – probably even someone who was at the planning meeting.'

They drank for a few moments without speaking, Karen looking vindictive and Deepa correspondingly uncomfortable, before Dr Clarke shifted the discussion a little.

'So what now? Is the rent strike dead in the water, do you think?'

The two girls exchanged glances and then they both slowly nodded.

'I fear so,' Karen sighed. 'Rycarte seems to have talked pretty well everyone round on Saturday night with his succour-to-those-in-need speech. Support appears to have crumbled more or less completely.'

It was Dr Clarke's turn to nod.

'As I suspected. Kate Beasley has been positively crowing about all the rent cheques she has had in this week. The percentage of accounts still outstanding has apparently fallen away sharply.'

Deepa looked wistfully up over the rim of her Perrier bottle.

'He *was* extremely persuasive. Those things he had to say, it all made a lot of sense. I mean it's true, some of us can afford to pay, can't we, and if resources are stretched . . . ?'

She met Karen's withering gaze and fell quiet.

'You're right, he is persuasive,' conceded Dr Clarke. 'He's a formidable operator, and that's why we need to regroup and consider how best to oppose him next. The rent strike served a purpose for a while but now it's over. The Alvau benefaction: that's the thing. It has always been and still remains the key means by which to thwart and discredit him, to undermine his authority and standing in the college community.'

'Yes!' said Karen.

'Y-yes?' said Deepa.

'I shall, of course, do my best to fight accept-ance of the money through the Development Committee and the Governing Body, but the question is, what can be done at student level?'

She rose from her seat to fetch three more drinks from the bar and by the time she returned Karen had it.

'I'll be her mother,' she announced with a flourish.

'Go on,' said Dr Clarke, pushing her glass of winebox Côtes du Rhône towards her and handing Deepa a second mineral water.

'Well, we always pair up the offer holders with an existing student, normally a first year in their own subject, who makes contact – usually just an e-mail to begin with – and answers any questions they might have about the college and Cambridge in general. So they know someone already when they turn up – you know, feel loved and all that. We call them college mothers.'

Dr Clarke was smiling broadly. 'Very good. And so?'

'And so maybe there won't be enough first year linguists to go round all the offer holders in that subject. As President of the SU, naturally I would consider myself duty bound to step in and fill the gap, wouldn't I?'

'Oh yes, naturally, I agree.'

'But what—' began Deepa. 'I mean, how is that

396

going to help with the argument about her father's money?'

'Oh, who knows?' replied Karen with an expansive sweep of the hand. 'How can we say what little Miss Alvau might reveal, if suitably prompted? About her father's relationship with nice, kind Mr Rycarte. The small favours rendered, the promises made, the strings pulled. It's how things work in Italy, isn't it? I can't believe Rycarte will have managed to remain above it all.'

She took a deep pull at her wine and raised an eyebrow at Dr Clarke.

'I bet we'll discover he's her bloody godfather or something.'

Even Deepa laughed with them at that, and they finished their drinks in relative harmony. But as Ros Clarke rose to leave Karen was heard to mutter, 'I'm still determined to root out that mole.'

And Deepa could not help but picture her, standing motionless and glittering-eyed, poised to strike with the back of her spade.

At three a.m. Martha woke sweating from a dream. Untangling her legs from the cloying twist of sheet, still damp with her fear, she hauled herself up and over to the window; there she threw up the sash to let in a slice of night air, the January chill a sharp recall to reality – then quickly closed it again, mindful of her sleeping husband in the bed.

Pacing her breathing with care, she continued

to stare down into the dark garden, the familiar shapes known even by their murky outlines, charcoal on black. The shed containing Lucia's unused bicycle; the rose bushes surrounding the blotched, uneven lawn, which she should have found time to cut one more time before the winter; the willow tree with the platform on which Douglas had never finished building the promised tree house, and the tyre dangling below on its frayed rope like a hangman's noose. More than fourteen years they had lived in this house, since Lucia was a chubby-legged toddler; their first and only married home, first home of any sort since postgrad digs where they had shared a rented room with the cot.

Time telescoped in on itself, just as it had done in her dream, which came pressing back to superimpose itself on the half-visible garden. In the dream she was not sure whether Lucia was her almost adult self or the child she had been, only that she was Lucia and that she was in the water. She also knew that Douglas was dead – already drowned. But she knew it distantly, the knowledge no longer touching her closely, like something known from long ago, before the first chapter opened, before the first reel began. Martha was in the boat – not so much a life raft as a wooden rowing boat like the ones on the boating lake at Thorpeness where they had holidayed when Lucia was small. Douglas was gone and Lucia was in the water, yet Martha knew that she could save her if only she would turn.

Martha cried out to her. She just needed her to turn and reach out her hand to bridge the small distance to Martha's stretching arms; then she would be safe. At last the dream Lucia did turn; she looked straight at her mother and then away again, her body lying limp and passive in the water, arms flat to her sides. And in her face there was nothing – not the accusation Martha might have expected, nor desperation to reach her, nor hate nor love nor fear, but only a blank, expressionless nothing.

CHAPTER 26

I t was unusual if not quite unprecedented, according to the annals archived in the box file, for the Development Committee to have to take a vote on any item of its business. Being on the receiving end of such small sums as they were able to raise had generally been something about which they could agree to be grateful. Today, however, a division was always going to be inevitable.

Rycarte had pinned Luigi Alvau down to business on the telephone. It had been three months now since the offer had first been placed on the table: time enough even for an Italian to talk figures without the suggestion of *maleducazione*. And the figure in question had not fallen short of expectations: one and a half million euros, which at current conversion rates equated to just a few spare thousand over the million pound mark. In the very next breath, Alvau had raised again the question of his royal progress with Paola and, while the elision of the two matters again gave Rycarte cause for some discomfort, a date for the visit had been fixed for the end of February, shortly before the meeting of the Governing Body.

Sitting down the next day with Kate Beasley and Martha, he had devised a blueprint with them by which this sum could be made to pay for the library renovations and to fund in perpetuity seven full-cost entrance scholarships and twenty rental bursaries. Another call to Rome, the promise of an engraved marble slab let into the wall of the Alvau Library and of annual drinks with the poor but radiantly grateful young recipients of his largesse, and the donor was on side. Next step: to secure the support of the Development Committee.

In the end it was surprisingly unproblematic. Susie James spoke with flush-cheeked vigour in favour of taking the benefaction; Kate Beasley went in punching like a cruiserweight and Martha added her quiet conviction. Joan Tilley turned out to be on the side of the angels, eschewing moral purity for a solid Anglican pragmatism, and, when a judicious Maggie Trent announced herself persuaded forty minutes into the discussion, Rycarte proposed the motion for acceptance, to Kate's emphatic seconding. Hands were duly raised: six ayes and only Letitia Gladwin's steadfast nay.

The rest of the agenda was dispatched in short order and ten minutes later the committee members were issuing into the corridor outside the SCR. Rycarte, who had been waylaid for a moment by Kate about some detail of tax on covenanted giving, hurried to outflank Martha

401

before she made it back to her office, diverting her instead towards his own. Closing the door behind them and turning round, he almost bumped into his secretary who was issuing from her own office with outstretched hands. Such was his levity of mood that he toyed for a second with the idea of seizing them in his, before handing over instead his handwritten notes on the proceedings just concluded for her to type up into minutes.

'No hurry, Miss Kett-Symes. We don't need to circulate them before the end of the week.'

Inclining her head in acknowledgement, she retreated to the other side of the internal door. Had she this morning been wearing, in addition to the green boots and patterned Fair Isle sweater, that matching silk scarf like a daffodil meadow?

Once they were alone he switched to Martha a face of undisguised delight, overlaid with not a little relief.

'Success! Just one short of unanimous. An all but ringing endorsement from the Development Committee to take forward to the full Fellowship. So far so quite unexpectedly good.'

But therein lay the catch, of course: the unexpectedness. Why only one voice against? Why, this day of all days, had Ros Clarke sent her apologies?

'Do you think Ros is really ill or something? She can't have had anything more pressing to do, surely, than to come along and cause trouble?

Do you think she knew the writing was on the wall and would rather not face defeat?'

Even as he uttered them, the words had a hollowly over-optimistic ring. It was not like Ros Clarke to duck a fight, however long the odds against her. Martha's teeth were whitening her lower lip, making him want to bite his own in sympathy; her soft brown eyes spoke concern.

'I'm not sure.'

He eyed her searchingly. There was more there – a warning, perhaps.

'What's her game?' he demanded; then, more gently, 'Martha?'

Her gaze slanted down and away, then back up to his face.

'Well, I honestly don't know, but if I had to make a guess . . . She knew that numbers in the committee were against her. I think she had spoken to Susie; she knew the score as well as we did. But I don't believe she missed the meeting to save face.'

'No.' It was true: there had to be more to it, 'So why, then?'

'To keep her powder dry for Governing Body.'

He did not like the sound of that at all, but he waited quietly for her to explain.

'The St Rad's convention is for the members of a college committee, once a decision has been reached, to stand together behind that decision. A version of collective responsibility, if you like. Having had their say at the committee stage and been outvoted, it is not usual for them to speak out against the agreed view when it comes to the larger forum.'

'I see.' He blew out his cheeks, letting the air escape in a slow deflating hiss. 'So by not being here today, she has escaped being implicated in the committee's decision – reserved her position, saved her fire for the bigger stage? Not having been present in Cabinet, so to speak, she can oppose the motion on the floor of the House?'

She nodded unhappily. 'That's more or less it.'

In spite of himself, he was entertained once again by the quirkish formalism of this place.

'No room in the procedure for the registering of a dissenting judgement, then? No separate minuting of majority and minority views?'

Smilingly she shook her head. 'All for one and one for all.'

'In which case,' he realised, brightening further, 'that means Letitia Gladwin won't feel free to speak against the gift at Governing Body. She has already said her piece in Development Committee and now must hop on board with the majority.'

'I'm certain that Letitia will respect today's vote, yes.'

Often, amusement was just below the surface with Martha, but not today, it seemed. In fact she looked so gravely serious that he found he wanted to embrace her, to twirl her round the room and shake her into laughter. He wanted to make her stay and talk a while, maybe sit her down and show her the ultrasound photograph of Paul's baby which he carried in his wallet. Instead, he merely thanked her earnestly for her advice and let her go – hoping it wasn't male vanity which prevented him from showing a very attractive woman of forty-one the evidence that he was about to become a grandfather.

Taking down the Development Committee box file he carefully clipped today's agenda back into its place. Replacing it on the shelf, he then selected the Governing Body file, turned to the complete membership list which was glued inside the front cover and picked up a pencil. It seemed to him that this afternoon he might have won a preliminary skirmish, but his enemy had escaped with minimum casualties and withdrawn to secure the commanding ground for the final battle.

The reason Martha did not feel much like laughing that afternoon despite the victory in the Development Committee had nothing to do with her own scruples about the Alvau donation; having decided to back the gift for the sake of James Rycarte and the college unity which only his defeat of Ros Clarke could hope to secure, she had put all personal doubts and misgivings behind her. It had to do, rather, with Lucia.

She had gone home at lunchtime: a rare event, necessitated by her having forgotten to bring with her to work that morning the draft chapter she had been reviewing for one of her PhD students and which she was due to discuss with the author later that afternoon. She had thought the house empty. Calling through to Douglas in the sitting room and upstairs to no reply, she concluded that he was out who knows where. Lucia, she knew, was working the ten 'til six shift. Even Maynard was not at his post to greet her at this unexpected hour.

On impulse, wandering up the stairs just to check in case Douglas was asleep on their bed, she decided to look into Lucia's room. It was an occasional surreptitious pleasure of hers, when alone in the house: to go in and sit on the bed and inhale her daughter's scent on the sheets. She never tidied; nor did she pry – would hate, indeed, the idea that Lucia might for one moment view it that way – but simply took a quiet delight in running her eye over the visible evidence of her daughter's rumpled, lived-in life. Recently, of course, in these last difficult months, the delight was somewhat tarnished, so that if anything the pain was greater than the pleasure, but still she liked to go in and sit down amidst the muddle. It was a reaffirmation of connection, a touching of base; had she analysed it at all, she would have said that it had become almost a reflex, like Douglas's Aunt Frances silently fingering for reassurance the rosary at her wrist.

Pushing open the door, she did not at first notice the hummock beneath the candy-striped duvet, which Lucia often left bunched up or wildly strewn on her eruption from the bed. Nor did she open the curtains, it being her habit to touch nothing on these clandestine visits, and so she found herself sitting down next to Lucia almost before she registered her presence.

'Mum?' said the duvet. The voice was gravelly with recent sleep and wholly lacking in animation, whether of surprise, guilt or affront.

'Lucia – are you OK? You know it's almost one o'clock? I thought you were meant to start work at ten today?'

The pause which followed this stretched out so far that Martha almost began to wonder whether her daughter had sunk back into sleep. Her own thoughts began to drift, so that when the answer came the meaning did not at first register.

'I've left.'

'What?'

'Qwikmart. I've left the job.'

Martha surveyed the striped hump in dismay. *Why didn't you tell me?* But she knew why not. *You'd only have gone ballistic, Mum.* And it was right: she probably would have, wouldn't she? She wanted to now; shouting would have done her good, but only temporarily. Instead she searched for something she could safely ask.

'What did they say?'

A movement from the duvet which was manifestly a shrug.

'Not a lot.'

'It's been barely six weeks, love.'

The endearment was insufficient to disguise the note of complaint which she could not entirely suppress.

A silence; the body under the duvet lay rigid. Then a hand appeared and a forearm, swathed in the sleeves of two different-coloured cardigans despite the central heating and the bedclothes. An edge of duvet flipped back; Lucia's eyes surfaced, their expression a brick wall.

'Dad didn't mind.'

'Dad?'

Martha's voice sounded as though it was coming from somebody else, somebody with a painfully constricted chest.

'Yeah. I told him last week.' Lucia's tones were flat and unantagonistic.

'Last week?'

At this there was a mirthless giggle which did nothing to ease the tension in the room.

'You sound like a parrot, Mum.'

Martha could barely raise an answering smile, but pressed ahead, determined to pick the scab and expose the wound.

'What did he say, exactly?'

She watched as the shutter of defensive loyalty came down in Lucia's eyes. They were allies, father and daughter; it was futile to attempt to divide them. Once again the words formed themselves unbidden in her head. Corrosion; atrophy.

'Where is he now, do you know?'

But even that question was a step too far into

the protective zone which was cast about the two of them. The hand drew back beneath the duvet, which nudged upwards over Lucia's nose.

'I'm tired.'

It was a dismissal, a pushing away which she felt like the screw of a fist in her gut. Why then, before she left the room to set off back to college, did she lean down and straighten the duvet, tucking it in around her daughter as she had done when she was six years old?

That evening, on a secluded bench by the tennis courts on the boundary between St Radegund's and neighbouring Robinson College, Darren and Julia sat entwined together, kissing and kissing and kissing. It was odd, reflected Darren, that after all those weeks of being so reluctant to be kissed, Julia now seemed to want to do nothing else.

It was not that they didn't talk.

'Are your lips sore?'

'Not really.'

He kissed her some more.

'They taste sore.'

'It's the cold. It's nothing – I don't care.'

Having first embarked upon the activity out of doors, it occurred to neither of them to go anywhere else for the purpose; or at least it seemed not to have occurred to Julia, so Darren did not like to propose moving to an indoor location, which might have been taken as suggesting more than was intended. And this was an excellent spot for it. They were largely concealed by overgrown planters and nobody was likely to come here anyway. The red of the all-weather Novacrylic was rimed to a treacherous mauvish pink, deterring play; besides which, it was usually dark. Even on nights like tonight when the fenland chill was sharp and clear, seeming to descend from the stars rather than rising damply from the river as it so often did, they created their own microclimatic fog by the mutual exchange of heated breath.

'Your face is always more prickly later at night,' said Julia presently.

'I shave in the mornings, that's why.'

'Mmm,' she murmured, so that he felt the slight vibration of her mouth against his.

Pulling away a little, he asked, 'Does it bother you?'

She gave her answer consideration.

'No. No, I like the contrast. Your lips feel rough on the outside and then smooth and soft inside.'

'I hope it's not that which is making your lips sore. I could take my razor to work, I suppose, and shave in the evening, before I leave the lab.'

'Wouldn't Jefferson think it a bit strange?'

It was said with a giggle, which meant he had to kiss her again. Their hands were buried inside each other's coats for warmth and both of them were content with that for now, making no attempt to delve further beneath the muffling layers of clothing.

'Thank you,' she said suddenly, surprising him

with the divergence of their thoughts. 'About the sit-in. For not saying anything, I mean.'

He rubbed his smile over her cheek.

'What happened, exactly, in the end? I never heard the story properly – didn't like to go back and ask Martha.'

'Well, it basically just fizzled out, I think. Karen was spitting blood. I gather Martha just sort of sat there so they couldn't begin properly at all, and then the Master came along, too, and talked to them and stuff. Now the whole rent strike seems to have died a death.' She nuzzled his chin. 'I'm glad you didn't have to get involved.'

'Well, um, of course I would have done . . . I could have done but, you know, I didn't want to risk anything that might lead back to you.'

A few minutes later he broke the silence again.

'Your nose feels cold. Are you cold?'

'No, I'm fine. The cold is nice.'

'Your mouth still tastes sore.'

It was the combination of wet lips and the chilly night air. Saliva must be particularly damaging, he hypothesised; salivary amylase digested protein, didn't it? Probably it attacked the surface of the chapped skin, exacerbating the soreness.

'Maybe we ought to stop kissing.'

'Oh no, please let's not. Not yet.'

Behind the planters Anna Axelsson, sprinter and high hurdler for the Cambridge University athletics team, crouched with a camera and tried not to listen. She wanted to join the Tigresses because she enjoyed a drink – and with her near six foot frame she could take a good few without much adverse effect – but she did not share Karen's vindictive desire to 'out' the Dean. She had only run into Darren Cotter on a couple of occasions, but had always found him completely inoffensive; she had even noticed that he had kind eyes. What did it matter if he was gay? She was fairly catholic in her own preferences, if it came to that, favouring a lean and muscular body but not hidebound by narrow constraints: she liked sex and was not bothered about gender. In any case, it seemed that Karen had got it wrong, because the second person on the bench was definitely female. Her voice, in fact, was decidedly familiar. Wasn't she one of the SU executive, the attractive, curly brunette?

Parting the scratchy twigs of firethorn and ceanothus, Anna peered into the darkness beyond. Faintly lit by starlight and a sliver of crescent moon were the commingled figures, Darren and what's-her-name, Judy or Julie. It was going to be difficult to disguise the flash, but impossible to get any kind of shot without it. Maybe if she waited until their mouths were locked again, which by every appearance could not be long. The girl, at least, had her eyes closed, though his she caught glinting, open and fixed myopically upon his companion's face. Seizing her moment, she depressed the button, holding her breath at the click and whirr, the momentary effusion of light . . . then

412

releasing it again in a soft sigh. They were still imperviously joined. Rearranging the branches with care, she backed away from the planter, pocketing her camera in some satisfaction. She had the picture which would make her a Tigress. What she did not know was that she might at the same time inadvertently have unearthed Karen's mole.

CHAPTER 27

Having the members of the Development Committee in the bag – with the none too honourable exception of Ros Clarke – James Rycarte spent most of the short, cold days of the short, cold month of February working his way outwards into the Fellowship as a whole in methodical swaths, courting hearts and minds. At times he was reminded of a hand-operated lawnmower he had owned when he was first married, handed down from an uncle of his wife's; it was the kind which had neither electric motor nor petrol engine to assist operations, working entirely on force of muscle, and the blades were crooked and awkward to keep sharpened. Frequently he would lay the small back lawn into beautiful, even stripes of paler and darker green and be putting the mower back in the shed when the grass began to spring stubbornly up again, a little thinner and more raggedy, perhaps, but basically as long as before. The St Radegund's Fellowship was much the same: he would think one group converted, only to find that the next day or the next week the same dons were opposing the Alvau benefaction as vocally as before.

'The benefits the donation will bring in terms of access seem impossible to argue against,' Warsha Ramachandra had conceded only last week after dinner, while Carolyn Gallagher nodded sagely. Yet five days later at lunch he had overheard the two of them doing exactly that on either side of poor Susie James, restating in most emphatic terms the case for keeping the admissions process tightly immured from the contamination of parental giving.

The reason, he strongly suspected, was that as fast as he could make the grass lie flat, Ros Clarke was going round after him standing it up again – though she managed to do so invisibly, so that he was never able to glimpse the imprint of her hands upon the resurrected opinions which she left behind. He did, though, have the solace of knowing that Martha Pearce was actively enlisted, wielding a pair of shears on his side. On one recent occasion Adeola Onoge, the new Research Fellow in African literature, had been sitting with Dr Clarke at dinner and he had been sure she was lost to the cause, but he had subsequently seen her talking to Martha over coffee and before the end of the evening she had come up to him with the open promise of her support.

He had photocopied the list of members of the Governing Body and taken it home with him; every night, propped up amongst Dame Emily's sprigged and ruffled pillows, he checked up and down the names again, totting and retotting the fors, againsts and undecideds. It was going to be a close-run thing, of that there was no doubt, but slowly and inexorably he sensed that the tide of opinion was turning in his favour. And whichever way you looked at it, the point of make or break was bound to be the visit of Luigi and Paola at the end of the month.

He said as much, for approximately the tenth time, to Martha one morning over coffee in her office.

'It could be the thing that clinches it for us, I really think it could. Or it could be a complete disaster.'

Frequent repetition of his first inopportune incursion seemed to have cured the Senior Tutor of her scruples about his visiting her on her own ground, and he had fallen into the habit of doing so regularly at an hour when he could be sure of coffee; she had even ceased to apologise for its being instant, and was far too courteous to allow him the slightest suspicion of all the more urgent things he was certain she ought rather to have been doing.

'It is our big opportunity, I'm certain of it, if we can only play it to full advantage. The donor himself, come to work his silver-tongued persuasion upon the floating vote.'

Her face was partially averted, spooning Nescafé into the crested dragon mugs, but he could read her amused scepticism of the efficacy of his friend's Latin charm. *Not all women are as inviolable as you though, Martha.* He recaptured a picture of Joan Tilley preening like a flattered schoolgirl on Alvau's previous visit, and Susie James pinkening more than was usual even for her.

416

'Certainly it will help if he comes here and shows that he has a genuine commitment to the cause of wider access which his money is to support,' conceded Martha, handing him a brimming mug with the handle towards him. Didn't the hot china burn her fingers, which spanned the mug delicately just below the rim? For the first time in longer than he could remember he thought with a tender pang of his mother, whose hands had also been seemingly immune to heat, at least until the last few years, when her skin retreated into papery frailty. The connection was a disorientating one.

'Um, yes, he will need to do that, certainly. Oh yes, I think we can rely upon him to say the right things.'

There was a touch of bravado about these last words, however; he knew the Italian well enough to recognise that he was far from guaranteed to stick to his script. And then there was the girl. He took a large, scalding sip and winced.

'The problem might be Paola. Susie tells me that offer holders rarely visit before they have an unconditional place confirmed – before their exam results are out, I mean. And she doesn't even sit hers until June.'

Martha looked at him evenly through the steam from her own mug.

'But that is because of not wishing to whip up expectations too much. To protect the candidate – not for any other reason. And actually, there might be much to be said for the opposite policy, in terms of sharpening offer holders' incentives.'

Returning her gaze with equal steadiness, he told her what she must already know.

'It doesn't matter what the reason is in other cases. The fact remains, they don't usually visit when they still have exams to get through. It may look . . . presumptuous.'

How could it not, in the circumstances, give the appearance of chickens already inappropriately counted?

She nodded, not denying the truth of this. 'It will certainly make a difference how Paola comports herself – the things she says – just as much as the father.'

And the daughter's conduct was surely even further beyond their power to control.

Martha had taken off her spectacles to avoid misting from the steam of the coffee, laying them on the arm of her chair, and he was grateful for the unencumbered view of her face – largely, but perhaps not exclusively, the better to read her thinking. Small lines of deliberation had etched themselves between her eyebrows and her gentle, dark eyes were withdrawn in thought.

'I suppose as Senior Tutor it might be possible for me to write to her,' she said slowly, her frown crinkling deeper. 'I do periodically have contact with those holding conditional offers, about accommodation and so on. I could send out a letter via the tutorial office.'

It was evident, though, from the way she was peering down critically at her mug, that she was far from happy with this solution.

'But what would I say? What possible way in could there be to warning her about how she behaves when she comes here?'

Not wishing to interrupt her contemplations, he merely sipped his coffee in silence.

'There is always her college mother,' she suggested at length. 'It's rather early, of course – there may well be nobody allocated to her yet. But I could have a word with Karen and see whether something could be arranged. Only because she is going to be visiting, you understand – to provide a bit of friendly contact before she arrives.'

He saw his smile reflected in her eyes, which were back with him now and dancing.

'And the person concerned might be suitably sympathetic about the difficulties of coming to look round when she is still uncertain of her place here?' he hazarded, sitting back in his chair with his mug between his palms.

'She might indeed – especially if I were to speak to her beforehand about Paola's awkward position, and the danger of raising her hopes too high prematurely.'

'Quite right. False hopes can prove so cruel, can't they?' He grinned wolfishly. 'As with that packet of chocolate digestives on the table there, for instance. I am sure it will turn out to be empty, dashing every wishful expectation.'

Nor could he quite regret occasioning her discomfiture, so delicious was the apologetic smile which she offered him along with the belated biscuit.

Meanwhile, Paola Alvau's self-appointed mother had had very little joy from her protégée, at least in the way of hoped-for incriminating material. The young Italian had not so much as mentioned James Rycarte, in fact, so that finally in her third e-mail, following detailed discussion of lecture timetables, sports facilities and kettles, Karen decided to refer to him herself. When the mere allusion to his name evoked no response, in her fourth e-mail (the two of them would soon be bosom buddies at this rate) she asked the question directly.

> *Mr Rycarte is an old friend of the family, is that right? It must be very nice to know that you are coming to study in a place where the Master is so close to your father. Home from home, in a way. And you'll always know that if you lack for anything, you can be certain of a sympathetic hearing from him. I'm sure he could fix anything for you, if you only asked.*

The reply left her even more frustrated than before.

> *I suppose it is good, as you say, to know that Sr Rycarte knows my father. But, you know,*

Karen, I haven't actually seen him since I was two or three years old. I think he worked here in Rome with British television at that time, and he did come to the house. It was when my mother was alive. But I cannot say that I even remember what he looked like.

That evening she flapped a print-out of the offending e-mail at Deepa with one hand, pouring blue curaçao into a large saucepan with the other.

'Can't even remember him, she reckons! But that doesn't matter, does it, not in Italy? A family friend is still a family friend.'

They were in Karen's room, the scheduled venue for that night's meeting of the St Radegund's Tigresses, and over at the hand basin Deepa was rinsing and drying every receptacle of Karen's out of which it was conceivable to drink a cocktail. She giggled and put on a most unlikely New York Sicilian drawl.

'You're my brother and I love ya. But don't ever take sides with anyone outside da family again.'

Karen grinned, set down the empty liqueur bottle and slipped an arm round her friend's waist.

'We'll catch them out, somehow, don't you worry. Even Mr Squeaky Clean James Rycarte can't be that bloody incorruptible. Have we got enough glasses and stuff here, do you think? We're expecting a pretty big turnout. I could text Sal and Josh and ask them to bring some more with them when they come.'

'Might be best.'

While Karen rummaged on the desk for her mobile phone, Deepa wiped thoughtfully with her tea towel at the encrusted interior of the last mug.

'Maybe you'll be able to dig up some dirt when she comes over.'

'What?'

Karen whirled round so suddenly that her mobile flew from her grasp, luckily landing on the bed with a cushioned thud.

'What do you mean, when she comes over?'

'When Paola Alvau comes to college to look round, with her father,' said Deepa; then, in the face of Karen's continued stupefied silence, 'Sorry, I thought you knew. I heard Martha talking about it. Of course I'd have told you, but I assumed she'd have mentioned it in her e-mails.'

'So . . .?'

She retrieved her phone but did not look at it.

'This is fantastic. Isn't her offer still conditional? It has to be, she's still at school, she was talking about working for her exams. The *Maturità* or something, she calls it.'

Setting down the mug with the others on the coffee table, Deepa eyed her doubtfully.

'So what? I mean, of course that means she isn't definitely in yet. But what do you intend to do about it?

'But don't you see? This is brilliant. Just as you say, she isn't even really in yet, and here's good old Uncle James having her and Daddy over to case the joint as if they already owned it. It looks really bad.'

'I suppose so.'

'Never mind "suppose". It definitely looks dodgy from where I'm standing. And it will look even worse if darling Paola seems to be assuming that her exam results are just a formality, won't it?'

She tapped the back of her mobile playfully against Deepa's shoulder.

'If, for example, she had been led to believe that academic conditions for entry are not treated very seriously by the college? If she thought that her place was as good as assured, whatever her scores in the Maturiwhatsit? She might give a really unfortunate impression, mightn't she?'

'You wouldn't.'

'Just watch me.'

'But . . .' Deepa's almond eyes were serious now, searching the SU president's face. 'That could be awful, couldn't it? If you really make her think St Rad's will take her even if she messes up her exams. It's not true, is it? Just think – what if she stops working or something, assuming she'll be OK regardless?'

Karen laughed, but Deepa's fine features hardened.

'You can't do that to her,' she insisted.

'Oh, lighten up,' flung out Karen, albeit sounding a little less comfortable. 'It's all in a good cause, remember? We want to get rid of that man, don't we? And why the sympathy for little miss rich girl all of a sudden? Don't you care if Rycarte is selling places here to the highest bidder?'

'Well, you know that isn't exactly what—'

'Yeah, yeah,' Karen interrupted. 'I've heard all the fine distinctions they like to make. But it comes down to the same thing: Daddy's money, Paola's good luck. Anyway, they'll be here soon – let's get the rest of these drinks mixed. And where are those crisps you bought?'

So they opened bags of ready salted and emptied bottles of gin and lemonade and Galliano into bowls and pans until the silence grew slightly less abrasive. Karen said something appeasing about the way Deepa had put up her hair and, when they discovered that they had forgotten to buy the blackberry brandy, Deepa made a joke about how it would have to be not so much Tequila Sunset as just plain Tequila Teatime and the argument was forgotten.

Grinning malevolently, Karen stirred a mixing bowl containing a high octane gin-based concoction of her own invention.

'Maybe we should call this one Dean's Downfall.'

Although with some reticence, Deepa joined in the laughter. Tonight's list of invitees included Anna the Swedish sprinter but it still did not include Julia. Very much not, in fact. From its place tucked inside her e-mail from Paola Alvau, Karen now drew out her print of Anna's covert snap of Darren Cotter, the back of his bent head not quite concealing the pale, smooth forehead and curly hair of his partner in crime, appropriately talpine in its dark glossiness. Karen glowered down at the perfidious villainess and her hapless consort.

'I wonder how Laura and Katie are getting on with the new task,' she mused.

The Tigresses' initiation test had changed for the second time this term. Aspiring entrants were no longer enjoined to produce proof of the object of the Dean's dalliance, but instead to uncover evidence which would incriminate the pair of them. Such was Karen's vengeful fury against the mole and her man that it would be satisfied by nothing less than public scandal and humiliation.

'I know they're at it. It's disgusting. I mean, she's only a second year, for God's sake. And he must be getting on for twenty-five!'

Rather like some glum, semi-hibernating mammal, Lucia had spent increasing portions of February asleep. It was a source of amazement to Martha, who rarely got the chance of more than six or seven hours a night, how her daughter could pass up to sixteen hours of the twenty-four not only curled up in bed but actually unconscious. Douglas, however, was neither perturbed nor unduly surprised.

'Why shouldn't she, while she's got the chance? Lucky girl, I say. Very pleasant way to spend your time.'

425

'But it doesn't seem natural, somehow,' Martha persisted. 'She's young. She ought to have more energy than this, surely?'

He looked up at her from his copy of *Poetry Now*.

'Don't worry about it so much. It's winter, isn't it? In winter our ancestors slept far more than we do today. It was dark half the time; there wasn't so much work to do on the land. Staying indoors and sleeping conserves heat and energy. So, "natural" is exactly what it is, I'd say. Much more natural than you, with your alarm going off at five thirty every morning when it won't be light for hours.'

Martha gnawed her lower lip and gazed at him, nursing the tea towel and wishing she were convinced. Sometimes she looked back with regret to the golden days of autumn when her daughter had been awake and merely tearful.

'Besides,' announced Douglas, closing his magazine decisively, 'the human body is self-regulating. It takes only the amount of sleep it needs. If she weren't tired, she would wake up.'

With that he left the kitchen and Martha in it, dearly wanting to believe him.

It was almost nine o'clock on a Sunday evening and, to her certain knowledge, Lucia had been asleep at least since four when she herself had returned home from sorting out a student's small personal crisis in college. She had slept through the time it took for Martha to prepare Monday's

426

lecture and write a paper for the University's senior tutorial working party on undergraduate finances, as well as cooking and eating the roasted vegetable bake which she and Douglas had just shared, before he opened *Poetry Now* and she mentioned her fears to him as she did the washing up. If she didn't wake her now, thought Martha with her hundredth glance at her watch, then before long it would be bedtime anyway; she would end up sleeping round the clock, and she wouldn't have had anything to eat. Surely she must eat, at least: admittedly she had done nothing to give her an appetite, but where could she hope to get energy from if she didn't eat?

Preparing a tray as she remembered her own mother doing when she was sick in bed as a child, with a bright linen napkin serving as a tray cloth, she spooned some of the leftover vegetable bake on to a plate, taking care to lay it with the crunchy cheese and breadcrumb topping uppermost; next to it she arranged a few leaves of lettuce and some radishes from the salad crisper. Lucia had always loved radishes, seduced by their cherry skin and noisy crunch even at an age when to like them was bordering on the deviant. A glass of cranberry and apple juice from the fridge, with the addition of a couple of cheerfully clinking ice cubes, joined the plate on the tray; she searched in the back of the cutlery drawer for the pink elephant's trunk straw Lucia had brought home from an eighth birthday party, but the effect smacked too much of desperation. Her own mum even used to include a flower from the garden in an empty glass meat-paste pot, when she was trying to coax Martha back into eating after the measles. Her smile at the recollection faded fast as she wondered whether Mum was managing to get her meals all right. From what Mrs MacDonald had said on the phone last week, Lucia might not be the only one to be mixing night with morning and forgetting about food.

'She's had a bit of a bad spell recently. Doesn't know if she's coming or going some days, poor lady,' she had told Martha, in one of the regular bulletins she had been prevailed upon to supply. 'On Tuesday she was in her nightie at half past twelve gone when I arrived, and worrying that there was no Weetabix. Just as well, really, because I know for a fact that the milk in the fridge was a week past its sell-by date; I poured it down the sink, later, while she was cleaning her teeth.'

Right now, though, it was her daughter who monopolised her worries as Martha climbed the stairs with the laden tray. No need to bypass the squeaky step; Lucia would have slept through pneumatic drilling on the stairs lately. She knocked, regardless, and shouldered her way in sideways with the tray. The room was not quite in darkness but pooled with dull sodium orange from beyond the undrawn curtains. And what struck her like a warm, wet flannel was the heat; the radiator must have been turned up to maximum all day.

'Lucia?'

She laid down the tray and found the radiator knob, screwing it clockwise as far as it would go. She would have liked to open the window, too, to let in a cleansing buffet of frosty night air.

'Lucia, love?' she tried again, but there was no reaction from the bed.

She sat down beside the sleeping shape of her daughter and gently drew back the duvet from over her hunched head. It was her winter duvet, a plump fifteen tog, but underneath Lucia was fully dressed as though for the outdoors, her baggy blue fleece revealing a glimpse of Aran sweater at the neck. Jeans, probably, too, if she had lifted the duvet far enough to see. Was her daughter's constant perception of cold a symptom of her psychological malaise, Martha wondered, or merely a side effect of inactivity? Either way, her balled-up and padded form reinforced the image of hibernation. Suddenly weary, Martha felt it would have been a relief to lie down with Lucia on the bed and pull the duvet up over both their heads, shutting out the world. But the supper on the tray was going cold, and she had come to make her daughter eat.

'Lucia,' she said again, gently rocking at the shoulder nearer to her. And then harder, shaking now; Lucia's eyes did not open but her body texture changed, the tension which seeped into her relaxed muscles telling her mother she was awake.

'I've brought you up something to eat,' she said

quietly. 'Dad and I have eaten already, and we thought you might be hungry.'

She heard what she had said and the disingenuousness of it: she knew Lucia was anything but hungry, and there was also that 'we'.

Nothing.

'It's that bake you like with the aubergines and peppers and the melted cheese on top.'

Then, too anxious to stop herself from pleading, 'Go on, love. I'm sure you'll feel better for it.'

Finally the duvet flipped back and she met, finally, a dull spark in her daughter's eyes which could have been anger, or at least frustration.

'Feel better, you reckon?'

'Well, of course I can't know how you feel, love. I don't mean that. But I do think that maybe if you got up and ate something. Maybe go out for a walk, even, to clear your head. You might sleep better for it tonight.'

Stupid, again. The one thing Lucia had no trouble with at all was sleeping. Her remark received the silence it deserved.

'Maybe we could go for a walk together. I'd like to get outside, too; I've been working most of the day.'

And that was wrong, too, wasn't it? Her bloody work, always her bloody work. Maybe she should just sit here and not say anything for a while. Maybe that would help – just being here. Lucia's eyes had closed again, and Martha straightened the duvet over her, letting her trailing fingers linger and rest where it covered her daughter's arm. She shut her own eyes, fighting the urge to lie down which came over her again. With closed lids she did not feel at once the prickle and burn as the tears began, not until the first slow gouts crept out to wet her lashes, making her grateful at least for the partial darkness.

'Go 'way, Mum.'

The knife blade words were twisted home more than they were softened by the apologetic exhaustion in Lucia's tone as she added, 'Please.'

Back down in the kitchen, with Maynard's weight against her chest providing a modicum of surface comfort, she allowed the tears to fall in earnest. Douglas must still be somewhere in the house; she could hear no movement but a light from the sitting room had registered distantly as she crossed the hall. She didn't seek him out, though, not yet; for the moment the blame she wished to cast was directed entirely against herself.

She had let things slip and slide away from her – had let her daughter slide away. Into the tangling, downward-tugging weed, beyond her reaching arms. And why? Why had she not grasped the problem sooner, taken steps to shake her daughter free of the smothering pull of her depression? Why hadn't she made an appointment with the GP, got Lucia to a therapist or on to some suitable drug treatment regime? Why hadn't she taken her in hand and forced her to stay at school and keep plugging at her A levels, while between them she and the doctors helped her to fight her way back up to the light? She knew why, knew it perfectly well if only she could make herself look it in the face. It was guilt: her own stupid, selfish guilt, serving nobody, damaging her daughter as much as herself. Guilt for all the evenings and weekends when she had been in college or at the computer keyboard when she should have been helping Lucia with her homework, or painting her toenails and hearing about her petty fallings-out at school, or discussing a movie they had watched together on TV. Those opportunities were gone; it was too late to retrieve them now. Tiptoeing around Lucia as she had done this last year would not bring those chances back; colluding in her drift away from schooling would not erase the tyranny which her own academic life had imposed upon her daughter. The past could not be helped: why was she allowing it to poison present and future, too?

Seized with determination to tackle things squarely for once, she put Maynard down on a chair and went through into the sitting room. Her husband's socked feet, propped on the nearer arm of the sofa, all but obscured the recumbent remainder of him, though not the trailing hand which caressed the bottle of wine they had opened to accompany supper, now standing empty on the carpet. Her anger suddenly switched direction, flaring up against Douglas, inveterate sidestepper of uncomfortable truths. Those few times that she had tried to circle in on the issue of Lucia and her state of drift, hadn't he always headed her off with easy platitudes? What was he doing about anything now? Drinking, of course. And using as an excuse for inactivity the gestation of poetry she could not read and which would doubtless never see the light of day.

She moved round to the front of the sofa, brushing off the last of her tears and bunching up her arguments into a tight fist. His eyes were not closed as she had anticipated, as they generally were when he was 'writing'. Open on his stomach was his laptop, from which he looked up at her approach. Something akin to amusement played around his mouth and he lifted one eyebrow inquiringly.

'He's your man, isn't he, Luigi Alvau? The television bloke.'

The transverse leap was so unexpected that Martha, as so often with her husband, was completely knocked off her stride, her gathered resolution all dispersed.

'Y-yes.'

'James Rycarte's *caro amico*, who is going to save St Radegund's?'

'Yes – why?'

'Because I think maybe you ought not to be counting on him too much after all.'

CHAPTER 28

In the lodging the next morning Rycarte broke the first two articles of the computer officer's catechism, checking his e-mails with a cup of espresso in one hand and a slice of buttered toast in the other. Fifteen unread messages, of which, amongst the routine and the vexatious, two caught his eye. One from Paul: a long, conversational ramble more than filling the text window which, having opened and scrolled briefly through, he closed again to save as a treat with his mid-morning coffee. The second was from Luigi Alvau: short and unconversational, verging upon the cryptic.

> *My dear friend,*
> *I am very much afraid that Paola and I shall not, after all, be in a position to visit your hallowed halls as arranged next week. Please never doubt however that, whatever the supervening circumstances and with the gods of business brotherhood on my side, I intend to honour in full the pledges that I have made in your regard.*

434

Wish me buona fortuna,
Luigi

He was still frowning in puzzlement at the screen when the telephone rang across in the hallway. Without closing the e-mail he went out and picked up the receiver, barking gruffly, 'Rycarte.'

'Look, I'm really sorry to disturb you so early – I would have rung last night but it was late – I didn't want you to go over into college without knowing.'

His tone warmed at once. 'Martha. Not at all – no, not early at all.'

The note of apology – or was it apprehension? – did not leave her voice, however.

'I'm afraid it's about Sr Alvau.'

For an instant he was more startled than he was concerned or curious. How on earth could she know?

'Well, of course it's a shame he won't be coming now before the Governing Body meeting, but it was always going to be potentially awkward with Paola.'

A moment of hesitancy at the other end of the line.

'So you've heard, then? Silly of me – I sometimes forget you were a journalist. You'll have seen the wires.'

Now it was his turn for confusion.

'Wires?' he repeated witlessly.

'Yes, that's where I heard about it. Well, in a

435

manner of speaking. Douglas – my husband – was browsing the Italian news networks on the internet.'

'Heard about it?'

He knew he was sounding like a particularly doltish mynah bird, but could really think of nothing else to say.

'Yes. His name popped up in the list of those arraigned, you know.' As soon as she said it, it was as if he had always known – it just had to be, didn't it? He almost wanted to laugh, if he could have trusted it not to emerge as a howl. Martha was still talking, anxiously, appeasingly, but he did not require her explanations in order to see it all: the latest round of corruption trials, the high profile arrests, the determination to root out and put to public shame another layer of Berlusconi's former cronies, unprotected now that their political godfather was no longer hand in glove with the judiciary. The ministers, the civil servants, the financial backers – and the media sympathisers. Irregularities, backhanders, plain and simple fraud. Luigi – *Luigi*. It was a disappointment – a crushing blow, in personal and in college terms – but hardly a surprise. Wasn't it Alvau himself who had once assured him, only half in jest: to Italians, the law consists merely of polite suggestions by the state.

Perversely, he felt a need to defend his friend to Martha, as if he also by association stood indicted before her. Yet there was no point in declaring Alvau's innocence; he knew even less about the matter than she and anyway, if he were honest, he thought it most unlikely that there would prove to be no substance behind whatever charges had been brought. Instead he found himself hanging on to the promise of this morning's e-mail, the one grain at least, in all this mess, of truth salvaged and honour still upheld.

'The donation is not under threat.'

That silenced her for a while; when she spoke again her words came slowly and hedged around with doubt.

'Are you sure? I mean, of course I don't mean to doubt your knowledge of your friend's situation, or question his word for one moment. But in such a case, surely his financial position must be open to scrutiny? Don't the courts have powers of sequestration—'

He cut through her words with something closer to sharpness than he had ever used with her before.

'Alvau has promised: the money will still be there. I believe we can trust him on this.'

He regretted the snap at once, occasioned as he knew by the very precariousness of his own belief; she showed no sign of offence but withdrew just a shade into circumspection and it was difficult to recapture the frank intimacy which he had learned to value so much from her.

'Well, I'm sure you're right. That's very good, then, for St Rad's,' she said, then added, 'Quite a relief,' in a tone suggesting anything but.

I'm sorry, Martha. Forgive me.

'Listen, I can see it looks bad – it *is* bad, and I'm certain Ros Clarke and her wolves will have a field day pointing out his every shortcoming – but he has said that the benefaction is safe. We still need the cash: the library is still subsiding, we still want the entrance scholarships. And he's still a prospective parent. Nothing has really changed, has it, as far as St Radegund's is concerned?'

She concurred with the first part of this speech if not the rest.

'It does look bad.'

Why the thoughtful seriousness? Since when did she care how things looked? This wasn't even like the admissions issue, where there were candidates' perceptions to take into account.

'I agree it doesn't exactly look now as if he's going to be a benefactor we can parade with pride. He'll hardly be making speeches to the other parents on graduation day if he's in prison.'

This did at least raise a laugh from the other end, followed by signs of softening.

'Look, I'm really sorry, James. He's your friend, and you must be devastated. It's going to be pretty unpleasant for you, hearing Ros blackening his name at every opportunity.'

Was that all? Was her anxiety only for his own sensibilities? Relief spilled into genuine amusement.

'Oh, I think my fragile psyche will probably hold

up under the ordeal. If Luigi can survive the full rigours of investigation by the Italian fraud squad, I dare say I can withstand a little ribbing from Dr Clarke.'

'I'm sure,' she agreed, her smile almost audible.

'Well, thank you so much for calling to warn me, Martha. It is very much appreciated. But I think I can handle the fallout all right, now that I am forewarned.'

When she had brushed away his gratitude and rung off, he walked back to his computer at the kitchen table, seating himself and recalling Alvau's message to visibility with a touch of the mouse. *I intend to honour in full the pledges that I have made.* The intention he did not doubt, but what of the ability to deliver upon it? Might Martha be right, with her talk of sequestration? Would there not be fines or criminal compensation to pay, civil suits to recover sums wrongfully obtained? Many who had faced corruption charges, even been found guilty and imprisoned, seemed to have survived with their fortunes surprisingly intact, but surely he had read of others who had faced ruin? Closing the e-mail he called up Google, typed in the words 'Alvau' and 'fraud' and pressed 'search'.

It was only half an hour and a second slice of toast later, walking across the college grounds towards his office dizzy with the arcane details of the Italian penal code, that it struck him what the ground for Martha's concern must really be. So instead of his own door he headed for hers and knocked, but to no reply. Probably she had a nine o'clock lecture. At his desk he could not settle to any useful task and comforted himself instead, once satisfied that Miss Kett-Symes was safely immersed in a substantial piece of typing, with reading Paul's e-mail. He had been through it four times at least before the clock showed it to be 10:10, the earliest time at which he judged she could be back from the Economics Faculty on her bike.

He was only slightly premature; they met at her office door. He sensed tension in her as she searched her pockets for her keys so he did not wait until they were inside but said at once, 'I am an imbecile.'

Her relieved smile bathed him in warmth.

'Far from it.'

Once across the threshold with the door closed, he began without preamble.

'They are going to say it's dirty money now, aren't they?'

She nodded briefly. 'That's about the size of it.'

He looked at her intently. 'Do you think it's dirty money?'

For a second her eyes met his, before they dropped away in the direction of her desk. He had the uncomfortable sensation of forcing her once again, for the sake of his position as Master, into a stance which did not accord with her own natural instincts. It was a feeling he hated with a vengeance, now even more than before.

'It doesn't matter what I think,' she replied at last.

But it did matter, it mattered enormously; he wanted to tell her so, but knew that instead he would respect her decision to put her feelings aside.

'What matters is whether *you* think so, or whether you still feel you wish to go ahead and accept the donation.'

His expression must have told her all she needed to know.

'And then how we are going to convince the rest of them.'

Ros Clarke, being neither possessed of an Italophile husband nor a regular on the news wires, did not discover the glad tidings of Alvau's indictment until six o'clock that evening. Her informant was Guido Giordano from the Department of Italian, a man with whom she shared a course on semiotics and the modern European novel, as well as the occasional night of discussion-fuelled passion. *Una ciulatina*, he liked to call it.

'Ros.'

'Guido. Always a pleasure. What can I do for you?'

'It's rather more a case of what I can do for you, I believe, on this occasion. As indeed on many other occasions, to my recollection.'

'As I say – always a pleasure.'

'Am I right in remembering that it was Luigi Alvau who was proposing to swell your college coffers, on the promise of a place at the seat of learning for his daughter?'

Ros's playful banter ceased; he had her un-divided attention.

'Yes. And?'

'And – I do not know if the British broadsheets will be covering the story in the morning, but there is talk of little else on the Italian networks – his own and all the rival channels.'

Not a patient woman at the best of times, Ros was now struggling to remain civil.

'What about him?'

'Fraud charges. Embezzlement, taking bribes, all the works. He and about a dozen others in the latest of the centre-left purges. Prodi has got the bit between his teeth – he isn't going to rest until all his predecessor's wheeler-dealing *compari* are in gaol.'

She drew a rapid breath. 'They've actually arrested him?'

'Last night, at his home. There are television pictures of him being assisted into the police car.'

Her eyes blazed; her mouth twitched, less a smile and more the curl of the predator's lips at the scent of blood.

'Guido, this is wonderful. Alvau under investi-gation by the *Guardia di Finanza* – actually in custody! This is the end for James Rycarte, it has to be. This is the kind of friend he has! He is finished – I shall have him.'

'Pleased that I could be of service.'

'Speaking of which . . .' Ros's carnivore eyes sparkled dangerously. 'I wonder whether you have plans for later on tonight? I think I may have a bottle of something Italian and corrupting in the wine cupboard. If you would care to join me, I feel in the mood to indulge in a little malpractice of my own.'

Darren and Julia were completely oblivious of the financial charges laid against the college's intended benefactor – oblivious of almost everything, in fact, except each other. Walking back towards Julia's room from their bench by the tennis courts they were leaning with their heads close together. This was not entirely just a symptom of affection; they were both connected, by one earplug apiece and a bifurcated strand of plastic-covered wire, to Darren's iPod. Julia had come to love Darren's singular electronic compositions. They reminded her strangely of his kissing: lumpy at first but, once you got used to it, slow, meandering and quite stirringly sensuous.

'Your hair seems fluffier today,' said Darren, his voice unnaturally loud in the darkness because of the music unfolding in his left ear.

'I washed it this morning. Sorry, is it tickling you?' replied Julia, also lacking volume control due to the earplug in her right.

'No, I like it. I meant fluffy in a good way. What's the shampoo? Smells like jelly babies.'

He rubbed his nose in her hair, inhaling appreciatively and knocking out her earplug. His fingers as he fumbled to reinsert it tickled her neck, making her giggle, but his face bore that familiar intense expression that suited him so well.

'They used to think that we identified different scents by the shape of the molecule. Jelly babies would smell like jelly babies because the airborne molecules they emit are a particular shape, designed to fit with a matching odour receptor protein in the nasal cells.'

'Sort of baby shaped, presumably.' She still felt giggly.

'Now, though, there's a new theory, about how smells might be vibrations, with the olfactory receptor cells recognising the various distinct frequencies.'

She wrinkled her nose. 'Is that why your aftershave sometimes fizzes in my nostrils and makes me want to sneeze?'

'Oh dear, sorry. I could change it. You never said before.'

'No, I like it. My receptor cells have got used to it. It smells like you now.'

Thus declaiming sweet nothings over the music as they strolled along, they were wholly unaware of Katie Parker following them at a discreet distance on her light trampolinist's feet. She had tracked them every day for a week without ever come close to being rumbled. Not that there was much purpose to these twilight shadowings, she

444

was beginning to think. Tonight, as on every previous occasion, the couple halted by the corniced doorway at the bottom of Julia's staircase. They drew together for a lengthy kiss, during which Katie politely scrutinised the stonework above the door – was that what they called an architrave, she wondered?

And then, as every night, Darren turned and walked away while Julia mounted the spiral stairs alone.

At around the same time James Rycarte was backing his Alfa Romeo out of the garage at the Master's Lodging, a bunch of flowers lying next to him on the passenger seat.

After months of trying to dissuade the Fellows of St Rad's from raising one objection to the Alvau donation, the earth had shifted beneath his feet and he found himself faced with countering a quite different one. The problem was no longer so much the perceived link to the admission of the benefactor's daughter; it was the character of the very money itself. Frustratingly, he had believed the former battle almost won. The firm pencil ticks on the Governing Body membership list by his bedside now outnumbered the sum total of crosses, question marks and fainter, bracketed ticks by a slim but decided margin. And all seemingly for nothing, due to the unpredictable plate tectonics of St Radegund's College. Now, it appeared, the issue was the shady provenance of Alvau's millions, his alleged fraudulent dealings tainting every euro standing to his credit in a bank account, Swiss or otherwise. Were they to be offered the contents of the piggy bank from Paola's dressing table at the present moment, he believed, the Fellowship would treat the cash as suspect.

What he was finding hardest to do was to locate his own feelings on the subject. For a start, there was the difficulty that he was genuinely fond of his old comrade and sparring partner; perhaps he had always known or suspected that the man lacked the most solid of moral cores, but he was match-less company and a kind and loyal friend. And then there was Martha's reaction: the distress she had not quite been able to hide at his stupid failure to apprehend at once the nature of the danger and, equally ill concealed, her own sympathy with the objection which she had nevertheless committed herself to overcoming, if that be indeed his wish. More acutely than at any time since his arrival at the college, he felt the need of somebody to talk to. That Martha, in fairness to herself and her own scruples, was out of the running on this occasion, increased his sense both of the value of her trusted confidence and of his own isolation. What a horribly lonely job this could be.

Really, the more he considered the matter, the more clear it became that there was only one person he could talk to about his dilemma. There was only one person, he realised, who would truly understand, one person who stood neutral above the fray. And that was when he went out to buy the flowers.

As he swung the Alfa to a halt beneath the eponymous beeches in front of the Edwardian cottage hospital, it came almost as a surprise to Rycarte that he had never visited before. Pressing the central locking and glancing up subconsciously to check for starlings, he mounted the three shallow steps in one stride. At the glass-fronted reception desk he waited patiently for the purple-nailed teenager to finish what sounded very much like an unauthorised personal call.

'Dame Emily Froud?'

It was the first time he had spoken her surname aloud.

'Emily? Yes, ground floor, room seventeen.'

The shock at hearing the illustrious archaeologist stripped of her title by someone the age of Martha's undergraduates must have shown on his face, but the receptionist was unperturbed.

'Along the corridor and it's on your left.'

He nodded his thanks.

'Numbers are on the doors,' she added helpfully, evidently expecting visitors to be as dazed and confused as the patients; then, chattily, 'Quite a stream she's had, today.'

'Oh?'

'Well, there was her secretary of course, she almost never misses . . .'

Her secretary: it was funny how unchallengeably true that still seemed.

'. . . and then that man that comes, used to be just Fridays, but recently he's taken to coming other days as well. They are often in there together. Somebody to talk to, I suppose, because Emily still can't get her words out, poor dear.'

Poor dear! This verged upon desecration.

'Well, thank you. Right. Room seventeen, you say?'

Locating the room and receiving no reply to his knock, he pushed the door gently open and stepped inside. She was asleep.

'I have a feeling these might be your favourites,' he said, loosening the tissue paper and laying down upon the bedside stand the flowers he had brought with him: two dozen tightly budded pink roses. There was probably something he ought to do about tracking down a nurse to fetch a vase and water, but he hoped his gender exempted him from the obligation. Somebody would find them later and see to it, no doubt.

The one-sided conversation he had come here to have would not, Rycarte decided, be made any harder by Dame Emily's being asleep; on the contrary, her complete lack of consciousness might even make things easier. He leaned over the bed and examined his predecessor's colour-less features. With her muscles relaxed in sleep it was impossible to gauge the extent of her debility when awake; the only clues were the slightly slacker texture to one side of her face and the thin strand of saliva which found its way out of the corner of her mouth and down the deeply creased indentation which separated chin from lower cheek. If Martha had been here she would of course have had a tissue; she would have wiped away the thread of drool, without fuss and without injury to the dignity of either woman. But the task was too intimate for him, too great an intrusion, even (or perhaps especially) in this place where the invasion of personal space was a daily starting point. Instead he sat down in the metal-framed visitor's chair and addressed the inert figure in the bed.

'So.'

Where to begin?

'I suppose Miss Kett-Symes will have told you about the library foundations?'

Because that was what it all came back to, whichever way he thought the problem through. The library was still falling down; they still needed the benefaction, however discreditable its source might now prove to be. Could they really afford to be so squeamish – to keep their hands snowy white at the expense of watching the collapse of the college's infrastructure? He opened his mouth to say something of this to Dame Emily, to try out on her his arguments for the Governing Body – and was taken totally unawares when something quite different came out.

'I can't get her out of my head.'

He recognised the inescapable truth of it only as he said the words.

'It's a joke, isn't it?' he said bitterly. 'Male head

449

of a women's college, falls in love with his Senior Tutor. His *married* Senior Tutor.'

He stared at the innocent rosebuds on the night stand, then back into the world-worn face on the pillows. Somehow he had a feeling he knew what she would say if she could speak.

'Infallible argument against men, really.'

But no, that was unfair. From everything he had heard, she was a liberal and forbearing woman.

'It's all right – don't worry. I have no intention of acting upon it. It wouldn't be fair to either of us. I shan't even say anything. What could I possibly say, after all? Leave your husband, run away with me? Destroy your family and bring scandal and disgrace upon your college?'

For fully five minutes he sat there, gazing at the sleeping former Mistress of St Rad's. Even thus diminished, hers was a face of intelligence, of good judgement leavened with compassion. It was odd, but having acknowledged his feelings for Martha, and the hopelessness of their being either expressed or requited, he felt the release from his mind of a clamping pressure of which he had not even been aware. It freed him to think clearly at last about the tarnished Alvau money. He was right, he decided. The case for accepting the donation was compelling and he must try to make it; he would throw his weight behind it and would succeed or else fall in the attempt. This time the arguments from the position of purity simply would not wash with him; the cash might originally have been come

450

by less than honestly but now it would be put to a use that was beyond reproach, in furtherance of the cause of education. What better, what more redeeming end for at least a portion of the dishonoured Alvau fortune?

Rising from his chair, he bent forward and hesitated for only a second before he leaned down to plant a respectful kiss on the crown of Dame Emily's white head.

'Thank you,' was all he said, but there was considerably greater determination in his step as he left the Beeches than when he had entered.

CHAPTER 29

While the arrival of March brought breezes loud and shrill to less water-bound landscapes, in Cambridge the daffodils, undancing, were merely shrouded in more fog.

No great clarity was thrown upon events, either, by Luigi Alvau, once Rycarte was able to get hold of him on the telephone. His release on bail had been almost immediate, but somehow the placing of a call to his private line proved to be problematic. Alvau's staff, it seemed, were as over-zealously protective as he would have wished his own to be, had he ever found himself in a similar situation. It did occur to him to feel that maybe Luigi might have phoned him, but no doubt there were other more pressing calls upon his time and attention.

He finally got through on a Monday afternoon, two days before the meeting of the Governing Body. He had been hanging on as usual, running up bills the college could ill afford and being stalled delightfully by a succession of *segretarie personali* with accents like honey, when suddenly he was startled to hear his friend's voice, fresh and cheerful in his ear.

'*Ciao*, my dear fellow. But perhaps I should not address you so. I believe you explained to me once that *il Padrone di Casa* is not a mere Fellow, did you not?'

'Luigi. I am sorry for . . .' What was the established formula for commiserating with one caught out in illegal business dealings? 'Well, I'm sorry.'

'No need, no need, I assure you. I have the very best of lawyers; all that can be done will be done. I am far from being discouraged. I very much hope to avoid incarceration, if only for the sake of my angel Paola. As a lone parent I must think of my responsibilities, you understand.'

That the man could speak thus without irony would have astounded Rycarte, had he known him less well than he did. Sheer gall had always been part of his charm.

'But of course *la mia piccola* will be very soon flown the nest, and in the care of others: in fact, in your own very excellent care. That weight, at least, will be removed from my mind. One does worry so much about the young. As no doubt you worry about your own dear Paul – your Paolo, my Paola.'

'Yes,' he agreed. 'It doesn't stop when they are no longer children, that's for certain.'

He found himself within a breath of telling Alvau about his grandson-to-be, two minutes into a conversation which might so easily have resembled an inquisition. To call him 'disarming' did not begin to do justice to his talents.

'But it is of the money that you wish to speak,

I am certain, even if in your English way you do not like to mention so delicate a topic to a person in difficulty. Well, be assured, I never go back on my word to a friend. It is the very first precept with me.'

Perhaps that was the problem, reflected Rycarte: personal loyalty as a guiding rule of conduct, even before the laws of the land. Yet such a position did have attraction; it was not easy to condemn out of hand.

Did you do it? he wanted to ask. He wanted to hear Alvau tell him the extent of his crimes, and hear from his own mouth how he justified them to himself – wanted, almost, to believe him, to be convinced. But he knew it to be impossible; friends they might be and he hoped would remain, but they inhabited different moral universes. *Are they going to be able to pin it on you?* That was the best he could hope to discover.

'What's it looking like, the case against you? What have your lawyers had to say?'

'Oh, they have some ideas, never fear. If you give a fee to a lawyer, he is never short of an idea or two. Pay him enough, and you will certainly find yourself wholly innocent in his eyes.'

Pity that is not so true of the judges since the change of government, thought Rycarte wryly.

'There is some evidence, I believe. But nothing that we cannot call into question, no prosecution witness who is quite above suspicion. Please do not be unduly anxious on my account, old friend.

454

And soon – very soon, once this unpleasant business with police and lawyers is out of the way – I shall come for that visit to St Radegund's with Paola. Having twice sampled the product of your fine kitchens and cellar, I am most to eager to come for a third taste, believe me.'

'You'll be most welcome any time you care to visit, I hope you know that. And good luck. *Ciao*.'

Only when he had replaced the receiver did it occur to Rycarte that Alvau was very likely not in present possession of his passport.

It was a telephone call from a woman named Amanda which led to Martha's delivering Douglas his ultimatum. Just plain Amanda without a surname, apparently, as was the current vogue within the smoked glass and steel workplaces of the City of London. In this case, it was a headhunting agency: Amanda worked for Murchett Webb & Associates, leading players nationwide in the executive recruitment market.

The call came when the tide of Martha's affairs was at a low ebb. Lucia had barely left her bed in a week and when Martha, finally able to bear it no longer, made an appointment for her to see the family GP, Douglas had accused her of interference and unnecessary fuss, urging her to 'back off and give the girl a break'. She had stuck to her guns and Lucia, at least, had not demurred, dragging herself up and out to the surgery with sluggish indifference, the wordless equivalent of the hated 'whatever'. They had returned to a house filled with bitter tension, punctuated by shafts of sarcasm from Douglas, which Lucia had escaped by the simple expedient of going back to bed. Then there was James Rycarte and the Alvau arraignment; he seemed set upon pushing ahead to accept the donation, irrespective of the shadow of felony which must now hang over the money. She had committed herself to supporting him, and would do her best, but they had only a very short time in which to try to win over the members of the Governing Body against what must be the instinct of almost all. She sorely feared the defeat of this proposal which he had advocated so strongly and so publicly, and with it the loss of all confidence in his Mastership. If Ros Clarke then went on to claim the Senior Tutorship un-opposed, the power would all be in her hands. She could not see James surviving for long after that.

It was these most immediate concerns which were occupying her mind, and not worries about her own future, when, home from accompanying Lucia to the doctor's, she picked up the phone in the kitchen at six thirty p.m. that Monday.

'Martha Pearce.'

'Dr Pearce, this is Amanda from Murchett Webb & Associates. Glad to have caught you in. I have been asked to approach you on behalf of our client, the University of Marlborough.'

Her distracted mind, very naturally, focused first upon the word 'university' and not on the unfamiliar name of Amanda's employers. A faculty seminar perhaps, or a series of guest lectures? Her research areas might not be much in demand these days, but she did still occasionally get such requests, and was always pleased to help out where she could. Marlborough – that was only fifteen minutes from Mum's. Perhaps she could fit in a visit at the same time, kill two birds with one stone. Nevertheless, her reflex was to hedge.

'Anything I can do, of course, I'd be delighted, though you have to appreciate that this term and next are very busy ones for me.'

'Er, right, of course. Anyway, our client is looking for a new Vice-Chancellor. That's why I'm ringing you this evening, Dr Pearce.'

'Yes?'

While her thoughts scrabbled wildly to find a foothold, the first idea which made any sense was James. They wanted to poach him, did they? Well, they couldn't have him – St Rad's needed him. Maybe they didn't all quite appreciate how much, but need him they did.

'Naturally I am always happy to provide a reference whenever I am asked to do so, but I have to inform you that in this instance—'

'Before you make any decision, may I at least put the details of the appointment in the post to you?'

'Yes, but—'

'The client was most anxious for you to understand the attractions of this opening. The University of Marlborough is about to embark, over the next five years, upon a major expansion of its operations; important funding links have been forged with the local and national business communities, and there have been many noteworthy additions to the academic strength, especially in the fields of applied science, technology and the human sciences. The institution is looking for strong but responsive leadership to take it forward into this exciting new era of its development . . .'

Why was the woman giving her what sounded like a sales pitch, she wondered? Did she really imagine that Martha was about to persuade James of the virtues of abandoning St Rad's after less than a year in favour of new challenges in Wiltshire? Her attention flicked back to the voice on the telephone in time to hear it saying, '. . . cannot stress enough that it is you that they want. They have watched your Cambridge career with great interest, academic and administrative, and they are firmly convinced that you have exactly the skills and experience they are seeking . . .'

Her? Not James Rycarte – her! That she should even have been heard of in Marlborough was a wonder to her, until she remembered Jack Merryck from the Economics Faculty who had moved there for a chair at the newly opened business school three years ago. Doubtless Jack had put in a word. Vice-Chancellor: she found the notion absurd, surreal, terrifying – and extremely exhilarating. Mustering her wits and the remnants

458

of civility, she thanked Amanda for her call, assured her that she would look forward with great pleasure to receiving further details of the post, and rang off.

With Lucia asleep and Douglas still sulking in the sitting room, she had time to think while she set about preparing supper. She took the packet of chicken thighs from the fridge and, with the smallest, sharpest knife, began to bone them. Vice-Chancellor . . . By leap-frogging to the top job she would neatly avoid the demand for professionalism which applied further down the administrative ladder; you didn't need to be a qualified accountant or personnel officer to front the show. She could be head of a new and expanding university, already well rated by HEFCE for both teaching and research, within the constraints of its intake and resources, and improving steadily, by all accounts. It was not mere puff when Amanda had mentioned recent high profile appointments: not only Jack Merryck but Tony Bircher from Oxford, who was making quite a media splash running Marlborough's Engineering Department.

Discarding the chicken bones she rubbed the inner surface of the thighs with salt and rosemary and drizzled on some olive oil before rolling them tightly, each in a slice of prosciutto, and securing them with a threaded wooden cocktail stick. She would be able to stop teaching, she thought, as she lined up the neatly wrapped chicken pieces one by one on a plate. Not that she didn't like teaching, in fact she had always loved it (something found rarely enough in higher education), but increasingly the content and assumptions behind *what* she had to teach meant that her heart was no longer in it. It was economics she loved; she had no desire to be a maths teacher. And it would be near Mum. A quick phone call, and Martha could be at her side in a quarter of an hour. She could pop over in the evenings to check she was all right, maybe drop off a casserole from time to time. Lucia could go round there and sit with her sometimes – they would both like that. It would be a new start for Lucia; maybe she could even get her back into school. Housing there was expensive, no doubt, but it couldn't be any worse than Cambridge. They would find something, surely.

The oil in the frying pan was starting to spit now, and she laid in the first piece of ham-wrapped chicken, adjusting the heat as it sizzled and browned. It was then she remembered that, in all probability, university Vice-Chancellors were paid considerably more than mere college officers; that should cushion the costs of moving. And it wasn't as though Lucia was in school here, or Douglas had a proper job. Only those bits and pieces of supervising he still did for other colleges – and he could write his poetry anywhere, couldn't he?

When all the meat was cooked through she turned the gas off completely and put a lid on the pan.

She could do some vegetables later, but first she needed to go and talk to her husband.

Such a lot seemed to have changed since she went into the kitchen that Martha was surprised to discover that with him their earlier argument was still alive and smarting.

'What did he say, anyway, the doctor? Have any miracle solutions, did he?'

Disorientated, and with no time to think up any more subtle reply, she told the bald truth.

'He said she is clinically depressed. As we all knew.'

He made a very Italian noise in his throat.

'Oh, we knew it, did we? Depressed like half the teenagers in the country are depressed! And putting a nice, tidy label on it is going to make everything better, I suppose?'

Breathing as evenly as she could, she answered quietly, 'He hasn't prescribed any anti-depressants yet. She isn't keen on taking psychotropic drugs and I agree, I think she's sensible to be cautious. But he has referred her to a specialist.'

'A bloody shrink! Oh, Christ, that's all she needs.'

Actually, yes, it probably was what Lucia needed right now: the chance to talk to a professional about the way she was feeling. To talk about strategies to help her to get through the next few months or weeks – or sometimes simply through the day.

'Well, it can't do any harm to see somebody, can it?'

His laughter was fingernails on a blackboard.

'No harm? Oh, no – except he'll make her think she's abnormal, won't he, and that wanting to write is a sign of pathology.'

But she doesn't write; I wouldn't mind if she did, but she doesn't. And neither do you, not really. What had Douglas written since coming back from Florence at Christmas? A few completed stanzas, two months ago.

'He'll get her all wound up, analysing her own perfectly ordinary unhappiness, thinking it's something to make a song and dance about instead of just getting on with things. And I dare say he'll give her all that Freudian crap too, about it being the parents' fault.'

Which of course it was, thought Martha. *Because I haven't been here, I've been too caught up with work. And Douglas . . . Douglas . . .*

Something inside Martha seemed to stop oscillating and harden into resolution. She had to get away, to start again. And, more vitally, she had to get Lucia away.

'I've been offered a job. At least, I haven't actually applied yet, but I've had an approach about it.'

This, at last, seized his attention away from his own grievances and he looked at her properly.

'What job?'

'Vice-Chancellor at the University of Marlborough.'

He stared. Then, to her dismay, he began to laugh – until he saw her face and stopped.

'Well, I suppose it's flattering, in a way. Might

have been interesting. And I dare say they were paying a few bob, were they?'

Might have been . . . But she had allowed him to pull the rug from under her feet often enough. This time her mind was made up, and she wasn't going to be swayed and sidetracked and blind-sided out of her decision.

'If they do offer me the post, I'm going to take it. A change of scene is exactly what Lucia needs to get her out of this rut. It will be closer to Mum. And the job would be great for me, too.'

His eyes narrowed; his voice lost its brittle edge and was rich and thick as chicken soup.

'And what about me? Do I fit anywhere into this beautiful plan?'

She drew a deep breath and resisted the urge to close her eyes against the pain, her own and his.

'You can join us. But only on one condition.'

It was the hardest thing she had ever done. Steeling herself, she looked him directly in the eye as she said, 'You've got to get a job, too. You can't come with us until you've found one.'

The 493rd meeting of the St Radegund's College Governing Body began promptly at eight fifteen p.m. with a lively and comparatively weighty discussion, under matters arising from the College Council, of college provision for grad-uate students. Rycarte was very much relieved; he was in a state of some agitation about the main debate to follow and did not think he could

463

have borne it if they had decided to talk about the curtains.

'With graduate teaching all being provided at the faculty level,' Letitia Gladwin was saying, 'postgrads quite naturally begin to ask what exactly it is that their college does for them. Yes, we house many of them, especially those coming from overseas. They can take their meals, and join in the social side of student life.'

This already sounded quite a lot to Rycarte, whose own provincial university, all those years ago, had provided barely that, and then only in his first and third years.

'But a Cambridge college should be more than merely a glorified hall of residence,' she went on. 'We are an academic community, and our graduate students ought to be at the heart of that community.'

There was general approval of this sentiment, though not much in the way of suggestions as to how to put it into practice, until Ros Clarke spoke up.

'What about a regular graduate seminar, here in St Rad's? Just for grad students and Fellows. Our PhD students could give research in progress seminars on their work, but aimed at a general audience.'

'What a wonderful idea,' agreed Martha. 'I'm sure a lot of us would be fascinated to hear what our doctoral students are working on, and at present there is so little opportunity for that kind of interaction. Maybe we could hold them fort-nightly or so during term, and alternate arts and sciences?'

Rycarte allowed consideration of the proposal to range around the room: what time of day would suit best, whether to combine the seminars with drinks or dinner, and whether these might be offered free to the students as an incentive to encourage attendance (this last fancy being rapidly quashed by the bursar). When all had had their say, Rycarte rounded things up by proposing a working party to look into organising the semi-nars, consisting of Ros Clarke, Martha and Carolyn Gallagher who, amongst her other hats, wore that of Graduate Tutor.

'May I say,' he ventured to add, 'what an excel-lent idea I think this is, Dr Clarke. I for one will be very pleased to hear about some of the research the students are doing, if a "general audience" may be taken to include one as untutored as myself.'

Ros inclined her head chivalrously, though the glint in her eye was not amusement.

'Of course, Master.'

It was the ritual salute before entering the lists.

Rycarte had arranged the agenda to ensure that the Alvau donation was the first substantive item, and on to this he now moved. He had chosen by way of introduction to stick to the speech he had prepared after last month's Development Committee, addressed to the utility of the money in terms of both the library refurbishment and broader access, countering unspoken objections based on the admissions issue and specifically ignoring those regarding the questionable provenance of the gift. Let the moral hawks raise the point themselves; any importance accorded it would not be seen to come from him.

'. . . seven full-cost entrance scholarships annually, each giving the chance of a completely free place at St Radegund's to a student who might well otherwise be deterred from applying by reason of cost. Surely this opportunity to do something to widen access – unrivalled currently by any other Cambridge college – is one we cannot turn down, especially for the sake of mere appearances . . .'

When he had said his piece, Susie James, pinkly earnest as ever, was the first to jump in and second his arguments. He was doubly heartened – both to have the Admissions Tutor on his side, and because he had not been entirely sure of Susie since the news of Alvau's fall from grace. Then Martha spoke, highlighting in particular the value of the rental bursaries, but by now it was clear that they were preaching to the converted, at least as far as a comfortable majority was concerned. Neither Letitia Gladwin nor Ros Clarke entered the fray, the former due to the collective responsibility of the Development Committee and the latter, presumably, because this cause was lost and she was saving her breath for the real battle to come.

And come it very soon did. Debate of the access question subsided for the briefest time, and the space was filled not by Ros but by Letitia Gladwin (supervening circumstances since the meeting of the committee presumably freeing her to voice her dissent on this point), though Rycarte thought he caught her glance at Ros as she began to speak.

'It is very pleasant to sit here spending Sr Alvau's euros, is it not? But I must say that I find the whole basis of the discussion so far to be misplaced, if not indeed disingenuous.' Here she clucked loudly and darted a look at Rycarte. 'Are we all to continue to ignore the soiled source of this benefaction?'

It was the cue for which Ros had evidently been waiting.

'Well said, Vice-Mistress. Are we really so destitute, both financially and morally, that we have no care at all where money comes from, as long as it is readily available for us to spend? Have we no care that the gift we are being offered is the fruit of illegal activities on the part of the donor: of fraud, of bribery, of political and financial chicanery of the worst kind? Is this the kind of conduct with which St Radegund's College seeks to see itself associated?'

Even though he had been primed for the assault, Rycarte sincerely wished that she were not delivering it with that smile on her face. Miss Kett-Symes, at his side, was scribbling dutifully.

'What example do we wish to set to the young

people in our charge? We are a place of education. Should we not be giving our students a grounding in proper standards of behaviour before we send them out into the world? For myself, I certainly believe that we would be failing in our duty if we taught our undergraduates only literature or languages, science or philosophy. Do we not also wish to inculcate certain values? Rigour in research, for example, and the importance of not plagiarising the work of others, nor distorting one's results to fit a theory; tolerance for the views of others; integrity in all one's dealings. Every year the Heads of House of all the Cambridge colleges certify their graduands to be of good moral character when they present them to the University for the award of their degree; even an outstanding payment on a college bill will prevent a candidate from going forward, such is the importance we place upon regularity of conduct.'

Nods were beginning to spread around the table as Ros continued.

'What contrary message, then, will it send out if we are to get into bed with this man Alvau? To be seen to be accepting his money with gratitude and according him the status of an honoured bene-factor? What statement will we be making about our attitude to business ethics, not to mention plain legality? This is dirty money we are being offered, and we should not take it.'

The standard being thus raised, one or two more of the Clarkean tendency nailed their colours to her flagpole.

468

'I must admit that I, for one, wouldn't feel comfortable about publicly taking his money,' said Maggie Trent – another Development Committee rebel. 'Hosting him here, as Dr Clarke suggests, as an esteemed friend and supporter of the college – quite frankly, it would stick in my craw. The man may even find himself in prison very shortly, for goodness' sake. It would be rather ironic, wouldn't it, if he had to send his apologies for the Benefactors' Feast because he was behind bars?'

There was a ripple of laughter at this, and a couple of assenting mumbles of 'quite right' and 'hear, hear', before Adeola Onoge timidly volunteered her maiden speech.

'If I may? I don't think it's ever right to turn a blind eye to where money comes from. Wealth buys all sorts of things in our society, and what we are selling here is not material goods or power or even real influence, so much as status. I suspect Alvau wants to be associated with Cambridge because it gives him a sort of spurious respectability, a veneer of authenticity, of solidity. Do we really want to be used in such a way by a man like him?'

Having played out the line to let his fish run, Rycarte now judged the moment right to begin to reel it back in. He was far from gratified, however, when the first voice to be raised on his side was the forthright one of Kate Beasley, the Bursar.

'What a lot of nonsense! Who is to say, necessarily, that just because the man has been involved in some uncertain dealings, all his money has been less than honestly earned? His fortune is the result of a career's worth of talent and hard work in television – a few backhanders once in a while may be reprehensible but it doesn't make all his money suspect.'

It was not an argument calculated to appeal to the academic purist.

'Like the proverbial curate's egg, in fact?' Ros Clarke grinned to the table at large, amidst renewed laughter.

Waiting until the titters had died away, Rycarte grabbed the moment and stepped in.

'You say that my friend Luigi Alvau's donation is now tainted, and of course there are many who would view it in that light. But I would beg leave to ask you just one question. What money, when examined closely, is ever wholly clean? Is there any other kind of money, really, than the dirty kind?'

As he had anticipated, this somewhat outrageous proposition sent a small frisson round the gathered Fellows. Miss Kett-Symes's fountain pen faltered to a standstill.

'Luigi Alvau runs a commercial television network. It must make a profit to survive. Do you suppose that it has never carried advertisements for alcoholic drinks, or junk food that will make Italian children fat and rot their teeth? Do you suppose that it has never run a mindless game show instead of an experimental drama in order to be sure of advertising revenue?'

One or two faces were now registering open disbelief, but Ros Clarke, he saw, looked sombre.

'What enterprise,' he carried on, 'designed to return a profit, can claim to be wholly beyond reproach? Show me a single manufacturing firm which can claim to break no rule of ethical conduct, in its sourcing, production and marketing, in its employment practices, in its boardroom politics. It is very easy for us to sit here, I shall not say in our ivory tower, but at least in our cosy moral security, and to condemn the way that other people make the money which we wish to spend. We are educators and researchers: we need never soil our hands.'

He allowed a brief pause for uncomfortable shuffling.

'Unfortunately, however, we live in a capitalist society.'

He had been looking forward to this bit. Not that he had succeeded in making it all the way through one of Ros Clarke's articles on literary theory, but from what little he had been able to decipher, it was clear that she came from a position of unreconstructed Marxism.

'And out there in the capitalist world, profit comes only at a price. All money is dirty, because all money is implicated in the inherently exploitative capitalist system. And what if the wealth is inherited, at least in this generation? That doesn't exactly make it squeaky clean either, does it?'

Ros had picked up her pen and was rolling it

471

between finger and thumb with intense concentration.

'Therefore, we have to make compromises. We make them all the time – the compromises we make when investing the college's endowment, for example' – he smiled at Kate Beasley – 'and conversely also the compromises we must make when we are on the receiving end of a potential investment ourselves, as in the present instance. The question is not whether the donation is soiled, but whether it is so irredeemably soiled that we are genuinely justified in refusing to touch it.'

There was more, much more, but he was conscious that he had held the floor for a long time, and he felt a sweet pang of something he tried to pretend was merely gratitude when Martha, after first catching his eye for permission, picked up the baton.

'There's the University's new Deshimaru Centre for Nanotechnology, over on the Science Park. Mr Deshimaru is over ninety and it's an old family firm, been in engineering for a century. Do you think the Council of the Schools of Technology have asked him precisely what he was doing in the 1940s? But the centre is doing groundbreaking work, putting his yen to excellent use. I have heard nobody in this room speaking out against it. Several of us attended the opening, when Mr Deshimaru unveiled the statue of himself in the foyer – Dr Clarke, I seem to recall seeing you there?'

Ros's pen was now taking a severe pounding. Joan Tilley chipped in next.

'I'm much afraid that the Church of England cannot claim a record of moral purity in terms of the donations it has received down the centuries. Some of the most wicked men in Christendom have been our sponsors. But I like to think we have used their ill-gotten gains to very good purpose. If we had been unduly fastidious I doubt that there would be much of a church at all today. I'm all for compromise.'

'Look at King's College,' suggested a normally reclusive medieval historian by the name of Mary Farder. 'The visible symbol of all things Cantabrigian. But what about its founder, Henry VI? The Plantagenet family fortune came mainly from taxing the poor to within an inch of their lives and a reign of imperialist plunder on the Continent. The man himself was weak-minded to the point of insanity, inspired rebellion during his lifetime and left a legacy of civil strife after he had gone. But the Provost still lays roses and lilies every year on the anniversary of their benefactor's death.'

'Even the Puritan colleges cannot claim to be above criticism in this regard,' Carolyn Gallagher agreed. 'Places like Emmanuel, for instance. Most of their original lands and wealth came from earlier monastic institutions, sacked during the Reformation and handed out to the new Protestant foundations. Difficult to maintain the moral high ground when your endowment was stolen by force from Catholic monks by the state.'

Much as he was enjoying the history lesson – and much though Ros appeared to be hating it – Rycarte felt he should bring them back to the central point.

'If no Cambridge college – nor even the sainted Church Commissioners – can quite hold its head up high with respect to the sources of its endowment, then how can we at St Radegund's afford to be any different? Why does it fall to our part to make a lonely stand? Ought we not to be learning to make compromises along with the rest of the world?'

He ran his gaze with slow deliberation round the perimeter of the long table of which he sat at the head, commanding the attention of all.

'And if money be tainted, if the earning of it be thought to have been ignoble, how better to employ it than in pursuit of charity? Rather than the money corrupting the cause which it supports, instead might not the cause be seen to cleanse and purify the money?'

Ros Clarke's eyes flashed; her lips shaped a word which looked suspiciously like 'laundering'. Martha smiled gently.

'The Department of Agricultural Engineering,' she said, 'last year accepted a contribution towards their appropriate technology research budget from a leading aerospace conglomerate. I believe there was talk of turning swords into ploughshares.'

Through the laughter and nods of approval, Rycarte pressed ahead with his case.

'We are the trustees of this institution for a short

spell in the span of its life; ought our task not be to think first of preserving and enhancing its educational future, for the sake of Radegundians yet to come, rather than using our position to make our own personal moral statements, however strongly held our private beliefs?'

Talk of trusteeship always struck a resonant note with the Fellows. Even Letitia Gladwin ceased her clucking and several of their number, led once again by the loyal Martha, spoke in support of this understanding of the nature of their trust. Perhaps most surprising in the robustness of her approach was the Revd Tilley.

'I agree. What matters is maximising our resources in order to carry out the pedagogic task entrusted to us. We owe it to our students. What right have we to get all precious about where donations come from, when it isn't us who will gain or lose in consequence? It's not we who are going to suffer by our high-minded squeamishness, is it?'

The final shot, however, went to Susie James – after Rycarte had teed it up for her.

'What do you think the kids would say at those comprehensives you go out and visit, Dr James? What would they tell us to do? How would their parents advise us in our dilemma? These are the people to whom we owe our duty of trusteeship, are they not? They are the future beneficiaries of the St Radegund's endowment. Do you think they would insist upon our refusing Luigi Alvau's defiled million?'

She coloured more deeply than ever, but her brow fell into shadow for only a moment before it cleared.

'I think they would laugh at us, to be honest – laugh at this whole discussion. It would never cross their minds for a moment that anyone would turn down the offer of a million pounds. Especially when it could be put to such fantastic use.'

As music to Rycarte's ears came the sound of Ros Clarke's ballpoint snapping.

CHAPTER 30

'So,' said Martha, raising her beer glass to him as her eyes smiled into his, 'you seem to have won them over.'

They were back in the side-street pub near the railway station where they had once before repaired for a drink. Rycarte was struggling to rid himself of the feeling that this was a clandestine meeting. He knew it was nothing of the sort, yet he was thankful for the cover of both the swirling fog outside and the swirling fug within – no-smoking bars were a concept yet to hit this area of the city.

'It was quite an emphatic vote in the end, wasn't it, though I say it myself?' he replied with a grin. Then, swallowing a long draught of bitter far too quickly, he added bravely, 'No small thanks to you.'

Shaking this away with her head, she said, 'Did I see Ros Clarke cornering you after the meeting? Was she congratulating you, by any chance?'

He laughed. 'Funnily enough, yes.' Then, ruefully, 'I expect it's all part of her next clever move. When she's nice to me, that's when I have to worry the most.'

She helped herself to a crisp from the packet he had split open on the table between them, crunching it reflectively.

'I think Ros has come to have a lot of respect for you,' she said slowly. Embarrassment crept into her cheeks. 'And quite right, too.' Then she grinned, breaking the moment of tension. 'Mind you, it would kill her to admit it – properly admit it, I mean.'

They were laughing together but his next question was serious, and she treated it as such.

'So I still shouldn't trust her?'

'Trust . . . Actually – and you may find this odd – I would say that I would trust Ros completely. Not that I think she will ever be loyal to you; don't expect that. But she is true to herself, in her own way. When she is committed to something she is a force to be reckoned with – as you have seen. I suspect that she has come to terms with your Mastership, and as long as she thinks you are treading the right path, you will have her support. If not, well . . .'

'God help me?'

The shared merriment backlighting her brown eyes made his heart dance.

'I'm very glad to hear you say all this, Martha.'

She cocked her head interrogatively.

'I have been thinking. About the Senior Tutorship.'

Her eyes dropped at once to her beer, discomfort crossing her features. His voice was very gentle.

'I know you and I haven't talked about it, not since that evening in the lodging at the beginning of term. So I'm rather guessing that your answer for me is no.'

She raised to him a face flooded with relief. 'I haven't been able to find quite the right moment to tell you.'

He smiled, understanding completely. 'It's OK. Because since I cannot have you . . . I have decided to have Ros.'

Dumbfounded was the best word to describe her expression.

'I mean, of course, if no other candidates put themselves forward, and subject to the approval of the College Council. But if that's how things work out, I'm happy to have her.'

It came slowly, but when her smile broke it took his breath away.

'You are a courageous man, James – but I think the decision is an excellent one. The two of you will be a formidable combination, when you are united. And when you are divided – as you surely will be, from time to time – well, checks and balances, I suppose. It can only be good for the college.' The smile widened into a grin. 'What was it Lyndon Johnson said, about having people inside the tent?'

'The analogy I would prefer is something rather more elevated. Like King Arthur offering the vanquished Pellinore a place at the round table.'

'Hadn't Pellinore beaten Arthur, in the story?'

'Not in my version.'

For a minute they drank their beer and munched their crisps in easy silence, but then it seemed to him that she had something she wanted to say, and at length he found out what it was.

'I've been offered a job.'

He took a deep breath.

'In the University?'

'In Wiltshire.'

Shit. A10, M25, M4 . . . it must be at least two hours away, even in the Alfa at a constant seventy-seven miles per hour.

'That's great. What's the job?'

'University of Marlborough. They want me to be their Vice-Chancellor.'

'But that's terrific, Martha,' he said, almost meaning it.

'I know. I'm incredibly flattered. It's only because of this man Merryck who used to be in the faculty here.'

'I bet it isn't!' Really meaning it this time.

'I'm very excited about it. Such a great new challenge. The university is expanding rapidly, and their HEFCE standings are improving just as fast. Mind you, it's a scary prospect, too, having the top job. Where the buck stops, and all that. I imagine it must be lonely – is it?'

For an answer he merely smiled and said simply, 'Not if you have people around you like I have had you.'

That made her awkward, so for something to

say and with very little forethought he asked, 'What about your husband? Will he be able to find a job down there all right as well?'

Not that he knew much about the man, Rycarte realised. She had never mentioned him at all, to his recollection. People had said he was a poet but he had never seen any of his stuff. Mind you, his name wasn't Pearce, was it, and come to think of it he wasn't sure what it was. Thus distracted, it took a second for her next words to register.

'I don't think he's coming, as a matter of fact. I think I'm leaving him.'

The hands holding his pint seemed suddenly to be somebody else's, somebody at a quite different table.

'Good God.' Then, remembering himself, 'Christ, Martha, I'm so sorry. I really had no idea.'

She looked up; her eyes were dry but their usually bright focus was softened with a liquid haze.

'Neither did I until just recently. It just sort of happened, all of a sudden – though I guess it's been coming for a while. I gave him a kind of ultimatum.'

She pulled a face, and he saw what it must have cost her.

'And?'

'And he didn't like it.'

Even this limited venture into disloyalty had clearly made her uncomfortable, and she stared back down miserably at her almost empty glass. His heart ached for her. He wanted to comfort her, to put his arms round her, but knew it was impossible. Everything about it was impossible, as it had been from the start.

But her marriage was over. The revelation blotted out everything else – almost blotted out reason. That knowledge seemed set to drive away all the cogent arguments as to why this was the last thing she needed to hear right now, when what she wanted above all was not more complication but simply a friend. He could all but hear himself speaking the words.

Martha. If you can't be my Senior Tutor, then maybe you can be something else.

Without needing to say it out loud, though, he knew how the rest of the scene would go, knew what her answer must be. Her beloved college: she could never do something which would bring St Radegund's into such disrepute. To leave her husband and go off with the Master, not yet a year in post – it was utterly scandalous, and therefore utterly unthinkable.

Instead of voicing the hopeless truths in his heart he drained the last dregs of his beer and sat in submissive silence while Martha went to the bar for another round. And, as they lifted their drinks, he clinked his glass against hers with a simple cheeriness he vowed should become reality.

'Your very good health, Martha. Here's to the University of Marlborough – a bloody lucky place.'

'And here's to a long and prosperous Rycarte Mastership.'

★   ★   ★

Never before had Martha had the experience of putting off going home. There had been many times when she had been torn two ways about it, conscious of the pressure of work still to be done and frustrated by the need to leave her desk and get back to her family, but always, as she loaded her folders into her bicycle basket and unpadlocked the chain, the feeling of going home had, finally, been an indulgence. Never once had pedalling back towards the house given rise to this sense of foreboding: not when Lucia was a baby, threatening a night broken by wailing; not when she was a toddler, punishing Martha's absence with tantrums on her return; not last spring when her depression first began to rear its head, and there were all the arguments about her abandoned schooling. Not even at Christmas, with Mum nagging, Lucia withdrawing and no Douglas there in bed at the end of the day to tell her not to fret.

This last week had been the most painful one of her life. She had been very glad of the Governing Body meeting to keep her thoughts busy at least during the working day; grateful, too, for her evening in the pub with James Rycarte, celebrating his victory. But eventually, whatever distractions St Radegund's might throw her way, she had to go home and face them: face Douglas and Lucia.

'He didn't like it,' she had said to James of Douglas's reaction to her ultimatum. A self-evident understatement: James had doubtless taken it as an indication that she wished to say no more. But at the time it seemed there had been very little more to be said, at least on Douglas's side. 'You can't come with us until you've found a job,' she had told him, quaking inwardly at her own temerity, amazed by her ability, at last, to beat a path through all his evasions and say what needed to be said.

'Fine, you go. Great job. You'll have a ball.'

His words had been shards of ice, even while he was swinging his legs down off the sofa with casual grace, and rising with deliberate slowness. Douglas never raised his voice – *never* – and perversely she wished he would now. Instead, he was very nearly smiling.

'I'm not getting some pointless, time-wasting job just to please your notions of proper usefulness. You can keep your Protestant work ethic, Martha. I'm staying here. Just as I am.'

And that was all, that first time; he simply stated his position and walked out, taking the time to pick up his jacket from the kitchen and barely even slamming the front door.

That night she had been asleep when he came in – not feigning but genuinely and exhaustedly asleep – and when she had risen shortly after six he appeared to be the same. Nor had the anticipated fireworks come the following evening, or not with more than a token, damp fizzle. She had made sure to get away from college by seven so as to be free of any charge of evading the issue herself; on her return she had encountered him in the kitchen, eating a Marks & Spencer beef stroganoff for one, straight from the microwaveable plastic tray. She had wanted to castigate him with the fresh cooking ingredients in her bag but stopped herself in time from rising to his bait. Focus on what matters, she had warned herself; stick to your position.

'Douglas, look, I've decided I'm definitely taking the Marlborough job if I'm offered it. I'm sorry—'

Her voice was perilously close to fracturing. He could not know how sorry. Or perhaps he did know, and only shielded himself from the knowledge.

'I'm really sorry, but I'm convinced it's the right thing. For me and for Lucia.'

'Lucia?'

His voice was measured but crackling with submerged menace.

'Y-yes.' She must not falter now; she must be strong. 'Lucia is coming with me.'

She must sound confident, however unsure of her ground, however unsure that her daughter could really be persuaded – steamrollered, if that was what it took – into this move which was, after all, for her benefit as much as Martha's own. That Lucia might choose to stay with her father was a dread she refused to entertain even for a moment.

'Oh, you think so?'

His quick, harsh laugh told her that he did not

need to ask whether Lucia had said so. Then she had wanted to beg him: come with us, let's all go together and make a fresh start. Jobs, school, we'll begin again. Please, Douglas: put this life of dragging dissolution behind you and be a father to Lucia. One she can look up to and seek to emulate without its being a canker which poisons her own life's ambitions and leaves her empty and listless.

Little of this, of course, could be given expression, but she had tried to explain some part of it as best she could: Lucia's need for structure, for productiveness and purpose around her; how Martha believed it would somehow rub off.

'Nothing could be worse for her than your example at the moment,' she had forced herself to say. 'You know she idolises you – she always has done. Maybe if she saw you making a new beginning, deciding to turn your life around, it could be just the incentive she needs to do the same.'

There was no angry reaction; his eyes held only cold pity as he tossed the empty stroganoff tray in the bin and his fork in the sink, repeating, 'You think so, do you?'

That was six nights ago. Since then things had been much the same. She had tried to remonstrate, tried not to plead; he had refused to react, fending her off with bitter sarcasm whichever way she attempted to approach the problem. Each evening despite her early return he had contrived to eat earlier and alone, enduring briefly and grudgingly her attempts to talk before going out – she did not know where – and returning in the small hours. She was frankly afraid. Was it not frightening enough that she had decided to leave St Radegund's, the college which had been in a very real sense her home for the whole of her adult life? Was she also – as she had announced to James in the pub, trying out the words for fit – was she really leaving her husband?

Braking to a standstill at the end of the drive, she wheeled her bike over the cracked concrete towards the side passage with a heavy step and a heavier heart. Already she was beginning to rehearse the phrases she would use tonight – *not going to change my mind*; *for Lucia*; *for the best* – as well as one she would not: *please, for me, Douglas, please*. But for once both kitchen and microwave were empty; Maynard was curled in a self-comforting ball on a chair. Of her husband there was no sign. With a wave of panic which had the physical smack of nausea, she wondered if tonight he had gone out earlier still with the purpose of avoiding her, avoiding even the appearance of pursuing their argument. This could not really be it, could it? Discussion over; marriage at an end?

There were tears blotching her vision as she mounted the stairs to Lucia's bedroom. She knocked, then entered at the faint 'hello'. Lucia was out of bed, at least, but was enfolded in her duvet like the outerwear of some Arctic explorer where she sat hunched at the desk. In front of her was a pad of writing paper, though there were no words visible on it.

'Hello, love,' said Martha gently. These last few days she had felt as though she were tiptoeing even more gingerly around Lucia than previously, acutely aware of the effect her parents' stand-off must be having on her already precarious sensibilities. She had no idea what, if anything, Douglas might have said to his daughter when they were in the house together during the day; she fought down the fear that he might be persuading her of the wrong-headedness of Martha's ultimatum, convincing her to stay with him in Cambridge and continue their directionless father-and-daughter existence. She herself had said little as yet; Lucia was aware at least in essentials of what had passed between herself and Douglas and up until now that had seemed enough. But now, tonight, was it still enough? She sat down heavily on the bed, bare but for its crumpled sheet. She ought to say things, reassuring things. The comforting bromide of all separating parents, she thought bitterly: *we both still love you.* Separating parents . . . Separation; divorce: was it really thinkable?

'You OK, Mum?'

Lucia's words shook her from her gloomy reverie. Self-pity she had always deplored; she would not give in to it now, when her daughter was in sore need of her empathy.

'I'm fine, love; just a bit tired, that's all. You look brighter tonight, if you don't mind my saying.

Have you eaten? I could make us both a sand-wich and we could eat it up here, have another picnic – if you don't feel like coming down to a proper supper, I mean.'

Lucia shook her head swiftly. ''S all right. I had one earlier with Dad.'

Martha smiled, shrugged; she considered drawing attention to the pad of paper, decided against it. There was such a lot to be said, to try to make Lucia see why moving to Marlborough was right for them all, but she felt too weary and daunted to know how to begin.

'You look pale,' said Lucia.

She felt pale. For all her resolutions against self-pity, one touch of her daughter's concern and she had to admit she felt pale and tired and old. She always seemed to feel old these days, further removed from the students, older than her almost forty-two years. Only James Rycarte occasionally, like in the pub the other night, looked at her in a way that made her feel twenty again – ironic really, since he was fifty-six. But you're not twenty, she told herself, you're forty-one; practically old enough to be a Vice-Chancellor, she thought with a wry smile, ceasing to wallow.

'We probably won't have to sell the house quite at once.'

It was something which had been in her mind, one of the many possibilities and impossibilities which had been knotting themselves inside her this week, and suddenly it seemed the one which was the safest: the most comforting, allowing room for compromise, making things contingent, deferring finality.

'The university have said they will pay for a flat for me to begin with and you and I could move down there, at least during the week.'

Lucia's eyes were scanning the room and Martha's were drawn with them, lighting on books, strewn clothing, Old Ted, Stripy Ted.

'So I wouldn't have to pack everything up just yet?'

Martha intuited the overwhelming lethargy which invaded her daughter at the thought of packing, of moving; for a second she could almost have shared it. Fourteen years in this house, twenty-three at St Rad's: was she really ready to leave it all behind? *And Douglas, and Douglas, and Douglas.*

'Not yet, no. I'd need to go down there in the summer, probably as soon as term ends here. We'd put the house here on the market. You could come and go. But it would be nice if . . . maybe in September . . .'

September: the new school year. Should she say something? Was it the time? But she did not need to decide because it was Lucia who looked across at her with frightened eyes and said, 'I miss school.'

Ought she to get up and go over to her, put her arm round her? But she was scared to make a move and rupture the fragile moment of confidence. Her breath halted.

'Not the work, I don't mean the A level stuff, nor really the people, not how I'm feeling now. But just going to school, you know.'

When she was nine she had had almost three weeks off school with a severe bout of tonsillitis; Martha had stayed at home to nurse her, and at the outset Lucia had revelled in the luxury of days watching old *Pink Panther* cartoons and being fed bowls of Heinz cream of tomato and melted raspberry ripple ice cream. But by the third week she was pleading with her mother in a voice still scratchy with pain: *please can I go back to school?* It had not been her friends then either, nor the desire to learn, although she often had her nose deep in some book meant for fourteen year olds. It was just school. Routine; a reason to get up, tasks to achieve, a reason to be. Take that away and what was left? Disorientation, drift. Bad enough for any school-leaver, but for Lucia, depressed, her education incomplete . . . ?

'Mum, I'm scared.'

Her voice was so small, she could have been the tonsillitic nine year old again. Then Martha did rise and cross over to her daughter, pulling the two ends of the duvet up closer round her shoulders as if she were in bed and leaning her cheek against the top of her warm, mussy head.

'I know, love.' *I'm scared, too.* 'You're not the only one who's not feeling hungry tonight. Shall I make us a cup of tea? I can bring it up if you like.'

Two duveted arms came out and round Martha

where she stood, so that they were both enclosed in the same sweet, stale, familiar warmth.

'Thanks, Mum.'

For the first time in more than three months James Rycarte wheeled his bicycle out of the garage at the lodging. It was dark and the two lamps above the garage door lit up twin haloes of drizzle. He did not mind; in fact, all the better: nobody would see his ancient tracksuit or his hitherto unused, somewhat gaudy French waterproofs. He just felt the need to get out, clear his head and think.

It took him a little longer than anticipated to get on the road because he discovered, on investigating the clip-on bike lights which lay still encased in card and plastic at the bottom of the kitchen drawer, that he must first assemble and mount brackets, front and rear, on to which they might then clip. Batteries, inevitably, were not included. Eventually, however, he was pushing the machine, fully lit, down the driveway, scooting it up to an appropriate speed and throwing a leg wobblingly over the saddle.

Discounting a short assignment in Beijing, he had not ridden a bike regularly since his twenties and, if central Cambridge on a wet Wednesday evening was anything to go by, levels of traffic had increased quite alarmingly in the intervening three decades, while levels of courtesy towards other road users (the two-wheeled variety in particular) had correspondingly decreased. After ten rather

492

hair-raising minutes, though, he was clear of the city centre and out on the open road. He was heading towards Histon, for no other particular reason than that he knew that from Cambridge north meant flat, and he remembered the Histon Road as including a cycle path. Once inside the safety of the solid white line, with the contrasting red tarmac stretching in front of him, he forced his fingers to relax their clench upon the handlebar grips and clicked up a few gears.

Since Martha's bombshell about leaving her husband, he had found himself unable to locate his habitual equilibrium. He had even lain awake at night as he had not in years – not even during the aerial bombardments in Kuwait City – not, in fact, since the last wretched days of his own marriage. Exercise and the resultant physical tiredness might help him sleep: that was one hope. Already the unfamiliar angle of pressure which he was exerting on the muscles of his calves and thighs was creating a pull where it was not normally felt; that tingle and tug at every depression of the pedal promised soon to become an ache. He would probably not be able to walk tomorrow. And yet the stretching felt good. He was not so old. Fifteen years older than her, perhaps, but very far from an old man. Positively youthful for a Head of House. And she made him feel, if not young, then at least that the years between them were of no importance.

But that was not the problem, was it? A mere

age gap was not the reason why he had said nothing to her since coming back from his visit to Dame Emily, nothing in the pub the other night when the opening was there. She had been sitting opposite him, cradling her glass and smiling at him with warmth and confidence and – he hoped it was not vain imagining on his part – even admiration. Being fifty-six was not what was stopping him from speaking.

It may be that Ros Clarke, Letitia Gladwin *et al* thought him a man without principle, an inveterate pragmatist, but if so they were mistaken. There were things for which he would dig in his heels – as indeed he had dug them in to get the money to save the library and launch Susie James's full-funds scholarships. Top of the list of what he cared about and would go to the scaffold for, whichever way you looked at it, was Paul. He had witnessed the cost to the teenaged Paul of one broken marriage; he shared half the blame for it, indeed, though not through infidelity or any other crime beyond being much absent and much changed by his experiences. That river had long since flowed by, but he had no intention of being implicated, however indirectly, in inflicting the same pain upon Martha's Lucia. How odd, it struck him as he braked at the red traffic lights of the A14 roundabout, that he had never met the girl – any more than he had met Paola Alvau since she was a ruddy-cheeked toddler of two or three, cross-legged at his feet on the Carrara marble floor of a Rome apartment.

He sat through the leisurely phase of the lights, grateful for the chance to regain his breath, conscious only now that he had stopped of the scalding liquid which somebody appeared to have tipped into his chest cavity, preventing the normal passage of air. Paul was right – he needed to get out and do this more often or he really would be turning into an old man. Martha might rejuvenate him . . . but it was impossible. Or was it? Was it really, he wondered, as the lights changed to red-and-amber?

Green, and he plied the ball of his right foot to the pedal with a will, ignoring the discomfort in his knee and trying to block out the sports page medical terms which sprang unwanted to mind: cartilage; cruciate ligaments. She had told him she was leaving her husband, leaving Douglas, the poet. If her marriage was already over, did that not make everything different? He was gradually picking up speed, his legs beginning to pump most satisfactorily as he moved up through the gears, gaining momentum. She was moving away, and her husband was not going with her. The distance between Cambridgeshire and Wiltshire, which in the pub had felt like a blow to the midriff, began to take on a new complexion in his mind. She would no longer be in St Radegund's; she would no longer be his colleague, his Senior Tutor. Would it really be so much of a scandal if a relationship were to begin, quietly, six months from now? Just at present she must be confused and unhappy;

she needed, she deserved, no more than his steady friendship and support. For now he wanted no more – no, that was too strong a claim, but he was at least content to be no more than a listening ear, should she ask it of him. But in six months or a year and in a new location, separated from the college gossipmongers by a hundred and forty miles of motorway, with Martha finding her feet as a single woman: who was to say what might not be possible then?

After another mile or so the houses ended and with them the street lighting, plunging him precipitously into virtual darkness, all except for the ineffectual oblong of yellow bouncing along the tarmac in front of him. Bike lamps, it seemed, were designed to enable the cyclist not to see but only to be seen. His purblindness, combined with the way the horizontal fen rain, unfettered now by man-made windbreaks, whipped against his chest and face, persuaded him to turn round at the next junction and head back towards the light and shelter of town.

For the last few hundred yards back towards the entrance to the lodging he put on a sprint, standing up on his pedals and tilting his weight forward over the handlebars like the King of the Mountains crossing the final col. The muscles in his legs were going to be stiff and sore in the morning but for the moment he felt only a pleasurable burn. Alternate thighs pushed, alternate knees straightened with barely a creak, driving him forward towards his own drive and a hot soak in Dame Emily's Victorian bathtub. He could wait, he could follow Martha to Marlborough and woo her at weekends, buy her dinner, bide his time. It was not impossible; he refused to believe it to be impossible.

He just needed to wait.

Coming down the stairs to put on the kettle for two cups of tea, Martha was surprised to see a low light on in the sitting room where she had not noticed it before.

'Douglas?'

He was reading almost in darkness, with just one of the low energy uplighters shifted round close to his head. It was too dim for her unadjusted eyes even to read the title of his book. She hovered close, unsure how to open the evening's inevitable round of unproductive recriminations. Not by asking if he had eaten, as she normally would, anyway: it would only give him the opportunity of saying that he had, and on his own. Clutching at straws it might be, but the only approach she could think of was to try the same line which had worked, to a point, in soothing Lucia.

'We won't need to sell the house straight away.'

Down here, though, the words sounded confrontational in a way she had not anticipated. The house bought with the mortgage which she had always paid: her house, her decision.

'I mean, it's only me who will need to move to Wiltshire to begin with, in the summer. You can stay, finish . . .'

Finish what, exactly? What did he need to do here that he could not do equally well in a flat in Marlborough?

'Yes, I can stay. Not just stay to "finish" anything. I am staying – I told you.'

His voice was toneless, final. Disconcerted, she stumbled on.

'Well, and, as I say, we needn't sell the house, not at once. They will pay for a flat so we could afford two places. For a while.'

And then, after that 'while', what then? She swallowed hard.

'Then when we do sell, we ought to raise enough to get a smaller place here as well. Maybe flats in both places. If necessary.'

'If necessary,' he reiterated heavily.

It was too much for her: the separate flats, the separate lives. She could not force out any more words, but only stand there miserably, silently imploring him not to make it so. The split; the end.

Incipient tears were blinding her but she heard a different note in his voice when he next spoke: tired, as tired as she was.

'You look pale.'

It did not trigger self-indulgent melancholy as it had when Lucia had said the same thing. Instead, his small attention set the tears flowing in earnest, not for herself but for the two of them, for everything that they had been to each other and that she desperately wanted to believe they still were. But she would not say the words which he would read as begging; she glanced off instead towards the nearest thing.

'Lucia loves you.'

Still unable to see his face through the blur and the gloom, she pressed on regardless.

'She needs you – but not like this, not the way things have been here.'

I need you, but not like this.

The semi-darkness seemed welcome now and, letting exhaustion rise over her head, she subsided into an armchair at right angles to Douglas's sofa, closing her eyes and making no effort to hold back the tears. She would have sobbed aloud, but for Lucia in the room above. Again and again, hopelessly, she traced the three sides of the impossible triangle; just as in Reutersvärd's illusion, she was never able to make them meet. Lucia needed her father, but not as he was; Martha needed him, too – but he promised to remain stubbornly what he had always been. And yet not always, she reminded herself. There were times when he had been a good father to Lucia, a proper father and not just an ally in idleness. Maybe he had never worked in the structured way which she herself found a necessity for existence, but it was not only Lucia who had once had a vibrancy, a vivid vitality. This dull inappetence was something recent, something neither inevitable nor inseparable from who he was. A new start – a kick-start for all three of them – she was sure it was for the best. *Please, Douglas.*

Unaware of his presence until he was right before her, she looked up through laced fingers and swimming eyes to find him bending forward over her chair. The touch of his fingers was light but insistent on her arm and it was he, not she, who pleaded.

'And me? Do you ever think about what I might need?'

CHAPTER 31

Bloody hell, it was cold. Katie Parker had come straight over to the tennis courts from trampolining practice to begin her evening's vigil behind the tub of shrubs, and a light tracksuit was not the best outfit for *al fresco* sleuthing at the beginning of March. Darren and Julia both had warm jackets and scarves as well as each other; tonight Darren even had a woolly hat. Katie had nothing. Moreover, the streak of sweat between her shoulder blades which made her tracksuit top cling to her skin was no longer warm but clammily cold, making every slight movement of air feel like a blast straight from Siberia.

It was a pointless exercise, anyway, wasn't it? Shortly after her arrival they rose from the bench, still closely linked, and began their regular walk towards Julia's staircase. They were talking, intermittently, over the sound from that iPod they shared. The fragmented conversation was loud enough for her to have caught their words, had she cared to listen, but she had long since given up expecting to overhear anything of an incriminating

501

nature. The colour of Julia's eyes, it had been the other night, and something about the optokinetic reflex.

All the way to the entrance of the stairway she trailed them at a safe distance and with light step – although she strongly suspected she could have stamped her feet and flapped her arms against the cold and they would have noticed nothing, so absorbed were they in each other. There, as every night, they pulled together once more and kissed for another long moment, and then Darren left Julia to go up to her room by herself. As usual, Katie had been freezing her fanny off for nothing.

She had a hunch that she would find Karen in the college bar, and it proved to be well founded. There she sat at a corner table, laughing with her deputy, Deepa Dasgupta. Arming herself with a tot of Southern Comfort from the bar, no ice (the very idea of it made her shudder), Katie joined them.

'Jeez, I'm cold.'

Looking up from her drink, Karen raised an interrogatory eyebrow. 'Anything?'

'Nope. Usual drill – bit of snogging, then he sees her home like the perfect sodding gentleman.'

'Dear oh dear, what are the youth of today coming to?' Karen pondered with a sad shake of the head. 'You'd think there'd be a bit more sex and drugs, wouldn't you?'

Katie unfroze sufficiently to giggle.

'Well, there's usually rock and roll. Unless that's *The Archers* they always listen to together.'

Deepa spluttered into her Diet Coke, but Karen's eyes were serious.

'Trouble is, you're never going to become a Tigress at this rate, are you?'

Katie took a swig of Southern Comfort, which was orange fruit pastilles in the mouth but liquid fire all the way down inside her chest. It made her brave.

'Look, I'm not sure why we're doing this whole stupid gumshoe bit anyway, to be honest.'

'Sorry?' Karen laid down her glass with exaggerated care.

'Well, it's not as though he's her Tutor or anything, is it? He doesn't teach her: he's in Electrical Engineering and she's a social anthropologist. What's the problem, actually, even if he did follow her upstairs? They're both adults.'

The look on Karen's face was making Katie feel very far from adult, but she pressed on regardless.

'I know he's Dean and she's the SU ents officer, but that hardly constitutes a major conflict of interest, does it?'

Deepa laughed again and, for once, faced down Karen's disapproval. There were times when she drew on reserves of courage which, in her case, had nothing to do with alcohol.

'I agree with Katie. What is it with you, Karen? Enough is enough! I think it's time you got a life and left poor Darren Cotter in peace.'

Karen was still marshalling her resources for a

503

reply to this piece of insubordination when she caught sight of Dr Ros Clarke entering through the bar's double swing doors. She attracted Ros's eye as it panned round the room; Ros came over to their table, drew up a chair and sat down.

Her lack of a drink discomfited the students somewhat; it blew any attempt at cover for being here on junior member ground. Karen and Katie wondered whether they should offer to get her one; Deepa did offer, but the suggestion was waved away. Evidently Ros was here on business, and did not mind who knew it. In fact, altogether she had an unconspiratorial air quite unusual in her. She did not even appear to care whether Katie had been vetted.

'Don't seem to be able to get anything out of Paola Alvau,' essayed Karen at length. 'Been e-mailing her non-stop. She now knows more about the dryers in the laundry and where to sign out the dark room key than most third years. But nothing in return – or nothing we could use, anyway. Just girly chat about school and how much she's looking forward to coming here, usual tripe. So grateful for my motherly interest, all that sort of thing.'

She drained her wine glass and replaced it none too gently on the table.

'Not even any premature assumptions about her place. She spends half her time fretting about her exams and whether she'll get the grades she needs.'

Ros nodded with little apparent concern; she did not speak.

'So what now?' persisted Karen.

'Nothing,' said Ros.

'Nothing?'

'That's right.'

Karen and Deepa both stared; Katie, who had very little idea what they were talking about but was enjoying the spectacle, sat forward and took another mouthful of Southern Comfort.

'Because of the vote in Governing Body, is that it?' was Karen's surmise. 'They are taking the money so now the fight is over? Too late, even if we find out he's been sending her a gold charm for her birthday every year since she was a baby? Even if he's the one who's going to pay her fees?'

This provoked Ros to a smile, at least – even if Karen was left with the uncomfortable feeling it was not her remarks which were the source of the amusement, or not her remarks alone.

'It's over,' said Ros in the simple, imperious tones of one calling off her dogs.

Katie had finished her drink but a return trip to the bar would have meant missing some of this, and that was out of the question.

'Not just because of the vote. It's what it represents.'

Victory for James Rycarte. Ros had set him up to be defeated by the democratic processes of the college; she had encouraged him to fly in the face of the entrenched beliefs of the Fellowship and instead he had turned them round to his own way of thinking. He might be a man but he was also a politician, and Ros respected that. It was a messy world now – no longer the simple universe of academic truth which Dame Emily had inhabited. St Rad's needed a politician.

'So, we're stuck with him as Master, you mean?' demanded Karen, scandalised. 'We're giving up, just like that?'

Ros smiled at her. 'I prefer to think not in terms of a surrender so much as a settlement.'

'You are settling for Rycarte as Master.'

The smile broadened. 'That's it, Karen. Precisely.' Then, as if noticing the empty glasses on the table for the first time, 'More drinks, anyone?'

When Ros arrived back with a brandy for herself and replenished glasses for the three students, she seated herself and commanded their attention again.

'Mind you, it doesn't mean I am going to let him get away with anything. I'm going to watch his every step; every time he turns round I shall be there.'

'And we can help?' Karen asked eagerly, while Deepa looked away and sighed.

'Yes, why not?' said Ros.

But her normally hawk-like eyes were oddly distant; her demeanour, if it were possible for such a woman, could almost be described as dreamy. She had arrived at the college bar tonight fresh from an encounter with Guido Giordano of the Italian Department. Her unusual detachment of

506

manner might be ascribed partly to the strenuous diversions in which they had been engaged together. But it was also at least partly due to something Guido had told her: a further piece of intelligence from the web-based Italian news networks. It did not give her quite the burst of vengeful glee it would have done a week or two ago, but it did give her a quiet, ironic satisfaction.

'Shouldn't I still be keeping an eye on Paola, then – just in case?' said Karen.

Ros laughed silently into her brandy, having nobody with whom to share the joke.

'Paola Alvau may yet be a candidate for one of her own father's entrance scholarships. If, that is, they ever exist.'

The formal offer to Martha Pearce of the Vice-Chancellorship of the University of Marlborough, together with her formal acceptance of that offer, presented itself to James Rycarte as an opportunity to host a dinner at the lodging in her honour. Really, as Paul liked to say, it would be rude not to. And then, with it being the last week of term and colleagues at their frantic busiest, what better than that the assembly should be confined to just the two of them?

Her departure for Wiltshire in a few months' time, which at first hearing had seemed like the loss of a limb, he had now come to regard as an occasion for celebration on his own part, too – or at least an occasion for hope. The only matter giving him pause was the tricky issue of what to feed her. He had prepared coq au vin for a Frenchwoman at Christmas without blenching but now discovered that the idea of cooking for Martha had him as self-conscious as a schoolboy. Nor could he exactly ask the college kitchens to send over supper à deux. In the end he phoned for a Chinese.

The problem with this strategy was the timing. If he ordered the food to arrive before his guest he risked serving it cooling and congealed, or else matted and soggy from being kept warm in the oven; if he ordered it to arrive afterwards, she would come into a cold and empty kitchen and he would have not so much as a prawn cracker to offer her with her beer. (Or maybe wine – did the moment call for wine?) Arranging for both to arrive at eight o'clock had seemed the best solution, but in the event it created the worst of disorder. How could he have forgotten that, uniquely, Martha did not work to Cambridge time, in which everything took place five minutes past the appointed hour? The takeaway delivery girl was also unexpectedly punctual, so that he was juggling notes and change and dropping foil cartons from brown paper carriers as Martha walked up the drive, and had not even a hand free with which to take her coat.

She had brought beer, which resolved that dilemma, and as soon as she was installed at his kitchen table, exuding her usual warmth and making him think she should never sit anywhere else, he was able to begin to relax.

'So, no other nominees for Senior Tutor, then?' she began almost at once, pouring her beer with her usual aplomb.

'No. Ros's appointment will go through at Monday's Council without needing to take a vote.'

She nodded approvingly. 'That's good. A split vote is always nasty. It inevitably gets out, and makes things uncomfortable for the incoming appointee.'

Catching her eye, he decided that she was teasing him, and acknowledged the point gracefully.

'As I am a living, breathing example.'

'And still very much breathing, in your case. You have certainly lived to tell the tale.'

His own glass was still full of slowly subsiding froth, but she clinked hers against it anyway.

'And have you spoken to Ros?'

He nodded. 'Yesterday, when the window for nominations closed.'

'And?'

'And she was very gracious. Said she was looking forward to working with me, almost as if she meant it.'

They laughed.

'She probably is looking forward to it,' said Martha. 'Ros enjoys a challenge.'

'We had quite a productive discussion – perfectly amicable – mainly about her ideas for the post-grad research seminars. In fact, there was only one point when something I said seemed to get up her nose. I was telling her what you and I had discussed, about looking for a full-time Senior Tutor. I said I'd decided against it, but that I appreciated how she would have other calls on her time, with her department and so on. Said I didn't want her shouldering too heavy a load.'

His voice dropped a few keys as he sought her eyes and added, 'I have seen the hours you put in here, you know, Martha.'

She shrugged this away. 'But what was it that annoyed her?'

'Well, I told her I'd be happy to try to take on some of the work. Unlike Dame Emily, I *am* full time, and I thought maybe there might be some senior tutorial functions which I could usefully undertake. Maybe chairing some of the committees which you currently convene, that kind of thing. Anyway, she was up and at me at once, defending her territory like a vixen. Clearly wasn't allowing any encroachment on her patch. You'd think I'd suggested disbanding the Governing Body and ruling as absolute monarch, by her reaction.'

'If she's going to do a job, she'll want to do the thing properly,' said Martha. 'You can be sure that she is going to keep everything you do under the closest scrutiny, and as Senior Tutor she will have an excellent vantage point for doing so.'

She was biting her lip; he experienced an urge to lean over and free it, to smooth his thumb

510

across it where it had been marked white by her teeth.

'But I don't think it's personal. I mean, if she had been anybody's Senior Tutor she would have done the job to her utmost, counted everything in and out. It's the only way she would know how. In fact—'

Those dark, earnest eyes held his and his heart forgot its rhythm.

'—I think she rather likes you.'

Was she teasing again? It actually seemed not.

'I don't know,' he mused. 'I feel as though I can never tell exactly where I stand with Ros. Even yesterday, I just had this sense, I don't know, as if she was holding something back. Something she was aware of and I wasn't, that altered the ground in some subtle way.'

He detected a flicker of amusement.

'Or maybe I am just delusional.'

'Maybe.'

'Anyway,' he said, fetching two dinner plates which he had forgotten to warm and bending back the foil from around the cardboard lid of the nearest container, 'what about you? You've definitely accepted the job, then? Congratulations.'

'Yes. Thank you.'

She didn't sound very much like a woman who felt she should be congratulated, so he reminded her, 'A Vice-Chancellor. Only just into your forties, and you'll be heading a thriving, upwardly mobile university. It's brilliant, Martha.'

When hearty felicitation produced no smile, he allowed himself the indulgence of something more personal.

'I'm proud of you, you know.'

There was a response this time, but by no means the one he had intended. Her lips remained marble and her eyes filmed over. God, but he was crass – he was the damnedest clumsy fool! Of course the move to this new post meant for Martha the end of her marriage, the break-up of her family. And here he was, expecting her to toast her success and embrace her future without a care in the world.

'I'm sorry. This move, I know it isn't . . . well, things are not the way you would have chosen.'

Oh, worse, far worse. The oblique reference was enough to send a tear spilling over and down her cheek, though her face remained unmoving.

Without a thought he let go of the beef chow mein and seized her hand across the table.

'I'm sorry, Martha. Really, so sorry.'

She did not meet his gaze but her hand twisted within his grasp until her fingers curled round his. *Trust* was the word which sounded in his head, so sweet and yet at the same time a warning. But this time he couldn't help himself, he had to speak. The feel of her fingers intertwined with his own catapulted him beyond all reasonable judgement.

'Martha—' His fingers tightened. 'Martha, I know this is not the right time, and I know there are a thousand reasons against it, against even letting you know how I feel, but I can't help it, I—'

She looked at him then and even before he met the compassion in her face he understood what her answer must be, just as he had before, in the pub. The college – the scandal. The wrong moment – too soon. But although he was right about her answer, he was wrong about the reason, or at least not entirely right. Looking him in the eye, she told him matter-of-factly, 'I love my husband – Douglas, I still love him. I still hope that things might work out with him. I – I don't think I can change my mind about what I have said to him, but he may, I'm hoping he may . . . I'm hoping it can still be mended.'

She gazed at him almost pleadingly.

'We are talking. Not much, not yet, but we are starting to talk. And even if it doesn't, if we can't . . . well, I'm afraid I still love him.'

After that, of course, both of them competed to apologise for things which they could neither of them help and, when they had run out of ways of saying sorry, Rycarte went to the drawer for knives and forks and spoons because nobody ever gets anywhere with the chopsticks they bring you. By the time he came back they had both recovered themselves sufficiently to finish opening the containers and scoop fried rice and shrimp and bean sprouts on to their cold plates. They forced themselves to eat, even if talking was beyond them. Until, laying down her fork, Martha smiled – a real, warm, Martha smile, even if it was still a little shaky.

'There's one good thing, anyway.'

He smiled back quizzically, brows raised.

'I can't see you having the same problem with Ros!'

After that, there was a return to something of the camaraderie which had developed between them during these last two terms and he discovered himself nursing dearly the more modest hope that her departure would not mean a cessation of their friendship. They talked about anything and nothing, to begin with, as they passed cartons of noodles and sweet and sour back and forth and forked up stir-fried vegetables. And then she told him for the first time something of her daughter's inertia and depression and he was moved by this deliberate extension of confidence on her part, the very opposite of what he expected or felt that his indiscretion deserved. Over coffee he succeeded in restraining himself from taking her hand again as he asked, 'Can I come and visit you?' and she replied smilingly, 'Of course.'

At the front door, saying their goodnights, he leaned down in defiance of Cambridge practice to plant a kiss on her cheek and, straightening again, he said, 'Martha . . .'

'Yes?'

Lips slightly parted, lit by lanternlight, she looked completely beautiful.

'Would you accept one piece of advice, from a senior colleague?'

The lips twitched; she smiled expectantly.

'If you love your husband, don't tell me. Go and tell him.'

The Lent Term was winding to its end when James Rycarte took the call from Luigi Alvau, one afternoon in his office. The call to tell him that there was no money – that, for all that could be ascertained, it was entirely possible there never had been.

'I hardly know how to tell you this, my friend – believe me, I would give anything to make it otherwise. But it is quite beyond my power.'

'Will you have to go to prison?'

'Ah, on that point I do remain sanguine. My lawyers tell me that they very much hope that unpleasant eventuality can be avoided. But this business has cost me dear, old friend, very dear.'

He talked of his trial, thought Rycarte, as if it were nothing more than a risky investment which had suffered an unfortunate downturn.

'So the money has gone.'

'Money, money! What money is ever really there? It is as ephemeral as a figure on a bank statement, is it not, and who can place his trust in a piece of paper? The wealth which appears to stand to one's name is only as secure as the commodity in which it is held, is that not what your university economists would tell you? Your fair Dr Pearce, for example? And these sequestrators, they are a flock of hungry seabirds.'

'Gannets.'

'Gannets, is it? I could not recall the proper phrase. But I would sooner see them as herring gulls, I think.'

'And Paola? Will she wait now to visit the college until she has the results of her *Maturità*?'

'Ah – yes, I think perhaps that may, after all, be for the best.'

The man was a rogue and a charlatan, mused Rycarte, as he put down the phone. Nothing but a mountebank. How absurd, then, that he should remain so inordinately fond of him.

He walked to the connecting door and attracted the attention of Miss Kett-Symes.

'Could you possibly find me the *Directory of Grant-Making Trusts*, please – I believe you have a copy in your desk?'

Then he reached down the box file containing past proceedings of the Development Committee and every sub-committee and working group reporting to it. They had work to do, raising money for the library refurbishment. St Radegund's would survive without Alvau's million. It would survive on the occasional windfall and the steady goodwill of its alumnae at the rate of twenty pounds here and fifty pounds there; it had done so for a hundred and sixty years and would continue to do so for a good time yet.

Miss Kett-Symes came through with the requested directory and laid it on his desk next to the Development Committee minutes.

'Back to the drawing board,' she said.

Was that a note of dry sympathy in her voice? It was certainly rare enough for her to refer, however obliquely, to any issue of policy. Idly, Rycarte considered the possibility of asking her what she thought: seeking her opinion of Alvau's disappearing donation and the political wild goose chase which it had occasioned, with the perspective of her almost twenty-four years' experience of this place to his not even one. But something told him he might be better off in the dark – even if, as was most unlikely, she were so unguarded as to enlighten him.

Nothing had changed, had it, as nothing ever seemed to change, over the centuries, in Cambridge? Except of course that it did – and it had.

As he pondered this, his eye fell upon her left hand, still gripping the directory. Specifically, her third finger, now unmistakably home to a ring: a gold band set alternately with diamonds and something reddish which might have been garnets. Or possibly carnelians: he was never quite sure of the difference. She caught the direction of his stare and shifted in pleasurable agitation between her two suede-booted feet.

'Miss Kett-Symes, are you . . .? Am I to offer you my congratulations?'

She flushed. 'Yes, indeed, Master. Colin has asked me to name the day. We are going to wait, of course, until Dame Emily is well enough to attend, but we hope it may be some time next year.'

'That's wonderful.'

Sincerity did not require any mustering and his warm handshake was accepted with the appearance of pleasure, though she was soon pulling her hand free and heading back to the dividing door. She spoke over her retreating shoulder.

'There's another thing too, actually, Master.'

He waited, and she reappeared shortly carrying a medium-sized cardboard box.

'I found this in the bottom of the cupboard when I was having a bit of a sort-out. I don't think it's been used for some while – it will probably need a good rinse. But it did occur to me that you might like to have it in your office. Though please mind that you always remember to unplug it when you go home at night, won't you?'

Somehow he had an inkling what might be inside the box, even before he took it from her arms and folded back the dusty cardboard flaps. A twist of black flex; a curve of stainless steel discoloured with spots of limescale. An old electric kettle.

Although many of the undergraduates had already dispersed for the Easter vacation, the members of the St Rad's Tigresses were assembling that evening for their final cocktail party of term. Those gathered on this occasion did not include Deepa, who was reading a book in the library instead. For their third change of initiation test they had gone back to the tried and trusted, resurrecting two decades of Tigress tradition. Katie Parker and

518

Laura Graham had each brought along to this, her maiden meeting, a boy with a double Blue to his name, and was staking her claim to membership of that coveted elite by consuming from his navel, to the squealing applause of the witnessing throng, a double Tequila Slammer.

Julia barely remembered that the Tigresses existed. As Katie and Laura were licking up the last traces of tequila, she was peeling herself away from Darren Cotter's kisses and leading him by the hand in through the stone-corniced doorway and up the spiral staircase towards her room.

James Rycarte was walking slowly home to the Master's Lodging. He was composing in his head a letter to Paul, inviting himself over to visit at Easter. After all, it would be his last chance before the baby was born, and after that Paul would be busier than ever. He was also determined to meet Marie-Laure's parents. A trip to the mountains would be a tonic; he might even rent a bike. Besides, they might never be his in-laws but his grandson shared their genes, and Paul wasn't going to get out of it that easily.

Locking her office up at a more characteristically late hour again, Martha was heading for the Fellows' bicycle shed. She had a copy of the *Swindon and Wilts Property Gazette* under her arm and a look on her face, if not of peace with the world, then at least of peace with herself. In her bag she carried a greaseproof parcel of soft herring roes from the market; having gone home from the lodging and acted upon James's altruistic advice, she had bought enough for three tonight. Fried in butter and parsley, she decided, and served on toast with lemon wedges and plenty of black pepper. They were Lucia's favourite.